The Lost Books of Benjamin
3 Benjamin 4:1–63

THE RICHEST THAT THERE CAN BE

Novel 4 of 12 in the 3rd Book of Benjamin

B. ALBERTILL

The Richest That There Can Be, Published April, 2025
Editorial and proofreading services: Taylor Morris; Gina Sartirana
Interior layout and cover design: Howard Johnson
Cover and interior images: Ruth Angulo Cruz

 SDP Publishing

Published by SDP Publishing, an imprint of SDP Publishing Solutions, LLC.

ISBN-13 (print): 979-8-9885439-9-2

ISBN-13 (e-book): 979-8-9922388-0-8

Copyright © 2025, B. Albertill

Printed in the United States of America

CB, My abilities as a writer pale in comparison to your gifts. You have transformed into a beautiful human being right before my very eyes. You humble me with all you manage to do that I fail to get done. You are my hero.

☼

For I know the plans I have for you, says the Lord, plans for welfare and not for evil, to give you a future and a hope.

—**Jeremiah 29:11**

Acknowledgments

The Richest That There Can Be, the fourth novel in the Third Book of Benjamin (3 Benj. 4:1-63) within the Lost Books of Benjamin (LBoB) series, could not exist without the support of so many people. Hence, sincere gratitude must be given to many, including my wife, the Lorelei, who helped me shape and hone characters, served as my plot-sounding board during writing, and traveled across France to reconnoiter key locations. To my creative editor and contributing author, Cathleen Salsburg-Pfund, *Kreative Kraken*, who has been there to mitigate the swinging pendulum to ensure the novel's creative delivery. Thank you, Cathleen, for joining us on the terrain walk both at Château Royal d'Amboise and Château du Clos Lucé, and down along the river's edge at Chinon. To my developmental editor, Taylor Morris, who held me to task with confident guidance ensuring novel depth and structure, as well as for the eagle eye proofchecking help. To my illustrator, Ruth Angulo Cruz, who took my author's image concept and artistically converted them to powerful images, both within the novel as well as the external cover. To my interior layout and cover design guru, Howard Johnson, who provided me the mallet and chisel to release my literary work in aesthetically-sound hard copy. To my publisher, Lisa Akoury-Ross at SDP Publishing, who very early believed in the beauty of this novel and the series and has patiently allowed me the pacing to make an idea tangible to the masses. Also, I must give thanks to my triune God who has blessed us and kept us in His hands, as well as being the inspiration for all things done in this novel and throughout the LBoB series.

Table of Contents

Prologue

Russell is gone and probably dead. Hunting for answers, Suzanne has abandoned Team Vermandois. Struggling in the wake of the Dragon Incident, Team Vermandois finds themselves still managing unresolved issues. What will result from the loss of these two critical players and significant Templar leaders?

On the positive side, Tepes is a happy memory. Also, Team Romania has shown remarkable resilience in the face of adversity. But nowhere is safe from evil. Team Romania has been crippled with casualties. Team Vermandois is weakened without Suzanne. So much more still needs to be uncovered from the Missing Art Project. Has a modern-day Haman gained enough ground to build back up the Amalekites, once defeated by Moses? If so, what is his nefarious plan? Can the remnants of these two teams be enough to contain yet another attack that is shifting its crosshairs closer to home? Team Vermandois must lick their wounds and dig deep to find strength where little remains.

1

Hating Mother Fleming

US Army Hospital
Heidelberg, Germany
Current day

I *don't remember falling again or breaking anything else.* DCS shook his head in the dim lighting, squinting his eyes to focus on the medical equipment around him. "Hello?" *This is Radiology. Why am I in the Radiology Department again?* He rotated his head. "Is anyone here?" DCS scanned over to his gauze-wrapped right arm which was taped down to an arm board. *Plastic tubing?* Following this tubing left and upward, he shifted his gaze to a shimmering at his periphery. *An IV bag?* "Why do I have an IV?"

"Your IV?" a voice with a British accent answered. "Oh right, all seems to be going in juh-jolly fine. I know folks wah-worry about skin reactions to the adhesive tape." The Brit tore off a wide swath of tape. "Duh-don't worry too much. Once your airway shuts off, the whole adhesive tah-tape issue goes away." The Brit slapped the tape over DCS's mouth. "Quite clever, wouldn't you say?"

"Wyrr dng dss tmee?"

"What's that? I'm sorry. I have trouble understanding you cuh-cuh-colonials. Okay, granted, that tah-tape over your mouth might indeed be the prah-problem. For that matter, if your arms weren't tah-taped down to the wheelchair, you could remove the tape or even stop the IV. Oh well, sah-some workdays are more challenging than others. Eh?"

"Whz nn de infzn?"

"I realize this must be fru-fru-frustrating for you. Please understand, I am fuh-finding this very stressful too. I really do wuh-want to know what you are saying. But you are just not cuh-communicating very well. You seem a trifle upset about the IV solution. Is that what you're trying to say? Here, leh-let me help you. No yelling, now." The Brit acknowledged DCS's head nod before ripping off the tape.

"Is that...?" DCS craned his head.

13

"An antibiotic? Yes, it is." The Brit scratched his face. "Peh-penicillin is what the vial said."

"Whoa! Stop the drug!" DCS repeatedly pointed his chin toward his chest. "Please, please stop the infusion!"

"The red dog tags? Yes, I saw them. I fuh-fully understand you have a severe reaction to peh-penicillin. Why do you think I'm giving you this wah-wah-whopping dose?"

"Please, I beg you. Stop!" DCS felt his face flush hot.

"Oh, go ahead, DCS. Feh-feel free to stop the IV yourself. As the dispensing cah-chemist here, you certainly must know how bad it is to have throat closure." The Brit crossed his arms and watched the man struggle for his life. "I'll bet you could pedantically en-enthrall the two of us for hours about Alexander Fleming's discovery of puh-penicillin in nasty old bread mold. Couldn't you?"

"Look, Mr. ... I'm the hospital's chief pharmacist."

"Yes, I know. The te-technician said so."

"If it's drugs you want...."

"Drugs? No, I duh-don't do drugs."

"Please. Why are you doing this?" DCS whimpered.

"You really don't remember?"

"No," DCS shook his head, his eyes wide.

"Right. I'll ask again like I did buh-before this messy IV business started." The Brit reached toward the surface of a small table. "I need you to sah-sign this document and this note." He affixed papers to a clipboard. "I promise. I will release you juh-just like I released the technician."

"What IV did you give him?"

"None actually. Deh-didn't have to." The Brit placed the clipboard in front of the man.

"Wait! This note is blank."

"Yes."

"I'm signing a blank note?"

"If you don't mind, DCS."

"What will the note say?"

"Does it matter?" the Brit leered, wiggling the IV tubing.

"All right, all right, I'll sign." DCS pointed with his lips. "Release my left hand."

"See?" The Brit loosened DCS's left arm. "A little cooperation goes a long way." He watched as DCS scrawled his signature, finishing with the tail of the *y* underlining the name.

"Thank you, Meh-Mr. Sweeny," the Brit swiftly cinched down the left arm again. "Or do you still prefer the name DCS?" he chortled.

"Release me, please. I've done what you asked."

"Of course, I am a mah-man of my word." He bared his teeth. "I will release you ... juh-just like I did the technician." He paused with mock confusion. "Wait now. I thought you wanted me to stop the meh-medicine first.... What to do? What to do?"

"Stop the IV!" DCS gagged. "Stop the IV now. Please hurry." DCS watched as the Brit moved to stop the infusion.

"One more thing. Your mah-mailroom, where is it?"

"Mailroom? Stop the drip and I'll take you there myself."

"Thank you, Mr. Sweeny. No need to truh-trouble yourself. Just the location, if you don't mind."

"North end of the caserne. It is the old single-story building next to the European Medical Command Building. It is right across from the soldier's club."

"Thank you." The Brit nodded and stopped the drip. "That wasn't so deh-difficult now, was it?" He reached for a large syringe.

"What are you doing?"

"I stopped the peh-penicillin as you asked. I just have one more thing to do to release you."

"What's in that syringe?"

"Don't fret yourself, Yank. Your duh-dog tags said you were allergic to peh-penicillin. It didn't say you were allergic to air."

"Don't do that. That bolus of air will kill me!" DCS felt the tape being secured back over his mouth.

"You wanted to be released. So did the teh-technician. I just thought I would accommodate you in the same way."

"Pehzze dohnnt!" DCS muffled, tears rolling from his eyes.

"I'm guessing you are a wee bit suh-sad wondering what happened to your radiology staff, aren't you? Don't worry. By the looks of the cah-color of your skin, you will be seeing him real soon. When you see him, teh-tell him one thing. Tell him Haman sends his thanks for the … how is it that you Americans say it? Juh-John Hancock, right?"

2

Sugar Daddy and Baddie

Cafeteria
Maternity hospital
Saint-Quentin, Somme River Valley
Vermandois region, France
Current day

"You'll know when you know, Mickey." Dr. Douglas Coletrane turned away from the food service counter and Mickey's glare. "And not a second before." Douglas beelined for a table with a solitary chair.

Colonel Dr. Mickey Peronne hastily ordered a coffee then followed Douglas, bearing down on him the same way he had since the moment Mickey had barged into his wife Loni's barricaded hospital room a few minutes ago. Mickey placed his disposable coffee cup down across from Douglas, grabbed another chair with his unbandaged hand, and slammed its metal legs down against the tile. "Is this seat taken?" he snarled.

Quietly Douglas watched Mickey's accentuated behavior over the edge of his paper cup as he took slow, steady sips. He kept his face neutral and said nothing.

"Back in the room, I said we need to talk," Mickey's voice was low and threatening. He dropped down into the seat and leaned over the table.

"Is Clarisse staying in the patient suite with Loni while you chase me down?"

"Probably. I'm sure at least Clarisse will want to be assured that, between conscious hypnoses, Loni is adequately resting," Mickey grunted. "However, Douglas, I said that we need to talk."

"I told you then and I'm telling you now, Mickey. I can't."

16

"As an army colonel and deputy commander, I'm not used to people walking away when I request to talk to them."

"*That* was a request?" Douglas scoffed. "Don't worry, Mickey, you're having twins soon, and I bet you'll be an expert at dealing with this situation in, what … about fifteen years?" Douglas rotated his cup to avoid a section of soggy rim. "You can't intimidate me and certainly have no authority over my Defense Intelligence Agency mission regarding the Missing Art Project or its tracking of the Rods of Power—Staff of Moses and Rod of Aaron. You know this about the DIA, Mickey. Just give it up."

Mickey pressed his lips together until the tan skin around his mouth tinged white. "Fine. You're right." Mickey threw his hands up. "But Douglas, you cut deep when you withhold situational data from me." Mickey selected a sugar packet tube from the condiment holder at the center of the table. "Minute by minute I must make critical decisions based on data provided to me by Team Vermandois. This information is the pulse of our effective teamwork."

"C'mon, Mickey. I'm sure you understand my predicament. You know all about privileged information, both as a doctor and as a soldier." Douglas blew at the top of his hot coffee. "There are things that are known by me that cannot be shared with folks like you not having a need to know."

"Yes, Douglas, I do understand," said Mickey, struggling with the sugar tube, unable to gain leverage due to his splinted hand, "but the way I see it, you have information regarding some *personal* secret stuff—involving my wife—and you feel the need not to share."

"I don't know what you mean by personal secret stuff, but yes, whatever involves the work that Loni and I do as DIA colleagues, I don't feel any obligation to share."

"Do you see us as rivals?" Mickey shrugged. "Maybe it's just that you are feeling uncooperative. But either way, I thought we were supposed to be a team in there. Ouch!" Mickey's hand slipped from the failed sugar-packet-opening and it banged into the table. "We're supposed to be a team to help Loni."

"I agree. But Dorothy, we aren't in Kansas anymore. Sometimes we must ignore the man behind the curtain." Douglas locked his gaze. "In this case, it's both Loni and me behind that curtain."

"Fine." Mickey dropped the plastic sugar tube and glared at Douglas. "I'll just come out with it." He took in a deep breath. "What is it that you and Loni were doing in her room behind the closed and barricaded curtain … er … door?"

Conjuring the image of Loni's and his hands tightly cupped around each other's when in their remote viewing mode, Douglas lowered his eyes. "It's not what you're thinking." Douglas stared into his cup and the dark reflection on the surface of the coffee.

"I'm thinking to tear the top of your head like this sugar tube." Mickey waved the unopened, mauled packet at Douglas.

"Well then, I guess I have no fear of personal harm." Douglas snatched the sugar tube from Mickey's hand and opened it. "Here, you're killing me with this whole sugar opening–comedy show."

"I told you, Douglas." Mickey selected another unopened tube. "I don't need your help."

"Really? You don't want my help." Douglas wiggled the sugar packet in front of Mickey. "But you want… " he tapped the contents into his coffee to punctuate each word, "my … helpful … information."

"Something like that."

"Look, Mickey." Douglas raked his hands through his hair. "How do I put it gingerly? The activity involving Loni and myself behind a closed door transpired because what we were doing needed privacy, quiet, and no interruption." Douglas scrunched up his nose as he played back his dialogue in his head. "Wait. That doesn't sound too good."

"No, Douglas." Mickey squeezed the sugar packet tube. "It doesn't, and I'd like to do more than speculate. After all we've been through here, whatever that was you were doing seems suspicious to me."

"I get it, Mickey. You know Loni and I are colleagues—"

"Which I *just found out*, if you recall." Mickey then added in a mumble, "Yet another secret."

"Yes, we are colleagues. And we share occasional clandestine activities." Douglas winced. "Hmmm, that isn't much of an improvement."

"Douglas, before you get yourself wound up too much tighter, I don't think you and my wife are … you know."

"Exactly, Mickey, everything we handle … that is … manage together is done so most professionally." Douglas fronted a grin.

"Stop trying to clarify." Mickey leaned forward. "Can you give me any information that you have submitted into intelligence channels?"

"No, I can't." Douglas swallowed the last of his syrupy coffee.

"Why, Douglas?"

Douglas rolled his lips inward. "Look, Loni and I access raw information and intelligence impacting the Department of Defense, okay? We perform an initial analysis and then we report it for contextual analysis. The last thing we need to do at our level is to forward unsubstantiated, uncorroborated information and intelligence which has not been compared against the greater pool of knowledge. Speaking of which," Douglas circled an upward, open palm, "feel like sharing what you were doing at the police station in Péronne?"

Mickey answered with a glare and a shrug.

"Maybe you were concerned about the status of Asaad's exhibit or information regarding his next of kin?"

"Tell you what, Douglas." Mickey licked his lips. "Quid pro quo."

"Quid pro *no*," Douglas hissed.

"Then I guess you'll know when you know, Douglas."

"Fine, I can live with the fact that I don't have a need to know."

"You know what, Douglas? I give up."

"Good. I am more than happy to help you with the sugar packet."

"No, not with this. I've got *this!*" Mickey grunted and then broke into a smile as shimmering crystals of sugar skittered across the table. "See? I told you I could do it! What do you think now?"

"Well," Douglas pointed to the floor, "I think you should order another cup of coffee."

3
Confirming Alpha and Omega

Château Royal d'Amboise
Loire Valley, France
1500

"Keep up, ladies." With her hands clasped in front of her, a solemn Queen Anne moved through the adjoining rooms which led to the great hall. The slight inconsistency in the cadence of her clacking shoes was muffled by her voluminous skirt. She walked until she reached a mirror positioned just prior to the hall's royal entrance door. "Clare, come up here and tell me what you think." Queen Anne dabbed at the corners of her brown eyes and then lightly brushed the upturned tip of her nose. She rolled her lips inward while pivoting her face from right to left.

"Majesty." Clare centered the headpiece over the chestnut widow's peak high on the royal forehead. "You are as lovely as the day you were born."

"Clare, I asked you to tell me what you think, not what you think I want to hear." The queen stood, her arms akimbo. "Please, Clare. Times are hard. I am their queen. I want to look regal, not opulent."

"Majesty, rest assured," Clare bowed low, "your ambiance is richly regal but appropriate." She stood and moved behind her queen, speaking to the ruler's reflection as she indicated elements of her royal attire. "Your lace-trimmed headdress frames your face aptly. It cascades and hangs perfectly. Look, these shadows highlight and soften your features." Clare stood back at arm's length. "You look queenly but quietly so."

"Good." Queen Anne exhaled loudly. "The people look up to me. I need to be worthy of their admiration."

"You are, Majesty. Out of love for you, the people spend days making your clothes and mere hours on their own. It would be a great offense to them if you did not show the world the incredible attention to detail given to your vestment, from the broad, delicately hand-laced collar to the lengthy cathedral train that dusts the polished floor behind you. It warms their hearts to see their work appreciated by their queen."

"I so trust your words, Clare." The queen made eye contact with the woman over her shoulder in the reflection. "More than any other." Clare smiled demurely in response. "Come," the queen continued, "let us not keep the people waiting." Queen Anne proceeded to the door and her royal entourage respectfully followed, annotating with great attentiveness every one of her regal comments, observations, and opinions.

As the cavalcade arrived at the great room and the queen took her seat, the entourage shifted into their appropriate places in an orderly and well-rehearsed manner. Queen Anne's primary ladies-in-waiting arranged themselves between the queen's chair and the royal entrance door. Clare moved to the queen's left armrest. The queen's eyes, however, remained distant and locked upon the white stone fireplace at the opposite end of the hall, making eye contact with none in the room. The crowd hushed as Clare leaned toward the queen's ear.

"On Your Majesty's left are your counselors."

"As per usual?"

"Yes, Majesty."

"On my right?"

"The artisans that you requested."

"Very well."

"In the center, amongst the pillars, all the way back to the entrance door and beyond are your subjects. All await the unveiling of the tapestries."

Queen Anne gave a minute nod. "Let's hope that I made a wise choice." Clare took a step back to her designated location, slightly behind the back edge of the throne. Queen Anne drew her eyes down into the large space before her, smiled at the gathered crowd, and stood.

"Greetings, advisors, artisans, and my loyal subjects. Seven tapestries, which have been five years in the making, will receive royal evaluation today." The queen pointed to the grandly carved display rack situated at an angle to her right. "Here we will see the works of art displayed, one at a time, in order, and you shall all learn of the tale they tell. Artisans and assistants, raise your hands."

Along the right side of the hall, many hands rose into the air. Queen Anne's eyes roved over the group slowly. "Skilled Lowlanders, I see you. Flemish artisans, drop your hands. Good. Belgian artisans, I see you as well. Drop your hands." Queen Anne narrowed her gaze. "You there with your hand still raised, from where do you hail?"

"France, my queen."

"Which tapestry did you work?"

"None and all, Your Majesty." The man cleared his throat. "I served as counsel to any artist upon request."

"You are from Tournai?"

"Where else?" The man bowed as the room chuckled.

"I am happy to see all of you today." Queen Anne clasped her hands. "I recognize all your faces. I give thanks to God that your health has maintained through this project that has spanned half a decade. I thank you again for the many voyages that you have made in preparation for this momentous day." She motioned to her left. "The royal treasurer, master of coin, is here today. Rest assured. You will all be given payment after we have together examined the details of your work. Please be patient. While you are here, you will be treated as honored guests. Let us begin with the first tapestry!"

Queen Anne sat in her high-backed chair and surveyed the artists as they moved amongst the seven chests in the far-right corner of the room near the cold, empty fireplace. Slowly the first tapestry was removed from its heavy wooden chest and brought to the display rack. An elderly woman accompanied by a very large boy worked to hoist up the tapestry.

Quietly Queen Anne rested her chin in her hand and waited patiently. She had learned that as a queen she was allowed a certain measure of contemplation, even when amid her court and public.

Caradoc, it has been many years since we stood together beneath the megalith stones in Carnac. I told you then that one day I would capture our lives in a great masterpiece. Oh, how I wish that you could be here to see it. I know we have been apart these many years, but our eyes have always shared the same vision—we see the same things in the same light. As such, I trust that someday, somehow, you will find the symbols placed by my heart for us.

"Majesty," Clare whispered, "the royal governess has arrived."

"Madame de Bussière, what have you for me?"

"Majesty, I have your lovely little plum, Claude."

"How is it possible? This one-year-old princess has grown more beautiful within the passing of the day!" Queen Anne received her daughter and held the small child on her lap.

"Will there be anything else, Majesty?"

"No, not from me, Madame de Bussière. Stay within sight of Clare. Otherwise, that will be all."

Clare stepped forward and spoke softly, "Majesty, the artisans of the first tapestry await."

"Quite so." Queen Anne smiled and rotated slightly in her seat to easily see the display rack while still speaking to the room at large. "Madame, how do I know that this is the first of the series?"

"Your Majesty told me that it was," the elderly woman answered, biting nervously at her lower lip. The crowd softly chuckled as the queen kindly hid her smile.

"Indeed, my good woman, I did. Let me rephrase." Queen Anne cleared her throat. "When we are all gone and many generations yet to come have discovered these beautiful works of art completed in the year of our Lord 1500, how will anyone know that this is the first in a series of seven tapestries?" Queen Anne's gaze was firm and unyielding.

"Again, Majesty, you told me to do so." Shuffling her feet, the woman coughed. "You said for me to place a symbol on the tapestry." The artisan dropped uneasily to her knees. "Have I not done what the queen asked?"

"Have you, gentle artisan? Rise. Show me now. In fact, show all of us now that mark which guarantees that the future will always know that the story begins here."

"Yes, Majesty." The old woman motioned to the large lad to help her stand then whispered, "Pass me the stick, my son." She pointed to the tapestry with the stick and though her hand made the pointer tremble, the woman's voice was confident about her handiwork. "Here, Majesty. These are the symbols you asked to be placed."

"I see that it is so." She smiled at the woman. "Well done." Then she raised her voice. "Artist of the seventh tapestry, can you hear your queen?"

"Yes, my queen," a voice croaked.

"We haven't come to your work yet, dear sir. However, can we all surmise that the same symbols occur on your tapestry with the exception that they denote closure?"

"Indeed, my queen. As you have requested, I have put into place the symbols which will tell the world that the story ends here." He patted the lid of the trunk holding his work.

"Very well." Queen Anne shifted the squirming Claude to the other side of her lap. "I have a story to share which has been a lifetime in the making. Listen well." *Caradoc Freichfras, wherever you cast a shadow, know that this story is the fulfillment of my sincere promise given at our beginning. With all my heart, dearest, it is dedicated to you until all ends.*

4

A Brush with the Devil

Château du Clos Lucé
Château Royal d'Amboise grounds
Loire Valley, France
1519

"*L'amour triomphe de tout,*" whispered the old man standing on an elevated platform near the chapel ceiling. With paintbrush in hand, the old man gazed up at the fresco of the *Assumption of the Virgin Mary* and smiled. Even in his advanced years, he was a remarkably handsome man. His eyes were strong and focused. Their rich, deep, coffee brown coloration was haloed by a light blue luminescent ring, publicly confessing the numerous passing of years. The creased skin of his face wrapped a bony facial frame, highlighting a high forehead cascading downward to a stern brow. Defiantly bristled eyebrows bracketed a long straight nose which almost overhung a downward curved mouth. The snow-white hair fell from his scalp, swallowing his ears, and blended almost inseparably with his marvelously thick beard. Framed by a plush of gray-white hair, the old man's lips silently mouthed his affirmation.

"Love triumphs over everything." A new voice translated from below the platform.

"Hello, Salai." The old man croaked his reply without looking down from his perch. "Why are you lurking in the shadows of the hallway?"

"Where else but in this small chapel would I find the person here who is longest in the tooth?" The old man's senior protégé, Salai, stepped through one of the paired wooden lancet-shaped doors.

"Indeed, my teeth have grown long," the old man nodded. Brush in hand, he made his way carefully down the contraption he had designed which allowed him to reach the arched ceiling of the cramped chapel. Salai reached out a hand to steady the old man as he made the final step to the slick, tiled floor.

The old man nodded his appreciation. He then crossed the width of the oratory in two strides, wrested back the tarp covering two prayer benches nested together along the left wall, and eased himself down into the seat. He

leaned back against the ornately carved wood and sighed deeply as he looked up again at the fresco. "You said that I would be a great painter by the summer of 1519, Salai. It is now the end of April, and I still believe that I have offended God and mankind—the vision in my mind is far greater than what my hands can accomplish." The old shoulders shrugged. "If I had more time, I know I could do better."

"Your skill is highly polished and deeply developed, Old Father," Salai smiled. "It harbors within you alone, excepting the portions you have graciously shared with me. However, you must know, time belongs to none of us."

"The short days of winter have passed, Salai." The old man picked at the paintbrush bristles. "Sadly, along with time, my skills seem less and less to belong to me."

"Do you want me, as your senior protégé, to help with the paintings here or, do you wish to work with Melzi?" said Salai, biting his lip and hoping he would not have to work with Melzi, the old man's junior protégé.

"Melzi?" The old man cocked his head. "Where is that fool of a rascal Melzi?"

"Now that's a great question," Salai sighed. "He *said* he was going into town with your manservant Battista to replenish kitchen stocks."

"Why wasn't I told this, Salai?"

"I don't know, Old Father." Salai propped himself against the wall. "How do I say this nicely?" Salai rolled his lips inward. "Your junior protégé, Melzi, is young, frivolous, and flighty. He rarely tells anyone anything."

"It's because he probably doesn't know so himself, Salai."

"Yes, that could be it." Salai smiled. "As for Battista, now there is a manservant with his head fixed squarely on a proud set of shoulders."

"Battista knows—"

"Indeed, Old Father. He does." Salai pushed himself off the wall. "Battista knows but, in his stoicism, doesn't want to share."

"As your manservant in waiting, Battista has a proud ownership over the doings of the household. This is his bailiwick." The old father pointed and Salai moved a teetering worktable closer. The mentor leaned forward, carefully rinsed the paintbrush, and then placed it in a tray.

"Yes, but why should one have to use a pry bar to get the least tidbit of information from him?" Salai laughed. "Know this, Old Father, whatever you need me to do, tell me. I'll do it. Whatever your heart needs or even remotely wants today, instruct your waiting woman, Maturina, to tell Head Housemistress Clare or me. We will make it happen."

"So both Maturina and Clare, Queen Anne's—God rest her soul—former chief lady-in-waiting, stayed behind?" The old man brushed at his beard. "Just as well, there should be servants in the house to tend doings. I can't manage everything."

"You're not a visitor in the house."

"I know, Salai," the old man groused.

"Then why act so?"

"I don't."

"Old Father, you act as if you are an eternal visitor in this house."

"I was brought here to do the bidding of King François I." He pulled his white beard to the side, out of his way, as he fumbled through the brushes in the tray. "I am the king's guest."

"Guest?" Salai scoffed and placed his hands on his hips. "Hardly. You are the king's chief designer of royal court festivals, his architect, his civil engineer and military engineer, the town planner, beloved artisan, royal advisor … must I go on?"

"It has been three years since Margaret, Duchess of Alençon, convinced the king to allow me to live here."

"Yes, the king's sister knows how dear this place is to His Majesty."

"That's my point, Salai." The old man's wild eyebrows bristled. "No matter how much I try to make Clos Lucé my home, everything in it and in Amboise itself echoes the eternal presence of Queen Anne. This place is hers, not mine."

"Queen Anne has been dead five years, Old Father."

"Physically passed, yes, but spiritually, no." The old father gazed around the chapel. Its warmly tinted walls and wooden paneling were soft and inviting, nothing like the chapels made of stark, unyielding stone. "Not one living soul completely disappears into the void. I have said this to you before, Salai. The greatness of this queen will never die." The old father pointed upward. "Though she and I never met, her essence permeates every rafter in the ceiling and every sinew within my soul. I have rarely known such a woman to possess this capacity, alive or not." The old man winced and swayed a little in his seat.

"Easy now," Salai whispered as he squatted down in front of his master. "Old Father, what is wrong?"

"I … I…." The old father forced his eyes open and looked squarely into the younger artist's eyes. "I fear that my body has grown so frail. It won't be much longer before the sixty downtrodden will follow me down the hill to Église Saint-Florentin."

"Stop this nonsense about funeral processions, Old Father. Sit a bit longer. I will have Battista bring nourishment to you here."

"As a well-spent day brings contented sleep, so a well-spent life brings a peaceful death." The old father's sharp eyes blurred, and he rubbed them gently. You're a fine person and a fine artist, Salai. But it wasn't always so. Was it?"

"No, it wasn't," Salai sighed, recognizing the approaching reminiscence, and stood. "When you first found me, Old Father, we were still in Italy."

"You went by your given name, Gian Giacomo Caprotti da Oreno."

"Yes, I did."

"But Salai … the little devil … that was the name you *earned* as you joined my household."

"*Il Salaino*, or Salai, you called me. I was only ten—"

"And a culprit with many vices when I took you in," the old man interrupted, shaking a finger at the young man.

"I was," Salai conceded.

"You stole money and valuables from the house."

"Allegedly, Old Father."

"Don't add lying to theft, Salai," the elder chuckled. "How could you explain the sudden appearance of expensive clothing and footwear in your wardrobe?"

"Miracle?"

"Hardly."

"I know … I was a pain," Salai squatted again, resting a hand on the man's knee.

"Yes, but all that energy, once redirected, produced this specimen in front of me." He reached out and took the young face in his veined hands.

"A brilliant apprentice and talented artist?"

"Easy on the accolades, Salai." The old man laughed softly. "You have developed into a master in your own right." He patted Salai's clean-shaven face. "How could I not forgive and forget?"

"We've worked together many years since, Old Father."

"Yes, we have."

"Do you think you will ever suspend calling me the devil?"

"You want me to pass the name on to Melzi. Yes?"

"He certainly is the best example in the house now," Salai shrugged. "If it weren't for Maturina, Clare, and I, who would reliably provide you your daily sustenance?"

"Sustenance is not what I need right now." The old father gripped the bench and heaved himself up.

"What is it that you need, Old Father?" Salai stood and offered his arm to the master.

"I need to share some information."

"Very well, I'll go get some parchment and ink. I'll scribe for you." Salai turned to leave but the man's rough hand grabbed hold of Salai's tunic, stopping him.

"Time flees," he whispered, and the weathered hand relaxed.

Salai came close and steadied the old man's crumpling frame.

"Old Father!"

"Salai, I need you to listen carefully." He gripped the young man's shoulders. "You will soon hear the answer to questions that will be asked for time unending."

"Good Lord, Old Father, this is more than just mere scribing."

"Yes, Salai."

"What's this about?"

"Two eyes, two ears, attend my words. Go to my room. In the corner of the bed frame, where the near sideboard meets the headboard, you will find an item bound with string. Retrieve and carry it, but do not unbind it. Bring that item to me, here, now, and we shall begin."

"Is the chapel the best place?" Salai whispered as he cast his eyes around the tiny room. "We can go elsewhere if you like. There is hardly any privacy with the main hall just there," he thrust his chin to the lancet doorways.

"This chapel is perfect, Salai." The old man gasped and sat again on the prayer bench. "Once you have this information, I will give you the next step," he whispered. Then, suddenly harsh, the old man barked, "Do I have your full attention?"

"You do, Old Father." Salai squatted, his concerned face immediately gripped again by the master.

"Your full attention?" The old man's eyes were fiery, both pleading and fierce.

"Yes, Old Father. Yes," Salai nodded.

"Go now." The old father released Salai and dropped his eyes to his lap, his fervor all but extinguished.

What has Old Father so troubled? Salai paused in the shadow of the right-side doorway as the old man intently studied his calloused hands, finally resting one inside the other and then both in his lap. *Minutes ago, the weight of the world burdened him. Now something new has been added.* Worried for his mentor, Salai stepped back through the tunneled doorway and leaned into the chapel with one hand on the center support of the double door. *What could it be?* Salai watched as the old man lifted his head and locked his gaze.

"Go now, Salai." The old father motioned. "But first, take the brush there and set in on the easel in the corner of my workshop."

"The one with the unfinished portrait of—"

"Yes, Salai. That one. Hurry now, please, the world waits on tenterhooks."

5

Taking of the Horn

Château du Clos Lucé

Château Royal d'Amboise grounds
Loire Valley, France
1519

I *could peek inside. Who would be the wiser?*
Salai lifted the corner of the mattress and felt beneath it. "There you are, my elusive little treasure."

"Salai!" scolded Clare, standing in the doorway of the bedroom. She surveyed Salai warily as she leaned a broom against the nearby wall. Recentering herself in the doorway, she sharpened her steadied gaze. "What are you doing?"

"Hello, Clare." Salai deftly withdrew his hand and stepped away from the package's hiding place. "The old father asked me to bring him an item from his room."

"Does it take unmaking the bed that neither he nor you made this morning?" Clare stood with her hands on her hips, a glare in her eyes.

"He wanted this." Salai held up a wrapped package.

"I know it. Hand it to me now," Clare demanded.

"But he asked me to retrieve it."

"Now, Salai." She tapped her foot.

"All right." Salai handed the package over. "But the old father *did* say...."

"So *you* say, Salai." Clare inspected the knotted strings. "Have you returned to your devilish ways, Salai?"

"I am telling you the truth," he answered defiantly.

"Are you telling me that curiosity isn't burning within you to release this string and let the opaque wrapping paper fall away?"

"It could happen, Clare ... accidentally, of course."

"See that it doesn't." Clare slapped the package back into his open hand.

"You still don't trust me, Clare?"

"I trust the mischievous Melzi less, if that's consolation." Clare wiped her hands on her apron. "Take the package directly to the old father. If he trusts you, so should I. However, Salai, know that I keep a wary eye on you."

"Do as you wish with your eye, Clare. However, believe me, you'd do better to keep both eyes on Melzi." Salai left the room muttering to himself all the way down the stairs and to the chapel.

Meanwhile, wondering where her housekeeping helper middle daughter was, Clare tidied the old father's bed alone. *Why can't Salai and Melzi fully appreciate the depth of the old father, Master Piero?*

"Can I help you, Mother?" said a female pre-teen voice from the doorway.

"There you are, Camilla," Clare said. She motioned to her middle daughter. "Where have you been? Chores? Errands? Never mind. Finish tying up your apron and then go to the other side of the bed. Help me tighten these sheets."

"Why was Monsieur Salai grumbling as he left?"

"It doesn't matter." Clare stopped suddenly and sat on the edge of the bed. "Come here, *cherie*."

"Am I in trouble?"

"No. Come here. I want you to stand over here and look around the room." Camilla did as she was told, coming to rest beside her mother. "Tell me what you see."

"I see tables, a desk, and bookshelves, Mother. Same as always."

"What do you see on them?"

Camilla's eyes roved over the many wondrous items in the room. "Sketches, drawings, journals, and notes. Shells, strange shapes of wood and stone, small wooden structures." She paused in thought and then giggled.

"Tell me, Camilla. Doesn't it look like the Master Piero's drawings and figures snuck out of his cluttered study and crept secretly up the stairs to have more room to lay about up here in his chambers?"

"Yes, Mother, it does."

"What do you see on that bedside table?"

"It looks like two knives fixed together, Mother."

"What is it used for?"

"I've seen the Master Piero cut with it."

"He calls them," Clare struggled to mimic the unfamiliar words, "paper cutters. He made that pair."

Camilla laughed at the sound of the words. "Did he invent it?"

"I don't know." Clare tussled with her apron strings as she mused, "He invents many things … things I cannot imagine."

"Is that why he works for the king?"

"I imagine so." Clare smiled at her middle daughter's insights. She squeezed Camilla's shoulders with one arm while she pointed with the other. "Underneath the paper cutters, what do you see?"

"I see a sketch of the same paper cutters."

"What about that sketch over there?"

"It is a unicorn drawing held down by a sculpture of the same unicorn."

"*That's* why he works for the king. Master Piero makes things *real*. Whether they are his own ideas or the ideas of others, from pictures or drawings, he can form thoughts into real things." Clare clasped her hands firmly. "Could you do this?"

Camilla shook her head. "No, not me, Mother." She paused as her eyes traced over the room's curiosities. "Why are you showing me this?"

"I know you're just short of your teens and quite young yet, but I want to see if you can appreciate the greatness of Master Piero more so than the two troublesome protégés he has chosen."

"Is Salai being a devil again?"

"I guess that is for the Master Piero to decide." Clare stood and stretched her back. "Here, child, finish helping me make this bed before you scamper off to attend to your chores and errands."

✠ ✠ ✠

"Salai, what took so long?" the old father asked as he inspected the string's knots while the apprentice closed the doors leading from the hallway to the chapel. "You were tempted to open this, yes?"

"I would be lying if I said no." Salai briefly shifted his weight from leg to leg. He tried hard to keep eye contact with his mentor, but his gaze ricocheted back to the doors with their decorative cuttings. *They're hardly doors at all, more like screens.* For the first time, he wished they were solid doors so that whatever was in the package could be kept between himself and the old father.

"I can see that you didn't open it," the old father smiled congenially. "What stayed your hand?"

"I can't say." Salai stared at the tiny parcel, nervously picking at his cuticles.

"Salai, I am asking if the only reason that you didn't open the package was because you knew I would find out."

"Yes, I know. I am thinking, Old Father."

"Hurry, Salai. I'm not getting any younger."

The young man sat beside his mentor. "I would have to say that as a human animal I am entitled to have curiosity. This is not unhealthy or wrong."

"Curiosity does lead to learning, Salai." The old man leaned back on the pew and stroked his long white beard. "Come, sit down." He held the small package in his hands, rotating it so the light from the two windows cast small shadows around the knots. "However, it is the *control* that one exercises over such urgings that makes one respected and trustworthy."

"I can't say that I worried whether a new knot tied would exactly replicate the one which initially existed," Salai sighed. "I can't say that I worried that the creases in the paper would lay in perfect alignment in the manner originally folded." Salai took in another deep breath. "It is a stark reality that as I get older, I have learned that I do stupid less well."

"Ah, yes. We all learn this over time."

"For me, this makes doing right the priority. I don't want to do stupid things. I can only say to you now that I want to do what *you would do* if you were standing here in my place. I want to try to do what is honorable in the eyes of He to whom we all answer." Salai gave a small bow of his head in the direction of the altar.

"Does this make you a better person, Salai?"

"It certainly makes me feel better about myself. So I guess it does."

"Well, it does and doesn't." The old father grimaced and repositioned himself on the bench. "Salai, I can see you are no longer completely a little devil as your Italian nickname suggests." The old father set down the parcel and gesticulated with his hands above his head, one finger up on each, like horns. "I think I shall rename you Unicorn because you have at least lost one of your devil's horns." He brought down one hand. "I'll give you this to think about. The unicorn, through its intemperance—not knowing how to control itself—for the love it bears to fair maidens, forgets its ferocity and wildness. It lays aside all fear, will approach a seated damsel, and go to sleep in her lap. Thus," he brought down the remaining hand from his head and jabbed the young man gently in the chest, "the hunters take it."

"What does that mean?"

"It means that our character strengths are nothing but our character flaws in disguise. Vices—everybody has them."

"Even you, Old Father?"

"Yes, even me, Salai," the old father chuckled. "You must decide for yourself whether you own your vices, or they own you. What you do today changes your history tomorrow." The old father tapped the top of Salai's head. "You were once a little devil with a record of transgression that we both well remember."

"I remember, Old Father."

"Now you are a unicorn." The old father touched his own glabella. "Note, Salai, I did not take away both your horns, only one. It is the intemperance and lack of control that you exhibited which has bred distrust in others."

"Yes, that was bad, but it is now in the past."

"It is bad and good." The old father shrugged. "It is bad because you must learn to trust and be trusted. Our past informs our present. It is good because you are a unicorn who holds one horn in reserve so that you don't become so trusting that the evil of the world—in this example, the hunters of the world—would take you as your head sleeps in the lap of a fair maiden."

"So I must hold on to being bad?"

"You must accept your badness, your vice, and exert control over it. Even a blood-sucking parasite knows when to pause feeding on his host."

"My single horn on my head is a symbol of my residual vices." The young man touched his forehead, frowning.

The old mentor reached up and with his thumb he smoothed away the worry lines on the young man's forehead as if anointing him. "Your single horn is a symbol of your strength which is your control over internal evil, the sins of Adam."

"Does the horn give the strength for control?"

"The horn points upward," the old man said, raising his hand toward the stained-glass windows above the altar, "in the direction from which we all receive strength."

"I think I like being a unicorn."

"Whether you like it or not, dear Salai, in my eyes you have become that beautiful creature."

Salai placed a kind hand on his mentor's shoulder. "I love you, Old Father."

"And I, you." He picked up the package and reached over to the tray of tools. "Come, let us read together what was bound and wrapped."

"What is it?"

"It is beauty beyond measure. It is the beauty that the queen has given to us with the pen strokes from her own heart."

As the old father snipped at the first strings, a form which had been lingering in the shadows just beyond the wooden doors slowly edged into the light.

6

Devil and the Unicorn

Château du Clos Lucé

Château Royal d'Amboise grounds
Loire Valley, France
1519

"A unicorn, you say?" The old father, Master Piero, started at the unexpected voice. "Oh, Clare, you caught me off guard." Piero held up the book, the corner peeking out from torn wrappings and glanced toward Salai. A few cut strings dangled but most were still intact.

"Are you saying the little devil lost a horn, Master Piero?" Clare opened one of the doors and moved fully into the chapel doorway. She dried her hands on a towel as a little girl followed her in, clinging to her dress.

"She's sharp, Salai," said the old father, Master Piero, laughing. "Don't cross her."

"You and Clare may see a unicorn, Old Father, but I fear otherwise. Change is not easy."

The old father nodded sagely and then placed the partially unwrapped book in his lap. "Who do you have helping you today, Clare?"

"This is my youngest daughter, Master Piero."

"What is your name, little one?" Master Piero spoke kindly, but the girl clung tighter to her mother's smock, not daring to pass the edge of the tunnel-like doorway.

"Answer Master Piero, *cherie*. It's all right." With another step, Clare walked the girl into the chapel and closer to the bearded man with bright, curious eyes.

"I am Little Clarisse," said a little girl of no more than five years of age. She pulled at the hem of her sundress, twisting side to side.

"Do they call you Little Clarisse because you are so tall?"

"That's silly." Little Clarisse giggled. "I am Little Clarisse because my sister is Big Clarisse."

37

"Now that is quite interesting," said Master Piero, looking up at Clare. "Two children named Clarisse, Clare?" His eyes flashed. "A stepchild?"

"Yes, Master Piero," said Clare. She smiled down at the girl. "Little Clarisse expanded our number of Clarisses when her father and I married."

"Have I ever met Big Clarisse?"

"No, Master Piero, she teaches riding at the palace. Her father says that since she was Little Clarisse's age, she was drawn to animals and horses especially." Clare chuckled. "The fact is that now as a young lady, Big Clarisse spends more time with the saddled animals than she does with us unsaddled people."

"Well, Little Clarisse," Piero shifted his gaze back to the little child, "I must say that your name is very pretty." He tapped his chin, pretending to think hard. "I still think your name is very much like your mother's."

The amused child piped up, "My mother's name is Clarisse, but she calls herself Clare."

"Clare," Piero looked up at her through his bushy eyebrows, "I don't believe I ever knew that. Is there yet another secret in the unfurling?"

"It isn't truly a secret." Clare rolled her eyes, exasperated. "I may have mentioned it once or twice to Maturina and Battista."

"I see, Clare." Piero leaned back in the prayer bench and sharpened his gaze. "Please tell me what information is worthy of Maturina and Battista and yet fails in worthiness to be shared with the master of this house."

"Master Piero, it's not like that." Clare's face twitched. "It's hardly worth mentioning," she sighed.

"And still it isn't mentioned to me even after a request?"

"It is no more than a long-standing family tradition."

"Tradition?"

"Yes, Master Piero. This tradition has been in the lineage of the ladies in my family longer than anyone can recollect." Clare folded her towel. "My mother's name was Clarisse. Her mother's name was Clarisse. My great-grandmother's name was Clarisse, and so forth."

"How very interesting, Clare." Salai tapped his finger over his pursed lips.

"To some, Salai," said Clare. "However, as I said to Maturina just the other day, for those of us so named it can be quite confusing. To help overcome this confusion, we alternate generations where every other Clarisse is called Clare. Every other Clare and Clarisse is then termed by their title."

"So, Clare," Salai scratched his chin. "your great-grandmother named Clarisse has a daughter—your grandmother, Clare."

"Yes, we called her Granny Clare," Clare nodded wearily.

"Her daughter is your mother, Mother Clarisse, whose daughter is you," Salai pointed, "and you, in turn, go by Clare. You now have the responsibility, nay, the obligation, to call your daughter—"

"—Big and Little Clarisse. What a clever system." Piero chuckled and then paused, looking quizzically at Clare. "The only flaw lies in the absence of a female in the sequential generation."

"True enough, Master Piero." Clare nodded. "The amazing thing is that as far back as anyone can remember, there has always been a female to carry the name in every generation."

"Each and every generation?"

"Yes, Master Piero." She looked up at the fresco of the *Annunciation of the Virgin Mary* behind the old man. "Each and every generation."

"Well maybe not *every* generation." Piero's eyes sparkled.

"No, sir. Every generation has a representative Clarisse."

"Well, you might be correct. It might have been that the first people were not Adam and Eve."

"See, Master Piero?" Clarisse laughed. "Your cleverness is why I choose not to share my name oddity."

"So there is a hidden secret."

"Yes," Clare whispered behind her hand, "most do not know that after being thrown out of the Garden of Eden, Eve did indeed change her name to Clarisse so as not to be associated with her impertinent deeds." Clarisse grinned as both men burst into laughter. Little Clarisse jumped up and down and laughed along though without understanding.

"Ahh, Clare," Piero nodded, "you possess a sharp wit indeed."

"To be a good housekeeper, especially in this household, one must keep a quick wit with humor fit." Clare beamed at the second round of laughter until it faded, then continued, "Master Piero, the only reason I interrupted you and Monsieur Salai was to ask you about your dinner. Battista, Maturina, and I are preparing for the evening meal."

"Melzi is not with you, Clare?"

"No, Master Piero, should he have been?"

"Well, where the devil is he?" Master Piero, the old father, grumbled.

"I, for one, do not know," answered Salai. "But as a devil-turned-unicorn, I can offer a best guess. I am quite sure that wherever he is, he is up to no good."

"I resent that remark," a new voice chimed in from the hallway.

"Don't you mean you *resemble* that remark, Melzi?" Salai stood, widened his stance, and crossed his arms over his chest.

"I can tell you what *you* resemble, Salai." Melzi slunk into the doorway, paused there, and slouched against the wooden paneling.

"Gentlemen! That is quite enough bantering." The old father, Piero, pursed his lips and snapped his fingers. "Clare, please tell Battista and Maturina to prepare the meal for three tonight. Use an extra pair of hands if you must."

"Oh, Master Piero, Big Clarisse is feeding the stable animals and Camilla is gone on an errand for the rest of the day. I am sorry, but Little Clarisse is still too young to be a valid help in the kitchen."

"Worry not, Clare. The helping hands belong to my junior protégé, Melzi. Although he does not demonstrate such, I am convinced that he is quite of age to qualify as valid kitchen help. I am sure there are some onions that need to be cut."

"You have been bad, Monsieur Melzi," Little Clarisse spoke, shaking her finger condescendingly, one hand on her hip. Then, as her confidence faltered, she scooted back behind her stepmother's skirt. She whispered up to Clare, "He might end up going to bed without any dinner."

Master Piero's sharp ears did not miss a word. "What an excellent idea, Little Clarisse. Clare, have Maturina, Battista, and Melzi prepare dinner for only two. Melzi will be fasting this evening." Piero leaned around Clare to smile at the half-hidden face of Little Clarisse. "Thank you, little one. Like your mother you are equally insightful and a good judge of character."

"Old Father," Melzi held his cupped palms upward, "have mercy."

"The kitchen awaits you, Melzi," the old father barked. "Don't let me hear that you have been sluggish in your help either."

"What if I die of starvation, Old Father?"

"See to it that your body falls without disrupting meaningful work."

"I don't deserve such a harsh sentence."

"Agreed, Melzi." The old father nodded. "Unfortunately, it's the harshest one I could provide."

7

The Hunt Begins

Château Royal d'Amboise
Loire Valley, France
1500

"A prince becomes king when the father dies." Queen Anne's voice rang out clearly though the palace hall. "But even with death," she shook her head, "there is no guarantee." The shuffling noises in the crowd had diminished now to an occasional clearing of the throat or rare cough; all ears hung on the queen's every word. *They are curious. Good. For some, this tale will be entertainment.* Queen Anne smiled. *But for the knowing, it is the landscape of my soul.* Queen Anne noticed how the crowd went silent awaiting the tale.

"At Ludlow Castle, on an island far away, there lived a twelve-year-old prince who was heir to the throne. His father had been growing ill for some time. The king's lungs were failing. The prince knew the time for succession was coming but he also knew that jackals would try to steal the throne. The prince feared for his existence. Then, one day in the second week in April, the news came. The prince's father died far away at the royal castle in London. Upon hearing the news, the prince and his closest advisors boarded their coach and set off for London." The queen shifted in her seat, pausing for all her constituents to absorb her words.

"The prince's two advisors were his mother's brother, Uncle Anthony, called the Earl of Rivers, and the prince's half-brother, twenty-five-year-old Richard Grey. Halfway to London sat Stony Stratford, and in this small hamlet they all stayed the night at the comfortable Rose and Crown Inn." The queen paused to calm the fussing toddler princess in her lap.

Meanwhile in the crowd, a young girl tugged on her mother's dress and whispered, "I don't see a king, a prince, or a coach on the queen's tapestry."

"Hush, Louise," said Lady Anne Pot, realigning her flowing skirts. "Do you doubt your queen?"

41

"No, Mother." Louise de Montmorency stood on her tiptoes, bobbing and swaying in an attempt to see the tapestry. "It's just that—"

"Silence. The queen will explain all to you in her time. Just look and listen."

"But, Mother, I can't—"

"But nothing, child," Lady Anne Pot whispered harshly. "Quiet!"

Disgruntled, Louise dropped to her heels. Once again, her view became the backsides of adults and a narrow strip of the top of the tapestry. She huffed and rolled her eyes. A martin darted by the open window to her right. Louise listened to the twanging, swooping song of the birds and thought of the nests of the daring birds. A smile crept across her face. Backing herself up to the corner near the window and leveraging her weight against her hands and feet, she moved up the wall little by little. Wedging herself against the walls like the birds build their nests, Louise hoped to gain a better view. Her shoe slipped ever so slightly, and, in a flash, Louise's mother had both the child's feet firmly on the ground. Louise looked up at her mother and gave the most pitiful, pleading face she could muster.

Her mother huffed and twisted her lips as she peered around the room. "Behave," the mother growled in a low voice near Louise's ear. With a nod and a pat on the back, she understood she was free to negotiate to a better viewing spot. Louise slipped between the standing people, making her way to the second of the four pillars running down the center of the room. She wrapped her arms around the white column and stepped up on its plinth, lifting herself up a little higher on each successive decorative curvature. Finally, she could see the tapestry, and with its view came the direct gaze of Queen Anne. Louise flushed with fear; she shut her eyes, and her legs went weak. She waited, but no reprimand came. She forced herself to open her eyes. To her surprise, she saw only kindness in the queen's gaze. Louise smiled timidly to the monarch. Queen Anne gave a wink and the girl smiled broadly, locking her little arms around the column tightly.

"Despite the late arrival at the inn," Queen Anne's voice filled the hall, "the travelers rose early the next morning before dawn to journey onward."

☩ ☩ ☩

"Will it ever get light, Uncle Anthony?" The prince peered out the window, moonlight reflecting off his pale face. "I think this coach ride is a never-ending journey in darkness."

"I know you're exhausted." The uncle patted the prince's shoulder. "Come. Close the curtain. It is perilous out there. You mustn't be seen."

"I'm glad you and Richard are making this journey with me."

"We are your mother's family and therefore your family too. Our purpose is to ensure that you make it safely to your mother, Elizabeth Woodville, and Duke Richard. Before your father died, he named the duke as your official protector. Sit back and rest, my dear prince. Soon you will be within the strong arms of your family."

✠ ✠ ✠

Queen Anne motioned for a drink. Meanwhile, a pair of misfit scraggly dogs sauntered in, sniffed the tapestry, and then proceeded down the long hall. Queen Anne watched the animals over the rim of her flagon of cool drink. She waited for the canine pair to disappear down the hallway and for the shuffling crowd to be still before she continued.

"Two of the prince's sisters, Elizabeth and Cecily, were older." The queen counted on her fingers. "His three other sisters, Anne, Catherine, and little Bridget were younger." Movement in the hall distracted her, and she looked up. Everyone went still under her keen, piercing gaze. The people had been shifting slightly here and there, making room for someone she could not yet see. Queen Anne continued the story while her eyes discreetly surveyed the crowd more closely than before. "The prince didn't worry too much for them. However, there was one sibling that caused him great concern."

✠ ✠ ✠

"Uncle Anthony, is Richard safe?"

"Your brother Richard of Shrewsbury?"

"Yes. Both he and I are the male heirs to father's throne. I think there are people who would do him harm."

"I can't speak for the safety of your brother. He's in God's hands."

"I wish he were here with us. He's nine but he has a timid, diffident nature. It's probably my fault. In his life, I've tried to shelter him too much. I believe that was the reason Mother kept us separated."

✠ ✠ ✠

The queen paused in her story telling; she could feel her pulse quickening. She nodded to a lady-in-waiting who passed the monarch a damp cloth so that she could moisten her lips. The queen was well used to being observed and scrutinized by a crowd, but there was something different today. She could sense it even if she could not see it … yet. Queen Anne looked over at Louise clinging to the second column in the hall and raised her eyebrows playfully. Louise aped the action back and beamed.

"As the prince sat in the coach, he heard a new sound which quickly overtook them. It was a tumultuous thunder of hooves. The night air was split with raucous shouts, horses whinnying, and the clamor of metal on metal. The prince cautiously pulled back the curtain which covered the coach's window and again peered out into the night. He saw a great number of moonlit men on horses. Though he didn't know them, William Hastings and Henry Stafford, the Duke of Buckingham, were there. He craned his neck searching for his brother, Richard. Not seeing him, the prince hoped against hope that his younger brother was safe."

✠ ✠ ✠

"Halt!" a voice among the horsemen shouted. "Who attempts to pass this way in darkness?"

"Do not delay His Majesty's coach," the driver called back gruffly. "It is on dire business. Yield the road to your king."

"How do we know you possess His Royal Highness?"

The prince watched his uncle open the coach door and block it with is body. "Rogue horseman, the coach driver speaks the truth! Richard Grey, half-brother to the king, and I, the Earl of Rivers, will flay any man who hinders His Majesty. If you don't accept that answer, then unsheathe your swords. I'll have no more words with you!"

"Then have words with me," a new voice calmly spoke. "I acknowledge your presence and question only that this indeed is a vehicle in the king's service."

"Who dares speak such disdain from the shadows?" Anthony groused. "Show yourself, man."

"It is I, Richard of Gloucester," a horseman eased forward, "the good brother of our departed monarch."

"We are saved!" the prince shouted from within the coach.

"Easy, Highness." The coach driver leaned over the edge and spoke toward the window in a harsh whisper. "I'm not so sure. It seems that one side of your family doesn't trust your safety in the hands of the other."

"What happens now, good driver?" the prince whispered back.

"We will leave that to your father's brother, Duke Richard."

✠ ✠ ✠

"The driver was correct," Queen Anne continued. "Each side of the family distrusted the other. However, Duke Richard was the official protector of the prince and had the king's backing, so he used that authority to have Richard Grey and the Earl of Rivers taken away. With the king's horsemen as security, Duke Richard led the boy prince, his nephew, toward London to be kept in a secure protective custody." Queen Anne passed Princess Claude to the governess with a smile. She then stood and motioned to the ladies-in-waiting to remove the train from her dress. Unencumbered, the queen resumed the story and began to pace. *Perhaps now I will be able to see that which approaches through the crowd.*

"Anticipating that this rift between the families would occur once the king died, the widowed queen had already gathered most all her children and took them to sanctuary at Westminster Abbey in London. This included the younger prince, Richard of Shrewsbury, Duke of York.

"To protect the two princes, Duke Richard increased the security in the Tower of London. In charge was a trusted English knight named Sir James Tyrrell. Duke Richard believed that unlike the questionable Richard Grey and Earl of Rivers, James Tyrrell would serve better as security."

✠ ✠ ✠

"Once in London, where are we going?" the boy prince whispered to the driver through a crack in the curtain.

"Duke Richard will direct us to the place of greatest safety in London."

"Sanctuary at Westminster? That's where Mother would choose."

"Maybe, my prince. The Tower of London is also a place of safety. It'll be up to Duke Richard to decide. I know you are alone in there, but you've got me up here, Sire. You should try to sit back and rest. We have much more traveling ahead."

✠ ✠ ✠

Queen Anne sat and accepted her little daughter in her lap again. She panned the crowd and found what she was looking for. *Ah, yes, the little face that hangs on my every word. And beside her, the one I've been sensing.* Now that she was sitting on her raised throne, she could observe the young man more closely. He was striking. He had a shoulder-length pageboy haircut, and she could just barely make out a gold-and-black checkered pattern on the shoulders of his vest. Queen Anne furrowed her brow. *Smart in appearance, but foreign dressed as though from southern Europe. Why here? Why now?*

"Young man," Queen Anne raised her voice and pointed, "what justifies your presence in this audience?"

"Forgive me, Majesty. It was not my intention to disrupt."

"Maybe. Maybe not. You have waited until each break in the story and eased yourself forward time and again. I assume you have an agenda." Queen Anne motioned to a pair of armed guards. "Either you are a hunter or a messenger. Which is it?"

"I am no hunter, Majesty." The young man slowly approached center court, bowed his head, and knelt. "What agenda can a messenger have other than the one entrusted?" He remained motionless, subservient.

"I don't know, and I don't know you." Queen Anne motioned the guards to pause their advance. She observed the man's vest, skirt, and pantaloons, each boldly patterned in gold and black. "A hunter would blend in with his surroundings and you certainly did not intend to blend in here."

"As I have said, Your Majesty, I am no hunter."

"That remains to be seen. In God's grace and gentle pace, tell me—what message so dire do you possess that leads you to hunt the Queen of France?"

8

Today and to Knight's Tomorrow

Château Royal d'Amboise
Loire Valley, France
1500

"Do you deny being a disrupter as well as a hunter?" Queen Anne pierced the kneeling man with her formidable gaze.

"I deny only any intent to disrupt." The messenger remained kneeling; his eyes respectfully averted. "As etiquette demands that a request be answered, so then a queen's request must be answered with greater intent."

"So your intent is only to relay a message."

"My intent is only to relay the answer to the queen's request."

"I send out many requests."

"I bring only one answer, Majesty."

"Let us not be delayed further. Stand, approach, and tell me the message."

The young man stood tall and walked with a powerful presence but spoke with a humble tone. "The message comes from the Republic of Venice. It was my best intent to deliver it to you at your residence at Château de Blois. I was redirected by the servants there to you here."

"Is it about the defeat of the Venetian fleet at Zonchio by the Muslims?"

"No, Majesty, I was unaware of this."

"Well, you should know that the fate of your republic currently hangs in the balance. Venice's naval commander in chief has been imprisoned and faces death. Given this situation, is your message more urgent?"

"It is only if the queen deems it to be."

"How will I know unless I have heard it?"

"There is no way to know, Majesty. Am I free to speak?"

"Is this the correct forum to relay your message or should I seek a chamber with more privacy?"

"Rest assured, Majesty, I believe that there is nothing of a personal or sensitive nature that would cause embarrassment to you. Mind you, Highness, if this is something which you feel may wait and be entertained at another time, I will resume my wait infinitely until only your hand releases me from it. My intent was only to let you know that an answer to your message awaits, nothing more."

"I confess that my curiosity is now aroused, messenger. Come now. Out with it. Let us all learn that which, at this point, is known only to you." The queen looked out over the silent audience—some eyes were watching the messenger while others were puzzling over the mysteries locked in the first of the queen's tapestries.

"Highness," the young man widened his stance and projected his voice, "the honorable artist Vittore Carpaccio graciously accepts your request to paint a young knight. He is overwhelmed that in the presence of so many great painters, you, a queen with the world's greatest treasury, chose him. As such, he wishes to do your bidding to absolute perfection. Thus, he sends me on a fact-gathering mission."

"So there's more than just a message." Queen Anne eyed him shrewdly.

"Master Carpaccio wonders if Your Highness would be willing to provide any specific guidance that will make the final painting more pleasing to your eyes and acceptable to your taste. He wished for me to tell you that he could not accept one coin of payment unless the queen was perfectly satisfied."

"I heard this about the artist. It is this very reason for his selection. If you will make yourself comfortable, I will briefly pause in my story of the tapestries at this time. I would like that we speak at length as to the painting's specifics. You can then leave at your earliest convenience."

"Your Highness, may I make a suggestion?"

"Speak warily. An ill suggestion could end an art commission before it begins."

"Before I stepped forward today on my mission, I was captivated by the story you were telling. Would you at least allow me to finish hearing the tale that spans the seven tapestries? Perhaps it will help me better understand the specifics of your guidance for Master Carpaccio and the commissioned art." The young man bowed with a smile.

"Perhaps," the queen answered. "To garner such understanding in the next few hours you will have to learn to see with your ears and hear with your heart. For the painting I have in mind, I will need you to feel my words in the marrow of your bones. You must relay to the art master subtleties about the painting that I cannot."

"Highness, say no more. I believe God has led you to Master Carpaccio and, thusly, me to you for an expressed purpose. I assure you that the words you have just spoken course through the veins of this Italian messenger." The messenger gestured to the display rack. "I believe that as I listen to the story of the tapestries, I will come to understand things that cannot be written on any paper anywhere. Upon my life, I can promise you that neither I nor my

Latin art master will disappoint you when I return with the finished painting. I promise you my death before any dishonor."

With difficulty Queen Anne broke eye contact with the proud, well-spoken man and glanced back to the smitten ladies-in-waiting within her court. She drew in a breath then redirected her attention to the little princess on her lap, whispering to her and stroking her hair for a few moments. She spoke again without looking up. "I have considered your suggestion." She could almost hear collective breath being held behind her. She looked up. "I choose it not."

"As you wish, Majesty." The messenger bowed deeply.

"Kind messenger, you intrigue me." She locked her gaze on the messenger. "You are no more than twenty years, yet you speak as one who has weathered many lifetimes past and may yet weather many lifetimes more into the future. There is something within you that is familiar, but for the life of me I cannot guess it. May we start with a name?"

"Of course, Highness. My name is Ottaviano Visconti." Ottaviano hesitated.

"Is there more?"

"Yes, Majesty." Ottaviano shifted his feet. "I am from Forum Livii. You might know it as Forlì." Ottaviano drew in a deep breath, then said, "I hail from the House of Riario della Rovere Sforza." Squeals and chatter immediately emanated from the queen's female attendants. A wave of Queen Anne's hand yielded silence.

"So you have deceived us. You are not just a messenger."

"No, Highness, not *just* a messenger. By birthrights based in Rome and the dignity of the house of my family, I am not just a messenger. However, yes, I am a messenger defined by the message, which is carried, not the birthright of the hand that carries it."

"How so, Ottaviano? Standing before me is a soul christened by the hand of the Holy See himself."

"It is true that the pope did christen me, Highness. Of this honor I had no control and therefore the event deserves no trumpeting."

"Maybe, Ottaviano, but you are no less a nobleman of Milanese royalty, which now is subject to France. That means that you are my messenger imbedded in the service of a foreign national. This is an interesting quandary. Isn't it, Ottaviano?"

"Yes, my queen," Ottaviano nodded. "I am nobility that serves two masters. For one year now, Milan lies within the auspices of France. Although my heritage lies in Milan, my present affiliation is with Venice. The story is long, and the telling of my tale would only distract from my mission."

"Why were you sent on a page's errand?"

"It didn't start out as such. As you know, the lands between Venice and Blois are most treacherous. No page could survive lest he was protected by a knight."

"Knights are in the service of nobility, not artisans. Whom do you serve?"

"Today I am in the service of Guidobaldo da Montefeltro." The tittering resumed from amongst the ladies but stopped immediately as the queen lifted her hand again.

"The Duke of Urbino." The queen nodded. "Impressive. You are a member of the elite armed forces." The queen narrowed her eyes.

"I am, Majesty."

"Are you a spy?"

"All who have eyes to see, ears to hear, and a mouth to report can be said to be spies."

"Are you a spy in the service of Urbino?"

"I have eyes, ears, and a mouth. I am a knight and thus I know the value of gathering military intelligence. It would be difficult for me to deny that I have been asked by the Duke of Urbino himself to keep my ears perked and my eyes sharp."

"So, you are a spy."

"With respect, Majesty, if my eyes need to be blinded, my ears to be cored, and my tongue to be ripped from my head in order to achieve your acceptance, then I submit myself gladly but only in the name of a messenger."

"Shall I meet that need?"

"If you did, Majesty, rest assured I would ask the Lord to enkindle my heart with the fire of the spirit that renewed the essence of the Blessed Sibyllina."

"I'm not sure that this queen would have much use for a deaf, blind, and dumb messenger, even if our Lord renewed his essence."

"Fear not, Majesty." He held his arms out, palms up, in submission. "I am no spy. I am only as the queen and the Lord desire me to be. Nothing more."

"Such charm follows well in the footsteps of your relatives. I think that sharpened ears, keen sight, and a skilled voice can be brought to acceptable use in the service of the queen of France. My only request is that you execute your mission to me with the same diligence that you soldier for Urbino."

"I hope one day to be a captain general myself."

"Proud aspirations for a proud knight." The queen smiled. "I like that."

"Aspirations are what drives us from within."

"You mentioned a page who was with you at some point, Ottaviano."

"Yes, there was, Highness." Ottaviano nodded.

"What became of the page?"

"He died as we crossed through the alpine passes."

"So with a page's messenger errand, we have a young, honorable knight standing before us."

"No, my queen, you have only a knighted messenger of a royal house who humbly wishes to serve you by completing an assigned mission for the great Venetian artist Vittore Carpaccio."

"Hmmm," the queen mused, "a knighted lord from Forlì acting as a messenger on behalf of an artisan from an unfriendly city. There is much I need to learn about you and this mission. I believe you are right. This is not the forum."

Queen Anne shifted her gaze to the assembly and raised her voice. "Kind artisans, there is a matter before me that needs the queen's full attention."

She then spoke again to the knight standing before her. "Ottaviano Visconti from Forlì and the House of Riario della Rovere Sforza, there are some insights that I possess which must be given to your ears only. It will be these that will add ultimate depth to the final commissioned painting. After I have given you this information, you are welcome to stay and enjoy the rest of the story regarding the seven tapestries. However, tarry not. Your art master will have a challenging task. And trust me when I say that I will hold him to the highest degree of his reputation."

"I fully understand, my queen," Ottaviano replied before he bowed and backed away.

"Clare," the queen motioned to her most trusted attendant, "prepare the guest rooms for every artisan and courtier here. Have all the comforts provided for several nights of stay. Use the houses and buildings throughout the castle grounds as necessary. For the artisans with animals, pay the local inns to provide comfort for them, their animals, and secure storage for their personal belongings. As for my knighted messenger here, he will stay here in the main palace. Ensure that his horse is well kept as we must ensure it will be strong for the long ride back to Venice."

"Yes, my queen. It shall be done."

"Clare, there's more. Have the kitchen prepare a banquet feast this evening which will feed everyone here to their utmost satisfaction."

Clare's eyes widened. "Everyone, Majesty? Not just—"

"What good is it to have the richest treasury in the world if there is no one upon whom to bestow it? Have everything prepared as I have said."

"Yes, my queen."

"And Clare, have one of the artisans, the last one, sketch the banquet itself so that we can expect a tapestry honoring this event for all time."

"Highness," Clare whispered, coming closer, "will you commission a tapestry for all time which has the queen here without her king?"

"The king is at war, and the banquet is here and now. What am I to do?" Queen Anne stroked her pleats with one hand. "However, your point is well taken. Have the artist include the king in the banquet tapestry. Have the artist also include a tree filled with green plums and a funny little frog." Queen Anne pinched the nose of her giggling toddler.

"Yes, my queen. Will there be anything else?"

"Yes, one last thing, Clare. Find Monsieur Commines, the royal scribe."

"Philippe de Commines, envoy to the Papal States?"

"Yes, the same. Please have him meet me at Chapelle Saint-Hubert. I may need his expertise."

"I hear all and obey, Majesty." Clare bowed and departed as the queen addressed her court.

"Ladies, gentlemen, courtiers, artisans, and any individual I might have inadvertently missed in oversight, we will defer further story telling at this

time. We will resume later. Lodgings are being prepared for one and all and a banquet will be served this evening." The queen passed Claude to Madame de Bussière's capable hands and then stood. "Ottaviano, please now accompany me to the palace chapel. Together we shall pray for the soul of the lost page and then thank our God for Venetian artistry. We shall then request a blessing on the work yet to be done."

"I shall pray for sharp eyes and ears to hear what you wish to share."

"As will I."

9

The Good, the Bad, and the Envoy

Chapelle Saint-Hubert

Château Royal d'Amboise grounds

Loire Valley, France

1500

"Even a healthy appearing onion can have a rotten core, Ottaviano." Queen Anne picked up a book from a narrow shelf in the chapel. In a few strides she crossed the length of the nave and then sat in the middle prayer bench.

"Have I given you room for mistrust, Majesty?" Ottaviano, following suit, sat on the edge of the same bench.

"You present a perfect blend of charm, character, confidence, and kindness, Ottaviano."

"You say that as if it is a bad thing, Majesty." Ottaviano held his riding cap, which he had removed upon entering the chapel. His rosy-brown hair shimmered red as it drank in the lights from the high-vaulted, stained-glass windows. "I had the feeling you had a different opinion of me as we spoke in the great hall."

"Yes, well, we aren't in the great hall now and I am not surrounded by my court."

"I know well the many masks we must wear, Majesty."

"How can a person so young exude such polish and wisdom?" The queen's eyes slid from the tanned skin on the knight's broad forehead to the thin wisps of his eyebrows. His widely set caramel eyes were casted down toward the shadows on the floor. "It's remarkably uncanny, Sir Knight."

"It's no mystery, Majesty." Ottaviano flickered a smile, causing the dimple of his chin to deepen momentarily. "I was well tutored."

"Yes, that much is evident, but to what end?" said the queen, squinting pensively. "Although similar, you are no Caradoc Freichfras."

"Who?"

"Never mind." The queen surveyed him astutely. "I see intelligence yet innocence. How is that possible?"

"Do you doubt that I can fully understand the information you wish carried to Master Carpaccio?" Ottaviano traced the margin of his chin with the back of his hand.

"No, that's not it." Queen Anne shifted toward him slightly. "I am uncertain about the transfer of the information between you and your art master when you arrive at Venice." Queen Anne opened her book of hours, flipping pages rapidly so the colorfully illuminated pages blurred, then stopped at a section near the back. Ottaviano watched carefully as the queen turned the pages in this portion of the book slowly. He noted that this part of the book was an addendum of sorts, individually laced and inset along the book's spine so that it was indistinguishable from the prayer book itself. The queen arrived at a blank page and then placed the entire book in the knight's hands. "This is my diary, ensconced amongst my prayers. I wish for you, in your own handwriting, to record the details that you will relay. Once I have heard my instructions read back to me, then I will know that the art master will fulfill my every requirement."

"I understand, Majesty." Ottaviano reached into a small satchel at his side and withdrew a stub of a graphite marking tool. "I am ready to write down your requirements."

"Excellent, Ottaviano." The queen sighed, drew in a deep breath as if to speak then fell silent.

"Majesty," said Ottaviano, dragging his eyes over the queen's facial features in profile. He ceased as he landed upon the tiniest of lip quivers. "Is there something that creates doubt?"

"Doubt?" said Queen Anne, rolling her lips inwardly.

"Your Majesty wishes me to have details of which she gives none. Has she reconsidered?"

"No, Ottaviano, as I said in open forum, you sincerely intrigue me."

"However, you lack a comfortable trust in me."

"Not in your abilities, Ottaviano."

"I know, Majesty." Ottaviano sat back in the bench. "You have reservations about me as a person. You will soon fill me with details I expect are known to none. How can you trust me?" Ottaviano held a fist to his mouth, drew in a tension-filled breath, and blew out into his fist. "You yearn to better know the vessel which is about to be filled?"

"Yes."

"The story is long." He dropped the graphite in the center seam of the book and set it on the bench between them. "Does the queen wish to hear it now?"

"Yes, the queen wishes to hear it." *Ottaviano is like a transient, makeshift Caradoc,* she thought, *albeit reborn Latin.* Queen Anne flushed with girlish delight, a feeling she rarely afforded herself. "This is not an opportunity any queen and messenger knight can say they have had." She reached over and gently touched his arm, "Begin now."

"Well then, if the queen so wishes, I am obliged." Ottaviano noticed how the diffused, midmorning light coming through the stained-glass windows of the chapel lit her smooth marble face with brilliant hues, softening it somehow.

"Go on."

Ottaviano cleared his throat. "As you know, Majesty, I am Roman-born and from the House of Riario della Rovere Sforza—"

"I know this; go on from there. Relate everything as if I have heard nothing before."

"Indeed. My family has ruled both Forlì and Imola as marches within the east coast of Italy."

"You were given this charge by the pope, yes?"

"Yes, Majesty, that was until last year."

"Last year? No. Not early enough." Queen Anne scowled. "Start again, this time at the beginning."

"As you wish, Majesty." He could not contain an amused chuckle. "I was born in Rome during the time that my father served as the captain general of the papal forces. For nearly nine years I had a splendid life growing up first in Rome, then in Forlì where my father was the lord ruler. It was twelve years ago in 1488, at the age of nine, when other children were playing with their toys, that I was placed on the throne of power upon my father's death."

"The year 1488, Ottaviano?" The queen put her hand to her chest. "That was the same year my father died. I was eleven. My father's fall from his horse led to his death and that placed me in charge of a duchy." Queen Anne shook her head. "One moment I was holding hands with my beloved amidst towering megaliths and dolmen, and the next I was laden with the chains of responsibility and the needs of my people."

"My deepest condolences for your loss, Majesty."

"Those words belong to you, Ottaviano. Forgive me. This is your story and yet I draw parallels in my life. Please, go on."

"There is nothing to forgive, Highness."

"Please."

"Because of my youthfulness at my father's death, my mother, Caterina, took the reins of power. She has held them tightly ever since. That is, until a few months ago."

A look of dawning comprehension swept across the queen's demeanor. "Your mother is Caterina Sforza, the Tigress of Forlì. She is quite the woman."

"She is an exceptionally powerful ruler, as was her brother, Ludovico, from whom the king of France has just wrested the keys of the Duchy of Milan."

"So, your uncle is Ludovico Sforza?"

"Yes, Majesty. He dwells now in the prisons of France."

"Are you here to see him and possibly attempt to free him?" Queen Anne leaned away, casting a wary eye on the knight.

"I will not deny, Highness, that as recently as one year ago my sword has dripped with French blood. I am a mercenary. I fight and kill the enemies of those who pay my salary. However, I do not come here today at the behest of any warlord."

"What of the Duke of Urbino?"

"I am in his service but currently excused of responsibilities to serve a skilled painter with a gentle hand. Instead of a sword, Master Carpaccio holds a brush. The red that drips from it gives life instead of taking it."

"A mercenary in service of an artisan. How unusual."

"Majesty, I assure you. I have no hidden agenda," Ottaviano splayed his hands wide in subservience, "and I would not dare to lie in the house of God. The power that France exerts over the city-states of Milan and Naples is a matter between them only. Even the king of Spain has chosen not to interfere."

"If the Italian city-states will not rule themselves as a nation," Queen Anne nodded, "then other powers will."

"Indeed, Highness." Ottaviano squeezed the hilt of his dagger and grimaced. "While in the direct service of Urbino, most days I am the muscle that the other powers wield."

"It's more than war and politics, Ottaviano." Queen Anne's eyes looked up and leftward; she tilted her chin. "My understanding is that France has rights to Milan through King Louis's father's mother, Valentina Visconti. May God rest her soul."

"Highness, I don't sit here before you to justify one political claim over another."

"No. You sit here before me because I permit you to do so," Queen Anne flared. She then shook her head and sighed. "I want to know the man who will bear my words forth. Please continue, Ottaviano. Tell me of your father's death. I remember it involving some intrigue."

"Your knowledge runs deep within the history of our peninsula."

"More than you know," the queen nodded.

One of the wooden doors of the chapel eased open. "Excellency," a new voice announced its presence, "you summoned me?"

"Monsieur Commines, thank you for your kind presence." The queen gently closed the book of hours next to her on the pew. "Enter and close the door behind you. This is Ottaviano from the House of Riario della Rovere Sforza."

"Riario, really." Commines scowled as Ottaviano stood and gave a curt nod. The scribe moved toward the front of the chapel and drew close to the queen. "I'm not sure I'm pleased to meet you, sir. Is Your Majesty aware of the company she keeps?"

"I am not, Monsieur Commines. That is why we all are here."

"What does Her Majesty require of me?"

"I need you here as an expert in the matter of Latin and papal affairs."

"As the queen wishes, I shall be the trained ears of Her Highness." Commines bowed to the queen. "Speak cautiously, young Riario," he sneered.

"Choose your words carefully. There is much I have seen in the world of Italian politics." Monsieur Commines sat in the front prayer bench with a sour-faced pucker on his lips. He turned slightly so his watery eyes could focus intently on every movement made by the young knight who had resumed his seat next to the queen.

"Your Highness," Ottaviano continued, "have no fear. My intent is honestly displayed. The presence of Monsieur Commines can only support the intent of my mission. May I continue?" The queen nodded and the young man cleared his throat. "My father was one of three involved in the Pazzi conspiracy of Florence."

"Pazzi conspiracy?"

"It was an attempt to eliminate the feud between papal and Florentine interests within Pisa and Imola," said Ottaviano. "The idea was to have the Pazzi family eliminate the Florentine leadership."

"Yes, Majesty," said Commines, "those who had been ordered to do the killing were signaled to do so at the very moment when the priest began singing the *Sanctus*." He leaned forward, grinning. "Majesty, things did not turn out as the conspirators had planned."

A creak of wood interrupted the scribe. "Highness," Clare stood at the door, "there is a person with me who has a note for the knight. He says it's quite urgent."

"Go ahead, pass it to him," Queen Anne commanded. "You know my definition of urgency, Clare. Please do not disturb us again unless it meets that criteria."

"Always, Majesty." Clare passed the note to the knight and left. As Ottaviano perused the note his features gradually sharpened. He glowered.

"Highness," said Ottaviano, his brow furrowed, "there appears to be something that requires my immediate attention. I beg your indulgence for a quick absence."

"Make it very quick." Queen Anne pursed her lips. "Monsieur Commines shall not wait for the tale." Queen Anne watched as Ottaviano left. She then turned to Commines and nodded.

"The hunters became the captives, my queen. The leadership of Florence did not kill them outright. The conspirators were executed by being disemboweled," Commines drew his finger midline down from his neck, "and hung from the balcony of the Palazzo della Signoria, the most public place in the city."

"Yes, Highness," said Ottaviano as he returned, closing the door behind him. "Francesco Salviati, the archbishop of Pisa, a conspirator himself, was executed from the balcony also."

"I imagine having his clergy publicly executed did not sit well with the Holy Father." Queen Anne shook her head.

"It did not, my queen." Ottaviano sat and sent a fleeting glance at the scribe. "After this outcome was communicated to the Holy See, he excommunicated the Florentines immediately."

"What became of your father, Ottaviano?" the queen asked.

"My father escaped. It was only later—as I told you prior—in 1488, that he was assassinated by the Orsi family from Forlì."

"I am sorry this happened to you and to your family."

"Thank you, Your Highness. My father lived the life of a marked man."

"How horrid for you, Ottaviano." Queen Anne reached out to place a comforting hand on Ottaviano's but then she thought better of it and reached instead to draw the book of hours close to her side. The brief, redirected motion did not go unnoticed by the keen-eyed young knight.

"It got worse, Majesty. After my father's death, the Orsi then captured my mother and us children. My mother left us. She escaped to a neighboring castle searching for help. The Orsi family tracked her down, threatening to kill all of us if she did not surrender."

"She left her children?"

"Yes, Majesty."

"What happened then, Ottaviano?" The queen searched the young knight's face.

"What she did then is not for your ears, my queen," Commines whispered behind his hand.

"Monsieur Commines, I will determine what is and what is not for my ears." Queen Anne glared.

"Of course, my queen," the beet-faced, Monsieur Commines yielded.

"Go on, Ottaviano."

"Highness, my mother stood on the wall of the fortress and lifted the front of her dress, displaying her most private female parts for the entire world to see. From the walls she shouted to our captors that if they killed us, it would be of little consequence since she obviously had what it took to make more children."

"How shameless of any woman to behave in such a manner!" The queen flushed, and then added, "And further, how heartless for a mother to speak such things about her children. Children are precious and should be protected."

"Think like an Italian." Ottaviano leaned closer and shrugged. "This brazen gesture saved our lives. The Orsi family saw Caterina as a hardened and heartless adversary. They released us unharmed since keeping us served no purpose. They felt that returning us to such a woman would alone be horrific punishment for both us and our callous mother."

"I can better understand Italian wisdom, though I have not the heart to feel the justification. What was the result of all this political maneuvering?"

"The death of the Orsi brothers became one of the grizzliest deaths ever to be recorded."

"I don't think I want to hear these details."

"That is a most wise choice, Highness."

"Ottaviano, you have grown up to be a knight of strong character."

"Others might disagree, Majesty."

"I see only strength in you."

"You know me only in a handful of moments. For years after my father's death, my character was weakened by the overshadowing power of my mother. When I became a knight, I fought not for honor, but for sacks of money. I became condottieri."

"This is the same as a mercenary, no?"

"It is the same, Highness—an Italian version."

"This doesn't tarnish the man I see before me."

"The eyes of the queen are obscured with kindness. However, I believe that you should know, from the onset, with whom you deal. These are important matters that you have at stake."

"Your basic character strength remains intact in my eyes, Ottaviano."

"What of my discredited past family history?"

"As Lord Jesus would say, I have no stones to throw."

"What of my time as a murderer for hire?"

"I am not hiring you to murder. I am entrusting a task to a man who has the honor to show the bad along with the good. I could ask for none better." The queen paused and turned to her envoy and scribe. "Your opinion, my good Monsieur Commines, is warranted now."

"This Riario here has presented himself forthright. I have no ill judgment or dispute with the lad. Your wisdom prevails, my queen."

With the queen's nod, Commines then stood to depart and made his way to the chapel entrance.

"Thank you, Monsieur Commines." Ottaviano stood and stepped into the side aisle of the chapel. "Unfortunately, I have an issue with you."

"I beg your pardon?" The scribe turned to look back, blinking several times.

"Sir, the horse which your coach injured upon your hasty arrival was mine. I am told that it will take weeks for his injured leg to heal. What say you to this matter?"

"I say," Commines hissed, "that a matter of a poorly hitched idiot horse daring to delay the queen's envoy is not one to be discussed in front of Her Majesty." As the envoy flipped his cape in Ottaviano's direction and made to leave, Ottaviano lurched forward momentarily.

"Gentlemen!" Queen Anne stood swiftly. "This can be resolved without bloodshed. Ottaviano, I command you to sheath your sword or else my personal guards will do it for you. Shall I call them?"

"No, Majesty." Ottaviano obeyed and knelt in the aisle.

"Monsieur Commines," the queen spoke over her shoulder, keeping her eyes on the mercenary knight, "is this true?"

"Majesty, the horse was poorly tethered. My intent was not to delay the queen's summons."

"I asked you a question." Queen Anne's voice, amplified by the close stone walls, made the scribe quail. "Don't make me repeat it!"

"It is true, my queen."

"Monsieur Commines, you will immediately see to it that your horse is unhitched from your coach and left for Ottaviano's convenience. Next, your people will find a horse equal in, or superior to, the quality of the one injured by your coach and give it to this knight. Until then, your coach remains here. Unless you purchase yourself an additional horse, you, sir, will remain on foot. Do you understand?"

"Yes, my queen." Monsieur Commines bowed respectfully to the queen's back and departed, pausing only briefly at the double doorway to glare back at the knight.

After the wooden door swung shut and the queen resumed her seat, Ottaviano rose and tapped his sword hilt. "Forgive me, Highness. I find injuring the defenseless shameful. Then again, threatening your envoy in your very presence was equally shameful."

"I have no qualms with your passion, Ottaviano." Queen Anne shrugged and motioned for the knight to sit. "Had it been me, I would have unsheathed both my sword and my dagger."

"Thank you for seeing the good in me, Majesty."

"Ottaviano, we are so much alike it scares me. I trust that at the end of writing these instructions, you will still see the good in your queen. Are you ready to write?"

The young man scooped up the book from the pew and opened it. "I am ready for the words from my queen."

As the colored light from the stained-glass windows crept across the chapel, the knight listened intently and recorded every word the queen told him. When she was finished dictating, she closed her eyes and listened as he read back his notes in her diary. Queen Anne nodded as his voice filled the quiet chapel.

"Have I fulfilled your expectations, my queen?"

"Indeed, you have, my dear knight," said Queen Anne as she opened her eyes and a small smile played at the corner of her mouth, "thus far."

10
Knight Unseen

Chapelle Saint-Hubert
Château Royal d'Amboise grounds
Loire Valley, France
1500

"I see a question in your eyes, Majesty," Ottaviano searched her face. "Where does its answer lie?"

"It concerns the knight for the painting, Ottaviano." Queen Anne cupped her hand over her mouth for a moment then returned it to her lap. "You see, the knight ... well he...."

"This knight you describe is not the king to whom you are married. Is he, Highness?"

"I had so hoped that these words would not have to leave my mouth in my lifetime, Ottaviano," the queen winced. "Yes, you are correct in your observation. That knight is not the king of France."

"Is he someone you love now?"

"Yes, very much."

"Is he someone to whom you have pledged your heart?"

"Yes, every cockle."

"Will you present this painting to him?"

"No. I cannot."

"I don't understand."

"I know, Ottaviano, but please understand this. That knight is the living manifestation of every beat of my heart, yet not part of my mundane world. I have been betrothed to four kings in my life." With her hand she motioned to the pendant crucifix on her necklace. "One queen spans the reigns of four kings."

"I still don't understand why you cannot give him the painting."

"When I was six years old, I was promised in marriage to the King of England. When he disappeared, the engagement was ended."

"As a six-year-old child, Majesty, could you even fathom the significance of being promised in marriage and then not?"

"I could."

"I'm surprised."

"That's understandable. Once you have heard more of my story, hopefully you will have better bearings."

"I know it's at a time gone past but I'm sorry for your loss."

"Thank you, Ottaviano." The queen smiled kindly. "I was then betrothed and married by proxy to the Emperor of Austria, a man I had never even met. It was he who sent me this crucifix pendant as a wedding gift. The church dissolved that marriage before I ever had any chance to meet him."

"Church politics, I'm sure."

"Yes, and royal politics as well."

"Sometimes they're one and the same."

"In this case, yes." Queen Anne nodded. "I was then married in secret to the king of France, Charles VIII, while he dissolved his previous engagement. The king died seven years later."

"Again, I'm sorry, Majesty."

"For him or me?"

"You, my queen."

Queen Anne shrugged and continued, "With no surviving heirs, I was bound by my marriage contract to marry Charles's successor. For two years now, I am married to Louis XII. You know him as the conqueror of Milan."

"Indeed, I do. So, the knight in the painting is a past king?" Ottaviano tapped the charcoal against the diary page.

"You asked for understanding, dear knight. You should have asked for patience."

"I am sorry, my queen. I am trying hard to fathom how your love, marriages, and paintings connect—but do not connect. I am already failing you."

"Kind Ottaviano, I ask for your silence for now."

"Yes, Majesty."

"With the absence of words, true understanding will arrive."

"Majesty, shall we now return to the palace and the tapestries?" Ottaviano returned the charcoal to his satchel.

"Presently. But before we go, please hand me my book of hours." Removing the pendant crucifix from her neck, Queen Anne placed it in the book like a page marker, then took it from him. "Give me a moment of private prayer. Please be sure both doors are closed. You may await me outside." She then proceeded past the front prayer bench and knelt at the altar.

She seeks so many assurances for these instructions. Ottaviano quietly moved toward the doors to give the queen all the privacy that she needed. In his last rearward glimpse he saw the queen deep in prayer at the foot of the altar. *There is no doubt that I cannot be the one to fail her in this quest.* Silently Ottaviano removed his deeply embedded dagger from the right-hand wooden door and sheathed it. *I cannot and I will not fail.* He left the chapel and closed the door behind him.

11

Knight to Queen's Book One

Château du Clos Lucé

Château Royal d'Amboise grounds

Loire Valley, France

1519

"That which was hidden shall now be revealed." The old father smiled, apparently re-energized since receiving the package and the banter with Clare. "Saint Luke said it, Salai. You should believe it." Now that the chapel was devoid of all but two, Salai again closed both wooden doors, and the old father lifted the partially unwrapped book.

"Here, Old Father, let me help you." Salai cut the remaining knotted string, allowing the opaque wrapping paper to fully fall away.

"This book belonged to Her Majesty—God rest her soul." In his hands the old father turned the thick little book over and back again. Protruding above and below the binding was a chain with a pendant crucifix, serving as a bookmark.

"It's not much more than a handspan in height is it, Old Father?"

"Yes, and look." Old Father placed his hand over the cover with his thumb tucked in. "It is narrower than my hand."

"So small, yet thicker than any book I have seen that size."

"It's Queen Anne's book of hours, Salai." The old father flipped through its pages. "Look here at all the writing and beautiful illuminations." Salai looked over his master's shoulder but did not touch the book even though he longed to. The old father let the book fall open to where the pendant served to mark. He read aloud. "'As Rigantona treasures Caradoc, so does the ermine endlessly admire the unicorn, even beyond death.'"

"What does that mean, Old Father?"

"This is part of the challenge I bring to you, Salai. I, myself, am not sure. It is a puzzle amongst puzzles and one that may place a burden upon us—upon you."

Salai cocked an eyebrow at the old father and shook his head. "I don't understand, how—"

"The *how* and *if* are for us to discover, apprentice. Look here, where the marker lies. What do you see?" He held the book open toward Salai who still dared not touch it.

"There is an additional section ... a separate bound part of the whole?" Salai whispered.

"Yes, and expertly made so that it aligns with the binding of the book of hours. It seems that here is where our path begins. Now, Salai, place yourself in the deepest artistic mind-set that you can muster." The Old Father sighed deeply, relaxing himself into the creative spaces within. "The first few pages here are written as if the author is the narrator of the queen's story—typical for a diary. But then the handwriting changes though the voice stays similar. I don't know who the other scribe could be."

"Why would she dictate to another in her own private book or diary?"

"I don't know, Salai. The other scribe's writing appears to have recorded a set of instructions for something. My guess is that a piece of art has been commissioned to honor someone."

"Who, Old Father?"

"I don't know. But, once we have discerned the meaning of this information, I need to know if there is a closing action yet to be done."

"What kind of closing action?"

"After dinner, I will tell you a story that only recently I have begun to understand. We shall see if you, my dear Salai, can help me. For now, just concentrate. I need you to taste colors and feel words. I will summarize the pages I believe to be instructions."

"Please, Old Father," said Salai, meticulously interlacing his fingers, "for my best understanding, tell me slowly."

The master nodded and then began, his quiet voice weaving through the warm light filtering in from the windows above the altar. "The instructions are adamant in that the artist must create a place where fantasy meets reality."

"Why, Old Father?"

"Come, Salai, as an artist yourself, you must know that sometimes reality can best be understood when found tucked within the folds of fantasy."

"I suppose," Salai nodded. "What else does it say?"

"It speaks to the importance of honor even to the point of death."

"Can that stark reality be expressed through fantasy?"

"Through the swirls of the artist's paintbrush, any message can be portrayed." Old Father gestured with his eyes closed, holding an imaginary brush. He then peered up and to his right, above the oratory's doors. "For example, I have not seen the Holy Virgin in heaven and yet there I have painted her— *Virgo Lucis*. Non-believers may call it fantasy—a woman taken to heaven body and soul, standing on the crescent moon—but to me it is real. Perhaps the fantastic and realistic elements each inform the other, perhaps their contrast helps us understand the miracle." The old father looked back to his apprentice. "The only limitation is in the mind and heart of the one who holds the brush."

"I have heard you say that many times before." Salai smiled. "What other instructions hide in the pages of Queen Anne's book?"

"There is guidance given for specific representatives from the animal world. Before you say it, Salai—for I know what you are thinking—let me add that the relationships of real animals to each other or even to other elements within the painting could still be portrayed in fantasy."

"Hmmm. I'm still not sure that I—"

"Consider a horse standing on the top of a man's head." The old father laughed. "Please don't. That sounds rather painful."

"I see your point," said Salai, chuckling. "Please, go on."

"It narrates requests for animal representations with very specific instructions."

"For example?"

The old father looked down at the book as he summarized, "The presence of a white ermine in association with a frog."

"That's very odd." Salai's forehead wrinkled. "Besides animals, is there a human representation requested?"

"Yes, and there's more." The old father beamed, enjoying every moment of the enigma before him. "She asks for specifics within a sea of ambiguity."

"How so?"

"Well, she has asked for a young knight which cannot be attributed to a single living person."

"So, this knight can be anyone?"

"Or, quite brilliantly, a compendium of everyone." The old father traced his finger along a line of text as he read aloud, "'She wishes him to be proud yet possess a hint of sadness. He must demonstrate balance in the face of turmoil.'" He chuckled and continued, "'She asks that the knight have the strong chin of the knight messenger.'"

"Strength with sadness," said Salai, nodding. "I like that. I can understand that."

"If you like that, then you will love this." The old father closed the book. "Above all, the painting must have heart."

"Heart … as in passion?"

"She doesn't say, Salai." Old Father reopened the book and flipped many pages. "She says," the old father pointed, "'Draw in a representation with heart because among all symbols, it is the richest that there can be.'" The old father again closed the book, folding his hands atop it. "Any thoughts, Salai?"

"Many, but where to begin?" The old father only answered with raised eyebrows and a shrug, so Salai continued, "I think that the scribe is a male, maybe even a knight himself."

"Why?"

"All these requests speak to chivalry. This concept would be well known to a knighted scribe."

"Yes, that is what I surmised as well … but why not, say, a female knight?"

"A strong chin speaks to fistfights and the ability to take a punch."

"Indeed, Salai. That was my conclusion as well."

"There is one part that burrs under my skin, Old Father."

"Just one part?" The old man's eyes twinkled. "Yes, go ahead."

"What involvement would a queen have with a knight who has permission to write about *another* knight—who is *not* the king—in her personal book of hours?"

The old father nodded smilingly. "Albeit a dubious musing, that, my dear Salai, is the right question."

12

When Right Has Left

Barclay Cottages
Barclayville, Liberia
Current day

"This isn't bathing! Brrr! This is freezing torture!" Mike Winnabe fumbled with the shower knobs. *This one should be the hot water, but it certainly isn't.* Mike rubbed hard on his gooseflesh. *More of this, ladies and gentlemen, and I am going from shake and flake to seismic shiver quakes.* Mike sprung out of the shower, slapped a towel around himself, and tremored for the phone. *This is incredible. Thirty minutes ago, warmly basking in my dreams, I was a bird flying through desert-baked air. Sand dunes emitted radiant fingers of shimmering heat rustling through my feathers. What would I give for that heat now?*

"Is-s-s this-s-s the fr-fr-front de-de-desk?"

"This is cottage reception. Is everything all right, Mr. Winnabe?"

"I'm being pelted by ice cubes in my morning shower."

"Did you flick the switch next to the shower head?"

"What switch?"

"There is a switch. It looks like a light switch. It will turn on the heating coil."

"What heating coil?"

"There is a heating coil that wraps around the shower pipe as it comes out of the wall."

"I saw that."

"Well, the coil heats the pipe, and the pipe then heats the water as it flows."

"But I'm wet."

"Yes, understandably."

"You want me to fiddle with a light switch on an electric coil while I'm dripping wet and standing in water … while showering?"

"Mr. Winnabe. I want nothing except what you desire." The receptionist paused; his voice muffled. "I'm sorry you were stung, sir. Always check your shoes before donning them. Please, read the warning on the back of the door."

"Hello?"

"Sorry, Mr. Winnabe, it's quite busy now. Where were we?"

"Sleeting rain as shower water?"

"Ah yes," the receptionist coughed, "if you want hot water, then you will have to turn on the switch. The switch will not engage until the water flows in the pipe." The voice sighed, "I realize this is not what you're used to, but things are a bit more basic here."

"I get that, but this still doesn't sound right." Mike stepped away from a scorpion scurrying across the floor. "The laws of electricity are the same here as in the rest of the world, aren't they?"

"Sorry, Mr. Winnabe. I'm tied up at reception right now. However, rest assured. I'll send maintenance right over."

"Have them bring a heating blanket!" Mike slammed down the phone. "Well, at least I'm lucky I got the room with the phone." He plopped himself in a plastic cushioned chair and glanced around the room until he saw his reflection in the mirror. Mike pointed at himself. "You, sir, should stop your whining. The shower water was much colder in '83 during Grenada operations. In '89 operations, the giant Panamanian roaches ate the scorpions for breakfast." Mike laughed as the room's doorknob dropped to the floor after a prolonged knock from the outside.

"Hold your horses. I'm coming." Mike fumbled the reseating of the knob.

"Mr. Winnabe?" A squeaky voice accompanied additional knocking.

"Almost there." Mike cinched his towel around his waist as he opened the door. "Who are you?" Mike peered out.

"Front desk sent me." An adolescent girl flashed a smile up at him.

"You're maintenance?"

"No, but I can show you how to work the shower."

"How old are you?"

"I'm eleven."

"You can't be. You aren't even tall enough to be eleven, much less reach the shower knobs."

"May I come in?"

"I'm half naked."

"Do you wear a bathing suit at the beach, Mr. Winnabe?"

"Sometimes," Mike adjusted his towel. "It depends on the beach."

"Well, you're probably more covered up now than at the beach."

"Are you sure you're eleven?"

"May I come in? Ike says I'm to pop in and out quickly."

"Who is Ike?"

"Ike says you're an American army guy."

"Who's Ike?"

"Ike is Ikenna."

"Who's Ikenna?"

"Ikenna runs the reception here at the cottages during the day. Adi runs it at night. Ike is the one who sent me."

"Yes, I am an American army guy."

"Ike says you work at a gas station in America."

"Where does Ike get this?"

"Is it true?"

"Well, yes, I own several gasoline stations in my hometown."

"Parkings Burg."

"Parkersburg. It's in West Virginia. How do you know all this?"

"I don't. I just listen to Ike when he talks on the phone."

"Who is Ike sharing this information with?"

"I don't know," the girl shrugged, "probably the cottage owner."

"Well, Leven, are you going to help me or not?"

"Leven?"

"I don't know your name. You said you were eleven. So—"

"I never had a nickname before." The girl smiled. "Leven it is!"

"Are you going to help me, Leven?"

"Yes, sir." Leven grabbed the plastic chair from the back patio and brought it into the shower. "First, you turn on the water."

"Which one?"

"It doesn't matter."

"Well, one says 'hot' and the other says 'cold.'"

"Yes." She turned a knob, and the icy jet of water began spraying again. "But they both run cold."

"I noticed that, Leven."

"See those two switches up there?"

"The ones with the dirty cobweb hanging between them?"

"Yes, one should be labeled 'right' and the other 'left.'"

"Both are labeled 'left.'"

"Really? You have two lefts?"

"Like a bad dancer."

"What?"

"Never mind, Leven."

"Well, you should flip the switch on the right side once the water runs." Leven placed the plastic chair near the shower.

"Are you sure it's safe?"

"Yes, I'll show you." Gripping the shower's tiny, slatted windowsill, Leven climbed up on the chair.

"Careful, now." Mike pointed up, "Don't nudge my neck chain off the sill."

"Never." Leven shifted her grip, reached up, and on tiptoes, flicked the right-side switch. "Now, we wait a bit."

"How long?"

"A bit," said Leven, smiling at him as she stood on the chair. She clapped some rust from her hands before shifting her position from standing to sitting in the chair. Now seated, Leven panned from the windowsill to where worried-looking Mike stood gazing up at the electrical switches and coils in juxtaposition to the water streaming down from the showerhead. "Is it true you are checking out in the next few days?"

"Maybe."

"Are you still going to Morocco?"

"Where did you hear that? Wait … from Ike?"

"Yes." Leven reached in and felt the water. "Where after that?"

"After Morocco?" Mike balked. "That is if I am going to Morocco."

"Yes, if and when you leave for Morocco."

"I don't quite know." Mike whispered to her with mock confidentiality, "However, when I do, I'll tell Ike and he can let everyone know."

"Great!"

Mike chuckled. "Is the water ready yet, Leven?"

"Yes, it should be." Leven again felt the water and smiled. "It's hot now."

"Let me see," Mike reached in and then raised his eyebrows. "Leven, I hate to tell you, but this is not hot."

"Yes, it is."

"No, this is tepid."

"What is tepid?"

"Tepid isn't hot."

"Is tepid cold?"

"No."

"Okay, well then tepid is hot."

"Will it get hotter than this?"

"No, Mr. Winnabe."

"Well, I need to talk to … you know what?" Mike shook his head. "It doesn't matter. At least it's not freezing cold."

"Do you know the trick to showering?"

"There's a trick, Leven?"

"Yes, once the water is hot, you turn down the flow until it is a fast drip." Leven tapped her head mimicking the drops of water. "Then scrub your hair with soap real hard. The scrubbing makes the soapy water warm as it trickles down your head and over your body."

"Actually, I knew that trick."

"Well, it works well here in the cottages."

"Thank you, Leven."

"Okay." Leven sprung to her feet. "I'll let Ike know you're all set."

"Thank you."

"Don't worry, I'll let myself out."

"The doorknob is on the floor again."

"I don't need it."

"Why is that not surprising?"

"Goodbye, Mr. Winnabe. Have fun in Morocco—if and when you go."

"I'll try, Leven. Thanks again." Mike moved the plastic chair back on the patio as the front door closed. He reconnected the knob and then looked at his reflection. "Imagine that, Mike, you were taught how to take a shower by an eleven-year-old kid." He laughed as he eased under the shower water. "Wow, that's still cold but not like before." He grabbed the soap bar and pushed open the filthy slats covering the bathroom window. *This should allow some of the hot out-side air to waft in.* He turned down the water to a fast drip, positioning himself so that the stream of water drops hit him on the centermost top of his head. Mike then took his washcloth and lathered it richly with the bar soap.

Why do you do this to yourself? Mike shook his head. *Mickey and I have been playing army since we were kids. Now, years later as a reservist, I am a special ops major in the boonies while Mickey and Bridgette are active-duty colonels sipping mai tais in a comfy garrison setting.* Mike scoured his scalp and skin.

"You did it for Zell, just to be close to her. Right?" Mike spoke out loud to himself as he rubbed hard on his body, trying to make the most of the warm water. *Yes but no.* Mike rubbed harder. *I haven't been anywhere close to Zell. Special Operations have had me globe-trotting. Today Barclayville. In a few days, Casablanca. Who knows after that?*

With his face lathered Mike shifted his position to allow the tepid water to drip high on his forehead and then cascade down over his brows and into his eye wells. The soap lingered. He had to flush his eyes several times. *How do third-world-people stand the harshness of the soap here?* Mike squeezed his eyelids tightly and kept rinsing. He never saw the fingers which crept between the lowest slat and the windowsill, nor the slow disappearance of his metallic beaded neck chain and the silver key upon it labeled *Right*.

13

A Chat with Cat

Office of the Command Surgeon
US Army Recruiting Command
Fort Knox, Kentucky
Current day

"No disrespect intended, Lord Doc, but are you nuts?" Major Oberstadtmeyer flashed his palms outward from both temples. "I'm going in there to pick up what? To carry to whom? And he's where?" Major O-stadt pulled hard on his chin, contorting his dark Greek facial features into a scowl. "Are you sure you've got the right guy?" His coal-black hair appeared in frightful disarray from all the pulling and tugging. *How is this the chance of a lifetime? Chance for what? Why don't they just paint a target on me?* Major O-stadt swallowed hard. "Let me see if I got this right, sir. My mission is to go into the bullion depository at Fort Knox, pick up secured classified documents, carry them through Europe to Africa, and place them in the hands of a special operative in Liberia in support of AFRICOM."

"Yes, Major O-stadt." Lord Doc handed him a business card. "On the way, you should pass through Germany. I'd appreciate if you would drop this card off at the European Medical Command Headquarters."

"Roger, sir." Major O-stadt read quietly. "But this is *your* business card. Will the recipients at ERMC know who Colonel Prentice Christiansted is?"

"I believe they will be quite familiar with that name—or part of it anyway."

"Sir, on the back side of the card is written—"

"I know what it says," Lord Doc groused. "Ensure it gets to the correct person."

"But, sir, how will I know who to take it to?"

"They'll know when you show them that card. Then you'll know."

"What if I get injured or killed en route?"

"Don't die until that card arrives at destination. And when you get directed to the right office, say you need to give something to the warden."

"The warden?" the major cocked an eyebrow.

"Yes."

"But sir—"

"Don't look so dour. If anyone should look gloomy, it should be me. I'm the one on the way to the hospital."

"Roger, sir."

Lord Doc twisted his lips as he looked the major up and down. "Are you worried about security?"

"Yes, sir. Of course, sir. Once the classified documents leave the depository, I only have my skills to ensure their protection. I then make a handoff in a foreign country and under unforeseen circumstances. Only after that handoff is completed—if I'm still alive—will all the secret squirrel drama end."

"It's probably not as dire as you paint it," Lord Doc laughed. "I'm sure the briefing you get will provide you a warm and fuzzy."

"Sir, warm and fuzzy is one thing. Having to personally defend the contents of a courier's case against unknown assailants weighs heavily on me." Major O-stadt wrung his hands. "I have no training in Special Operations. I'm not a spook."

"I'm aware of that. This works to your advantage. Your part in this is neither cloak nor dagger."

"My advantage? How so, sir? The eyes of the enemy are everywhere. Even if enemy agents don't know what I'm carrying, they know it's coming from America's premier security vault. Might as well stamp a bullseye on my back. Sir, plain and simple, this is a suicide mission." Major O-stadt paced the office. "Sir, I've checked in the mirror. I don't have *stupid* written on my forehead."

"Son, there is only a handful of people who would ever be trusted for a mission like this."

"Where are *they?*"

"Well, you should be aware, some *are* dead. Others are on other similar missions."

"So, not dead *yet*."

"No." Prentice Christiansted coughed. "If only I was younger and in better health, I would go myself."

"What exactly am I carrying?"

"It's classified."

"Classified to the extent that it has to be housed and protected where the nation guards its gold reserve?"

"I have no data to explain why the classified document, or documents, are housed at the Fort Knox Bullion Depository."

"Isn't it enough to know that this intel must be guarded by a massive fortress structure surrounded by redundantly emplaced steel fences? Each of the four corners of the fortress has mounted guard boxes with state-of-the-art weaponry."

"It's just a big safe."

"Sir, if a tower guard accidentally sneezes, what would be left of me could be served up in a thimble."

"Sneezing is unauthorized anywhere in the building."

"Sir, this isn't funny."

"No, it's not." Lord Doc stood to face the major. "Son, you dug yourself in a hole back in Romania. That wasn't my doing. I've now devised a way for you to pull yourself out. This is a good thing."

"Sir, I think you—"

"You're welcome, Major O-stadt. Now go and do yourself proud." Lord Doc watched as Major O-stadt stiffened, saluted, and left his office, heading toward the bullion depository.

In less than fifteen minutes by car, Major O-stadt arrived at the fortress. As he passed under the watchful eye of the hypoallergenic soldiers in the machine gun emplacements, he imitated Lord Doc, saying, "Sneezing isn't authorized. This is a good thing."

Upon passing the extreme external security of the depository, Major O-stadt followed a tabby cat as they both entered the inner sanctum. "What's your mission, Sir Feline?" Major O-stadt squatted down, but the cat merely gazed at him nonchalantly. "Not sharing? Well, me neither."

He stood and walked through the marble entrance at the front of the building, upon which he read the inscription *United States Depository* and saw the seal of the Department of the Treasury in gold. At the base of the archway was a saucer of milk.

"So, Mr. Cat, you do have an agenda." Major O-stadt lifted his gaze straight ahead as clacking steps approached.

"Major Oberstadtmeyer?"

"That would be me."

"This way, sir." Major O-stadt stepped off at a fast pace and was quickly directed to the door of the captain's office. A desk sergeant stared him down.

"How much of the one hundred and fifty million ounces of gold are you going to let me have today, desk sergeant?" Major O-stadt forced a grin.

"As much as you can lift with one finger, sir." The sergeant's pale, bland expression never changed.

"Do you have anything equally as precious that wouldn't be so heavy to carry out?" Major O-stadt leaned on the desk ledge.

"There are historical relics, articles, addresses, and stuff like that."

"Addresses?"

"I don't know, sir. Somewhere in Gettysburg I heard."

"Tell me, is it true that during the war, our Declaration of Independence and the Constitution were brought here and stored in a bronze storage container weighing one hundred fifty pounds?"

"I dunno. I was off shift."

"Is it true that the Armor School was here just so that there would be tanks to guard the nation's valuables?"

"Missed that meeting, sir."

"Is it true that this place has stored the English crown jewels, copies of the Magna Carta, the Gutenberg Bible, some Nazi documents from the Leaning Tower affair, and the ruling staff of Hungary?"

"Speaking of *hungry*. It's chow time." The desk sergeant stood abruptly. "Wait here. The captain will be here momentarily." He pointed down the hallway.

"I said 'Hungary,'" Major O-stadt iterated.

"Indeed, sir." The desk sergeant left the desk and, as he passed the approaching captain, thumbed back toward Major O-stadt.

"I see you met Cathy." The captain extended his hand in greeting.

"Cathy?" Major O-stadt shook the hand.

"Yes ... as in Chatty Cathy. Honestly, the guy never shuts up."

"Are you serious?"

"No." The captain motioned, and a guard approached, setting a large Pelican travel safe in front of Major O-stadt. "Clamshell design, dual locks, and waterproof."

"With the locks, Captain," Major O-stadt pointed, "why the thumb-rolled combination?"

"Sir, it's best if you just listen. I'll answer any remaining questions afterward." The captain presented a single piece of paper. "Documents have been placed in this container with attestation of such being verified by this certificate."

"What does the document say?"

"It says that the requested documents were verified and secured by two people whose signatures are on this certificate." The captain redirected to the case. "As you noticed, the container is secured by two locking mechanisms of which you will hold one key." The captain handed over a silver beaded chain threaded through a single silver key. "Be advised, sir, there is an imprinted word on the key."

The major held the chain in his hand and though in reality it was quite light, to him the burden was heavy. *More like a noose if you ask me.* He turned the key over and found the imprint. "Yes, I see the word 'left.' May I assume that the key that reads 'right' is not going to be issued to me but to another?"

"Yes and no. The key that reads 'right' has been shipped already and we have verification that it has been received. Now the remaining key may be issued to the courier."

"Understood. I take it that the other key lies at the destination."

"Yes, sir. It is already there."

"What about the combination wheels?"

"Sir, the mechanism is set so that once you have aligned the numbers in the sequence you desire, the memory chip engages. Only that sequence will unlock the Pelican."

"Seems simple enough."

"I would advise that you memorize the five-digit sequence before entering it. Whatever number you concoct, reverse it so that it has a greater chance of anonymity."

"Got it."

"Once you have passed a combination wheel and engaged the next, you cannot return to the ones prior. Ten seconds after you enter the last number, the memory chip is set. I would advise that you not use any number that could be presently associated with your name such as: your social security number, significant life event date, any form of registration number, credit cards, zip codes, telephone numbers—"

"I get the picture. If you will give me a moment, I believe I have the perfect number."

"Do you have the number?"

"Yes."

"Then reverse it and enter it into the combination lock after I have turned my back." The captain spun on his heel away from the major and waited.

"Okay."

"Finished? Good. I now need you to give the basis of the number and two distracters."

"I don't understand. You want me to tell you the number sequence?"

"No, sir. I don't have need-to-know. However, the number sequence you entered had relevance to something which you associated with a memory link. What I need to know is the memory link and two distracters."

"Got it." Major O-stadt's eyes went up and left. "Snyder Street garage sequence. High school combination lock. Romanian dance club bar tab."

"One of these is correct?"

"Roger. Only one. Do you need to know which one?"

"No, sir. I don't have need-to-know. However, if you are in a position where you have a memory lapse, you may contact us at the number on this card and we will read to you these memory links. Only you will know which link is correct and the number sequence attached to that link."

"I understand. Is there anything else?"

"As long as you understand that you do not have permission to access the document, or documents, within this case, I have nothing else for you."

"Oh yes. That has been made crystal clear."

"Well then, sir, I stand subject to any alibi questions or concerns."

"Are you going to open the case so I can attest to the fact that the documents inside are actually in there?"

"No."

"How do I know that the valuable documents are really in there?"

"The certificate states so."

"I see two names I don't recognize, on a sheet of paper I've never seen before, from a person I don't know, assuring me this is a valid certificate."

"Sir, you are a courier. You are responsible for taking this Pelican to destination. The contents are of no concern to you."

"For all I know, Chatty Cathy's lunch could be in there."

"I assure you that it isn't."

"Why, have you looked in there?"

"I will entertain any serious questions, sir."

"What if I lose the case?"

"Sir." The captain sniffed. "In the absence of any serious questions or concerns, I bid you a safe journey." The major reached out for the case. "I trust that there will be no need for me to hear your name again."

"What does that mean, Captain?"

"Courier missions like this are in the single event category. If I never hear word of you again, then all went well. I'm happy. You're happy. Chatty Cathy is happy."

"Chatty Cathy?"

"If your name appears here a second time, he will have to be the one to go get you."

"I'm serious, what if—"

"Sir, there are no what-ifs. In this business it is best never to have a second interface of any nature." The captain gave a quick, supplicating grin and then departed hastily.

Happy to meet you too. Major O-stadt nodded as Chatty Cathy approached. "Is the captain always like that?"

"Like what?"

"Never mind, Sergeant." Major O-stadt shook his head. "That was certainly a quick lunch. I guess you weren't as 'Hungary' as you thought."

"You have your Pelican. Are you ready to go, Major?"

"I was ready to go when I arrived here."

"Yes, sir, so were we."

14

Perkins and Peekings

Bullion Depository
Fort Knox, Kentucky
Current day

"Are you my escort out?" Major O-stadt scrutinized the armed civilian.

"I'm Perkins. I'm your security detail."

"I wasn't aware I was getting one."

"Are you ready to go, Major?"

The major nodded his assent. With the documents safely stored inside his Pelican travel safe and under guard, Major O-stadt traveled north to the reservation airfield. He repeatedly glanced at Lord Doc's business card as he waited for his hop to Louisville.

"Is that who you're meeting at Ramstein?" Perkins pointed.

"What?"

"The business card, Major."

"No." Major O-stadt slipped the card into a pocket and secured it.

Soon after, the pair boarded a specially arranged Blackhawk and passed east over the tiny town of West Point, Kentucky, on the way to the airport on the south side of the city. There at an undisclosed hanger, the two men waited.

"Do you know where we're going, Perkins?"

"Yes, Major. I have the flight plan to Ramstein."

"Care to share?"

"Negative."

"Come on, just a peek."

"Negative, sir."

"Is there a reason I'm being treated like cargo?"

"Sir, my job is to get you to your overseas connector. There my job ends. There will be other security elements along the way to assist you in getting to your destination."

"Until when?"

"Until there isn't."

"Where are we going from here?"

"Outbound."

"See? Was that so hard?"

"Sir, I'm going to get some coffee and a sandwich."

"Would you mind getting me a—"

"Tuna on rye. No mustard. Coffee black, two sugars."

"Well, you certainly did your homework on me."

"Don't wander off, Major. I need to keep line of sight on you." Minutes later Perkins returned. "Eat fast, we have to be at the heliport in ten."

"We're going outbound again in a chopper?"

"It seems so."

"I guess that would mean we're going to Wright-Patterson."

"I guess we'll know when we get there."

"Why so cryptic?" Major O-stadt chortled. "I'll bet your name isn't even Perkins."

Arriving at Wright-Patt, Major O-stadt watched as Blackhawk transport changed over to a military passenger jet heading for Germany.

"Proceed this way, sir."

"What? You're not coming along, Perkins?"

"No, Major." Perkins pointed ahead. "Your next security detail is waiting for you on board."

"Who do I ask for?"

"Don't worry. They'll know you." Perkins spoke into his sleeve as Major O-stadt disappeared into the plane. As soon as he crossed the threshold of the plane, Major O-stadt was engaged by another civilian security element.

"Major O-stadt?"

"Let me guess, ma'am, you're my security."

"Guilty as charged. I'm Perkins."

"Really, I think I know one of your relatives."

"Mother has a lot of us."

"So, what's the plan from here?"

"We're headed to Ramstein, Germany."

"Not being cryptic?"

"Why cryptic?"

"I don't know … the other Perkins wouldn't give me the time of day."

"It's twenty hundred hours." Perkins tapped her watch. "That would be eight o'clock civilian time."

"Sense of humor too."

"You'd best get to your seat, Major O-stadt."

"Sure. Are you going to need line of sight?"

"You'll be fine in first class."

"First class? On a military flight?"

"That's what they call first-row seating."

"Great." Major O-stadt rolled his eyes. He stowed his small pack overhead and settled into a seat in the first row as Perkins buckled in next to him.

"I'd recommend that you sleep while you can. You are going to lose your night in travel. We'll arrive at Ramstein in time for breakfast."

"Will you rest as well?"

"We'll see how it goes." Perkins smiled.

"What time do we arrive?" Major O-stadt asked but the only answer was a soft, slow breathing from his left. *Gosh they can even sleep on command. Mother has them trained well.* Major O-stadt closed his eyes until turbulence woke him.

"Perkins?" Major O-stadt craned around. "Perkins?" He noticed a blue blazer folded over the adjacent seat's aisle arm. *What have we here?* Major O-stadt pulled out a folded paper peeking out from an inner blazer pocket. He read quickly.

"That's not yours, Major O-stadt." The standing Perkins snatched the paper back.

"No, Perkins, but it should have been."

"I don't make those decisions, Major." Perkins put her blazer back on, secured the paper in a pocket, and sat down.

"Why didn't anyone tell me what I was carrying?" Major O-stadt whispered, leaning over the arm of the chair.

"No need-to-know." She cinched the seatbelt strap.

"And now, Perkins?"

"You know without need."

"Is this really what I'm carrying?" He kept his voice hushed despite his rising emotions.

"I don't know … for sure."

"Perkins, I have some questions. Time to level. Tell me what you *do* know."

"I know your full travel itinerary."

"Good. That's a start. Where do I go from Ramstein?"

"You will need to fly to Rota, Spain."

"From there?"

"You will fly into Monrovia, Liberia. There a chopper carries you to destination."

"Why not tell me all this in advance?"

"Well, first of all, there are a hundred variables that play out between Fort Knox and Barclayville, Liberia." Perkins looked at her watch. "Military flights are added and deleted like clockwork."

"So, the Perkins at Ramstein will have his or her hands full trying to manage those variables."

"There will be no further security element once you arrive at Ramstein. You will be totally within the military systems at that point, so there is no need for it."

"Okay, so, if a blue-blazered Perkins walks up to me at Ramstein and tells me that they are my security element…."

"Karate chop to the throat, sir. Then run."

15

Passing Perkins

Ramstein Military Air Terminal
Ramstein, Germany
Current day

"This is unacceptable, Perkins." Staring at the display headed Connecting Flights, Major O-stadt shook his head. "Half of these flights have changed since we have been standing here."

"That's what I told you."

"Look, now all flights to Spain are in abeyance for seven days."

"The airman at the help desk said that all flights destined to the Iberian Peninsula, including Portugal, had been diverted to the Middle East and Romania in support of ongoing operations there."

"When God closes the door, Perkins," Major O-stadt sighed, "he usually opens a window."

"God might find out that the Ramstein windows are closed as well."

"What happens to you now, Perkins?"

"Me? Normally I would catch the next flight to anywhere in the US. From there, I'd catch any plane back to Louisville."

"Normally, but not now?"

"No, I asked for this assignment so that I could take some personal time on this end and go visit my mother."

"Your mother lives in Germany?"

"No, France."

"Perkins is not a French name."

"You know quite well my name isn't Perkins."

"I guessed it was the name of your security firm. All you guys are named Perkins?"

"Yes."

"So out with it, Perkins. What is your real name?"

"I'll tell you if you promise not to laugh." Perkins fumbled at her blazer buttons. "And you'll have to tell me something equally embarrassing about yourself."

"First, I never laugh when on courier duty. Second, I have never had anything embarrassing happen to me, ever." Major O-stadt smiled. "So what's your name?"

"It's Pinkerton."

"Seriously?"

"Oh, it gets better."

"Really?"

"Yes, my married name was Brinks."

"Oh my. What are the chances of that?" Major O-stadt laughed. "Wait. You said *was*. You're not married now?"

"No, it didn't take." Pinkerton shrugged. "You?"

"No, I have never been named Pinkerton, Brinks, or any other security-related company."

"I was asking if you were married."

"You have the file on me. What does it say?"

"It only talks about some past deviations in Romania and Texas."

"Good Lord." The major pulled his hand across his face and groaned.

"Well," Pinkerton smiled, "it looks like you have some embarrassing things to share after all."

"Sure, how about over coffee, Pinkerton?" Major O-stadt pointed at a coffee bar.

"Fine." She watched as Major O-stadt brought over two tall beverages. "I really don't drink coffee. I'll just sit as you drink yours."

"Lucky for you, they were all out of coffee. This is some chai tea concoction."

"No coffee at a coffee bar?"

"The guy says here in Armed Forces Europe, this happens all the time."

"Guess I have been lucky to be in the USA so far."

"I guess so." Major O-stadt sipped loudly and looked out over the terminal.

"So, Major O-stadt, which do you want to discuss first, Romania or Texas?"

"Since the Romania incident is currently being made into a movie, I'll share the lesser known but equally embarrassing Texas massacre of my countenance." Major O-stadt leaned back in his seat, fiddling with the saltshaker on the table as he spoke. "It was in March of 2003. A certain Captain Oberstadtmeyer was assigned as a medical service support officer to the Task Force 1-63 Armor, which was being airlifted out of Germany into northern Iraq."

"I remember that."

"Yes, the strategic situation was such that the Third Infantry Division was fighting its way through southern Iraq. A pincer movement was planned with the Fourth Infantry Division to be inserted through Turkey into northern Iraq. The plan was to force the Iraqi Army to have to divide its war assets and fight a war on two fronts."

"That didn't happen."

"No, Pinkerton, it didn't." The major tapped one edge of the saltshaker against the table until the contents bounced out of the holes on top and dusted the table. "A political miscue led to the denial of US Forces in, or over, Turkish air space. The result was that the Third Infantry was left to fight without the support cavalry necessary to execute a pincer movement."

"It was a mad scramble."

"Yes, US Army war planners immediately shifted gears." He swept the spilled salt into piles. "They mobilized the European Quick Reaction Force from Vilseck, Germany—the 1-63 Armored Battalion. It was decided that these highly skilled warriors would be airlifted into northern Iraq along with an airborne brigade contingent to do the work of the mechanized infantry division which had been shut out of a Turkish port of entry."

"An armored battalion instead of an armored division."

"Yes. In this modified configuration, war planners included medical service officers to work with the two units to provide medical plans support which normally would have come from the division staff and its command surgeon. I was at the right place at the right time and thus received the nod to go into northern Iraq."

"You were here in Germany?"

"No. I was transported from my assignment at West Point Academy's Keller Army Community Hospital in New York to San Antonio, Texas. Once there I would fly out of Kelly Air Force Base. Before my week-long in-processing would start, I was given a forty-eight-hour furlough."

"This is when the Texas incident occurred?"

"Yep." The major took a pinch of salt and tossed it over his left shoulder. He swiped his hand across the table, pushing the rest of the salt onto the floor as he leaned forward over his cup. "I thought I could use the two-day layover time to drive over to Fort Sam Houston's Army Medical Command and receive a strategic and tactical briefing of the situation I was about to enter in Iraq. I coordinated this plan through the post garrison commander's secretary."

"Sounds benign."

"Yes, but no. Knowing I would be deploying from Texas in battle dress vestments, I left all my civilian clothes, including my warm, New York winter overcoat, back at West Point. This meant that I only had the jeans and short-sleeved guayabera that I reported in for deployment."

"It's a reasonable plan."

"I thought so too, until the Texas winter with March wind chilled me to the bone! Let me tell you, in Texas there is nothing to stop that wind except barbed wire."

"Is this when you made your mad dash, like the report said?"

"Almost. My rental car took me to the main gate at Fort Sam. The guard looked at me and saw that the car had a Florida license plate. He surmised that a Floridian had made a wrong turn."

"You showed him your military orders and ID card, right?"

The major rolled his eyes and continued. "He asked me where I was going. I told him Post Command Headquarters."

"That had to raise a red flag."

"It did, Pinkerton. Here's the second flag. Look at this face." Major O-stadt turned his head from side to side. "When the gate guard saw it, he began wondering if I was a terrorist. So he forwarded a suspicious car report to Military Police Headquarters as a precaution. Of course I didn't know that at the time."

"And there it is."

"Yes, as luck would have it, all the nearby headquarters parking was either obliterated in the name of force protection or marked as reserved. The closest parking spot was about a block away from Post Command Headquarters, just outside the Military Police's central station." Major O-stadt mimicked binoculars. "The Military Police desk clerk at the station observed a dark-featured individual, darting from a previously reported suspicious rental car, running with an object in hand toward the HQ. All patrol cars were immediately dispatched to intercept and mitigate the impending threat to post leadership."

"Did you make it inside?"

"Almost. I made it to the doorway when I felt someone slam against my side. The wind was knocked out of me. Before I could catch my breath, an MP rolled me facedown and cuffed my hands behind my back."

"Didn't the secretary explain?"

"No, initially she was stunned mute. Later I could hear her plea in my defense. But the damage was done, so to speak."

"So, I'm sipping chai tea with a known Middle Eastern terrorist."

"Is that what the report said?"

"More or less the same." Pinkerton laughed. "It's not often I have tea with a famous criminal."

"Well, Pinkerton," the major poured the rest of his drink directly into his mouth and gulped it down, "I can't wait seven days for these flights. It appears that I've got an opportunity to complete an obligation at Medical Command Headquarters," Major O-stadt winked, "and in the process meet an old friend at the hospital. So it looks like I need to head east. Care to join me at the rental car counter? Maybe we can get a BOGO deal."

"BOGO?"

"Yeah, buy one, get one. You still have to get to France to visit your mom, right?"

"Thanks, but I'll wait till you're finished at the counter just in case some of your *wanted* posters are still currently on display." She smiled. "Besides, I still have some chai left."

"Suit yourself." He stood, grabbed the Pelican case and his small bag, then gave a smiling nod. "Good luck, Perkins."

Pinkerton sipped her tea until Major O-stadt cleared the car rental counter and terminal. As he disappeared through the exit, she picked up her phone. "Package is en route to Heidelberg."

16

Tight and Uptight

Chief of Staff's office
European Medical Command
Heidelberg, Germany
Current day

"Lord, help me." Bridgette groaned as she stared at her husband's picture in a frame on her desk. "I'm wound tighter than a cheap pocket watch." She cringed as she caught her own reflection in the glass window. In it, she saw herself gnawing off all but the tip-end of a salami and gherkin kaiser roll sandwich. A peachy sunset painted the sky outside. *One would think that the European Medical Command's chief of staff, Colonel Bridgette Ward Christiansted, would have a fancier midday meal. And that she might actually eat it at midday instead of early evening.*

She looked from the window back to her desk. "No suggestions?" Bridgette spoke to both the picture and her own green-eyed reflection in its glass. She dropped the stump of the sandwich on her desk and wiped her face and hands with a napkin. With her elbows on the desk and her head held in her hands, she pressed at her temples then raked her fingers onward through her blonde bangs. With a massaging action she continued over the top of her pinned-up dark-rooted hair and down onto the nape of her neck inside her military uniform collar.

"What a whirlwind of vile events." She continued to add pressure to the base of her skull, her eyes closed against the fluorescent glare of the office lights. *First, word comes down that General Framingham is KIA during a bizarre series of events in Romania. What did they call it? Oh, yeah, the Fighting Dragon incident—whatever that means. This should all be Mickey's line—he's next in charge. But Deputy Command Surgeon Colonel Doctor Mickey Peronne is presently unavailable.* She pressed her thumb against the twitching nerve at the base of her eyebrow near her nose. *I can't blame him. He's in France on a medical emergency with his wife. So, by default, you, Bridgette, get to bear the yoke of command responsibility for all medical forces in Europe.* Bridgette rubbed at the pain in her temples which throbbed along with a pounding at her door.

"Come in, if you dare." Bridgette waited to hear yet another knock or the sound of timid feet scurrying away. Instead, she heard the metallic click of the door handle being engaged. She opened her eyes wearily. "Just remember. You've been warned."

"Ma'am, do you have a minute?"

"Never for most, Master Sergeant." She sighed and forced a grin. "Always for you. Is it important?"

"Yes, ma'am." Master Sergeant Francis Roman, the command's operations sergeant, paused in the doorway, nearly brushing the top of the frame with his dark hair. With one hand he massaged his jaw and high cheekbones as he spoke. "But I am unclear knowing just how important. I was hoping you would help me prioritize."

"Sure, Master Sergeant. I can delay my private wailing and gnashing of teeth for a bit longer." Bridgette waved him in.

"Appreciate that, ma'am." The master sergeant of Korean lineage, Suk Rho Minh, known in US Army uniform as Francis Roman, entered the office and closed the door behind him. "We received a security memo from Fort Knox."

"Those are always fun."

"Yes, ma'am. This time they wanted to alert us that there will be a courier passing through Europe en route to western and northern Africa."

"Okay," Bridgette clawed at her temples, "is the courier due to come through here?"

"No, but since we are in their path from Fort Knox, we are given a heads-up as a courtesy."

"Okay, but why?"

"I think," the master sergeant tapped the paper, "this courier is specifically carrying a Fort Knox storage item."

"Boom! There it is."

"Yes, ma'am."

"Okay, make sure we have all protocols in place to store any such item, or items, until it leaves our area of operations."

"Yes, ma'am." The master sergeant smiled. "Done and dusted."

"I figured." Bridgette stood and approached the master sergeant, matching him eye-to-eye in height. "So what's the beef?"

"I wasn't sure how tightly wound we should get when the chances of actually engaging such a responsibility are so remote."

"Understood. However, failure to plan and prepare is, indeed, poor planning and preparation. Doing nothing and hoping that they won't stop through here is not the best plan."

"The G3 came to the same conclusion, but I felt you should know why we were heightening our security posture despite the minimality of the situation."

Bridgette nodded. "Do you happen to know what is being carried?"

"No, ma'am, we never do."

"It's probably better that way. Nevertheless, tighten every one of our security measures like we did when Dr. Peronne returned from the Leaning Tower affair with the documents from Poland." She picked up her coffee mug and leaned against her desk.

"That was a momentous event, ma'am." Master Sergeant raised his eyebrows and blew into his fist. "Those Nazi documents that we secured temporarily had not seen the light of day for over sixty years." He smiled with boyish excitement.

Bridgette watched his reaction as she drank her coffee. "Oh, I remember quite well, Master Sergeant—a hidden underground bio-medical Nazi laboratory conducting secret Nazi projects about river people and immortality."

"It was the stuff of historical fiction," Master Sergeant grinned. "Leaning towers, secret intrigue, classified intel, world-class evil versus modern-day Knights Templar—"

"Fiction, Master Sergeant?" Bridgette cocked an eyebrow. "Not for a minute."

"Yes, ma'am." The master sergeant reigned in his excitement.

"It was real—all too real. At the conclusion of the Leaning Tower affair those Nazi documents were mandated to be secured at the Federal Bullion Depository at Fort Knox. There they went and hopefully, along with the Ark of the Covenant, there they stay."

"Understood, ma'am." He twisted his lips trying to stifle the hint of a rising smile. "For me it's kind of bittersweet. The Leaning Tower affair brought about an exciting OPTEMPO we haven't had in quite a while."

"You liked it, didn't you? That much is obvious," she half-chuckled, half-scoffed.

"Ma'am, as soldiers, we spend all our energy training and practicing our battle rhythms. Sometimes it is just nice to feel the breeze of battle intensity blow in our faces."

Bridgette nodded her understanding. "Well, let's hope this breeze stays in the past, Master Sergeant, or at least until we finish our watch."

17

The Big Uneasy

Maternity hospital
Saint-Quentin, Somme River Valley
Vermandois region, France
Current day

I don't remember ever seeing this much beauty so early in the morning. Loni kept her eyes fixed on the window as she paced around the big hospital bed in her room, intermittently tracing the tubing of the intravenous line taped down on her forearm. She brushed at the burnt sienna and café swirls of her shoulder-length hair. *What is this place? How did I get here? Is that me in the window's reflection?* Loni stopped and surveyed. *I'm a rather pretty woman—fair complexion; trim, dark eyebrows; keen brown eyes; a delicate, straight nose with a hint of an upturn at the end; full lips.* Her gaze slid away from her face and down her unfamiliar body. *Why would such a lovely woman be in such a hideous hospital night-gown?* Beneath the gown and robe Loni saw the outline of her robust breasts and exceptionally rotund, gravid belly. *Oh yes, I'm pregnant. They told me eight months pregnant—with twins no less.* Loni pressed her hands against the cool glass, blew her warm breath upon it, and drew a stick figure in the condensation. *I wonder where that man Mickey is now. He said he was my husband. He seems nice.* Loni drew a second row of stick figures. *But so are all the other male doctors and nurses who have passed through this room in the performance of their duties.* Loni lay her temple on the windowpane.

"Especially in this dim light," Loni spoke directly toward the window, "the river is breathtaking."

"It is indeed," said a voice from behind her.

Loni calmly glanced over her shoulder. It was a hospital after all, and people were always coming and going from her room. "What's the name of it?" Loni drank in the pre-dawn light. "I know I have asked you this before—and am sure you have told me numerous times—but it seems like I can't remember anything these days."

"It's the Somme," Clarisse answered as she wiped down the bedside tray. "The river is named La Somme."

Her accent seems French. English is not her first language. Loni turned and placed her back to the glass. She wrung her hands. "What's your name?"

"Clarisse," the woman smiled, "Clarisse Saint Vincent."

Loni repeated the sounds slowly, letting them roll around her mouth. "Sahn Vee-sahn." Suddenly self-conscious, Loni felt heat rise in her cheeks. "Sorry, Clarisse. I was never very good at French, but I like the sound of it." She glanced timidly away, but Clarisse kept a steady gaze. "Your last name, Americans might say it ... Saint."

"Vincent." Clarisse enunciated the hard *n* and *t* sounds.

Loni nodded and smiled. "Thank you for making the effort to speak English to me, Clarisse." Loni sucked in a deep breath. "So many French people here seem to find it a bother."

"I am *not* French, Loni." Her tone suddenly harsh as she mimicked spitting on the ground. "I'm a proud French-Canadian woman."

"Oh, I'm sorry." Loni flushed. "I, uh ... are you assigned to my room?" Loni bit her bottom lip as she surveyed the woman in hospital uniform. *Slim and petite, her delicate facial features look like mine except for her higher forehead.*

Loni relaxed a little as Clarisse answered kindly, "It is all right, you had no way of knowing."

"Still, I'm sorry. I don't want to offend you. I know so little right now about ... well, about me and this place. I've been here awhile it seems and yet it's like I haven't been here at all."

Clarisse nodded in understanding. Loni watched as the woman moved around the room tidying up. *I would kill for those hazel green eyes and that jawline ...*

those prominent cheeks. After some low-level dusting and picking up of discarded tidbits from the floor, Clarisse momentarily stood, arching her back before returning to the world below the knees. *She's much shorter than me, probably by a full handspan. I wonder if she knows how pretty she is.*

"Yes and no." Clarisse continued wiping the room's surfaces and gathering trash.

"Pardon?"

"You asked if I am assigned to you." Arising from a squat, Clarisse stood and looked directly at Loni. "I am and I am not. Today I'm helping the dark shift for housekeeping."

"What is the dark shift?"

"You know, from sunset to sunrise." She pointed to the room's window. Clarisse wiped down a chair, then perched herself on its arm. Briefly, she wiped her forehead with the back of her forearm.

"That's a long shift, Clarisse. Why are you on the dark shift?"

"Because I run the late-day floral shop."

"Floral shop?" Loni stretched her arms under her belly, relieving some of the pressure on her back and hips.

"Yes, it's the small flower shop around the corner. It's not much more than a closet but its plants are happy and blooming. The main floral gift shop is on the ground floor near the hospital's entrance. It is filled with life."

"I know what that feels like," Loni sighed.

"Very true."

"When do you sleep?"

"Sleep is not the problem, Loni. It's the waking and feeling rested. Like you, my sleep has not been so restful lately."

"You noticed."

"It's hard to miss."

"Well, Clarisse, I guess if I have to be hospitalized in France, there could be worse places."

"Yes and yes."

"What?"

"Yes, you must be hospitalized—at least until your memory returns. Yes, there are only a few medical facilities in France with an overlook of a beautiful river." Clarisse rose from her chair, walked over, propping herself against the right side of the window, joining Loni. "Look! There go the rain clouds."

"The weather here always seems to be moving away to the east." Loni tapped the glass indicating the direction. "Is that a Europe thing or just me being ill?"

"Your memory loss isn't an illness."

"How do you know, Clarisse?"

"As housekeeping, I am mostly invisible. So, I am privileged to every conversation."

"You have heard talk from my doctors?"

"I have heard talk between Douglas and Mickey." Clarisse edged closer, whispering, "They seem to think that trauma and injury took your memory."

"Where are they, by the way?"

"Getting some food and clearing the air, I expect." Loni gave a quizzical look, but Clarisse only wiped at the fingerprints on the glass and redirected, "Loni, do you remember anything of that day?"

"Clarisse, honestly, it's a jumble." She covered her face with her hands, speaking through the cracks in her fingers. "There are things I remember. Things I *want* to remember. And things I don't care to remember." Loni dropped her hands and moved to the reclining chair to sit.

She walked her fingers gingerly across the top of her belly. "There are some things that creep up on me with tiny cat's feet." She shuddered and reached for the blanket on the bed. Clarisse retrieved the blanket and brought it to her, covering Loni's shoulders. Loni clutched the blanket around herself. "Clarisse, I feel a vague familiarity with things that I don't have the right to remember. The fact is, my whole memory feels like a push-pull system of—" she put a hand to her temple, "of whispers … and shadows … and feelings … and sensations. I don't understand it."

"Push-pull?"

"Yes. It's as though whenever I try to pull and reach toward a certain memory of a person, a place, or an event—like that Mickey person or this accident you all talk about—instead I get information that is pushed to me from other people and places, from a time that's not this one." Loni wrapped the blanket around herself more tightly. "Does this make any sense?"

"Yes and no."

Standing up, Loni went back to the window. She tapped on the glass with one hand; the other clutched the blanket at her chest. "Look, Clarisse. Look at those fading clouds … the puffy ones just off the horizon. Do you see them?"

Clarisse approached the window. "Of course, *cherie*, I see them. One looks like … an alligator of sorts and the other," she tilted her head, "a round flower … a cotton boll."

"Okay. Well, right now in my head my memory is pushing the same pair of clouds but in a different place, maybe even a different time." Loni reached up and wiped her eyes laterally in a slow, steady movement. "The sky in my memory is a little lighter. Maybe it's a different time of the day. I can't be sure." Loni swooned forward, placing her forehead and open palms against the cool window glass. "Clarisse, hold me."

"I have you, *cherie*." Clarisse kicked away the fallen blanket from their feet and steadied Loni's shoulders. "What are you seeing?"

"I see an abundance of green hues. It's getting warm. Can you feel it?" With one hand, Loni pulled at the collar of her robe.

"Come sit down." Clarisse carefully guided Loni back to the reclining chair.

"Listen. There are voices in the greenery. Do you hear it? Soft voices murmuring over … over. It sounds like the tinkling of cascading water."

"A waterfall, maybe?"

"No, it's an overflowing rain gutter dripping water into barrels."

"Rain barrels?"

"No, no, no, it's none of these." Loni gasped. "I see it. It's coming clearer."

"What do you see, Loni?"

"I see … a … water fountain. Yes, oh Clarisse, it is a beautifully ornate water fountain. It is in the center of a warm, richly green courtyard." Loni extended her arm out, pointing around the hospital room. "There are cozy tables filled with chatty people everywhere. They are separated by clumps of decorative foliage. I can see the sky through the wooden fingers of ribbed pergolas and leafy alcoves. And Clarisse, the smell is so pungently earthy. Clarisse? Clarisse?"

"I'm here. I'm here." Clarisse took Loni's hand and squeezed it. "Where are you, Loni?"

"I'm alone at my table."

"That's not what I meant, dear."

"I'm alone at my round metal table. You know, like the kind you see in those sidewalk cafés. But there's something peculiar. Everyone's table is black, but not mine. Mine is an odd color—very dark weathered green."

"Where are you, Loni?" Clarisse's voice hinted at desperation.

"Yes, Clarisse, I am at the table whose paint is chipped and cracked. Look. See the craquelure?" She put her free hand out on a surface invisible to Clarisse. "There is rusty erosion on the edges."

"Old can be beautiful, Loni." Clarisse held Loni's hand tighter and forced calm into her voice. "Your table is special. You are special."

"You're so right, Clarisse. Dare I say it? It is deterioration with charm. Everything here pulses a steamy, sultry ambience of … antique charm. It's so intoxicating." Loni wriggled and tugged at her collar. "It warms me … to my core—"

"Loni, where are you?"

"I think it is a tropical outdoor café. Yes, it is. I see in the distance a young, well-dressed, dark-skinned girl giving menus to a growing line of impatiently waiting restaurant patrons. Her hair is cornrows … beautifully done. She speaks to them in a very strange accent … not yours and yet not entirely English … not entirely French … maybe Portuguese? Maybe, but mostly English. It's delightful. There is another girl, an assistant of sorts. She escorts select groups from the front of the line to tables. The tables are placed between the small bushes and trees which fill the entire expanse of this courtyard."

"It sounds lovely. I think I would like to be there with you. It sounds so—"

"Jazz."

"No, not the word I had in mind, Loni. But, okay—jazzed."

"Clarisse, I hear jazz … live-spirited jazz. I know where I am."

"Not the tropics, yes?"

"Jazz … outdoor café environs … English with a hint of French."

"Haiti."

"No, no. This environment is bathed in upbeat jazz. It echoes off the walls of the surrounding brick buildings. Clarisse, this can only be the French Quarter deep in the heart of the Crescent City."

"Crescent City?"

"New Orleans. The smells, tastes, and sounds are a mixture of heaven and earth. Nowhere else exists a place like this in the world."

"You seem sure."

"Oh, I am. I see a sign along the street." She pointed to the hospital room's wall. "I'm in New Orleans in the Vieux Carré, the French Quarter." Loni tilted back her head. "Smell it, Clarisse. The strong, earthy chicory. The Cajun spices—"

"Cajun? The succulent plant from Cuba?"

Loni shook her head. "No, no, no. Cajun *flavors*—garlic, paprika, cumin, mustard, and all those peppers. Where else in the world can the best of France be completely enjoyed outside of France?"

"Loni, why New Orleans?"

"I don't know." Loni panted. She blinked hard, eyes refocusing on Clarisse. "My memory pushed it to me. New Orleans is so unlike the Vermandois. Why do I reside in both places and yet it seems that I belong to neither?" She rested a hand on her chest and felt the chain of her necklace. She closed her eyes and drew in a deep, steadying breath.

Clarisse watched Loni carefully. "It's like being in France and not France at the same time. No?"

Loni nodded then opened her eyes. "Whoever I am and … and … wherever I've been seems somehow to be tied into France, or the French, or French places. But I am not French—I am clearly American. Yet somehow, all this Frenchiness must connect me back to America one way or another. I just wish I knew for sure." Loni's eyes welled with tears.

Clarisse patted Loni's hand, and then went to collect and fold the blanket from the floor so that the pregnant woman could have a moment to recompose herself. Loni watched Clarisse and the brightening daylight glowing on her face.

"The old clouds are gone beyond the far horizon, aren't they Clarisse? The alligator? The cotton?"

"Yes."

"Along with everything connected to them." Loni furrowed her brow trying to pull some wisp of her own life back to her.

"Worry not, Loni. There are new clouds to replace them."

Loni heaved herself up, walked to the window, and looked out. "These clouds don't seem as amiable. I look, but I find no friend among them." Loni sighed and rubbed her protruding belly. "I guess I should just be content that I am safe here, able to ponder their existence on a warm, friendly day."

"Luckily for you," Clarisse gently squeezed Loni's shoulder, "at this time of year in the Vermandois, the good weather days will be more frequent than the bad. Knowing this makes for happier days." Clarisse left the windowpane, returned the blanket to the bed, and migrated far across the room. "Loni, I have to go, *cherie*." She stood with her hand on the doorknob. "Duty calls."

"Are you really going to leave me alone, Clarisse?"

"Yes, unfortunately. I wish I could stay longer. Really, I do. There will be others dropping by. This is a hospital. There are always visitors. Try to rest."

"But Clarisse…." Loni watched the door shut with a quiet, but finite *click*.

I can't believe it. Clarisse up and left me swimming in a sea of French-speaking hospital staff. I never know what they are saying. Loni looked at the door again. *I'll be glad when Mickey and Douglas come back.*

Loni looked at her reflection in the window again. "Why can't you remember things clearly? You know, people would want to be with you if you had the decency to at least remember them."

Remembering…. I never thought that this would become the bane of my existence. My memory is so skewed. I'm fractured, that's what I am. I can remember many far away things. Loni studied her reflection. "You know, I'm named after an Armenian province. I've known that since I was a child. But how do I know that? You there," Loni pointed to the image in the glass, "tell me the last meal you ate. Tell me why you are always dressed in a patient's garb in a French maternity hospital?" Loni laughed. "What? You don't know?" Loni pointed back over her shoulder to the door. "Where are your English-speaking friends?"

Wait a minute. She turned to face the door. *Where are those English-speaking allies? Why did they leave me here? I don't speak French. Certainly, all of them can't be otherwise engaged at the very same time.* Loni looked at the wall clock. "Wait. It's still too early. They probably must sleep too." She glanced around the now familiar room. "Not many good spots to sleep in here."

Loni turned back to her reflection, ignoring the brightening day beyond the glass. "You should have known," she admonished. "People need sleep, right? Hey! Look at me. I am talking to you. Don't you turn away!" She struck the glass with her open palm. "You may just be my reflection, but I need you to be here for me. I need somebody. Hey! Move your mouth! The least you could do is talk back. What? There's no one here but me. Me and that incessant pregnancy monitor. Are the beeps scaring you off?" Loni glared at the monitor.

Oh God! It can't be true. Besides this silent reflection of mine, who doesn't care to talk to me, the only company I have in this room is that monitor. Loni cocked her ear. "Is it my imagination or are you developing a French accent too, you annoying little machine?" Loni gave up. She grunted herself into her reclining chair, trying hard to find an angle to provide some comfort for her strained body.

"What?" She looked up. "You don't care to sit? Go ahead, you stupid reflection! Stand there all by your lonesome." Loni massaged her scalp then buried her face in her hands to hide her tears. A few minutes later she looked up and saw the reflection remained unchanged—standing, staring. "Hey," she sniffled, "look, I'm sorry. I'm just lonely, ya know? I mean, look around here." She gestured to the empty room. "Please sit down. Thanks. Tell me, can loneliness kill? I mean, it certainly wounds." The reflection shrugged. Loni dropped her gaze to her hands. *I'm not lonely. I'm not. I'm just alone.*

Loni struggled out of the chair and approached her seated reflection. "We still have the memories of my dreams—the good ones anyway—for company, right?" Loni tapped on the glass. "What? You don't like the dreams?" Loni covered her mouth and gasped, "Oh no. I'm sorry. I didn't stop to think about it. No, no. Don't get up." The reflection looked away. "Really, I'm sorry. I didn't get it before. I get it now. You don't have the dreams." Loni spasmed a breath. "No, that's not it! You don't *want* the dreams, don't you? That's it, isn't it?" She put her hands on her temples. "Yes, I thought so. I understand." Loni turned and leaned her back against the glass. "I wish I had a choice." The reflection eased out of the chair and stood behind her. "You're right. The dreams have become disturbing lately." *It is as if there is someone or something inside me, other than the babies, trying to get out.* "You feel it too, right?" Loni looked over her shoulder and saw the reflection nod. Loni walked over and hovered over her chair. The reflection did the same. Together they both lowered themselves back into their respective chairs.

"You're afraid to sleep?" Loni nodded. "Yeah, me too." Loni closed her eyes. *There it is … the tower, always that horrid tower. It's dark and doleful, serving more of a prison than a home.*

With her eyes still closed she spoke aloud, "It's not a prison. It's not." Loni shook her head as tears began to stream down her cheeks. "If anything, prisons are safe. *This* tower is not safe." Loni squeezed her eyes shut, wiping the tears away with her palms.

There it is … the large bedroom surrounded by circular stone walls. I'm inside the tower. Where are they? I don't see them. There they are … the two boys with blonde pageboy cuts. The littler one holding on to his pet spaniel until … there it goes … it jumps to the floor. The younger boy clings to the older boy, both huddling in fear. Always cringing in fear … but of what? Look. The puppy is moving toward the doorway alternating sniffing and softly growling.

Loni's eyes popped back open. "Where am I?" she gasped. Loni looked back to the direction of the window. "I see you. New clouds chasing away the old." *Thank goodness. Those dark clouds have drifted farther away. I wish my dreams would drift away with them.*

Loni addressed her reflection again. "Why is it that you can remember, with such detail, this dratted tower dream and yet you cannot remember anything in the waking world?" The reflection shook its head. "What? Still nothing?" Loni rubbed her eyes. *Nothing about the real world makes sense. Everything in my dreams makes horrible vivid sense.*

Loni pointed to her reflection. "I may not understand you or even remember you, but you are quite preferable to my dreams." Loni fought off a yawn. "Oh, I just have no choice." Loni succumbed to a shuddering yawn. "I shall never sleep peacefully ever again." Her eyelids sank. "No, I won't…. I can't. The tower will be there."

Loni rose and sat on the edge of her bed. "I need to stand and walk some more." She heaved a deep sigh. "But it's the walking and standing that exhausts me. If I lay here, I can still rest but I must force myself not to sleep. I can control that. I can lay here and rest, without sleeping." Loni yawned again and so did her reflection. "No, I'm not sleeping. I'm just resting my eyes. I'm just resting my…."

18

Defiant and the Diffident

Château Royal d'Amboise
Loire Valley, France
1500

"Louise! Come here right now!" A voice rang out above the hustle and bustle of the disbursing artisans and courtiers within the grand salle. "Fine! *That child reminds me of...me. "D'accord!* Don't be late for dinner. Hear?"

Catching the last of her mother's fading words, Louise panted against the flow of pedestrian traffic. Skillfully she weaved her way back to the tapestry. *I'm almost there. The queen said there was a coach and horsemen and towers. I want to see them up close. I must see them.*

Louise pulled up with a lurch and shouted, "No, stop!" *They're rolling up the horsemen and towers.* "Please, I want to see—"

"Hello, little one." The old artisan smiled at the puffing little face. "Is there something you need from the queen's finest tapestry weaver?" She winked.

"I came to see you," spouted a winded Louise in a breathy exhalation.

"See me? Did you now? Hmm." With the gnarly fingers of an experienced weaver, the old woman tapped her chin. "Why on earth would you want to see an old tapestry-making codger like me?" The old weaver turned to the sweating lad and pointed, "Go ahead, Strong Charles, put away the tapestry." The boy reached for the frame hooks.

"What are you doing?" Louise whimpered.

"We have to put this away until the queen requests it again," said the weaver.

"But why?" Louise pleaded. "I'm not finished looking at it."

"Sorry, missy. I've got other work to do. This tapestry is coming down," said the old weaver. She turned to Strong Charles. "Go on, my son. In your fourteen years of life you've done as your mother said. Don't stop now."

"No! Wait, Strong Charles! I haven't found the things I'm looking for."

"What is it that you seek, child?" The old weaver's eyes sparkled with curiosity.

"Louise," the girl said, pointing to herself.

"There is no Louise in the tapestry," said the old weaver. She winked at the little girl. "I'm sure of it—and I should know! I weaved that tapestry myself."

"No, madame. I am Louise," affirmed the little girl with a stomp of her foot. "Louise de Montmorency."

"Mademoiselle Louise de Montmorency, I am no madame." The old woman weaver laughed. "I assume you are a mademoiselle."

"Yes, I am a mademoiselle for now."

"I am called Simone." The elderly woman's face crinkled into a kind smile. "How can I best serve the mademoiselle?"

"When the queen spoke, I listened as my mother told me to. But, Simone, I could not see the prince in the tapestry as the queen spoke about them. Please, help me find him."

"I understand, child." Simone nodded as she pulled a pipe from her pocket. "You won't find the prince."

"I won't, Simone? Why?"

"It is because you are looking with your eyes. The queen is speaking from her heart." Simone lit a match and the fire sparked, throwing fleeting shadows across the faces of both the young and old.

"I don't understand." Louise's shoulders slumped.

Simone puffed the pipe to light it. Looking through the smoke she said to the girl, "Of course you don't understand." The weaver pulled up a chair and patted her leg. Louise came and sat in her lap. "How old are you, Mademoiselle?"

"I'm six and a half."

"Oh, well!" Simone made her eyes big. "Are you sure you're not married already?"

"No," Louise giggled.

"Do you wish Strong Charles to leave the tapestry up? He is my son and listens to me...mostly."

"Yes, Simone, please!"

"Well, Mademoiselle, you best tell him before he wanders off from his spot there next to the tapestry display frame. Look. See that face? He's got a good mind to go forage for bread and drink."

"Now?"

"You better hurry." Simone winked. "He's looking hungrier and hungrier."

"I can't." Louise buried her face against the old woman.

"It is all right. I'll help you." Simone turned. "Strong Charles, Mademoiselle Louise wishes for you to leave the tapestry up."

"Yes, Mother," said Strong Charles standing with a stretch. He then unrolled the tapestry, mounting it on the hooks on the wooden display frame.

"There you go, Louise." Simone bit the pipe stem, holding it between her teeth as she spoke. "Your wish is our command."

"It is still up?" Louise peeked.

"Yes, dearie. You said that you wanted to see the unseen. Didn't you?"

"Yes, Simone."

"Very well. Let's begin." Simone shifted Louise toward the tapestry. "First, tell me what you see."

"Can Strong Charles move out of the way?"

"Strong Charles, move aside, my son," said Simone, motioning to the lad and then returning her gaze to a wide-eyed, beaming Louise. "Now, tell me, child. What do you see?"

"I see a white unicorn in the middle of the tapestry."

"Tell me about the unicorn."

"He is lying down in the middle of a fence which circles around him."

"Does he look sad?"

"No, Simone. He is all alone, though. I think he is a little lonely."

"Are you sure he is alone?"

"I think so. I don't see any friends for him."

"Hmmm." Simone puffed, observing Louise and her searching eyes. "Tell me about the fence."

"The fence forms a circle around him. It has a gate. Oh, Simone, there is no room for him to run and play so he just lies down in the middle. I think he does not like having no room to run around and play."

"What do you think about the round fence?"

Louise cocked her head, her face puzzled. "I've never seen one like it."

"Think about this, Louise." Simone bracketed her hands. "In a round fence, every bit of turf belongs to the animal. He can run and run and never worry about running into the fence rails. In a square fence, the areas in the deep corners are lost. The animal has to slow to turn at each corner."

"Are you saying he likes being in a round fence?"

"No, I am just saying that if he has to be in a fence, it is better to be in one that is round."

"Hmmm. I wonder if the fence is to keep him in or to keep children like me from playing with him. I would certainly want to play with a unicorn if I ever saw one."

"Ah, my little one. You are sharp." Simone smiled and tapped Louise softly on the nose. "So, tell me. Is there anything else in the fence with him?"

"There is a tree. He is chained to the tree. That cannot be fun to be chained to a tree. Please, Simone, tell me, why is he chained to that tree?"

"You see the chain as bad, Louise, yes?" Simone pointed with her pipe stem.

"How can it not be bad? The unicorn is locked up. Like a prisoner."

"Ahhh, but it may not be something bad." Simone placed the pipe at her lips. "Chains are sometimes a symbol of reward for acceptable and weighty service. When they come with a handsome collar, like the unicorn here has, it could mean that the owner of that symbol is chained by a sense of obligation to the people that he serves. Chains and collars represent honor for sheriffs and mayors and, in the past, for knights."

"I don't think I understand." Louise furrowed her brow.

"The chain that holds him to the tree may not be something bad—especially if he doesn't look so unhappy."

"Whether it is a good thing or not, Simone, I don't like him chained."

"You will understand more when you grow up, Louise. Adults have many things that chain them. It is called *responsibility*. Now, little one, tell me what you see on the unicorn."

She squinted her eyes. "There are spots of red on him," Louise whined. "He's bleeding. I think he is hurt. Maybe he cut himself."

"Does he look like he is in pain?"

"No."

"Maybe the red splotches are not coming from within him but instead are falling upon him."

"Oh, yes, I see. It could be that the red is dripping from the tree."

"Sometimes trees do that. What else do you see?"

"There is only one tree. He likes lying under it. I think it keeps the sun off him. Why would that tree be dripping on him?"

"Tell me what you see."

"I see a kind of fruit hanging on the tree. It is broken open. Maybe the fruit is dripping on him. I think I would move if a tree or its fruit was dripping on me."

"True enough. What else do you see?"

"There are lots and lots of plants both inside and outside the fence."

"Is that all?"

"There are some ropes making bows with letters and numbers."

"Do you know your letters and numbers?"

"Yes, I know my letters and numbers."

"What letters and numbers do you see?"

"In every corner and in the middle on the tree there, I see a letter *A* and a number three. It must be a three since it does not look like any letter I know."

"Did you say you saw the bows in every corner?"

"Yes, but I was wrong. There is no bow in the bottom-left corner. Maybe it fell off." She turned to the artisan questioningly.

"No, darling," Simone smiled, "it didn't fall off. I never put it there."

"Why?"

"The queen asked me not to do so. She told me this represents that this is the first tapestry."

"I think putting a number one on the tapestry would be easier."

"I agree with you," Simone chuckled. "In fact, I told this to the queen. However, she said she wanted me to do it this way."

"That's silly."

"It's a little bit silly, but don't tell the queen I said so."

Louise giggled. "I promise." The elderly artisan hugged Louise briskly.

"Did you find the friend of the unicorn, Louise?" Simone pointed with her pipe.

"No."

"Look carefully in the plants outside the fence."

Louise's eyes scanned the foliage. "No … no … yes!"

"What do you see?"

"I see a frog, a tiny little frog." Louise beamed. "How did you know it was there?"

"Honey, I put it there."

"Why?"

"Because the queen wanted it. She told me to place it in the area outside the fence."

"Why outside the fence? It cannot be with the unicorn that way."

"I don't know. She didn't say."

"But I think no one will ever see the frog."

"I know, Louise. He is hidden in plain sight."

"He is so tiny!"

"The queen wanted him to be small." Simone whispered, "He is almost a secret."

"I still see no coach or a prince."

"The coach isn't there. The prince is there. But you must not look with your eyes. Look with your heart."

"I don't know how to look with my heart." Louise put her hands on her hips and looked at the artisan exasperatedly. "It has no eyes."

"True enough." The old artist laughed hard. "What if I tell you part of the story that the queen did not get to finish? Would that help?"

"I think so."

"Well then, Louise, let me tell you the rest of the story, just as she told it to me."

"Yes, please." Louise sat herself upright. "I promise to listen with two ears and not to speak with two mouths."

"Fair enough."

19

Buffy the Raven Player

Maternity hospital
Saint-Quentin, Somme River Valley
Vermandois region, France
Current day

"Where am I?" Loni groaned as she tried to roll to her other side. "No, no, I fell asleep," she muttered incoherently. *Am I floating? No, I'm flying. What's that sound?*

Loni felt her consciousness being hurled through time and space until she arrived wherever something, or someone, saw fit to place her. *I know that sound; it's a coach. How can I know that? And I feel ... I feel a heaviness.*

A rumbling coach knifed through the darkness in the early hours of the morning surrounded by a galloping armed entourage.

Loni felt a sense of dread consume the coach driver. She saw the entourage veer away toward city lights as the coach approached a castle which overlooked a dark and murky river.

✠ ✠ ✠

"We've arrived, Majesty." The coach driver spoke loudly with a thick British cockney accent overcoming the rustling of his muddied travel wardrobe. "We made it safely."

"Is it morning yet?" The twelve-year-old prince yawned and rubbed his eyes, peering through the curtains.

"It's trying to be, Highness." The driver eased the horses forward, their hoof beats slowing from the previous rapid pace. "The sky is beginning to lighten." The driver pointed off to the side. "I see many guards milling around. I believe you will be safe here. They will direct you to warm accommodations and your family no doubt."

"Where are we?" the prince asked as the coach slowed to a halt at the castle gates. Quietly he slipped on his black travel jacket over his black puffy-shouldered velvet smock. His matching black velvet knee-length trousers cascaded downward into black knee-high stockings accompanied by black buckled shoes. A gold garter pinched at the junction of his trouser leg and stockings. Carefully, the prince tucked his gold cross on a gold neck chain against his chest. He peered out again. "Wait! I know these guards' uniforms."

"Of course you do, Highness. These are the guards of the royal palace."

"We're at the Tower of London."

"Good morning, Highness." A voice came out of the dark.

"Who calls me?" The prince pulled the curtain closed to a slim crack and peered out with apprehension.

"The name is Sir James Tyrrell, Highness. I'm the castle constable." Tyrrell approached the coach and opened the door. The boy hung back, pressed against the wall. His shoulder-length red hair cascaded rearward with each surge of the wind. "You'll be staying here in the Garden Tower. Your uncle says to remain inside until he arrives. He has much to explain to you." Tyrrell extended his hand to the young prince.

The boy leaned farther into view. "Have Richard Grey and the Earl of Rivers arrived as well?"

"There were none who came with, or before, you when your coach arrived."

"Could they be still on the way?"

"Possibly, Sire." The constable scratched his chin. "They may have been redirected in your best interest." He beckoned to the prince.

The boy stood and moved closer. "Have any other members of my family arrived at this Garden Tower?"

"Hurry now, we need to get you out of this dampness." He grasped the prince's arm and took him from the carriage. "It's not morning yet and you'll catch your death of cold out here in the night air." Tyrell pulled his constable's cloak tightly around his shoulders as he guided the prince through many sally ports, gates, bridges, and halls until they arrived at the Garden Tower.

"How many more flights of stairs up must we go?" the boy prince sighed.

"Just up that last flight and in the door at the top," said the constable, pointing. "I'll be leaving now, Sire. I trust you will find everything in order. It is as your uncle requested." The constable stood on the stairs watching as the door opened and the prince stepped beyond the threshold into the brightly lit room beyond.

"Is anyone here?" The prince shivered as his body embraced the warmth within the room. The sound of a high-pitched bark followed by the sound of shuffling feet broke the brief silence.

"Good morning, Sire." A disheveled eight-year-old boy in a rumpled shirt and breeches appeared beside the dog. "Are you the Prince of Wales or the Duke of York?"

"I am Edward, the Prince of Wales." Edward eased out of his riding jacket, hanging it on a hook poking from the mantel. Adjusting the puffed shoulders on his smock and the jewelry around his neck, Edward locked his gaze on the younger boy. "Who are you?"

"I'm Bran." The lad's bright eyes shone through a brown mop of tussled locks. "I belong to a castle yeoman. I live here."

"In this room?"

"No, Sire," said Bran, waving his dirt-stained callused palms, "not in this room. My family and I live in a dwelling on the other side of the castle."

"Why are you here now?"

"I'm here to make sure you have all you need to get settled in."

The young prince stood rigid, mustering up a commanding tone despite his exhaustion and anxiety. "Where is my family, Bran? I traveled with many riders. Have you seen anyone else arrive?"

"No riders or family await you here. Was there family traveling with you?"

"My stepbrother Richard Grey and my mother's brother the Earl of Rivers rode with me from Ludlow. I've not seen them since Stony Stratford."

"I have seen no one else before now, Highness. I was told to prepare the room for you and your brother Richard of Shrewsbury."

"Is he here?"

"No, Sire. I am expecting that he will be quite along though."

"Is this your dog?"

"Buffy?" Bran knelt to scruff the spaniel. "Oh no, Sire. She belongs to the castle grounds." He swirled his fingers through the dog's fur. "Everyone knows her, even the ravens. Besides me, Buffy is the ravens' number one playmate." Bran stood. "She followed me up here."

"Did your father say anything about other people arriving? Did he mention the queen, my mother?"

"No," Bran shook his head. "He said that two boys, you and your brother, would be arriving." A knock on the door startled the dog. Buffy responded with a tentative bark. Soon the door creaked open.

"Richard?" Edward craned. "Is that you?"

"Edward, I am so very glad to see you!" Dressed in the same velvet smock-over-knicker style but hued in a dark green, nine-year-old Richard of Shrews-bury dropped his cloak and rushed in to embrace his brother. Bran walked over and took Richard's riding cloak from the floor and hung it on a mantel hook. Quietly Bran stood with Buffy to the side of the fireplace as the brothers spoke.

"Hullo, Froggie," said Edward. "Glad to see you're safe."

Richard broke off the hug and crinkled his nose. "Mum said for you to stop calling me that."

"Have you seen Mum?"

"No, not since I left sanctuary at Westminster Abbey. How long have you been here?"

"Not long." He paused. "Father is dead."

"I know." Richard sniffed and swallowed hard. "Edward?"

"Hmmm?"

"You're king now."

"I don't feel like a king." Edward walked toward the fireplace. "Have you heard if Mum is coming here?"

"I don't know. I only know that Duke Richard sent for us." Richard noticed the other boy in the room. "Who are you?"

"You are Richard of Shrewsbury, the Duke of York," said a starstruck Bran as he slowly approached the younger prince, a boy just a year older. "I hung your coat on the mantel, Sire."

"Yes, I see." Richard crossed his arms. "Who are you?"

"I'm Bran. It is nice here. There are many guards who keep the grounds safe. They call themselves yeomen. My father is a yeoman. We have a raven's nest on the far wall. It is filled with baby birds and—"

"Bran," Edward stepped between the younger boys, "this is not a game. We were not brought here to play. No doubt we are preparing for my coronation."

"Coronation?" Bran's eyes widened. "I know that's important, Sire." The boy twisted his hands. "But until then, can't we play?"

Richard stepped around his brother. "Tell me more of the ravens, Bran."

"Well, there's a bunch of them. There is one raven with a hurt wing. One of the yeomen told me that it was a male bird. The yeoman said that he thought the wing was broken in a fight to defend his family."

"Oh! That yeoman seems to know a lot about birds," said Richard.

"Yes, Sire," Bran smiled. "We call him the raven master."

"Is the hurt raven all right now?"

"It seems so. He just can't seem to fly." Bran squatted down to pet Buffy. "There is another raven, a mother raven. She sits in the nest. Mother raven is always near the baby birds."

"I'd like to see the birds." Richard beamed as he leaned down to pet Buffy. "Have you named them all?"

"Heavens, no. Why would I do that?"

"My mother told a story of a king with injured arms. We could name the bird Caradoc Freichfras after the character in her story. It is not like any story you've ever heard!" Richard glanced toward the fireplace. "You do remember, don't you, Edward?"

"What?"

"Caradoc is the one with the short arms. Over time, they became very strong."

"I don't remember, Richard." Edward poked the embers in the fireplace, his mind far away.

"Of course Edward remembers." Richard smiled at Bran. "It was his favorite story too."

"I like this fellow Caradoc." Bran pulled Richard toward a bench at the foot of a large bed. "I would like the father raven's wing to become strong like Caradoc's arms. Could you tell me the whole story?"

"The whole story?" Richard paused thoughtfully. "Yes, of course, Bran." Richard shifted his gaze. "Wait. Edward, what do you think? Can we tell Bran's mother's story about Caradoc?"

"Sure, Richard." Edward stared at the flames.

"Bran and I want to name the hurt bird Caradoc. What do you think, Edward?"

"No word on my mother, Bran?" Edward turned his concerned eyes on the boy.

"Not since you last asked, Sire." Bran scratched behind Buffy's ears as she put her front paws on the edge of the bench. "But I heard the raven master say that she was at Westminster Abbey. I only hear bits and pieces from the yeomen though."

"Who is this raven master?" The fire cast sidelong shadows across Edward's face. "Why would he have knowledge about my mother?"

"I don't know his name or title. Everyone just calls him Raven Master. He doesn't talk much about anything except the ravens." Bran shrugged.

"And yet he knows about my mother." Edward hardened his face. "Do you know this raven master well, Bran?"

"No one really does. He has this look on his face. It's kind of strange ... scary." Bran shuddered. "No, Sire, not everyone knows the raven master and even fewer like him."

"Being so strange and scary," said Edward, studying Bran's face, "have you heard any good reason why the raven master still remains here?"

"I have heard some of the children around here say that the raven master is here as a punishment. Some say that he killed his wife and children and buried them here on the castle grounds."

"Really?" Richard whispered. "Have bodies been found?"

"Some say that the skeletons of children have been found in the work area. The raven master killed them in their sleep, then he took their dead carcasses and fed their meat to the birds."

"Did you see the skeletons?" Richard scanned the room with wide eyes.

"No, Sire, I can't say that I did. But my friend Sean, whose mother runs the kitchen crew, said—"

"Enough, Bran." Edward turned his back to the fireplace. "I hardly think that my uncle would have such a vile man working for him. What are we? Little girls who scare each other in the night? What I want to know is why this raven master has knowledge about my mother."

"Certainly, Sire." Bran clasped his hands and stared downward. "Blimey, I never said I believed the tales. I just said that there are a lot of unanswered questions about the raven master."

"Bran, can you please tell me why the raven master has knowledge about my mother?"

"Of course, Sire." The boy stood and riveted his eyes to his shoes. "I can tell you that he is the one yeoman who is allowed to go into town without question. He does not need special permission to leave. He goes whenever he likes to buy the food for all of us here at the castle." Bran chanced a glance at Richard. "I was told that he buys a little extra meat for the father raven to help him get better."

"Bran, you are making me so tired. Answer the question about my mother, your queen."

"Right. I was just getting to that. When the raven master goes to town, he listens to the townspeople talk about the news from near and far. He hears things at the market and then tells the other yeomen here in the castle."

"So he hears what others are saying."

"Yes, Sire. Without the raven master's trips into town, we wouldn't know what was happening outside these walls." Bran shifted his gaze to Richard again and added in an undertone, "What would you name the mother bird?"

The younger prince smiled broadly. "The name Rhiannon would be a nice name for the mother bird."

"Rhiannon?"

"Yes, Bran. What do you think, Edward? It's from Mum's stories."

"Rhiannon is fine, Froggie." Edward nodded to his brother then turned to the boy. "Bran, I really want to know about Mum. Tell me everything you heard."

"Maybe you should ask me that question." Duke Richard stood at the door. "I might be a better source for an answer, rather than a castle boy."

"Hello, Uncle. I didn't hear you come in."

"I prefer it that way, Edward." Duke Richard shut the door behind himself. "These are dark times, lads. Where were you going, my prince, when we met you on the road?"

"We were coming to London."

"It is good that I caught you when I did. You were completely unprotected by the House of York. I don't know what would have happened if the Lancasters had found the new claimant to the throne of England so ill guarded. I need you boys to stay quiet here in the Tower of London under my protective custody. There are many who want you two dead."

"Why would they want us dead?" piped up Richard.

"The *why* of it isn't important, young nephew. The important thing is that you're here with me and safe. Here in the Garden Tower you are protected by great walls. The soldiers here serve only within these walls. These guards have only sworn their allegiance to the crown. That crown belongs now to you, Edward."

"Did they serve Father?"

"No. I have newly organized them. I call them Beefeaters."

The nine-year-old prince laughed. "That's a funny name. Why do you call them so, Uncle?"

"Right now, young Richard, I have no money to give them. So I pay them in food. They earn a daily ration of meat for themselves and their families. They seem to like the beef the best. Just ask this young fellow here." Duke Richard pointed to Bran. "I see you've already made friends."

"Uncle," Edward fought to keep the quaver out of his voice, "I don't want friends here. I don't want to play with a dog named Buffy who plays with the ravens. I just want to know if Mother is safe and if she is coming to get us." Unbidden, tears welled in the eyes of the twelve-year-old boy.

"Edward, you are in line to be king now. Young as you are, you must expand your thinking beyond what you want. You must think of the needs of a kingdom. As lord protector, your father entrusted me to guide you in this. His death began my responsibility. I have put many wheels in motion—including the removal of many personages who might threaten you."

"Did that include Richard Grey and the Earl of Rivers?" Edward drew himself up tall.

"Yes and no." Richard looked the prince over shrewdly. "They are being held and questioned right now. Although their hearts may appear true, I cannot be sure they are loyal supporters of the crown under the House of York."

"If I am to be crowned king, then you are to be my subject, yes?"

"Yes, Edward." Duke Richard gave a curt bow.

"As my subject I command one thing now. I want my mother. Please, Uncle. Make sure my family is safe."

"I am already doing much to secure your family. You must give me the chance to settle these changing times. You must trust that I am doing the best I can."

"When I see Mother," Edward thrust his chin up, "then my trust will begin."

Duke Richard bowed again and, taking Bran with him, the boys' uncle departed.

As soon as the door closed, Richard joined his brother at the fire. "Edward, I'm scared. Why do I feel so scared?"

"Easy, Froggie. I'm here." Edward patted his brother's shoulder and then crossed the room to check the door. He plopped down on the bench. "Mother," Edward sighed. "I want our mother."

"I love you, Edward." Richard sat down beside his older brother and lifted Buffy to the bench.

"I love you too, Froggie." Edward rubbed the top of his brother's head and then stroked the dog.

"Will you ever stop calling me that name?"

"I don't think you want that, do you?" The older brother smiled.

"Why wouldn't I?"

"Remember, you are the frog who turns into a king when a princess kisses him." Edward arched an eyebrow. "I thought you didn't want to be kissed by a princess."

"You're right, I don't! Absolutely not!"

"Then you are still Froggie."

"I guess that's all right then."

"Come, Richard, it's late—or early? Either way, let's get some rest. Bring Buffy and let her sleep with us."

"Yes, she is probably a little nervous." Richard smiled at his big brother and flopped on the bed. Buffy followed.

"Besides, Richard, there are some ravens we must see when we wake. What were their names going to be?"

"Caradoc Freichfras and Rhiannon."

"Yes, Caradoc and Rhiannon." Edward lay down next to his brother and took his hand. "The same as in Mum's stories."

"I can hardly wait. I know we will like them."

"I already do, Froggie. I already do."

20

Racing Heart

Château Royal d'Amboise
Loire Valley, France
1500

"Mademoiselle Louise, did you like the rest of the story?" Simone, the artisan, smiled.

"I did so very much, Simone."

"As you heard the story, did you look at the tapestry with the eyes of your heart?"

"I did." Louise put her hand on her chest and closed her eyes. "I saw a tower. It was in a garden filled with plants. It had to be a Garden Tower."

"What symbolized the Garden Tower?"

Louise opened her eyes again. "The tower was the circular fence. Inside, it held the unicorn, but not Froggie. Froggie was outside."

"Why do you suppose Froggie was not in the Garden Tower?"

"Maybe he was with Bran playing with the ravens?" Louise smiled at the thought.

"Maybe, but maybe not. We will understand more, I think, as the story continues through the other tapestries."

"I really liked Froggie. He is the younger brother of Prince Edward."

Simone nodded sagely and then pointed at the tapestry with the stem of her pipe. "Where is the prince?"

"I know the prince is in the tower. The prince must be the unicorn."

"Yes. The prince is the unicorn. Why do you suppose that is?"

"I believe that the queen asked you to make it that way," Louise smiled proudly.

"She did indeed," Simone laughed. "Do you know why the prince is shown as a unicorn, Mademoiselle Louise?" A puff of smoke rose over Simone's head.

"I'm not sure but I have a guess," Louise shrugged. "I believe that Prince Edward is the Prince of Wales."

"Why would that make him a unicorn?"

"The family symbol for Wales is a unicorn."

Simone's forehead wrinkled in surprise. "How do you know this, Louise?"

"I have tutors."

"You have good tutors. I'm impressed."

Louise turned her gaze back to the piece of art. "Why is the Prince of Wales chained to the tree, Simone? Nothing in the story shows that he is chained."

"You are forgetting what I said about chains and collars, Louise. Maybe it is for the same reason that Froggie is outside the tower." She shifted the girl on her lap. "However, Louise, you are now listening with your ears."

"I know, I know. I must listen with my heart. Now my heart must have eyes and ears. Once it has legs then it will probably walk out of my chest."

"I dearly hope not," laughed Simone. "What would your mother say?"

"Tell me why the prince is chained, Simone."

Simone looked at Louise appraisingly then said, "Let us wait until more of the story is told, Mademoiselle. The only thing I can tell you now is that the unicorn wears a chain because the queen said it must be so. I believe we will learn more as the rest of the story is revealed in the other tapestries."

"I can't wait!" Louise bounced up and down. "My heart is growing legs. It feels like it wants to jump out of my chest!"

"Oh, but you must wait."

Louise touched her chin thoughtfully. "Do you know the artisan of the second tapestry?"

"Well … yes. I mean only that we have met. I really can't say I know him, but he seems nice enough."

"Would he be willing to show us the next tapestry so that with the eyes and ears of our hearts, we can understand the story of Prince Edward and Froggie?"

"You are a very determined young lady. Let me see what I can do. Go now and tell your mother what we are doing. I don't want her to worry about her Louise."

"I will be back soon." Louise hopped down.

"Hurry, but don't rush."

"I won't, Simone. But don't be surprised if my heart arrives here faster than the rest of me." Louise ran back through the milling crowd.

When she returned, she saw Simone standing with Vaast, the maker of the second tapestry, and Pollixe, the weaver of the third tapestry. She ran up and took Simone's strong, old hand in her own. "Is that the second tapestry, Simone?"

"You must be Louise." Vaast, the old master weaver, smiled and doffed his hat. His unkempt hair sprung out like white hoarfrost on a winter's morning. "Simone, Pollixe, you ladies must excuse me as I believe I have an appointment with this young bright-eyed wonder." He brushed away fabric lint from his sleeves in a failed attempt to look tidy. Last, Vaast stood as upright as age permitted and tugged firmly on his leathery vest adorned with two huge front pockets. Then, cocking his leathery ear, he lowered his head and repeated, pointing a gnarly bent finger. "Are ye that most curious little angel, Mademoiselle Louise?"

"I am, sir."

"I've heard quite a lot about you." Vaast winked. "It seems you have a genuine appreciation for tapestry art. Is that so, young missy?"

"Yes, sir." Louise nodded toward the tapestry. "Did you put this second tapestry up just for me, or is the queen coming here to continue her story?" Louise raised herself on her tiptoes and peered around the hall.

"No, darling," Simone smiled. "Queens busy themselves with queenly matters. When she returns, we will display the first tapestry should she wish it. We artisans are allowed a little leeway. I am sure we all wish to check our work one final time before the royal review. Am I right, Vaast?" she asked with a wink.

"Simone speaks the truth," said Vaast. Then, frowning down at Louise with a serious nod, he asked, "So, I ask again, are you ready for the tale to continue?"

"I am if Simone holds me."

"That sounds like an accord." Vaast turned and held out his slightly quivering hand. "Simone?"

"It's your tapestry, your time, and your treat, Vaast." Simone and Louise settled in a chair. "I will warn you though, sir. Mademoiselle Louise will ask the hard questions."

"Should I be afraid, Simone?" Vaast asked, tucking four fingers of his left hand into his vest pocket.

"I would be if I were you," she chuckled.

"Then I would be most afraid to delay."

21
Test of the Unicorn

Maternity hospital
Saint-Quentin, Somme River Valley
Vermandois region, France
Current day

If the fall didn't kill me, I would drown at the bottom. Flinching fitfully in her bed, Loni continued to sleep and dream. Her eyes moved rapidly under her closed lids. Her view was from atop a long castle wall stretching between two turrets. *At least the dreadful night is gone!* she thought. She looked over the edge of the wall. At the bottom of the sheer stone wall drop, the Thames flowed. Turning on the stony ledge, Loni felt the wind at her back. *The castle green on the inside of the wall is so picturesque.* On the grounds, the children played across the manicured lawn. Loni knew it was called the bailey, though she didn't know how she knew it. In the distance, workers cut the grass and clipped the hedges. Loni focused in on two boys sitting together across the courtyard. *What are they tending to with such intensity?* Realization crept into her mind. *It's a black bird with a bandaged wing.*

✠ ✠ ✠

"Caradoc, come to me." Edward watched as the bird hopped toward the food morsel in his hand.

"He likes you, Edward. He likes you best!" Richard's voice drooped.

"No, Froggie. He likes the food," Edward laughed. "Worry not, little brother. Caradoc, Rhiannon, and that conspiracy of ravenlings in their nest think of you as their dear Uncle Richard."

"Do you really think so?"

"Absolutely!"

"I believe he is getting better, Edward," Richard pointed. "I think he wants to jump off the wall and fly."

"I don't think he has the confidence to jump off the far side yet, Froggie. It is a long drop."

"He might." Richard watched as Caradoc hopped to the bailey just inside of the wall. The youngest prince tracked his eyes up the immensely tall fortification. "Then again, he might wait for a better day."

"Sure, Froggie. Maybe the winds are not right for him today."

"Maybe tomorrow, Edward?"

"No, not tomorrow either, darlings." The widowed Queen Elizabeth Woodville shook her head. The gossamer streamer from her conical headpiece fluttered as if greeting.

"Mother!" The pair of princes simultaneously rushed the queen, causing all to fall backward onto the soft green turf. Decked out in a black form-fitting velvet dress, trimmed only with a broad band of gold embroidery at the neckline and cuffs, the queen contrasted greatly against the verdant lawn. "Do you like the ravens?"

"They're lovely but not more than my two boys." She held their faces in turn, kissing each boy's cheeks.

"Caradoc is getting ready to fly!" Richard stood and spread his arms wide. "Caradoc?"

"The bandaged bird," said Edward.

"Oh, I don't think that bird is going to be able to fly for a while, Richard." The queen rolled to her side and smiled at her young sons.

"Will you be here when he does?"

"I can't say, Richard."

"I feared for you, Mother." Edward stood and extended his hand. "Without father or me to protect you from villains and scallywags, I had no guarantee for your safety."

"I knew that you would, my son." Elizabeth Woodville took Edward's hand and pulled herself up to a seated position, brushing off her dress.

"I did too, Mother." Richard knelt and wrapped his arms around his mother's waist. She stroked his blonde hair and smiled down at him. "Did you see Rhiannon?" he asked.

"She must be the mate of the one with the bandaged wing, right?"

"Yes, Mother." Edward sat and pointed. "The father bird is Caradoc Freichfras."

"Well, I can see you both remembered your Welsh mythology from my bedtime stories. I thought that you were asleep as I told you those tales." Elizabeth Woodville's tickles gave rise to boyish giggles and another tumble on the green grass.

After a few moments, Edward sat up, plucked a blade of grass, and began chewing it. "Are all the girls well?"

"Yes, my darling. Little Elizabeth came with me here to the Tower of London today. Cecily stayed back with the rest of the children."

"Elizabeth is here now?" Richard hopped to his feet. "Where is she?"

"I'll bet she found Buffy, Froggie. Why don't you bring them both here?" Richard nodded and was off like a shot. Edward and his mother watched as Richard ran off yelling aloud the names of both his sister and the dog.

"I'm glad all are safe, Mother." Edward nodded.

Elizabeth Woodville sat herself upright and beckoned Edward closer. "Are you boys well?" With her thumb she smoothed away the tiny furrow from the young prince's forehead.

"Yes, Mother, we are." He let the weight of his worries leave his face and leaned his cheek into her hand. But it was a fleeting moment of peace and comfort. Edward lifted his face, looking into his mother's eyes. "Why aren't all of you staying here with us?"

"We aren't contenders for the throne. So we are not in the same danger as you two boys." The queen sighed and straightened the seams of her black velvet dress. Her thumb pressed the velvet into greater smoothness. "Duke Richard greatly fears for you both. He says here is the safest place for you."

"I know why we are here, Mother." Edward frowned. "I'm just wondering why the rest of the family can't be here too."

"Duke Richard feels that the rest of the family being here would be a distraction and a security risk. I don't fully understand it, but I know he is wise in these matters. Your father thought so as well."

"Richard and I are the sole source of all the family's danger, aren't we?" Edward tugged some grass up by its roots and threw it down.

"Don't say that, Edward." The queen stilled her son's hands. "Know that you two are the crown jewels in the new kingdom. Jewels are meant to be protected—sometimes with extra special measures. It is easier to provide a focused security for two than for all of us, nothing more."

"Sometimes I feel we are chained prisoners, Mother." Edward glanced around uneasily.

"In some ways you are, but only with invisible chains. You are tethered here to the tower because of evil people who lurk beyond these castle walls."

"The House of Lancaster wants to hurt us, don't they?"

"There are many people, from many great houses, who would kill to sit on your father's throne. Duke Richard has sought out many of them and has put them to the sword."

"When will it be safe for Froggie and me to leave this place and join the rest of the family at home?"

"When Duke Richard has eliminated the threat to you and your brother."

Edward nodded and bit his bottom lip. He traced the embroidery of his mother's gown with a fingertip. "Mother, am I still engaged to marry Queen Anne, the Maid of Brittany?"

"Yes, why?"

"I was just wondering if it would be better to join our allies in Brittany. Would that better secure the throne and keep us—all of us—safe?"

"Edward, you are growing up so fast. You have not yet reached the day of coronation and already you have the thoughts of a king."

The boy's voice became a whisper. "Mum, please." He turned anxious eyes on the queen. "Please lead Duke Richard in the direction that best keeps our family together, even if it must be that we live in Brittany."

"We think the same, Edward, you and I." She stroked his cheek. "I have spoken of you to many of those who would hunt you down to harm you. I have spoken of your virtue, your kindness, your wit, and your likeness to the greatness of your father. I believe I have the *would-be* hunters appreciative of a young king who could stabilize England rather than split it into many factions."

"Well, if this is so, then should we be going home soon?"

"I hope so, darling." Elizabeth Woodville stood. "Edward, I need you to do something for me." The queen held out her hand. "Please say yes."

"Of course. Mother, there is nothing I wouldn't do for you." Edward stood and took the queen's hand.

"So you say yes even before you hear the question?"

"If the request comes from you, the answer is always yes, Mother."

"Good." The queen smiled. "When I was at the abbey, I saw as the Archbishop L. B. Balliert direct a man to undergo a challenge. Edward, I need you to do the same. It will be uncomfortable, darling. Are you willing?"

"Sure, Mother, I will do it." Edward paused. "Will it be painful?"

"Oh, darling, I admire your father's courage in you. I am grateful for it." Elizabeth Woodville put her hand on her chest. "The greatest pain that will be felt will probably be mine as a mother having to watch you while being unable to help, guide, or protect you."

Edward nodded bravely and lifted his chin. "Where and when, Mother?"

"Here and now. Come with me to the fountain on the green."

"Of course. I can show you the shortest and fastest way." Edward began to lead but rapidly concluded that his mother knew the way. As they arrived, he watched her stand next to the fountain, her body rigid with tension as it had not been moments before.

"Edward, take the bucket there and fill it to beyond the halfway point."

"Yes, Mother." Edward filled the large bucket.

"Edward, place the bucket on the ground. Good. Now, kneel over the water so that you can see your reflection, and only your reflection, on the surface. Can you please do that now?" The queen's voice trembled. "Very good, my son. Now I need you to close your eyes and pray to God for strength for what is about to happen. No matter what sounds may come, you must keep your eyes closed until you are told to open them. Can you do that?"

"Yes, Mother."

"Good."

Edward heard the shuffling of many footsteps along with the rustle of bodies in motion all around him. He clenched the rim of the bucket, his knuckles white. "Mother?"

"Yes, Edward?"

"Is everything all right?"

"Soon, my son." Elizabeth Woodville inhaled sharply. "Keep your eyes closed." Queen Elizabeth Woodville watched as Edward gave a slight nod.

"Mother, I hear things." Edward cocked his head as the rustling slowly surrounded him.

"Edward, you may open your eyes but do not, I repeat, *do not* look at anything except your reflection in the water."

"Yes, Mother." Edward slowly opened his eyes.

He could hear his mother whispering a prayer in angst. "Lord Jesus, be the strength in my child through this…."

"I hear heavy footsteps coming toward me, Mother." Edward's voice ratcheted higher.

"Yes, my son. Look at your reflection."

"Mother?"

"I need you to do as I say," a gruff, manly voice spoke.

"Mother? Are you still there?"

"Highness, it is my voice now that you must obey."

"All right." Edward visibly trembled after a deep sigh. "I'm listening."

"Place only the pointer finger of your right hand into the water, Sire. Hold your hand as steady as possible so that your finger doesn't cause the water to ripple."

Edward willed his clenched hand to release the bucket's edge. Raising his elbow up, he slid his hand down near his face to the level of the water. "Like this?" Edward steadied his hand in the water. *More people have come. I can feel their heat. I hear sniffing. It's a dog. I'll bet it's Buffy. That means Richard, Elizabeth, and probably Bran are all here too.* He took a breath to steady himself. With his finger in place, Edward locked himself into a comfortable kneeling position of absolute stillness. He then closed his eyes tightly.

"Edward, I need you to listen carefully."

"Mother?"

"Yes, Edward. It's me. Keep your finger in the water still and listen carefully. There are three questions to ask you. I need you to answer from your heart. God give you strength."

"I'm ready." Edward recited the Lord's Prayer quietly, his lips barely moving.

"Edward?"

"Yes, Mother?"

"Answer the man's questions."

"Yes, Mother."

"Sire, do you love England enough to give your life for her?" the gruff voice rasped.

"Yes, I do." Edward could hear metal clinking in the direction of the man's voice.

"Sire, will you be honorable in marriage to Queen Anne of Brittany and equally support and defend the people of Brittany to the death no matter what temptations or evils would lure you away from good?"

Edward swallowed dryly. *I don't know Queen Anne or the Brittany people. However, if honor and duty are at stake, I am bound by God to do the right thing.* "Yes, I will." Edward could hear the metal sounds drift away, replaced by the swishing of cloth.

"This is your last question, Edward."

"Yes, Mother."

"Keep your finger perfectly still and please think carefully before answering."

"I will, Mother."

Edward heard the clinking of metal draw close again, followed by a stern voice. "Will you love your family, be they English or Breton, more than yourself and never do harm to any of them, even if it means that you exchange politics for love?"

Edward drew in a calm, deep breath. *I would sacrifice everything for those I love.* "Yes, I already do."

Edward heard the shuffling grow steadily louder until it was replaced by happy chatter and, ultimately, with clapping. He dared not move.

"Edward." Elizabeth Woodville tapped her son's shoulder. "Open your eyes, rise, and open your eyes." The queen's voice cracked as she wiped away her tears. "There is someone here who wants to meet you." Tilting his head upward, Edward first opened his eyes and then stood slowly.

"Hello, Edward." A six-year-old girl curtsied.

"Hello," Edward answered politely with a nod. He then shifted his gaze to the man holding the child's hand.

"Prince Edward," the gruff voice issued from the man, "behold our duchess apparent, your betrothed, Anne of Brittany."

22

Of Truth and Unicorns

Château Royal d'Amboise
Loire Valley, France
1500

"Love, duty, and honor are beautiful, aren't they, mademoiselle?" Simone blew her nose and nodded her thanks to Vaast, the artisan of the second tapestry.

"Please, Simone, help me to understand it in the tapestry." Louise reached up and dabbed at the old woman's tears with her own embroidered handkerchief.

"Look, darling." Simone shifted Louise in her lap, sniffing back the remaining tears. "Tell me what you see."

"Hold on, little one." Vaast reached down to pick up an engraved metal flask and held it out to Simone. "Simone, m'dear, this will take the edge off."

"The edge off what?"

"The edge off most my tapestry working tools." Vaast winked and nodded toward his tool table which had been brought over when the tapestry was mounted. "So don't spill it on the tools or in my goblet."

"What is it?"

"A concoction I made with wine and cherry juice." He jiggled the flask. "Here, Simone, take it. You'll feel better."

"Can I have some too?" Louise sniffed as the flask passed.

"No, child." Vaast shook his head. "It's for Simone. However," Vaast pointed with his handmade beechwood tapestry pick-up stick, "you still have a question to answer. What is it that you see in my tapestry?"

"I see a unicorn kneeling in front of a water fountain." Louise hopped off Simone's lap and joined Vaast at his side. "It is surrounded by many people and strange animals."

"Tell me about the people, little missy. What are they doing?"

"I see many men in groups of twos and threes." Louise pointed. "They

118

are talking about the unicorn. Some of them look like hunters. Others do not."
Louise grimaced. "There are many of them I don't like. I don't know them,
but I don't like them."

"Ah, yes," Vaast nodded, "quite astute." Pointing with his tapestry stick,
he added, "Tell me about the animals. What do you see?"

"I see a lion, an ermine, a stag, many birds, rabbits, some hunting dogs,
and ... " Louise cocked her head, "some animals I have never seen before."

"Are the hunting dogs hunting?"

"No, they aren't. That's strange, isn't it?" Louise furrowed her brow.
"There are some real mean-looking animals too."

"These are probably not nice animals."

"I can tell you what I don't see." Louise waved her hand. "I don't see
Froggie or little Queen Anne of Brittany."

"You don't?" Simone's seat scraped on the ground as she pulled closer. She
passed the flask back to Vaast.

"No, Simone." Louise left Vaast's side and climbed back into Simone's lap.

"I know Froggie, Prince Richard, was there in the story. He was there on the bailey with his mother and the dog, Buffy. And he was in the first tapestry, but I don't see a frog here."

"What if I tell you that Froggie is Richard of Shrewsbury, the Duke of York, and his sister Elizabeth's name is Elizabeth of York? Does that help you see them?"

"I still don't see them."

"Mademoiselle Louise, just like the unicorn is the symbol for the Prince of Wales, the lion is the symbol for the House of York. Is there a male and a female lion?

The child peered intently at the menagerie of animals in the tapestry. "I think so. Yes, there in the front." She clapped excitedly.

"That's right, little missy," said Vaast. "Froggie, as the lion, is there with his sister, the lioness Elizabeth—except that in this tapestry they are pictured as animals."

"Yes, different animals." Louise crossed her arms in a huff. "Why is Prince Richard a different animal?" She tugged on Simone. "He was a frog before. That makes it confusing. How is anyone supposed to know the story if the people keep changing what they look like?"

"Because the—"

"—Queen Anne wanted it that way," Louise finished Simone's sentence with a sigh. "She sure wants to make it difficult, doesn't she?" Louise muttered under her breath.

Simone stifled a rising laugh as Vaast's face broke into a wide grin. "We have to keep an eye on this one," he whispered to Simone.

"Did the queen forget to have herself put in the tapestry? Little Queen Anne is not there. No grown women are there."

"No, she didn't and yes, she is." Simone held Louise by her shoulders. "Remember now, not all animals are animals."

"In the story," chimed in Vaast, "who did Edward first see when he opened his eyes?"

"He saw Queen Anne."

"What is in the line of the unicorn's sight in the tapestry?"

Louise leaned forward. "He is looking straight at the ermine, Vaast."

"Yes, the symbol of the Duchess of Brittany is a white ermine. Queen Anne is right in front of him—but as Annie, the six-year-old Duchess of Brittany."

"Yes, Vaast. I see her now. But I thought the queen's symbol is the fleck, the shape on two of the columns." Louise pointed over her shoulder toward the center of the hall.

"Again, as before, many symbols mean many things. And a person may be many and one all at the same time."

"If you say so, Vaast, but it just seems confusing to me." The girl rolled her eyes. "If Queen Anne is the ermine, why is she not looking at Edward?" Louise pouted her lips. "Simone, why isn't she looking at him?"

"Louise, you told me there were very mean animals around, remember?

Look at their faces. You said that there were many humans whose faces you didn't like either."

"Yes." The child huddled closer to the old artisan, half burying her face away from the tapestry.

"I think," Simone stroked Louise's hair, "Queen Anne is worried for the unicorn. I think she is worried that Edward is surrounded by the bad as well as the good. Maybe she is even a little afraid herself."

"I was worried for the unicorn before, but now I am worried for Queen Anne too." Louise looked up at the artisan with moist eyes.

"Don't worry too much about things you cannot control, darling."

"But I don't want anything to happen to Edward the unicorn."

"Nor do I." Simone wiped away Louise's tears. "This is when we place our faith in the hands of God. He will provide us the ability to accept that which may come our way."

"Promise?"

"Yes, honey, I promise." Simone sighed deeply. "Now, be brave. Look again. Tell me all about Edward the unicorn. What do you see?"

"He is exactly in the tapestry the way that I imagine him in the story. He is kneeling in front of the water fountain touching the water. Why does the unicorn have his horn in the water?"

"Because Edward had his finger in the water." Vaast tapped his index finger in his palm.

"Yes, I know, but what does that all mean, Vaast?"

"Well, Louise, unicorns don't have fingers. I had to depict the unicorn touching the water the best that he could."

"Why did Edward and the unicorn have to touch the water at all?" Then Louise drew in a sharp breath, her eyes wide. "Was the water magic?"

"I can tell you, dear, the water isn't magic." Simone chewed on the end of her pipe. "Well, it *is* but it *isn't*." Simone shook her head. "Oh dear, let me see if I can correctly explain it." She put her pipe down next to a goblet on the small tool-bearing table near her spindly-legged chair, then held her deeply creased palm up before Louise. "It's like a mirror. You can see yourself in water like it is a mirror, but it isn't, and that makes it kind of magical."

"Go on."

"Water is pure and clean. That is why we drink it, wash ourselves in it, and see ourselves in it. That is why the church baptizes us in it. Jesus turned water to wine and walked upon the sea. Water plays a part in his miracles."

"I understand."

"When you touch water with a finger, it knows when you are lying."

"Really? How does it do that?"

"Do you know the difference between the truth and a lie?"

"Of course, Simone, my mother says we should never tell lies."

"Remember the queen in the story? Edward's mother said she had a kind of test for him."

"Yes, Simone."

"When Edward's finger is in the water, if he tells a lie, the finger will slightly twitch causing little ripples in the water."

"So every time a question was asked, all the people were there watching to see if the water would ripple or not?"

"Yes, Louise, that is correct."

"He didn't lie, did he?"

"Look at the water in the tapestry," said Vaast pointing. "Is it rippling?"

"The water is still and smooth all around the unicorn's horn."

"That's right, Mademoiselle Louise." Simone nodded with emphasis.

"He didn't lie!" The girl beamed at Simone. "All the questions he answered were the very truth. Edward didn't lie."

"No, little one, he did not. The water never rippled. He told the truth before God, his queen, and his future family and bride, little Queen Anne of Brittany."

"Is that why his mother, the queen, started crying?"

"Yes, she was overjoyed. She had no control over what Edward would say. So she placed her faith in God that Edward would answer in the way that would be best for England. She was proud that she had raised such a wonderful boy as her son and future king of England."

"I was happy too."

"I saw."

"Is that why you were crying, Simone?"

"No, I was crying because Edward's mother was. I was happy and my tears flooded away." Simone dabbed at her eyes again. "Sometimes my best tears are when I'm happiest."

"That's powerful water too," Louise observed keenly. She turned her attention back to the tapestry. "Were all the people happy that Edward was truthful?"

"You tell me, little missy." Vaast pointed with his tapestry tool. "Do they all look happy?"

"No, they don't, Vaast. Many of them look like they are making plans to hurt the unicorn. I hope they don't."

"Me too, Mademoiselle," said Simone. "I guess we'll have to wait until the third tapestry to find out what happens to Edward."

"Oh, Simone, I knew you would say that."

"I cannot tell a lie, Mademoiselle."

"That's right." The girl smiled slyly and reached out for a goblet full of liquid on the small table. "I now know how to be sure."

"Indeed, you do, little one. You are growing wiser with each tapestry."

"Where is the third tapestry?" Louise looked around as she returned the goblet.

"I will have it brought from its trunk at the back of the hall, missy, as soon as mine has been retired." With that, Vaast gave a deep bow and began removing the tapestry with the help of Strong Charles.

"How long do you think the queen will be gone, Simone?" Louise whispered.

"I would not presume to know. She is so busy." Simone patted Louise's hand. "Anyway, I think it's special just with us."

"Simone, you are the best." Louise hugged the artisan tightly.

"You really think so?" Simone chuckled. "I also have ways to be sure."

23

Chief and the Arrow

Route to Heidelberg

Germany

Current day

"Why does ninety minutes feel like ninety hours after an overseas flight?" Major O-stadt gripped the steering wheel of his rental car as the Pelican case rode shotgun. The autobahn drive from Ramstein Air Force Base to Heidelberg passed through the Rheinland-Pfalz region of Germany. The highway remained flat for many miles but then eventually reached the western shoulder of the Upper Rhine River Valley. There the scenic panorama was gorgeous. Major O-stadt saw the tall towers of the bridges in the German city of Worms to his left. Straight ahead were the industrial cities of Ludwigshafen am Rhein and Mannheim. In the ridge-line on the far side nestled the city of Heidelberg. Major O-stadt's eventual goal of AFRICOM Headquarters in Stuttgart was not visible at his current location, but he knew it lay south of the far ridge, deep in the recesses of the Black Forest.

DCS should still be there at the hospital pharmacy. It'll be great to see him again.

As Major O-stadt descended the elevated plain, in the distance he could just barely see the communications towers to the right over the city of Heidelberg. *Perfect. The ERMC Headquarters is on the same Nachrichten Caserne as Heidelberg Hospital. I can store the Pelican in the safe there and then I'll be in a perfect posture to drop off Lord Doc's card. It'll be a quick stop and then I can spend the rest of my time at the hospital catching up with DCS.*

Major O-stadt took in the view of the vineyards as he descended into the Rhine Valley. *Tomorrow morning, I'll recoup the Pelican and then go visit AFRICOM headquarters down in Stuttgart to discuss the nuances of the plan to bring Liberia under the multinational auspices of AFRICOM. After a day or two in Stuttgart, I'll drive the two hours back to Ramstein and take the connector to Spain ... which had better be up and running by then.*

Major O-stadt adjusted the car's sun visor. *Once at Rota, Spain, if I have time, maybe I could drive up to Madrid and go to the National Museum of Art.* He shook his head at his foolishness. *Time? What time? What am I thinking?*

When Major O-stadt arrived at Heidelberg, the securing process of the classified documents went off like clockwork thanks to one Master Sergeant Roman. Almost immediately the major seemed lighter on his feet with the lifting of the weight of responsibility. Major O-stadt took the extra time and made a quick stop at the hospital to leave a message for his friend and afterward began to ask around for where he ought to deliver the business card. Soon enough he remembered what Lord Doc had said and then found himself back at the ERMC building, standing at a half-open door on an upper floor, craning his neck to better read the name plaque of the chief of staff.

"May I help you, Major?" a gravelly female voice echoed from down the hallway.

"I was looking for … " Major O-stadt read the name on the female officer's combat uniform and, noting the eagle rank, he stiffened his posture. "You, ma'am."

"Major Hugh's office is down the hall to the left." Staring down at a file folder, Bridgette breezed on into her office.

"No, ma'am, sorry, I didn't mean 'Hugh,' I meant you. That is, I was looking for Colonel Christiansted."

"What is that you need from the very busy Colonel Christiansted, Major?" Bridgette looked over the top of her reading glasses as she drummed her fingers on the inner doorframe.

"It's a personal delivery. Would the colonel have a moment to spare?"

"Now is as good, or bad, as the next moment." Bridgette locked her gaze on the major. "Close the door. Don't bother to sit down." In one fluid motion, Bridgette slid into her desk chair, adjusted her reading glasses, then peered over them in mild annoyance. "I'm sorry," she glanced at his uniform, "I have zero chance of correctly pronouncing your name, Major."

"Oberstadtmeyer, ma'am, Major Amos Oberstadtmeyer. Most folks suffer from the same malady and just call me Major O-stadt. In fact, just the other day when I was on the phone with my mother—"

"Why do I know that name?" Bridgette gave a flinty glare at the stranger in her office.

The major swallowed hard. "Romania, ma'am."

"Oh, yes. I remember." As Bridgette leaned back, her chair gave a squeak. "Your idiotic shenanigans in Constanta caused me to have to give my Joint Task Force command surgeon double duty—not a privilege I care to bestow on many."

"Yes, ma'am. That would be me. I deeply regret that."

"Not more than me." She dropped her glasses on the desk. "Last I read, Major O-stadt, my name plaque didn't say *all-night bar*. But let me check." She turned the plaque on her desk toward herself and back again. "Nope, still doesn't. I trust you know your way out."

"Roger, ma'am. I read you loud and clear."

"No, Major, I don't think you do. You're still standing in my office."

"Ma'am, the past has uniqueness in that it cannot be changed, no matter the effort made to change the present."

"Didn't I read that stitched on a pillow?"

"I'm sorry, ma'am. I can't change the past—"

"And the future?"

"Especially the future." Major O-stadt licked his dry lips. "Ma'am, if I may have a moment's more latitude?"

"A minor moment, Major, no more." Bridgette looked at her watch and clenched her jaw, drumming her fingers on the desk.

"As I said before, ma'am, I was asked to make a personal delivery … to the Warden and no one else." Major O-stadt tracked Bridgette's eyes as they darted to the framed photo on her desk.

Only Lord ever calls me by that name, she thought. Bridgette sat frozen as Major O-stadt slowly reached past a tray of propped military coins and the remnants of a half-eaten Gouda cheese, sliced gherkins, and hot sauce on baguette lunch. He placed a business card faceup on the glass near a tiny superhero figure pointing toward the framed picture on the desk.

"That's my husband's business card."

"Yes, ma'am." Major O-stadt nodded. "Turn the card over." The major watched Bridgette's eyes well up as she read the card. "Sorry for again soiling the sandbox, ma'am." Major O-stadt egressed as Bridgette sat transfixed.

"So much for a bright future," Bridgette murmured as she looked up, blinking back her tears.

In her doorway she saw that Master Sergeant Roman had engaged the major attempting to ease himself out of the office. Bridgette stared down at the business card while she listened.

"Thank you, Master Sergeant," said Major O-stadt. "Was anything else left accompanying this note?"

"No, Major, just this."

"Fine, Master Sergeant. Thanks." The master sergeant continued down the hallway as Major O-stadt timidly approached Bridgette's desk and tossed the crumpled note into the trash bin. Looking up, he saw Bridgette staring at him. "Did you ask me something, ma'am?"

"Yes." Bridgette sniffed hard. "I asked how well you know my dear Lord?"

"Well enough to call him Lord Doc to his face."

"I assume you meant that respectfully."

"Yes, ma'am, with the greatest degree of respect, and received that way too."

"You are Major O, aren't you?"

"I didn't know anyone else knew me by that name."

"That is the main way I know you. Lord thinks a lot of you."

"Ma'am?"

"I'm sorry, I should explain. I have always called him Lord. It is meant in the greatest ambiance of respect. I will say, though, that I like the epithet Lord Doc better—though it seems to be reserved for those with whom he works. It always troubled me in that calling him Lord I was verging on taking God's name in vain."

"Not a habit I would make, ma'am."

Bridgette nodded. "I guess I didn't know that you and Major O were one and the same person as the ignoble Major Oberstadtmeyer. Apparently, a belly flop in disgrace has done you some good."

"You really don't pull punches, do you, ma'am?"

"It's part of my charm." Bridgette wiped under her eyes with the knuckle of her index finger. "Now, why did Lord Doc give you this card?"

"He didn't say, ma'am."

"Did you read what he wrote on the reverse?"

"Yes, ma'am."

"Do you know what it means?"

"Ma'am, every soldier in the military knows what Broken Arrow means."

"Relative to him, I am asking you if you know what it means."

"Yes, ma'am. Relative to him, I know what it means."

"Even though he's calling in every possible therapeutic modality available to him, he believes he's going to die. Isn't that right?"

"No, ma'am."

"He's not dying?"

"No, ma'am."

"That's a relief," Bridgette let out a sigh but stopped in midbreath as she scanned the major's face. "That's not a relief, Major O-stadt?"

"Ma'am, he's not dying anymore."

"That's what I said."

"Ma'am, Lord Doc is already dead."

24

The Keyes or the Keys

European Medical Command

Heidelberg, Germany

Current day

"Major O-stadt, did you personally see my husband, eyes rolled up, rigor mortised, in a morgue?"

"No, Colonel Christiansted."

"Well forgive me for ignoring this rubbish. But I don't believe for a minute that Lord Doc is dead." Bridgette pounded on her desk, rolling the uneaten portion of her cheese and pickle hoagie sandwich onto the floor. "Seeing a corpse is key. You didn't see him dead. Did you?"

"No, ma'am. If you're asking me if I saw him with his dog tag wedged between his teeth and a toe tag on his foot, then I have to say no. He gave me this business card three days ago stateside in his office at Army Recruiting Command."

"That doesn't sound so ominous."

"He was on his way to a hospital bed at Fort Knox."

"Again, not dead, Major."

"True, he was quite alive when he wrote the two words on the back of that card. Ma'am, we both know that a Broken Arrow is a command given without any intent to survive."

"*Dying* is not the same as *dead*. We are all dying. From the moment we are born, we begin to die. You, Major O-stadt, were dying when you were ogling the strippers in Constanta. In fact, my dear major, even as you stand here before me, your death continues."

"Ma'am, I appreciate your strength, but this is that old river in Egypt."

"River in Egypt?"

"De Nile."

"Denial is the only thing I have Major O-stadt. I embrace it!"

"Ma'am. I wish, for your sake, that there was other news I could have

128

brought. To be fair, I didn't know that I'd be delivering this message to Lord Doc's wife. There was … is … a lot I wasn't told."

"I say again, Major, if you did not see him dead, how do you know—unequivocally—that he is dead?

"Ma'am, there is no reason to doubt the attending physician whom your husband echoed when he told me that he had only hours-to-days to live."

"If that was the case, why didn't you stay with him until the end?"

"Mission, ma'am."

"Mission?"

"Yes ma'am. I needed to hit my chalk line out of the country. Please understand," the major took a half step forward but froze at the stern look in Bridgette's eyes, "I would have stayed longer if I could have done so."

"There is some seriously bad logic here, Major. For example, why wouldn't Prentice have called me, his wife? Tell me that." Bridgette glimpsed Master Sergeant Roman gesturing from the hallway in the background. "Major O-stadt, ruminate on that." Bridgette stood. "Evidently, I have a previous key engagement. Leave your contact information with the master sergeant. Mind you, keep yourself tethered to this command. I *will* follow up on this with you later."

"I know you will, ma'am. Please let me know what I can provide. Be advised, ma'am, after a stop at the hospital I will be back later to retrieve the Pelican left in the operation's vault. Maybe by then, the information regarding your husband will be crystal. For my part, I believe he was the greatest officer I've ever known."

"Is—not was," said Bridgette, scooping her cheese and pickle sandwich off the floor and into her trash can.

"As the colonel wishes." Major O-stadt saluted and departed toward the hospital. Bridgette was not far behind. She pulled the beret from her cargo pocket, left her office, dropped off a couple of directives to Major Hugh, and swung past the G3 Operations office to speak to Lieutenant Colonel Luis Toro-Calderon, her acting second-in-command officer. Bridgette overheard Luis rigorously handling an issue regarding a missing hospital pharmacist. She paused in the doorway. *Do I need to address this before driving up the autobahn to Schloss Strahlenburg? The promotion ceremony for the command chaplain is important but….* She saw Luis shaking his head confidently and waving her out the door.

As Bridgette began placing her beret on her head and reached for the exit door, it opened unexpectedly in front of her, leaving nothing but night air to stop her fall.

"Bloody dah-daft of me, Colonel. Would have put you right down on your face, wouldn't I? Have a better rest of the evening. Guh-Guh-Good night."

"No harm, no foul," Bridgette mumbled to the stranger, keeping her beret in front of her face until the flush of embarrassment passed. *Stumbling down the stairs to a faceplant does little to bolster confidence in the acting installation commander, Bridgette.* She felt the facial redness start to recede. *The last thing I need now is a personal injury and hospitalization. Lord Doc's recurrent bouts with cancer have had enough of that for the both of us.*

Bridgett made it to her car in time to cry in private. *Prentice, why do you make decisions about your life for the both of us?*

"Ma'am?" A knuckle rapped swiftly on the driver's side window. "Are you okay?"

"Luis?" said Bridgette, trying quickly to recompose her bearing. She knuckled away tears with both hands and made a quick swipe of her nose and upper lip. Then, steadying herself with a deep breath, Bridgette rolled down her window.

"Are you okay, Bridgette?" Luis searched Bridgette's face, noting her typical stoic features rapidly melting into a face all aquiver.

"No, Luis." Bridgette exploded. "Prentice is dead." A river of tears filled the palms with which Bridgette covered her face. *Thank God for Luis, the friend I need who is a vault indeed. This outburst is safe with him. I know it.*

"That's impossible," said Luis, gripping the side of the vehicle with both hands. "There have been no Red Cross emergency notifications received saying that he is dying, much less dead. Ma'am, I'm sure you just got some bad info." Luis steadily tapped her shoulder with a closed fist. "Look, just because someone says it's so doesn't make it so, right? Loose lips sink ships, but not you, Bridgette. Your hull is watertight!"

"You're right, Luis." Bridgette knuckled at her eyes. "If I didn't know better, I'd think you were in the navy, not the army." She fronted a quivering smile.

"I guess my first assignment at the navy base in Spain had more of an effect on me than I realized," Luis chortled. "But at least my navy antics are producing a hint of a smile there, Bridgette."

"Luis, you're correct," said Bridgette, continuing to steady her breathing. "There has not been a formal notification of family member." She sniffed hard. "Why didn't I think of that?"

"Ma'am, I'm sorry to say, some people take a little information and blow it way out of proportion."

"Exactly, Luis." Bridgette forced a smile. "Wait. Why are you here? Why did you follow me out?"

"You forgot your promotion gift for the ceremony at Schriesheim."

"How did you know?"

"Honestly, I didn't. Amal, the housekeeper, found it in your office and remembered you mentioning it."

"Thank you, Luis." She took the gift through the window. "And thank Amal for me." Bridgette drew in a deep, steady breath. "I'm better now. Thanks." Luis nodded as Bridgette rolled up her window.

She was watching to be sure Luis cleared the rear of the car when a shadow shot by. "Whoa! What was that?" she half shouted. Bridgette locked her doors. She craned her neck. *That looked like a person, but taller and thinner than an average soldier.* Bridgette replayed the image in her mind. Her memory caught the atypical camouflage uniform pattern. *It was a soldier for sure … but not one of ours.*

"Go figure," she spoke out loud to herself, "with all the NATO officers here, why wouldn't one be moving around in the dark?" *He's probably a foreign soldier on his way to the NATO offices down the street at Campbell Barracks.*

Looking again to ensure the rear of the car was clear, Bridgette started the car, and its headlights kicked on. "Why can't shadowy figures restrict themselves to daylight hours?" She badly faked a chuckle to ease her apprehension more than anything else.

Bridgette proceeded toward the autobahn and her next appointment. Along the way, her mind wouldn't stop streaming. *Prentice was diagnosed with synovial joint cancer in his left foot over five years ago. Last year, Mickey, as our family physician, discovered its recurrence.* Bridgette accessed the autobahn. *Then came the surgery, the loss of the outer half of his foot, and the medical board. 'Fit for duty in his specialty but no longer deployable for combat duty,' that's what they said. Then came the reassignment—command surgeon for the US Army Recruiting Command—and off he went to Fort Knox.* She crossed the Neckar River. *Then came the lies. Prentice didn't tell me that the cancer had returned. He went stateside on the pretense of house hunting for us in Kentucky. Stupid me. I believed him even though nothing synched. Now, according to his Major O-stadt, there has been a downturn. The question is how much? How bad has he gotten?*

Before Bridgette could reach the exit to Schriesheim, her cellular phone rang. She glanced at the display and saw that it was the Heidelberg Hospital commander himself, Colonel Huston Birdsong. She answered on the speakerphone.

"Yes, sir?"

"Bridgette, I am sorry to be the one to have to wreck your night."

"What makes you think you are the only one with that honor tonight, Huston?"

"We have a death in the Patton Room."

"X-ray room number one?"

"Yes."

"Did you notify Luis at G3 Operations? I saw him there not twenty minutes ago."

"Yes, I did."

"Then why are you shooting this up the command chain to me?"

"The Military Police on-site seem to think there may be some foul play afoot."

"I see. Suicide? Homicide? Let me know when I'm getting warm."

"Negative knowledge, Bridgette."

"Who is the victim?"

"It was the hospital chief pharmacist."

"And that would be...."

"Dewayne Cameron Sweeny."

"Fine, Huston. I'm turning around now. Give me twenty minutes." Bridgette sighed and ended the call. *Death seems to be the top of the order in every aspect of my life.* The autobahn lights flickered past on the drive back to the hospital. *How could Prentice have evolved—or devolved—to such a point that he had to call in a Broken Arrow on himself without telling me? In all our communications since he left for Fort Knox, he said nothing about his cancer getting worse.* She pressed her thumb at the base of her eyebrow, relieving the building pressure in her head. *Even if he didn't tell me, why didn't Mickey say something about it to me?* She crossed the Neckar River. *Prentice's departure probably has less to do with our relationship and more to do with his illness. I just wish he would stop being John Wayne.* She hit the steering wheel in frustration. *But I know that's not going to happen. He hasn't changed since the day we married.* Bridgette's lips parted into a smile as she began to recall their wedding at the turn of the millennium.

We said our vows at eleven o'clock on New Year's Eve in the Wuerzburg Military Hospital's chapel. The celebration afterward was beyond phenomenal. The millennial fireworks lit up Festung Marienberg. The fortress looked stunning. Bridgette's thoughts shifted as signs to Heidelberg Hospital appeared. *I need to know why Major O-stadt was going to the hospital. I wonder if he saw anything significant.*

Bridgette Christiansted drove through the gate into the compound. *What have we here? Huston said there was a death—not a mass casualty scenario.* She noted people were bustling here and there with papers and specimen bags in their hands. Other people were just supervising. *Who are all these people?* Bridgette squinted in the darkness. *I need to find Major O-stadt to ensure he and his mission are not mixed up in this excitement, but first I need to find Colonel Birdsong who will be the on-scene incident commander. Maybe he has an explanation as to why the hospital campus has become a frigging zoo.*

Bridgette entered the hospital. *Let's begin searching at x-ray room number one.* Bridgette joined the throng. *Apparently, everyone heard an overhead page for a Code Blue.* Bridgette craned her neck. *No Major O-stadt ... but there's Huston with the Military Police.* "So the fun begins," Bridgette murmured. "Enter the Military Police." She joined Colonel Birdsong's side and listened to the discussion unfold.

"Dewayne Cameron Sweeny was a victim of an unclear basis of foul play, Colonel Birdsong." The MP tapped on his clipboard. "That is the only thing we know for sure."

"Could this have been a suicide?"

"No sir, he was taped into a wheelchair with an IV hanging on him."

"An assisted suicide?"

"Unlikely, Colonel."

"Do we know why he was taped to the chair?"

"No."

"Why was he being given an IV?"

"We don't know why, and we don't know who was administering it."

"No chance he was here for a radiological procedure?"

"None, sir."

"What was in the IV?"

"From what we can tell, it was penicillin."

"That doesn't sound so nefarious." Colonel Birdsong studied the MP's face.

"Well sir, I'm just wondering why the chief of the pharmacy, an unscheduled patient, would be taped down to a wheelchair with an IV solution of penicillin dripping wide open into his veins." The officer walked over and opened Sweeny's shirt. "Red dog tags, sir. He is allergic to penicillin."

"This was a deliberate act to wrongfully harm Dewayne Cameron Sweeny."

"Yes, Colonel."

"Is there a suspect?"

"We're pursuing a couple leads now, sir." The MP shook his head as he looked over his notes.

"Question, Sergeant?"

"There are a couple of things."

"Go on."

"Sweeny's wife was a former fiancée of a Major Amos Oberstadtmeyer."

"Yes, so?"

"Major Oberstadtmeyer appeared on the caserne earlier today."

"So?"

"This major just arrived from the US today and made a beeline straight for Heidelberg."

"So?"

"It's hinky, sir. I will need to talk to this major at first opportunity."

"I understand." Colonel Birdsong sighed deeply. "What's your other concern?"

"The duty officer's log had an x-ray patient signed in named Preston Michaels, Major, NATO."

"So?"

"Do you know why this person would be receiving late services?"

"No, can't say that I do. I would venture a guess that he was sent down from the ER for further imaging."

"That was my thinking also. However, the ER log has no patient Michaels as an entry."

"No help here, Sergeant." Noticing Colonel Christiansted had joined the group, Colonel Huston Birdsong turned and asked, "Any ideas, Bridgette?"

"Just more questions, Huston."

"Like?"

"What does the shift radiology technician have to say?"

"I'll check that out, ma'am." The sergeant scribbled. "Sir, we'll need to question your staff, patients, and any visitors who might have been in the area at the time." He clicked his pen closed. "I can offer you no more information at this time."

"On your list of people," Bridgette tapped on the MP's notepad, "you might want to note that Major Oberstadtmeyer came by my office earlier with a declaration that he had been at the hospital and had intent to return."

"You spoke with him?" The MP clicked his pen and began adding more notes.

"I did."

"Was he acting oddly?"

"If you're asking me if I think he's involved in a murder, I kind of doubt it. However, having been in, and around, the hospital after checking in classified materials, I would want to know if he might have seen something."

"Which office would that be, ma'am?"

"European Medical Command. I am the acting deputy command surgeon."

Colonel Birdsong cleared his throat, "Sergeant," he leaned in, "don't permit anything pertaining to DCS to be released until we know all the details. Not a moment sooner. The last thing we need is misinformation and a scandal based on hearsay."

"Clarification needed here, sir. When you say DCS, are you talking about the deputy command surgeon," he pointed his pen at Bridgette, "or the victim, Dewayne Cameron Sweeny?"

"DCS is the dead pharmacist, Huston?" Bridgette's eyebrows raised.

"Yes, Bridgette." Colonel Birdsong glanced at her. "However, Sergeant, my use of DCS in this case does, indeed, mean Dewayne Cameron Sweeny. Sorry for the confusion. Everyone here at the hospital knew him more by his initials than his name."

"Gentlemen," Bridgette tipped an imaginary hat, "if you'll excuse me."

Bridgette left out the north hospital stairwell. With an intense stride alternated with a quick trot, she shot across the caserne and into the European Medical Command building where her office was located on the upper floors. *I need to catch Luis before he pops smoke for the night.*

When Bridgette arrived, the G3 door was shut and locked. "Since when are soldiers permitted dinner?" Bridgette laughed softly. *Looks like it's just me and housekeeping.* "Wait! It's just me and housekeeping! It's time to talk trash." Bridgette bolted up the stairwell.

She rushed to her office and grabbed her trash bin. "Empty, with a new liner. Dang." She dropped the trash can and plopped into a chair, wafting the air around her. "Ugh, too bad the whiff of garbage couldn't have been eliminated with the trash. I can still smell that Gouda cheese. Wait! That's it!" Bridgette shot down the hallway sniffing and looking for housekeeping.

"Good evening, Amal," Bridgette smiled.

"How's my favorite colonel?"

"Amal, I need to retrieve a note that was dropped in my trash."

"Yes, Colonel, but it will be mixed in with all the trash from the offices in your hallway."

"Be that as it may." Bridgette snapped on some gloves from the supply cart. She and Amal sorted through rubbish until Bridgette lurched upward.

"Wait! Do you smell that?"

"Yes, Colonel. It smells like garbage."

"No!" she smiled. "That is Gouda cheese, gherkins, and hot sauce! And," she added with a flourish, "this is the note I'm looking for." Bridgette unfolded the note and scrutinized the words handwritten in scribbled cursive letters while Amal began gathering up the trash.

Meet @ Hospital Patton's Room. Left Keyes For You.

Bridgette shook her head. She looked closely at the *i* in the note. *A smiley face to dot the letter?*

"Is that what you needed, Colonel?" Amal interrupted.

"Thank you, Amal, yes." Bridgette shoved the note in her pocket and reached to help gather up the trash.

"It's okay, Colonel. I've got this."

"Thanks, Amal." Bridgette stood and put her gloves in the trash bag. "Sorry to have delayed you."

Bridgette walked back toward her office, pulling the stained note from her pocket. *This note is strange. Misspellings and smiley faces?* Bridgette stopped and held the note up to the light in the hallway. She leaned absentmindedly against the wall poring over her find. *This note was signed by Sweeny. He was probably just leaving Major O-stadt his house keys. But why would Sweeny leave house keys for his wife's former fiancé? Maybe his wife wasn't at home. Maybe Sweeny was at home waiting for Major O-stadt with a baseball bat. But if Sweeny was already dead, who delivered the note to the G3 desk? Maybe Major O-stadt is sitting at Sweeny's place right now, not knowing Sweeny was killed. Wait! Did Major O-stadt kill Sweeny for the promised keys?*

"Good night, Colonel." Amal pushed her cleaning cart down the hall. "Good luck with the note."

"Good night, Amal." Bridgette continued into her office and slid into her chair. "What mischief have you—yet again—gotten yourself into, Major O-stadt?"

Bridgette stared at the empty doorway. *Standing right there, Major O-stadt asked Master Sergeant if anything had accompanied the note. That means he was expecting something with this note ... it wasn't there. But what?* Bridgette looked at the note.

"What if *Keyes* was not a misspell?" she whispered. "What if *Keyes* was a British spelling like waggon, organisation, or defence?" Bridgette pressed the note flat in the center of her desk.

"No doubt the meeting at the Patton Room meant that Major O-stadt was meeting DCS in x-ray room number one," Bridgette nodded. "Tonight, it's the site of the dead pharmacist named DCS."

Did Major O-stadt make that meeting? If yes, that would mean he is a prime murder suspect. What importance do these keys have that would warrant murder? Bridgette leaned back with a rusty squeak; her brow furrowed.

Who is this Major Preston Michaels from the duty officer's log? Which NATO country does he represent? Was he just a patient getting an after-hours radiograph as a courtesy given to international officers? Is he a body yet to be found?

Bridgette rocked forward and sat upright. "I need to find out what G3 and the radiology staff knows. And I can't wait for the MPs to get around to it." *What do a missing radiology technician, this Major Michaels, and Major O-stadt have in common? And why can no one find them? They all may be sitting playing cards at Sweeny's place with Sweeny's wife serving up drinks. Then again, they might be stuffed in some remote dumpster.*

With an action plan established, Colonel Christiansted stood her full six-foot height and clamped on her war face.

"All right, Bridgette, it's back over to the hospital again." *Man, I hate playing ping-pong, especially when I am the ball.*

25

Lord's Silver Lining

European Medical Command
Heidelberg, Germany
Current day

"Lord, help me." Bridgette shook her head at the photograph of her husband as she reached for the note on the desk. "What would you do if you were in my place?" She shoved the note in her pocket.

"Did you call me, ma'am?" Master Sergeant Roman peeked his head into the office.

"No, but I'm glad you're still here. I was just on my way back to the hospital, but I could use some intel first. Come in and close the door." Bridgette pulled over a sticky notepad and sat on the edge of her desk. *Three variables; three missing people.* "Master Sergeant, what do we know about the disappearance of Major Amos Oberstadtmeyer? You saw him leave my office earlier—did you notice anything suspicious?"

"Nothing out of the ordinary, ma'am. Starting from the top, Major O-stadt came here and dropped off classified documents in a Pelican safe for the security vault. He left briefly then came back and spoke to you," the master sergeant said, pointing to Bridgette, "received a note," he pointed to the trash bin, "and then left."

"How did the note arrive? Was it delivered by someone?"

"Negative, ma'am. It came by PTT."

"The pneumatic tubes transfer system crisscrosses the caserne. The note could have come from anywhere on campus. That doesn't help narrow down where Major O-stadt might be now." She scratched a line through part of her notes. "Master Sergeant, how did you log in his Pelican?"

"Because he is US Army personnel, I thought about placing his Pelican into permanent party storage—but then he told me he was in courier status."

"So, his classified document went under the Temporary Military Visitor category?"

136

"Roger, ma'am. The Pelican is logged in and stored as TMV."

"Okay. Make sure every shift maintains an armed guard status."

"Done and dusted, ma'am."

"Well then, if everything is under control on our end, Master Sergeant, why in hell's bells do you suppose I have this pounding headache?" Bridgette tossed down the notepad and pounded the desk with her fist.

"Same as always, ma'am."

"I know, I know. We hold classified documents without the luxury of electrified fencing, armed crenation, machine guns, and roaming attack dogs." She began pacing her office.

"We aren't Fort Knox, Colonel. Granted, things aren't usually very exciting for us in the world of classified document security. However, when it does come about … well, you know the rest…."

"I do indeed. These blasted classified documents brought from Fort Knox have become notable only by the unexplained absence of their courier." *And his odd, tangential association with the foul play at the hospital.*

"On our watch, ma'am. Makes it our headache. That is, ma'am, your headache. For me, it's just a seriously sour stomach."

How could this have happened? What exactly has happened? Bridgette walked around her desk and scanned her notes. She tapped her husband's business card and looked at his picture. *Start with what you know. That's what you'd say, right, Lord?* She scrutinized the master sergeant, standing patient and attentively in her office.

"Sit, Master Sergeant, this may take a while." He took his normal seat and Bridgette continued. "This Major O-stadt is the same one we sent to Romania on assignment as the medical plans officer to support the Joint Task Force East."

It was a statement, not a question. The master sergeant knew how Bridgette worked, and he knew his part in her information processing. "Yes, ma'am. It was the Proof of Principle phase of the operation."

"On whose recommendation?"

"That would be Colonel Milton Sandhurst."

"Why did Sandhurst specifically want Major O-stadt?"

"I don't really remember. The medical operations officer's job description was to ensure medical support of the numerous military training missions round the clock in an international and joint service venue. Major O-stadt's job was threefold: to establish, and administratively support, a medical clinic; to coordinate medical support with local hospitals; and to plan all medical evacuation procedures."

"All these things are critical to guarantee a successful medical support operation." Bridgette tapped her pen on her palm as she continued to pace her office. "I just don't see why Major O-stadt was the primary consideration for selection."

"I see what you mean, ma'am." The master sergeant's eyes went up and left. "In order to get the mission rolling, the medical operations officer needed to set up prior to the main force arriving. If I recall correctly, Major O-stadt had to deploy from his airborne assignment in Italy to join the advance party of key players."

"For Romania, I imagine the position required the medical officer to be ahead of even the advanced party."

"You mean the torch party, ma'am?"

"When the lights come on, a medical ops guy should be there fleshing out the plan."

"Now that I think of it, I remember some folks saying that Major O-stadt wasn't happy to leave the Italian paradise to become part of the torch party in Romania."

"I can't understand why, Master Sergeant. It's an elite bunch—twenty hand-picked, highly skilled US Army personnel chosen to execute the mission of securing a toehold in Mihail Kogalniceanu Air Base. MK Air base is where the best of the best fighter pilots train for the Romanian Air Force."

"Major O-stadt should have been thrilled to get the nod."

"That's right. Being so selected meant he was seen at the top of his game."

"But playing devil's advocate, ma'am, there are two sides to that coin."

"I know. It isn't always fun to be perched high on a pedestal. After all, the drop from the top can lead to a huge thud."

"Like that cartoon coyote who manages to find the tallest cliffs in the road-runner's neighborhood?"

"Exactly, Master Sergeant."

"Joining a pristine torch party like the one going to Romania would mean that any soldier would want to have assurances that someone has their back if things go south."

"Enter Milton Sandhurst."

"That's right, ma'am. As commander of the JTF-E, Colonel Sandhurst selected and commanded the torch party."

"Sandhurst ... " Bridgette groaned and rubbed her forehead. "All those reports." Bridgette stopped at her window and stood silently staring into the stark night.

What a tough break for Major O-stadt. Colonel Sandhurst was not the most scrupulous of men. He was very Charles Dickens—his character attributes pretty much balanced out his character flaws. Bridgette tapped on the glass with her pen. *I remember seeing Milton accept difficult assignments, requiring truckloads of courage. However, this was mirrored by his documented willingness to step over into the dark side as well. In Romania, he was quick to pal around with his staff, taking them down to the local strip bar and whooping it up till dawn. Then he just as quickly reined in any officer who performed the same behavior without him or without his expressed blessing. Major O-stadt learned that fact too late. His trip to the all-night girl club led him to an altercation about the bar tab and ended in his incarceration at the local Romanian police station in Constanta. Sandhurst personally came to bail him out, and then immediately initiated dismissal actions. How could the very officer who showed him the location of the night club, sat with him through many nude performances, and barfed with him in the same dumpster pull a holier-than-thou act?*

Master Sergeant Roman cleared his throat to break her silent mulling.

"Well, ma'am, after all the reports, Major O-stadt's return from Romania to Italy was ignoble."

"I'm sad that this happened to Major O-stadt, but personally I don't feel that he was the only one to blame."

"Sometimes good things can phoenix out of bad, ma'am."

"This is true." Bridgette returned to her desk and sat down. "The Proof of Principle phase was successful in Romania. The major's absence gave Dr. Russell Lange the chance to gain even greater responsibility. And then, with the assistance of a logistics guru, Major Mike Winnabe, they became a very efficient torch party."

"Major Winnabe?"

Bridgette leaned back with a squeak. "Mike Winnabe and I actually go back as kids all the way to the same neighborhood. He was brought to Romania to replace Major O-stadt." She held her hands up like uneven scales. "The result was that huge kudos went out to Russell and Mike for a job well done, and Major O-stadt's name was mud."

"Well, I am happy for your friend Winnabe, but I am still curious about Major O-stadt. If he was a victim of a toxic combination of his poor choices and sour circumstances in Romania, how did he end up here as a courier with classified documents? There must be a silver lining."

"Actually, yes, there is a silver lining of sorts—if you ignore the dark cloud surrounding his current status as missing." Bridgette leaned forward over her desk, adjusting the framed picture of her husband, and considering how much to share about the man she knew as Major O. "Major O-stadt was transferred to Fort Knox, Kentucky, to the US Army Recruiting Command. He worked in medical officer recruitment."

"And that's positive, ma'am?"

"As you know, the Recruitment Command serves as a decompression assignment for those who have recently served overseas. It affords folks the chance to be stationed in their hometown and enjoy a place where they schooled or worked in the past."

"Major O-stadt was from Fort Knox?"

"Close. Major O-stadt was from Louisville, Kentucky, not forty minutes from where he hung his hat at Fort Knox. From what I understand, the problem was that the recruitment pace was intense. This decompression assignment turned out to be nothing more than a time and energy sinkhole."

"The silver lining, ma'am?"

"Almost there. Major O-stadt did well, despite the challenge, and quickly befriended the local command surgeon—another displaced overseas soldier who had just served his tour here and left his family behind. Major O-stadt became the surgeon's respected and admired protégé."

"Was this relationship the silver lining?"

"Kinda. Sorta. The command surgeon was known affectionately by all recruiters as Lord Doc. Apparently, Lord Doc admired the spunk and tenacity of this young officer and soon placed Major O-stadt under his wing. Major

O-stadt handled all the direct commissioning applicant cases who wished to have access into the army Medical Corps. Major O-stadt hand carried the files of the applicants with health issues and personally presented them to Lord Doc." At the look on the master sergeant's face, she clarified, "It was not a name the command surgeon cared to have, but even he had to admit to its accuracy."

"I was going to ask you about that. The nickname sounds a bit sacrilegious."

"Maybe, but there seems to be some substance to it. The way it was explained to me was that the title of Lord Doc was not attached frivolously. In the world of operational medicine, the command surgeon of Recruitment Command holds absolute medical power of accession over every worldwide army applicant. If an applicant has a disqualifying medical condition, only Lord Doc was fully authorized to act in behest of the commanding general and waive their disqualification."

"I'm not sure I knew that, ma'am."

"Most don't. Also, if a malcontent applicant rebutted to the inspector general, any general officer, any Congress member, the surgeon general of the army, or any politician in the executive chain—including the president of the United States—the letter of complaint eventually gravitates to one place for final action: the desk of Lord Doc."

"I guess in the eyes of recruiters and applicants alike, this command surgeon would be god-like with power. With great power usually comes great corruption."

"Contrary to the tenets of Machiavelli, in the case of Lord Doc, absolute power did not lead to absolute corruption. Within the reign of this command surgeon, his power was tempered by a kind heart and a King Solomon–like sense of fairness allowing the medical evidence to drive the waiver. Considering every medical shortfall, he worked hard to provide the best applicants through the front door of the US Army."

"Sounds like fiction, ma'am."

"Some say this goodness stemmed from Lord Doc's wife, the Warden, as she was nicknamed. She kept him in balance—even at a distance."

"You're the Warden and Lord Doc is Colonel Prentice Christiansted, isn't he?"

"Maybe," she evaded.

"So the silver lining is that Major O-stadt was able to work with your husband?"

"I could think of lesser silver linings. But no. This was not the silver lining. Anyway, how did you know I was the Warden, Master Sergeant?"

"I figured it came from an extrapolation of your maiden name, Ward."

"Well done, Master Sergeant." She gazed at him over her glasses. "However, when Lord Doc was asked about the moniker, he would always respond that it was because 'she held the keys to his heart.'"

"Yes, ma'am, that's what husbands say." Master Sergeant smiled. "Tell me more about Major O-stadt and Lord Doc. I am guessing the silver lining is close. And maybe it'll help us locate the missing major."

"Close, yes, very close. Lord Doc's office was a haven for Major O-stadt." She picked up her husband's business card from the desk and rubbed the sharp corners until they were smooth. "Even if, as the Warden, I have the keys to Lord Doc's heart, there was plenty he kept from me. He was—is notoriously secretive. He admittedly withholds information selectively. So from here on out my story of Major O-stadt is purely guesswork."

"Understood, ma'am."

"Well, as I'd imagine it, they're sitting there one day and out of the blue, Lord Doc reveals that he has recommended Major O-stadt for a specific tasking within the US Army African Command."

The master sergeant waited expectantly for a few silent moments before asking, "So, ma'am, Major O-stadt's selection for courier to AFRICOM came about because of his availability after Romania and the subsequent meeting of Lord Doc. That was the silver lining?" He looked at her skeptically.

"Yes, it could be. The special operations courier missions belong out-side the Recruiting Command, and within the auspices of the Army Medical Command at Fort Knox. However, the local hospital commander, like all commanders, was probably loath to give up any of his assigned officers for this special tasking. Upon hearing this, Lord Doc was most likely positioned to make a weighted phone call which then catapulted Major O-stadt into the slot. Hence, even though Major O-stadt had been dismissed in disgrace from Romania, Lady Luck yet again smiled in his face. We all know that while the Romanian mission has been uploading, so did the start of AFR-ICOM. As you would know it, Major O-stadt was again at the right place at the right time."

"That certainly seems to be good timing."

"It does indeed. But that's just the way Lord Doc is. Things tend to play out how he expects—or manipulates—them to. Anyway, few folks assigned to the Recruitment Command can work in a special operations capacity with its first stop at the fortress. I would imagine that Major O-stadt was probably thrilled beyond words knowing that the secrets held behind the high fences and gun emplacements of the Bullion Depository would soon be opened just for him." Bridgette laughed. "I know I would be chomping at the bit until the day arrived when I could see that which only a few Americans in all of history have ever laid eyes upon."

"Well, he was either thrilled or terrified. Either way, a second shot is what I call a mega silver lining, ma'am." The master sergeant smiled broadly as he stood and placed his hand on the doorknob. "You said that you needed to go to the hospital, ma'am. You'd better be on your way before the folks you need to talk to clear out of there."

"Right you are, Master Sergeant." Bridgette dropped her eyes as she retrieved her beret from her pocket once again. "You know, Master Sergeant, I'd give all of the treasures in Fort Knox and more just to be able to go back and spend time with Lord Doc." She set the business card down on her desk and stared at his name.

"It could happen." Master Sergeant glanced at his watch, opened the door, and stood in the doorway. "Who knows?"

"It's all in the hands of the Lord," Bridgette replied.

"Which one?"

"Exactly."

26

Never So EZ

Zimmerman residence
United States Military Academy
West Point, New York
Current day

*Y*ou can't put a baby's room in a kiln and fire it up to twelve hundred degrees Fahr-enheit, can you?* Jillian Zimmerman shook her head glumly. *This rain has been pelting down for hours. How will the paint in the twins' room be able to dry?* Staring out through the upper-floor windowpanes of the magnificent mansion which overlooked the Hudson River at West Point, Jillian propped her chin on her hands.

I don't know if I should have started this project. Maybe I should have left it to the pro-fessionals. I'm so tired all the time. What made me think I could do this room remodel alone? She looked down at her hands beginning to swell from water retention. *What does a commercial ceramist know about painting rooms in a mansion anyway?* Jillian took the eight-ball fortune-telling device from a nearby table and shook it. It read: *Not Today.* Jillian laughed.

This is the exact kind of behavior that Mother would say is so brilliantly Jillian. Jil-lian shook her head and put the fortune teller back on the table. *Dad says that I am—how does he say it? Oh, yes, Frida Kahlo meets chihuahua on caffeine.* She traced the path of a raindrop on the window as it merged and split its way to the ledge. *Maybe both parents are a little right, but Loni has me spot on—Jillian is artsy, tartsy, pud-ding, and pie.*

Jillian peered at her raindrop-splattered reflection in the window. *I don't look like an overanxious looney.* Her heart-shaped face still retained the two promi-nent, rounded cheeks from her youth. She had sparkling blue eyes and thick coils of golden hair that cascaded untamed, teasing at her collarbones. Like the *Mona Lisa*, she had a perfectly straight nose which ended right above the sweetest of sly smiles. Turning sideways, she looked at the profile of her body.

Look at my belly. You can't hardly tell. At twelve weeks, it is still mostly flat. She pressed her hands gently against her abdomen, pulling her shirt taut. Only the slightest hint of a baby bump could be seen. *It just looks like I had a big lunch.* She released the shirt and closed her eyes. *It's more what I feel rather than what I can see.*

Most women her age would be pleased with a mostly flat, firm belly. However, not many other fifty-year-old women had engaged fertility experts in hopes that this last-chance pregnancy would be sustained until delivery. Even now, her sister Loni was eight months into her trek toward motherhood.

What is wrong with our younger generation of Meriwether women? Why is it that it takes us so long to finally achieve any hope for sustaining a pregnancy beyond the first trimester?

"Be careful what you wish, you may indeed get it." Jillian smiled and began humming a song about green alligators and unicorns.

Why has the Zimmerman household remained a no-child zone? And why is that void such a difficult burden to bear—and share? She and her husband had been struggling with infertility for some time, but Jillian had never told her mother of all the pregnancies that started but were rejected within two months. *And only Loni knows about the one with Russell.* This time was so different, she could feel it.

Twelve weeks solid—and it's going to go through to completion. Imagine, two tiny heartbeats cuddled together inside me.

"Hang in there, okay?" she whispered to her tummy. "I'm making someplace special for you—the Unicorn Room."

Judging by this rainstorm, the walls might *be dry by the time the babies are brought home from the hospital.* Jillian's eyes combed the street below. She noticed a drenched, disheveled child spinning a tattered umbrella without a care in the world. The pirouetting green Eifel Tower design of the umbrella began to make Jillian feel nauseous. She looked back to the clouds.

I wonder how Mom and Dad are faring in France. They left days ago. By now they should be catching up with Mother's relatives in the wine country at Oger. Then it's on to Saint-Denis and Paris with the city dwellers. When will they meet up with Loni and Mickey and head back to Heidelberg to wait for the blessed delivery? I never got the full itinerary. She picked absentmindedly at her hangnails, constantly chalky white and dry because of her profession.

Eh, no matter, Frog Face will be so surprised when she sees Mom and Dad. She chuckled softly. *Frog Face. It's funny how nicknames persist on into adulthood. That one never really bothered Loni. As for Suzanne Coletrane, the nickname Viking Witch never went over well. But it was appropriate and thanks to small military communities, it has stuck with her all these years. She deserved it. After all, she stole away my first crush.* The hangnail she was tearing drew blood. "Dang!" She put her finger in her mouth.

Jillian sat down and stared at her watch as if she could stop the hands from moving just by watching. *Today is an office day at the ceramic shop. I don't want to go all the way to Marlboro. Marquis will want to review the books.* Jillian frowned. *Marquis Du Bois always wants to do the books.*

I just hate the monthly business review. Why can't every day be an art production day? Jillian fought off a sneeze.

Wait. What if I catch a cold from being out in the rain? What if I slip and fall on a wet patch of asphalt or curbing? Then again, she looked in the direction of the twins' room, *what if I breathe in too many paint fumes?* Jillian shrugged. There were a million pitfalls that could affect the success of this pregnancy.

I can't remain holed up like a hermit for the next six months of pregnancy. The shop must be open. It's best that I am there. She looked toward the rain smattering the glass. *Just maybe not today. Marquis is there. Who could have a better number two man in their organization? He's always there. And expert ceramists Salt and Pepper will be there too. It'll be fine.* Jillian picked up the phone.

"Hello? Hi, Marquis. It's raining."

"Yes, Jillian," Marquis answered dryly, "I know. It's raining here too."

"Is today's business review meeting still on the schedule?"

"You know it is, lovey."

"I'm just not feeling in a business review mode."

"You never are, pumpkin," Marquis huffed. "Look, Jillian, remember when Jillian's Ceramics was always in the red financially?"

"Of course, you never let me forget," she sighed and rolled her eyes.

"Is that sass?"

"Come on. How often must you remind me that you, Aunt Louise's star protégé, swooped in to help me out?"

"Whatever, Jillian. When I first arrived, we had to agree on many things. One of them was a monthly meeting."

"I never liked the idea of changing the shop's name, Marquis." Jillian doodled on a scrap of paper on the desk as she spoke. "Your husband, AnSim, agrees with me."

"Like you, AnSim's strong suit isn't business tactics. That's my lane at home and at work. So, Jillian, be honest now, which has made you more money? Tranche de Vie or Jillian's Ceramics?"

"Look, I am quite appreciative of what you've done with the shop."

"Changing the name to French attracted a wealthier demographic. Online capability heightened visibility. Jillian, your historical figurines are in demand worldwide now."

"Yes, Marquis, I am eternally grateful but…." She dropped the pen and huffed, "Who is the boss here?"

"You are, of course, but you won't be if you don't know what aspects of your art drives the highest income." Marquis cleared his throat. "Jillian, I know business meetings are not your forte and make you anxious. Also, I know this is not a good time in your life for you. However, neither was last month or the month before. If it's not rain, it's snow, or sleet, or darkness giving you excuses for truancy on monthly business review day. Honey, it does no good to do a review if you aren't here to do it with me."

"I'm the artist. I do art. Why can't that be enough?"

"I get it. You're an artist. But know what? Both Sally and Pippin are ceramic artists. I'm an artist too, Jillian. However, of all of us, only you have the gift of being able to make a household decoration into an affordable, desirable piece of historical art."

"But I'm tired of that, Marquis." She slumped back in the chair and mumbled, "Have Salt and Pepper do it."

"Do they know you call them that?"

"Excuse me. Have Sally Natrum and Pippin Bellflower make historical art. Is that better?"

"I still need your habeas corpus, Jillian."

"Marquis," Jillian groaned. "I'm tired of being historic. I want to move into the realm of fantasy with winged horses, griffins, and unicorns."

"I know, Jillian. You asked me to run the numbers and I have. That is part of what we need to discuss at the business review today."

"I know."

"I know you know, but do you remember?"

"Remember what?"

"We have the *Art of the Levant* show next month."

"I remember. It worries me."

"Nothing to worry about, Jillian. I have arranged for a very special pair of eyes to come view, review, and provide sage commentary."

"You're talking about Elior," Jillian sighed.

"Yes, dearie. Elior Yahel."

Jillian heard him tap on the mouthpiece. "Hello, I thought you would be excited and ... and ... well, at the very least ... happy."

"Marquis, this pregnancy is very important to me." She traced a spiral on her abdomen.

"No doubt. However, an energetic Jillian Zimmerman mustering the time to create two life-sized unicorns in the past six months shows me that you, Miss Thing, can make art *and* build toward a family at the same time."

"What about EZ?"

"What about him, pumpkin?"

"Is he going to lose his pregnant wife to a ceramic business with all its review meetings?"

"First of all, on many occasions, my husband AnSim—EZ's head chemist—has told me that EZ's plate is as full as yours, Jillian. You very well know that as head of the Chemistry Department, EZ has management, research, and education of the cadet corps on his docket."

"I'll wager EZ gives AnSim too much to do."

"No, not at all. As EZ's head chemist, AnSim expects to be kept busy."

"Maybe, Marquis, but I'm sensing that you and AnSim aren't getting enough couple time together. Maybe you should take the day off today and just spend it down in the chemistry lab with him."

"This isn't about your husband or mine, Jillian. Is it?"

Dang, he didn't take the bait. Jillian changed tracks. "I do have concerns about EZ lately."

"Okay, out with it. Tell me what concerns you have about your hubby, the great and wonderful Colonel Emerson Doyle Zimmerman."

"He and Mickey are knee-deep fleshing out a brand-new project."

"Another one?"

"It's something about a blessing hand."

"Blessing hand? That sounds like Mickey, not EZ."

Jillian sighed. "It involves some biochemical pollen studies and the Shroud of Turin."

"So?"

"Ever since they both happened to be assigned here at West Point, they have done collaborative research."

"Researching if their chemistry matches well with the Meriwether sisters— Jillian and Loni?"

"How did you know that Mickey re-met Loni at my wedding?"

"Because you tell me, Jillian, again and again," Marquis exhaled into a groan. "You talked about how much better the wedding was because you used ceramic flowers over live floral arrangements—"

"You should have seen my idea for a ceramic cake."

"I did, Jillian! "Marquis's voice strained. "Kill me now." Marquis took a beat. "Honey, I know that your memory wasn't always the greatest. You were already forgetful but now this pregnancy isn't helping it. I really need you to come—"

"Anyway, working along with Loni, Mickey, and EZ as they begin this blessing hand project has been taxing for me."

"Wait, I thought those three were doing a project on osteopathic medical assistants."

"They're doing that too."

"What a bunch of overachievers."

"Look who is calling the kettle black."

"Kettle smettle, Jillian. What does any of this have to do with you coming to work today?"

"I'm trying to make you understand how complicated my life is, Marquis. Sometimes I just need a day—one day in the month—as a mental health day."

"I'm fine with that, Jillian. But why does it always have to be on the day of the monthly business review?"

"Why can't life be fair, Marquis? Why can't the rain abate so that the animals quit pairing up two by two? Doesn't any of that worry you?"

"Enough of this Noachian nonsense, Jillian. Are you heading this way, or do I have to come get you?"

"All right, Marquis." She stood up. "I'm grabbing my bag now and coming to your silly meeting."

"Good. Call me when you are fifteen minutes out." Marquis chortled. "I'll put on a cappuccino for you."

"Marquis," Jillian sighed exasperatedly, "now look who's forgetful. I'm *pregnant* and that means no caffeine, remember?"

"Touché. Tell you what. I'll make it a decaf double cappu topped with ceramic dust just for you."

"It's raining, Marquis. Better make it a triple."

27

Cloistered Truancy

The Met Cloisters
New York, New York
Current day

Finally, the rain is letting up. Jillian rolled down the window of the parked car and stuck her hand out into the moist air. *I love that the air smells so earthy after a rain.* Jillian scanned panoramically as she took a deep breath.

This certainly isn't Marlboro, the location of my required meeting with Marquis. Jillian rolled the passenger window down and leaned over to look out. *No Lily Lamps by Tiffany or Urbino maiolica earthenware pottery in any nearby window.* Jillian nodded confidently. *We can rule out being near my ceramic shop ... definitely ... definitely rule it out.* Jillian snickered as she stepped out of the car and stretched her arms wide.

This is far from West Point. The question is how far? I wonder how long I was driving. She cocked her head, pulling a hand through her blonde hair.

Where exactly am I? How did I get here? Jillian peeked back into the car. *No, there's no one else in the car. I drove here all by myself. Why can't I remember where I was going, or where I am now?* Jillian ambled to the edge of the parking lot.

Wait. I know this place. She clapped and did a little hop. *I know exactly where I am! This is The Met Cloisters of the New York Metropolitan Museum of Art.* Her face went blank for a moment. *Why the Charles Dickens am I here?* Jillian went back to her car and plopped onto the driver's seat with her legs still outside the car.

Okay, let me think through this. Jillian placed her balled-up fists under her chin.

I remember back at the house I came to the realization that staying home doesn't make wet paint dry any faster. So I exited the north gate of the academy. But why? Jillian bent, picking up a twig at her feet and scratched out a map in the soggy dirt.

My plan was to go from here to there, she prodded, *to the ceramic shop.* Jillian furrowed her brow. *But why? Gosh, pregnancy really is making my brain Swiss cheese! Wait, I know*, she grimaced. *Marquis wanted me to sit in the monthly torture he calls* a business meeting. *But I wasn't going to do that. Was I?* She flipped down the visor mirror and spoke to herself, making her eyes as haughty as she could. *No, not me … not this month. No, I was going to excuse myself from the angst-producing meeting and slip off to the mud room and create. I can do that! Right?* She saw doubt in her own eyes. "I'm the boss," she said aloud, "and that's what bosses do." But she didn't believe herself.

She sighed and turned to look in the back seat. *Yes, there's the proof.* Her purse was tossed haphazardly on the back seat. A couple of art pieces peeked out of it as if begging for attention. Some designs and sketches that she meant to take to the office had shimmied out of her purse and lay about like fallen leaves. *Yes, I was taking those to the office, all right.* She pushed them into a pile on the seat.

The normal assortment of her tools littered the back seat: elephant-ear sponges, loops, needles, an old four-inch fettling knife, and pottery ribs. There were a few new tools too, conspicuous amongst the others due to their clean, metallic sheen. The six-inch fettling knife, the stainless-steel spatula, and the trowel glinted up at her cheekily, begging to be put to good use. Jillian pursed her lips harshly. "Well, that's not babyproofed is it?"

She leaned through the seats, pushed the tools around, and then scooped up her favorite old, wooden pottery rib shaped somewhat like a teardrop. "Well, maybe *you* are, my friend." She slid her fingers around the well-worn wood, smooth as satin from shaping earth with water and force. "You couldn't hurt a baby." She smiled and reached to return the rib to its mates, but it slipped off the seat. Jillian groped around the footwell, retrieved the rib and a wayward charcoal pencil, but then groaned as her hand bumped something. In the footwell on the passenger side stood the empty, pristine box EZ had specifically bought for Jillian to corral her tools. She sighed, and rolled her eyes. *Oh, EZ, bless your heart.* She shoved the pottery rib and pencil into her purse and then faced out toward the open door again.

She picked at her cuticles, pushing the toes of her wedge shoes through the dirt map that she had drawn on the ground just outside her car. *It's not just him. There's Mother. Jillian, she would say, you're being irresponsible and immature in the management of your business. Then she would throw it in my face that Marquis made special arrangements to bring in Elior Yahel to review the show next month. It's very important for you to be there, Jillian, she would say. Actually—though I hate to admit it—Mother is right. I do need to be there. However….* Jillian sat herself upright with the posture her mother always demanded.

I need to be prepared to be there. Mother always said never to go into anything without proper preparation. Since I clearly won't make the meeting today, I need to be looking for the resources I had mentioned to Marquis. Jillian's phone rang. She groped for her purse and dragged it into the front seat. After pawing through its disheveled contents, she found her phone at the bottom. *Ugh, It's Marquis.* Jillian put on her fake-happy voice.

"Hello, Marquis, I was just about to call you."

"No, you weren't."

"You're right." She gave up the peppy tone. "How do you know these things?"

"I have some bad news, Jillian."

"Bad news? What kind of bad news?"

"Elior is delayed. We need to postpone the meeting."

"Really? I was so counting on—"

"No, you weren't. So, darling, don't even pretend."

"Come on Marquis, you know I *live* for your meetings. They're so vibrant—"

"I'm not letting you off the hook that easy."

"What? You still want me to come in?"

"No, that's not efficient," Marquis sighed. "I need you to go into the city."

"New York City?"

"Actually, The Met Cloisters. There's a poster print there that I can't get online."

"*Unicorn in Captivity?*"

"Yes, how did you know?"

"Great minds think alike."

"Can you do that for me? Please. I need to stay here and redo the balance sheets for the month."

"Why? What's wrong with the balance sheets?"

"I found a handful of receipts that AnSim was supposed to give me, and he never did."

"Your life is hell."

"You don't know the half of it," Marquis sighed. "There are mustard stains on the receipts. I swear, the man is half Neanderthal."

"Ah, yes, but he's *your* Neanderthal."

"Right," Marquis coughed. "So, pumpkin, can you do a quick trip to the museum?"

"I don't know, it's awful far."

"Okay. Never mind. Come in and we'll wipe off the mustard and sort through the old receipts together."

"Know what? I'm in the car now."

"I figured you'd change your mind. Thank you, sweetie."

"No, Marquis. Thank you!" Clicking off the phone, Jillian hopped out of the car and did a little dance. "Two for tea; a unicorn and me.... Wait! she snapped her fingers. "I almost forgot! The museum has the new book I wanted." Jillian scrambled to roll up the windows. She slung her purse over her shoulder and across her body, closed the car door, and began trekking toward the museum. *There is no way this was an accident. This was all divinely directed. I leave West Point headed for work, next thing I know ... voilà! The car connects west, veers south, then east heading for the Tappan Zee Bridge and across to greater New York City.* She stopped midstride. *But why?* Jillian spotted a lovely outdoor bench facing the river and drifted toward it. *It's got to be for more than a poster and a book, doesn't it?*

A pair of sea gulls landed in the parking lot just as Jillian settled herself on the bench. "Didn't I just see you two on the Tappan Zee?" Jillian chortled. She watched the birds strut about.

The Tappan Zee. Oh how I love the Tappan Zee. It's closer to a work of art than a marvel of engineering. Jillian smiled. *EZ laughs when I call it an expanded concrete ribbon over water. Down river, you can see the impressive George Washington Bridge kissing its reflection in the twinkling waters of the Hudson River. Sitting upon a little round top on the upstate side of the bridge's connection to the eastern shore is Axe Castle bristling on the far-side bank.*

Jillian nodded toward the birds. "You two know better than me that there is one reason greater than all the others which makes the Tappan Zee the favorite for me." The gulls twisted their heads back and forth viewing Jillian from each eye in turn.

"That's right, you and your fine feathered friends habitually perch yourselves high upon the tops of the bridge's light posts. Loud and proud—that's the seagull way. Don't even try to deny it, fellas." Jillian scooted to the edge of the bench. "There is nothing more certain in life than the fact that every gull, on every lamp post, on the entire expanse of the bridge, will face in the *same* direction. Whether you all face left, right, front, or back, whatever one gull does, every gull does.

"You two may not know this, but I," Jillian tapped her thumb on her chest, "Jillian Zimmerman, am the sole proprietor of the widely unknown theory explaining the sea gull/light post phenomenon. My theory supports wind as an explanation for why the seagulls face the same way." Jillian stiffened in mock response to a seagull rebuttal. "What? You don't believe me? Tell me what you think." Jillian adjusted the wings of an invisible bowtie. "My argument is that the wind determines the direction faced while my husband, EZ, argues that it is the light. I'm correct. You two know that I am. However, even though I am right, EZ argues relentlessly." Jillian shrugged. "What is his lame rebuttal? I'm glad you asked."

Jillian shifted her seat direction, stiffened, and then deepened her voice. "You see, my fellow humans, the birds are not drawn by the air currents, but instead to the lighting—either from the sky or that which reflects off the Hudson."

Jillian reversed her position, relaxed her shoulders, and normalized her voice. "Oh no, EZ," she shook her head. "That would not explain those dreary winter days when the lighting is dispersed. No, honey, it is the windy updraft that draws the birds into facing the same direction. Therefore, the wind on the beak makes them all take a peek in the same direction."

Jillian shifted back and again deepened her voice. "But, Jillian, the winds off the river swirl in many directions."

She turned again, "Maybe so, but the birds feel the wind in their faces. This gives the birds lift into flight."

"You're wrong, dear, it's the light."

"Sorry, snookums, wind."

"Photons, sweetheart Jillian."

"Convection, darling EZ."

"Illumination."

"Aerodynamics."

"Jillian Rebecca...."

"Emerson Doyle?"

"I am a scientist, dear," Jillian barked in deep register, "I know these things."

"You play with lights, EZ. Four-year-old children play with lights. I won't hold that against you. I am an artist. I *feel* more than you will ever *know*."

"Ah, but Jillian, you can't see that which sits before your very eyes—"

"Honey, you can't even feel nature's breath lifting the lashes of those unseeing eyes."

"Jillian, I have seen how the light draws the birds."

"I can only tell you that when I feel the wind on my face, like those birds, it makes me want to fly."

"I can't win, can I?"

"Nope. Not if you only seek a victory." Jillian stood abruptly, her arms akimbo. "Women are just like the wind. We seek only to be considered." Jillian heard some whispering and the quick scuff of shoes on pavement. She broke off her one-woman dialogue act and looked around only to see a couple of quickly retreating tourists who kept glancing over their shoulders in her direction. "Hey, where did you two birds go?" *They're probably a pair of opinionated males. It figures.* "What's the matter? Can't stick around for a fight?" Jillian plopped down on the bench again, listening to the other birds in the trees.

Every time we cross the Tappan Zee Bridge, EZ resurrects his sad explanation from his previous defeat. Normally I must listen to his justifications during the full length of the Sawmill and Henry Hudson Parkways. But not today.

"Not today!" she said aloud, laughing at the advice from the fortune-telling ball earlier that day. She reclined back on the bench and put her hands behind her head, reveling in the soft breeze dancing across her face. *Today I am at The Met Cloisters, overlooking the Hudson River on the east bank at Fort Tryon Park.* "Hand to God! I got here not even knowing this was where I needed to be." Jillian sat up and reached in her bag for a compact.

I've read about people becoming so engrossed in their thoughts while driving that they end up somewhere else entirely. That's probably what happened to Father. Jillian powdered her face. *He avoided being at the Pentagon on 9/11 by driving in a distracted jet-lagged mental fog. Like father, like daughter. Though I think my fog took me to a much better place than his did.* Jillian adjusted her hair.

I just love everything about this place. The long stone tunnel leading me ever upward to the main cloister hall. Then, from the internal summit, all I do is turn right into the bookstore. Jillian applied her lip gloss. *There, in splendid majesty, sits a gold mine. The room is filled with a plethora of unicorn books, unicorn memorabilia, and yes, unicorn posters and prints. I can be in and out in a flash—poster, book, back again. Then I can be on my way upstate to where my work-husband, Marquis, awaits.*

"Wait a minute, if all I needed was the book, I could have easily ordered it online and a poster could have waited." Jillian snapped her compact shut. "Jillian Zimmerman, you were brought here to see the domed atrium of The Met Cloisters for a reason."

Could I be another Monty Meriwether who was divinely diverted from probable death to another chance at life, liberty, and pursuit of mission? Jillian shook her head. *No. I was brought here to experience something that neither a book nor a poster nor an online interface can provide. I just wish I knew what that reason was. Whatever it is, I need to see, hear, or feel it in person.*

Jillian walked determinedly for many minutes until she stood inside the museum at a crossroads. To her right was the entrance to the bookstore, bustling with patrons as usual. Directly ahead stood an archway revealing hints of stone statues and wall reliefs. Jillian peeked into the hall to the left and paused before two beautiful nudes in print—*Venus of Urbino* by Titian displayed right next to the *Sleeping Venus* by Giorgione. *Look, both are in the same exact pose, but subtle variations of a master painter's touch stir different emotions.* Backing out of the room's entrance she bumped into an easel holding a poster. "Oh, gosh!" She quickly righted the easel. *How handsome are you, boy knight? Sorry to have jostled you.*

Jillian eased embarrassedly back into the center of the main hall. *Right? Ahead? Left?* She spotted a map on the information desk, scooped it up and after a moment she gave a firm nod. *There's only one choice for me.*

She turned left across the expanse of the main hall antechamber and toward the Late Gothic Hall. Her footsteps echoed as she sped through the gallery. Jillian felt a tightening from within; her breath grew short.

What is wrong with me? My skin feels like plastic shrink-wrap squeezing my flesh against my bones. Is it my anxiety flaring? Fear? This is a museum not a morgue. She leaned against a wall and consulted the map. *Come on, Jillian! Pull it together!* Vigorously she rubbed her arms with her hands. She moved through the Boppard Room and took the last steps toward her destination.

Finally, here I am—at the entrance of the Unicorn Tapestries Room. Jillian sucked in a deep breath. *I just need to get past the female sentry dressed in that blue blazer. What if she needs another ticket? I don't have one. Maybe I should go back and check. No, that's silly. Deep breath. Easy does it. Just look like everyone else.* Jillian weakly smiled as she stepped tentatively over the threshold and into the dimly lit gallery.

It's darker than I expected here. She moved to the center of the room and allowed her eyes to adjust. Jillian's eyes were drawn to the left. *That unicorn is fighting for its life.* She swallowed dryly. *He's just like me. Fighting to escape. The world crashes all around. Fighting and escaping are the only way out. Fight or flight.* Her palms became clammy. *All my life I have been in flight mode. It began when I escaped Europe to go to America.* Jillian turned and faced the unicorn.

What choice do you have? What choice did I have? Home life was oppressive, to say the least. It was a burning cauldron of heightening emotion, constantly gnawing away at a home life already on the brink of total disintegration and collapse. She stared at the unicorn's eye.

You know, Russell Lange and I commiserated by forming a club of misfit rebels. We called it The Society of Sound and Sensibility. We buried ourselves in Renaissance art and the poetry of Alexander Pope. The unicorn's eye blinked.

Sure, we thought we were an autonomous collective free of any authority. Ah, youth. Lucky for the Meriwether clan, someone in Canada revered me and my talents. So I left Europe and the US military bases behind me. Unlike you, my dear unicorn, I had a way out. Jillian stepped closer to the unicorn on the tapestry.

No, it's not that Aunt Louise was less strict than my mother and father. It's just that we connected, artist to artist. Then, when Canada became home, I knew it was goodbye forever to Russell and the poetic heart who loved me for me. Jillian's eyes welled up. *Freedom comes at a price, my friend. You know that.*

Rascal knew how I hated the whole "beautiful girl" scene. He knew I would have gladly exchanged my beauty for plainness—at least then the friendships formed were genuine. Jillian stepped back and gave a minute wave. *And so, it was goodbye to Suzanne. I knew deep down that, as the Viking Witch, both her beauty and her beast would eventually conquer my poor Russell. Sadly, it was also a sad goodbye to little sister Loni and her academic brilliance.* Jillian sniffed hard, receiving a fierce glance from the museum guard. She wiped her nose on her sleeve. *On the upside, leaving Europe also meant no more parents shoving me into Frog Face's shadow.* Jillian adjusted her purse strap laying across her chest and then put her hands on her hips.

The Canada experience was good. It didn't solve all my problems. Even after all my schooling, when it came time to start up my own ceramic business, I floundered. Like you are now, unicorn. The ever-present Aunt Louise came to the rescue, sending me the brilliant business mind of Marquis Du Bois. Jillian sighed heavily.

You're right, my friend, you're right. Once again, I was fitted into the frame of a person who couldn't survive without help or assistance. Keeping her eye on the unicorn, Jillian paced back and forth ambivalently on the glossy wood flooring.

Then came Canada's last gift to me. She looked at her left hand, absent of her ring due to the swelling. *Strangest of all places, I met EZ in a cemetery at the gravesite of a mother and infant daughter. He immediately saw through all my façades and embraced the person deep inside. We connected instantly for a reason only known to God himself.* Jillian dabbed at her eyes with her sleeve's cuff. *No, not in the same way as Russell. Not better or worse, just different.*

But then I let him down too. I did, really. I always do. The one thing EZ wanted most from me that no one else could give him was a child. After a lifetime of trying to sustain a pregnancy, even that hasn't happened till now. She touched her abdomen. *And then what? If the pregnancy goes to term, then there will just be another little pair of people who will rely on me—and I'll probably fail them too!* Jillian dropped her shoulders and stared up at the ceiling. She heaved a breath, then squared off with the unicorn.

I know. I know. None of this explains why I was brought here. But we're all trapped in one way or another, right? A gilded cage is still a cage. A woven fence is still a fence. Fight or flight—that's all life is. But that's not all it should be, right?

Jillian closed her eyes and took another deep breath. *Be here, be in the moment, be present.* She opened her bright blue eyes and stepped closer to the tapestry. She tilted her head, studying the unicorn's eye.

All my life I have been connected to you. I'm not sure why, but for me it was an ability to find an inner strength—something beyond myself and the flaws I see manifested in myself. The unicorn flared his nostril. *Have I answered a call you somehow made to me?* Jillian shook her head. *No, it doesn't even matter. Whatever the source that brought me here today, I'm glad.* She held her hands out at her sides, palms out. *If you can accept my fragile, fragmented past, I'll tackle whatever lessons you have for me.* Jillian moved back to the centermost point in the room. She scanned all four walls.

Standing here between all the events in your life, I feel connected to every aspect of my life. Look at me standing here on a workday. Instead of creating small earthenware figurines of unicorns in a shop, my earthen self which is filled with the breath of life is being shaped by unicorns. That's it. Isn't it? Jillian panned the entire room noting the last unicorn, which was the first she saw upon entering the room. *That's why I'm here. Right, my friend?* It looked directly at her and gave a subtle nod and wink.

28

Somniphobia

Maternity hospital
Saint-Quentin, Somme River Valley
Vermandois region, France
Current day

"There's treachery in those faces." Loni's body twitched and flinched in the bed until she woke herself up with a gasp. As her eyes opened, she found herself in the full-faced gaze of Clarisse Saint Vincent.

"Are you all right, Loni?"

"Yes," Loni panted as she regained her bearings. She took a deep, shuddering breath. "No, Clarisse, not really. I am not all right. I am having the same dream again and again."

"Does the dream help you to remember the past?"

"Yes, it does, Clarisse. But not *my* past. I am reliving someone else's past."

"How do you know that it is not your past?" Clarisse tucked Loni's hair behind her ear and dabbed the sweat from her forehead.

"The time is different. The clothes are different. It is a time of castles, princes, and towers. There are queens and duchesses."

"That could still be today here in Europe."

"It might be, but it isn't." Loni put a hand to her temple.

"How do you know?"

"I can't explain it, Clarisse. But I just know it—I three-dimensionally know it."

"What do you mean—"

"Is your dream pleasant?" Douglas interrupted as he entered the room.

"Up to this point it is, Douglas. From here it will get ugly." Loni bit her lip. "I am so glad I was able to wake up. I hate the next part of the dream." Loni shook her head dolefully as she accepted a glass of water from Clarisse and took a few sips.

"Why, Loni? What happens?"

156

"I don't know, Douglas. I mean, I can't remember. Right now, all I have is this recurring image of backbiters and intriguers all plotting against the good." She handed the glass back to Clarisse then ran a hand up and down her other arm. "I can feel the tension in my body—it tells me that something terrible is ahead."

"But you can't remember what that terribleness is?" Douglas came to stand beside Clarisse.

"I can't. I know if I go back to sleep, it becomes revealed to me. I don't want to go back to sleep. Please, Douglas," Loni pleaded, grabbing Douglas's wrist with one of her shaking hands.

Douglas hated to see his dear friend like this. "You must sleep, Loni. Everyone must sleep. Without sleep we would be … we'd be…."

"Like me right now, Douglas?" Her eyes were wide, her voice strained. "I feel like my insides are gelatin. My core is shuddering with uncontrollable fear, and I hate it. But as much as I hate it, I also almost embrace the quivering because when *that* stops, then my terror begins." Loni twisted hard on the button of her hospital robe. "Yes, I must sleep. But I'm afraid. The fear of the unknown is better than the horror I know will come. Douglas, Clarisse, I know when I go back to sleep, I will start back at the dark tower."

"What happens then, *cherie?*" Clarisse asked, taking Loni's twisting hand and bringing it to stillness.

"I don't know." Loni cast her eyes around wildly. "This and that. There are children—royal children. All is nice for a while. There are ravens and green … so much green. Then it gets ugly. Children are in danger. I can't remember, but I know that it makes me hate to sleep." She set her gaze on Douglas and moved her grip from his wrist to his hand. "Please, you say we are friends, good friends, and I believe you though I don't recall the relationship. Believe me now when I say that I can't go back to the dark tower. I can't see it all again. Please, can you give me something to help me sleep past the bad part?"

"Actually, I can."

"I knew I could trust you, Douglas. Please do. Please do … " Loni's voice trailed off and she released Douglas's hand as a wave of exhaustion swept over her gravid body, and she sank back onto the pillows of the bed.

"Douglas," Clarisse said as she gently laid Loni's hand on the bed, "are we going where I think we're going?"

"Yes, Clarisse."

"Well then, I guess I'd better go get Mickey." She started for the door but stopped abruptly.

"No need. I'm here," Mickey's voice rasped. Stroking the length of his arm brace, Mickey trudged sluggishly into the room. "I was trying hard to rest. It seems, of late, that this is a task doomed to impossibility. Maybe that cafeteria coffee wasn't decaf. Either way, God knows we could all do with some decent sleep."

"Well, it seems that all the players are here." Douglas nodded around the very familiar room. "Loni doesn't want to sleep, Mickey can't sleep, Clarisse feigns sleep, and I fight sleep. Since we all have a common enemy, and we're all awake—more or less—let's get to work on deciphering yesterday's today."

"I agree, Douglas," Mickey nodded as he rubbed his bloodshot eyes. "It's the only way to get to tomorrow."

29

Inside and Outside Queens

Maternity hospital
Saint-Quentin, Somme River Valley
Vermandois region, France
Current day

"Loni, you do you hear me, don't you?" Douglas rubbed the surface of his hypnotizing medallion. "Loni, if you hear me, I need you to—"

"I hear you."

"Good." Douglas rocked back in his chair and took a beat. *Here we go.* He licked his dry lips and swallowed. He spoke in his calm clinician's voice: "Loni, do you know where you are?"

"I am in the Chapelle Saint-Hubert. Where are you?"

"Describe what you see, Loni."

Loni's head turned side to side, her eyes roving the space before her. "I see the interior of my palace chapel. As far as I know, there is only me here. I don't see anyone named Loni." She paused and then demanded, "Who is this?"

"This is Douglas Coletrane."

"Very well, Monsieur Douglas Coletrane, given your state of address, I am forced to assume that you know not to whom you speak."

"You are correct, I do not know, but I meant no disrespect."

"Monsieur Coletrane, I am Queen Anne of Brittany." Loni paused for effect, her posture regal. Douglas and Mickey nodded to each other. It was as they suspected. Loni continued, "Why is it that I hear you, but I cannot see you?"

"Majesty, that tale is long and complicated, but know this: I speak to you through a person named Loni who has lost her memory. I am trying to help her regain it and the process brings me to you in your chapel. Can you tell me what year it is?"

Loni raised an eyebrow. "You have the power to speak within my head, yet you know not the year. What kind of wayward sorcery is this?" Loni wrung her hands in her lap.

"It isn't sorcery, Majesty. It is a hiccup in time." Douglas shifted forward. "I did not direct any power to seek you specifically. Whatever mechanism that guides me has taken me to you. I am hoping that, through you, I can find the reason why you are a part of Loni's memory. Please, can you tell me the year?"

"I know no one named Loni. Does she have any other title or name?"

"Yes, she has the title of doctor and the name Meriwether. Does that help, Majesty?"

"I know of no one named Meriwether. I am disinclined to cooperate with mysterious voices in my head. Sorry, I cannot help you," said the queen as Loni raised a dismissive hand and turned her face away.

"Look, Queen Anne," Mickey cut in, "Loni Meriwether is *my wife*, and she carries my name as well as our unborn children." Mickey's voice broke, "Please, help us."

"Strange voice," Loni did not turn to acknowledge the outburst. Instead, she spoke off to the side of the hospital bed. "I can sense that you love this Loni Meriwether and the children she carries. I feel it in your voice. I, however, do not condone your tone," she added sharply. "Who are you? Who without permission speaks so boldly to a queen?"

"Highness, you are hearing the voice of a man teetering on the edge of an emotional cliff," said Mickey, his voice aquiver. "Forgive me my impertinence and poor manners and allow me to start again." He drew in a deep breath and exhaled it slowly through gritted teeth. "I am Mickey, Mickey Peronne."

"Peronne?" Queen Anne whispered. "Mickey Peronne. How can a Peronne come to be in my mind?" she muttered.

"Is there something amiss, Majesty?"

"Amiss?" Loni faced them finally. "No, Mickey, there is nothing amiss. This Loni Meriwether, who connects us, she is Loni Meriwether Peronne, yes?"

"Yes, Majesty. She is indeed."

"Well, then, I *may* be able to help you. What is it that you need of me here in the year of our Lord 1500?"

"Highness, excuse me." Clarisse stepped forward. "I would like to introduce myself. I am Clarisse. I am—"

"—a housekeeper, I am guessing."

"I ... I ... " Clarisse's tongue froze to the roof of her mouth.

"Am I correct, Clarisse?"

"Yes, Majesty." Clarisse shrugged her shoulders at the Americans, her hands upward. "How could you know this?"

"When one is queen, especially at the beginning of the sixteenth century, one must possess great knowledge, Clarisse." Loni smiled kindly.

"Indeed."

"Further, I am beginning to see the threads of the rope that binds us."

"I'm glad someone is," Mickey whispered to the other two.

Queen Anne continued, "What plagues me is I that am not sure exactly how to help you all. Maybe we can sort through more details. May I continue to inquire?"

"Yes, Majesty." Douglas nodded eagerly. "Let me give you a little insight into—"

"Mickey Peronne, I suppose you know the name Piérronne. It comes from Brittany—Piérronne la Bretonne," said Loni as through her voice Queen Anne dominated the room with a comfortable, practiced ease. Queen Anne was unlike the timid, reverent Jehanne d'Arc or the volatile, formidable Vlad Tepes of the past two encounters linked through Loni's subconscious.

"Yes, I know it, Highness," said Mickey.

"Clarisse, I believe that your mother is named Clarisse, but she goes by Clare."

"Yes, Highness."

"Her mother's name is Clarisse. You would probably call her Grand-mother Clarisse."

"Actually, Granny Clarisse, but yes, Majesty."

"Your daughter's name is Clarisse, but you call her Little Clare."

"No, Highness." Clarisse directed her eyes to the floor sheepishly.

"Then I am postulating that you have no daughter."

"Correct, Majesty," Clarisse nodded solemnly.

"As of yet," the queen added in a kindlier tone.

"Majesty," Clarisse redirected, "I feel it is my turn to ask: What kind of sorcery is this?"

"Not sorcery. I have knowledge of your namesake, my good woman, and of Mickey's as well. That is all. Based upon these facts and this clandestine connection, I am ready to help you all the best that I can. However, I still know not how."

"That part," Douglas coughed, "falls into my expertise. May I suggest what we do next?"

"Yes, Douglas Coletrane, I await your suggestion."

"Please, call me Douglas. It's easier that way, Majesty."

"As you wish, Douglas."

"I need you to remember a time in your past. A place with a dark tower and children. Possibly with ravens and grass?"

"Douglas, ravens and grass and towers could only be connected to one time in my life. I was a six-year-old child sent to England to meet my future husband on the bailey within the Tower of London. I vaguely remember the happening. I'm afraid I cannot help you with details from 1483 that I cannot sharply recall."

"Majesty, I get the impression that your knowledge runs deep with regard to the castle visit that day. Perhaps there was also fear and anxiety associated with these memories. Particularly regarding a dark tower?"

"Where do you get this impression?"

"From what we know of you."

"Know of me?" Loni tilted her head in perplexity. "What do you, voices in my head, know of me?"

Douglas looked to Mickey and Clarisse signaling that they should pipe up.

"Majesty," said Clarisse, "there are people who have studied the unicorn tapestries associated with you—"

"You know about my six tapestries?"

"Yes, Majesty," answered Clarisse with a wry smile, "and there are seven, not six."

"Correct." Loni as Queen Anne smiled. "Well said, Clarisse. But still, I wonder why my visit to the Tower of London would be important to you."

"Majesty," Clarisse continued, "what we need may be found in the most subtle, seemingly insignificant details unconsciously captured by the eyes and heart of a six-year-old bride. All things seen are mentally recorded, but not necessarily remembered."

"Well, I remember that I was not Edward's bride." Queen Anne's voice saddened. "I was only his betrothed. He was to be my future husband, nothing more at that time."

"Highness," said Douglas, "if we have learned anything during our search to help our friend Loni, it is that nothing is ever quite as it seems. If you are willing to help us, Majesty, I will ask you to close your eyes and listen only to the sound of my voice. I am going to take you back to the days that you spent in the Tower of London."

Loni's eyes were wide open, her mouth a thin line. "What will happen to me here and now where I sit in prayer?"

"Nothing, Highness. I will place you in a special state of slumber and you will see through the eyes of yourself—your six-year-old self. When we have found that for which we seek, I will wake you up and you will be back as you are now—Queen Anne in the year 1500."

"Will I remember the things that you help me to see again?"

"I cannot say for sure, but I believe that you will." Douglas sucked in a breath. "I must warn you, Majesty. The human mind has an innate ability to suppress aspects of painful past experiences. In this state of slumber that we call hypnotism, all things, both pleasant and painful, will come to light. The choice whether to help us is yours, but it is not without emotional consequence."

"I feel that this is something I must do. I can't explain it, but I have a strong feeling about this."

"Then, Majesty, with your royal permission, we will begin."

"I am as ready as I can ever be. I just hope that what I learn doesn't change the work that my artisans have spent so much time completing for me." Loni, as the queen, drew in a deep breath through her nose and sat proudly, her back straight and her hands folded gently over her full belly. "Very well, your wish is granted."

"Queen Anne, I need you to close your eyes and listen only to the sound of my voice," Douglas began. "When I say, I need you to open your eyes and tell me what you see." Loni nodded and closed her eyes. Within moments the slow, deep, rhythmic breathing of the queen was demonstrated through Loni's corporeal body.

As the queen retreated into a guided hypnosis, Mickey handed over his notebook and pen and headed out of the room. *Douglas won't need me for a bit.* Mickey dragged his hands across his haggard, sleep-deprived face. *He and Clarisse can handle a six-year-old personality and some unicorns.* Mickey walked over to the hallway window. *Dr. Douglas Coletrane has the undisputed lead and has kept it this whole time even over Suzanne, the MD, and me, a DO. However, despite his metaphysical prowess, even Douglas has his limitations, and I think we might be approaching them soon. No discredit to him or his training, but I need to prepare now for what may be coming—for when I must take the lead.*

Mickey moved to the far end of the hall with his phone clutched in hand. For a moment, he contemplated calling Monty, Loni's retired army general father. *Wait. That would be a clear violation of the agreement that we made. Monty and Monique's arrival is supposed to be a surprise for Loni—no matter what.* Mickey wrestled with his promise and his need for help. *Maybe if her parents were physically here in this hospital, their presence could jog Loni's memory.* Mickey shook his head.

No, I remember Monty clearly saying that before they would meet up with us, they had other personal plans in Europe. Something special for Jillian. Monty's exact words were, "I must get a gift for my firstborn befitting of her love for fable and fantasy ... something to excite the creative mind while setting a standard among all gifts." Probably some Jillian's love for unicorns thing.

"That's it!" Mickey shouted. He glanced sheepishly up and down the hallway hoping he hadn't disturbed the hospital staff. Mickey flew through the address list in his head. *If these tapestries are connected to Loni, her sister is the one person who can speed ahead past Queen Anne, Douglas, Monty, and Monique. Those tapestries are right there in New York! And when it comes to knowledge about single-horned or wing-bearing horses of fantasy, Jillian is the only one.*

He punched the green button. The phone connected. Again and again it rang. Mickey's heart quickened. *Maybe I should hang up and redial. No. Hold the course.* Four more rings and the thought of hanging up returned. Mickey's thumb reached for the red button. Just then, the phone clicked.

"Hello, this is Jillian."

Yes! Pay dirt! "Hello, Jillian," said Mickey. "We need to—"

"Sorry, I'm not available. Please leave a message."

30

Wall to Wall and Unicorn All

Unicorn Tapestries Room
The Met Cloisters
New York, New York
Current day

*T*hey're alive. Jillian reveled in being surrounded by unicorns. Standing in the center of the room, she panned circumferentially looking at the life-sized woven unicorns in the twelve-foot-tall tapestries. *I can feel the movement, smell the pungent florals and greenery, and hear sweating men and beasts rustling through the foliage.* Jillian felt her heart shifting in tempo. The pulsing thrum in her neck and temples began to make her dizzy. Jillian staggered. A pang of sharp pain coursed through her body. One hand went to her abdomen, the other to the small of her back. *It feels as if my knees are going to buckle.* She took a deep breath then placed both palms against her face. *Hot and flushed.* Jillian closed her eyes, trying to master her own heart, her own pulsing life force. "Please legs," Jillian muttered, "don't fail me. Not here. Not now."

Certainly, there is a bench somewhere. Jillian took tiny, pivoting steps and frantically scanned the room. *Not even one seat? Really?* Her eyes furtively darted from corner to corner, wall to wall, finally resting on an oddity. *There! That's a seat ... of sorts.* Separating a pair of tapestries were two windows of moderate height on the cloister-side wall. Each window was blessed with a pronounced windowsill. *Windowsills can also be window seats.* On the right sill perched an elderly Asian couple. At the left window sat an elderly, mildly disheveled, Caucasian man, his eyes shadowed by the brim of his hat. *There's room for one to sit but ... ugh.*

Jillian moved toward the Asian couple. The pleasant pair bested Jillian's honorable effort to procure seating. The couple smiled, nodded, gestured, and returned her queries with musical Mandarin gibberish. However, there was clearly no intent to budge.

I'm going to have to either squat in place or sit down next to the solitary gentleman. The man never stirred or moved his limbs. Jillian stepped closer. *His wife will no doubt ask me to move. No. No woman heading this way. Maybe a grandchild? No. No child heading this way.* Jillian steadied herself before moving to the next logical step. *I need to ask him if I can sit here.* After a few moments of standing nearby, Jillian tapped the man's shoulder.

"Sir, forgive my rudeness," Jillian said with a winning smile, "but I don't feel well." Jillian leaned in. "May I sit here for a bit?" The man never even moved. Only the slightest hint of snoring escaped his well-set lips. "I see." Jillian laughed softly to herself. "I promise not to wake you if you promise not to use me as a pillow." Jillian slid her purse from her side to her lap, sat down, and took in the view from her new home.

Leaning forward a bit she could inspect the two tapestries separated by the windows. To her left was the fenced-in unicorn and to her right was the tapestry showing the start of the hunt. Past the tapestry of the captive unicorn, on the wall to her left was the unicorn and fountain scene. Its wall ended in the doorway from which she first entered the room. The blazer-wearing sentinel could still be seen posted outside the doorway in the Boppard Room. The far wall displayed two more tapestries separated by a beautiful marble fireplace. In the front of the fireplace was a stool intentionally placed behind the stanchioned ropes. *I could have used you moments ago.* A large tusk adorned the left side of the fireplace. Since unicorns are mythical beasts, Jillian knew this tusk must have come from some animal which gave rise to the unicorn legend. *Probably a narwhal.* The spiraled tusk was about three inches wide and stood at least four feet tall. *If that belonged to a unicorn, he'd be larger than this room.* Displayed to the left of the fireplace was the tapestry depicting the unicorn jumping out of flowing water. Positioned to the fireplace's right was the tapestry showing the unicorn kicking and fighting.

Jillian's eyes continued to rove clockwise to the far-right exit doorway in the corner of the right wall. Above the doorway was a small tapestry fragment showing a maiden standing next to a seated unicorn. *Those torn bits always bother me. Maybe it's because I hate to see art in ruins, or maybe it's because the intent is so unclear. Is the maiden helping the unicorn or trapping him?* Though she knew which tapestry she had not yet seen, and dreaded it, she couldn't stop her eyes. The remainder of the right wall was covered with the most horrific tapestry scene in the series. There, in graphic detail, was the enactment of the slaying and death of the unicorn. *I can't even … I just can't.* Jillian pushed away a tear as she doted on the face of the fallen beast.

Before she could begin the circuit again, a humming began in her left ear. Instinctively, her left hand rose to the activation button on her hands-free phone device, then paused abruptly. *Oh no.* Jillian glanced at the sign prohibiting cell phone use and pulled the humming device out of her ear. *Wait,* her mind raced, *what if this is an important call? What if it is EZ and something happened*

at West Point? There could have been a horrific accident in the laser lab and now he needs me at his side. The incessant humming of the earpiece beat a rhythm into her palm. *Then again, it could be Marquis at some impasse only I can resolve. Maybe it is about Elior. Maybe one of the kilns caught fire and exploded, injuring dining patrons at the next-door restaurant, Raccoon. What if it is Mother or Father calling from Europe? Maybe something's wrong? Being exhausted after losing hours of sleep, they could be vulnerable.* Jillian's eyes were drawn to her left and landed on *Unicorn in Captivity*, homing in on the tiny frog outside the fence. *What if it is Frog Face and something bad happened?* The humming ceased.

"Dang," Jillian whispered to herself, "it went to voicemail." She shoved the earpiece back in place, then precariously balanced her bag on her knees and began frantically digging for her phone. "Oh, God … which catastrophe is it?"

31
Tusk and the Task

Unicorn Tapestries Room
The Met Cloisters
New York, New York
Current day

"Pick up already, darn you!" Jillian muttered. With her hand at her ear, Jillian nodded interactively toward the sleeping, elderly gentleman next to her on the windowsill. He was the perfect faux conversational companion.

The line clicked, and Jillian heaved a sigh of relief. "Mickey? Are you there?" Jillian placed her right hand under her left elbow, keeping her left hand over the earpiece. She continued nodding and gesturing in pantomime. "I trust everything is fine with Frog Face?"

"Jillian, I'm so glad you called back," Mickey said. "I need you."

Jillian heard the rustle of movement and noted the forced calmness in her brother-in-law's voice. "You need me?"

"I know this is most likely a bad time, but I need to scratch your gray matter."

"You didn't answer my question, Mickey. Is Loni okay?" Jillian's eyes scanned the narwhale's giant tusk near the fireplace across from where she sat, pondering the museum's intent to have unicorn fiction meet a deadly reality.

"Loni is okay. And," Mickey coughed, then continued in a hushed voice, "the doctors say that she is stable."

"Stable?" Jillian's pitch heightened. "Mickey Peronne, if something has happened to my little sister, or the babies, I'll...." Jillian scowled at the tusk.

"Jillian, I am trying to be everything to everyone, okay?" Mickey's voice wavered. "I have beat myself up because on the trip to France, Loni gave me every sign, every indication that she was not well. Nevertheless, I brought her into harm's way. After doing so, I responded to her needs as a husband, not like a soldier or a doctor."

169

Jillian imagined a hole in the dike of Mickey's normal calm-and-in-control resolve. Somehow that was just as distressing as the potentially bad news of her sister. "Mickey, I—"

"I have failed at being her physician, her husband, and now you are going to tell me I have failed at being a brother-in-law as well. It's too much. I really can't deal with that right now, Jillian. I can't."

"Okay, Mickey, calm down. Put a finger in the dike, all right? I admit. I got crazy for a minute. I do that. You know I do that. Right now, my world is a little topsy-turvy too." She heaved a sigh. "Can we start again?"

She heard a breath escape between his clenched teeth. "Yeah, I'd like that."

"All right, you called me." Jillian licked her lips. "This is what I know. Loni has undergone something bad, but now she is okay. I know that she is okay because of you." Jillian took a deep breath. "What happened?"

"For now, Jillian, can we just say that Loni is having a memory issue?"

"Are the babies fine?"

"Yes, babies are fine." Mickey took a deep breath. "We need you to help Loni in a way no one else can."

"Whatever it is, I'll do it, Mickey."

"Where are you, Jillian?"

"I am in New York."

"Yes, I know that. It's a big state."

"No Mickey, I am in the city."

"Really?" said Mickey, reversing himself in the hallway back toward Loni's suite. "Where in the city are you, Jillian?" He shuffled quickly to Loni's suite doorway, framing himself within its arch.

"I am at the Metropolitan Museum of Art."

"Fifth Avenue?" Mickey stepped through Loni's doorway.

"No, not downtown," said Jillian. "I am at the Cloisters near Fort Tyrone."

"The Cloisters?" Mickey parroted loudly.

"The Cloisters?" Douglas echoed.

"Douglas," blurted Clarisse, "that is where the—"

"Shhh!" Mickey interrupted Clarisse. He then nodded emphatically and mouthed, *Sorry*. She scowled a response. Tapping Loni's arm as a pre-arranged stimulus, Douglas quickly put Loni into stasis. Confident that Loni remained linked to young Queen Anne of Brittany, Douglas turned toward Mickey.

"That wasn't Loni," said Jillian curtly. "Who else is there, Mickey?"

"Douglas Coletrane."

"No, I heard a woman." Jillian's voice dropped an octave. "Is Suzanne there?"

"No, Jillian. Suzanne had to go. I'm putting you on speaker, okay?"

"Uhhh…."

"Hi, Jillian," Douglas mimicked Mickey's strained calmness. "You're at the Cloisters. Right?"

"Yes," Jillian said, stretching the sound. "What is going on, guys? Why does it matter where I am? Who else is there, and why do I need to be on speaker?"

"No one else you know," said Mickey, easing over to the head of Loni's bed. He tussled with her gown's collar.

"Mom and Dad aren't there, are they?"

"No, only Douglas and Clarisse. You don't know Clarisse."

"Is she a friend of Loni?"

"No … well, yes … kind of." Douglas looked at Clarisse and shrugged. "It's hard to say exactly."

"Clarisse is an acquired acquaintance of Loni's," said Mickey, bouncing his gaze between Clarisse and Loni.

"Why is she there, guys?"

"She has joined us in our hopes to help Loni," Douglas said.

"What kind of help, Douglas? I thought Mickey said Loni was stable. I'm kinda freaking out right now."

"Jillian," Mickey said, swallowing hard, "from a medical standpoint, Loni *is* stable." Mickey stroked Loni's shoulder. "However, we needed Douglas's help to reach Loni's mind."

"Why? Besides a memory issue, Douglas, what's wrong with Loni's mind?" Jillian's pitch heightened then retracted immediately. "Can you just tell me straight? I can't keep blurting out … this museum guard is giving me the evil eye."

"Sure thing, Jillian," said Douglas. "Mickey rightfully concluded that the maternity and medical staff alone could not solve Loni's problem." He shrugged. "Apparently, Loni has fused memory experiences with a sixteenth-century French queen. I'm here trying to bring her back."

"What in God's name does that mean?"

"It means that Loni is here in body, a healthy pregnant body. However, she exists to us only through the historical figures with which her mind has combined."

"Figures? As in more than one? Plural?"

"Yes, Jillian." Douglas cleared his throat. "It began when Loni hit her head, developed amnesia, and then began talking in the voice of a four-teenth-century French king … via a certain Maid of Lorraine. And then Vlad Tepes."

"Oh my God, what is going on over there? Wait. Where is there?"

"We're in the French Vermandois."

"What does that mean in English?"

"We're in a maternity hospital in Saint-Quentin, France."

"Okay, that accounts for her body. But her mind?"

"Best we can figure, her mind is now fused with a sixteenth-century French queen who was in England as a child in the late fifteenth century."

"I don't even know what to say right now." Jillian's voice quavered as she could feel her heart rate quicken. "Assuming that you all haven't entirely lost *your* minds, what help can I possibly be here at the Cloisters?"

"Where in the Cloisters are you?" Clarisse interrupted.

"I'm guessing that would be Clarisse?"

"Yes. My apologies, Jillian—if I might call you Jillian. I am Clarisse Saint Vincent."

"Yeah, sure, call me whatever you want, Clarisse Saint Vincent, just tell me why on earth is it important that I am in the Cloisters?"

"Are you in the Unicorn Tapestry Room?"

"I am," Jillian gasped.

The stunned silence in the hospital room was broken by Jillian's voice coming through the phone. "How could you know?"

"None of this is coincidence," Mickey muttered to his awestruck companions. "We all ought to know that by now."

"What was that, Mickey?" Jillian asked. "Wait, never mind. We're making headway. Continue, Clarisse."

"The room contains the seven beautiful tapestries commissioned by Queen Anne of Brittany, yes?" Clarisse asked.

"It does."

"Well, for you to help Loni, there is no place in the world better than where you now stand."

"Well, sit in actuality. But yeah, what do you want me to do?"

"Jillian," Douglas chimed in, "I have a task for you." Douglas paused to steady the delivery of his remarks. "I need for you to talk to Queen Anne of Brittany."

"Say what?"

"Well, actually, listen first and then talk."

"You want me to *listen to* and then *talk with* Queen Anne of Brittany—*the* Queen Anne?" Jillian scoffed. "How *exactly* do you propose that I do that, Douglas?"

"Leave it to me." Douglas blew into his cupped hands. "It is why Mickey called me to the Vermandois in the first place. I have been using hypnosis to help Loni span the time bridge in her mind."

"That's who Loni's mind is linked with?! Queen Anne?"

"Fly on the wall, Jillian," Mickey cut in as Douglas prepared to bring Loni out of stasis. "No matter what you hear through this phone line, you must be silent until we call on you. Got it?"

"Of course, Mickey," said Jillian, steadying her breathing. "Look, I know Loni's your wife, but remember, she was my sister long before that."

"Understood, but you've got to keep your emotions in check." Mickey exhaled loudly. "We need you. Your sister needs you."

"Okay, okay. I only hope and pray that I am in the right state of mind to be of some use. You know anxiety plus these pregnancy hormones are … well … challenging, but I can calm myself down, Mickey. It's been known to happen—occasionally."

"Well then, it's time to prove it. Mouth shut and ears open, Jillian. It's a huge task you're facing."

"Probably, but no more than you all are facing."

32

Strangers and Stranger

G3 Operations Office

European Medical Command

Heidelberg, Germany

Current day

"Sir, I fully understand what you are saying." Master Sergeant Roman placed both hands on the customer counter. "It's clear to see that this release document has the signature of Major Oberstadtmeyer. However, since I cannot get Major O-stadt to verbally verify this request, I must decline it. That is, unless you know his whereabouts so that I may contact him?"

"I have not seen him since he signed this document," Colonel Worjedee answered impatiently.

"I see, sir. Well, therefore, as I said before, without verbal confirmation from the major I cannot grant you the right to access secured material. I trust you understand."

"Well, Master Sergeant Roman," Colonel Worjedee postured at the counter, "regarding Major Oberstadtmeyer, he commented to me that he was having an issue with his phone chip from the USA. He stated that he planned to buy a disposable phone for the time he intended to be here in Europe."

"I need to hear that from him, sir."

"Based on what I just told you, that is unlikely."

"Nevertheless, sir."

"Are you doubting my word?" Colonel Worjedee pounded his fist on the counter. "I am a colonel of the Liberian Armed Forces in possession of a properly signed paper."

"Sir, I have no way of making it clearer to you."

"Is it because I am Liberian? We may be a small African country, but I assure you, your American government has shown great interest in us as of late."

"I have a great appreciation for Liberia." The master sergeant kept his voice cool and collected. "Your country's capital is named Monroe, after an American president. However, even if James Monroe walked through that door and himself requested it, I could not grant you the right to access the document or documents."

"I see." Colonel Worjedee's jaw clenched as he drew in a breath through his teeth and held it for a moment. He exhaled slowly, etching a new resolve into his face. "Will you grant me a moment? I have a colleague that may be of assistance."

"It's your time, sir. I'm here all night." Master Sergeant Roman returned to his desk, watching Colonel Worjedee step out into the hall and reaching for his phone. He watched the colonel sit, sorting through some papers in his briefcase. Several minutes later, another person appeared. Together the pair returned to the G3 desk.

"Good evening, Master Sergeant." The British accent accompanied a Cheshire cat smile. "I'm Major Doctor Preston Michaels-Kuh-Keyes. I was the cah-cah-command surgeon and chief NATO medical advisor to your brigadier before his untimely demise in Romania."

"Evening, sir." The master sergeant rose and walked to the counter in no great hurry.

"I regret being late to this discussion." Major Michaels-Keyes's smile widened. "We would like to access the document that you have in your vault. I believe your DCS, Acting Cah-Cah-Commander Colonel Peronne, would support this request."

"Sir, you may be everything you say you are. I further appreciate your relationships with Dr. Peronne and the late General Framingham. But the issue here is one of authorized access. With one valid signed release document," the master sergeant held up a finger, "I need voice verification." He then held up the second finger. "With two valid signatures supporting release procedures, and the presence of the unlocking measures, there is some latitude for access. However, it's still a sticky wicket."

"A sticky wicket?" Michaels-Keyes frowned.

"The fact that the request originates from two international officers means that these procedures could fall under other potential limitations." Master Sergeant rapped his knuckles on the counter. "At this point, other than your spoken word, I have no acceptable objective verification. Thus, your right to access documents remains only an inaccurate perception."

"I guh-guh-guessed you would say as much. You leave me no choice." Michaels-Keyes reached down toward his hip. "I have a duh-duh-document supporting the release of the vaulted document signed by a second American officer, Cah-Captain Dewayne Sweeny. I spoke with him earlier and he was kah-kind enough to provide a signed duh-document … just in case."

Master Sergeant received the document. "It certainly seems as you say," he replied slowly, taking his time in reviewing the forms and keeping his finger over the MP alert switch which, if activated, would bring a security response within minutes. "I just need to first verify that these signatures belong to Major Oberstadtmeyer and Mr. Sweeny."

"Cah-Captain Sweeny."

"He's a deactivated reservist, Major Michaels-Keyes. However, as a signature, I will accept his rank as if activated."

"Excellent." Michaels-Keyes nodded. "Regarding the dispensing chemist, Cah-Captain Sweeny, even if you desired to ta-talk to him, he would be inaccessible. He said something about having to puh-push through a major drug deal." Major Michaels-Keyes laughed.

"Pardon?" The master sergeant froze.

"Sorry." Michaels-Keyes sniffed. "British humor often falls puh-poorly on the ears of you colonials. Never knew a Yank that truh-truly understood our humor."

"What's the joke?"

"Cah-Captain Sweeny is the chief of pharmacy at the hospital. Every action he does *is* a duh-drug deal…."

"The joke?"

"Right." Michaels-Keyes sucked his teeth. "Well, anyway, we have the wherewithal to open the Puh-Pelican. All we need is your assistance for access."

"Roger, sir. With two verified valid signatures and current possession of the keys, I will grant limited access."

"What do you mean by 'limited,' Master Sergeant?" Colonel Worjedee scowled.

"I will retrieve the Pelican and access the materials. However, I will provide you no more than a copy of the secured document or documents."

"Oh, really?" Colonel Worjedee puffed his lips and turned away.

"I'm sorry that it's not all that you desire, but it allows me to report that although copied, the document itself was not released. If this is unacceptable, I'm fine with leaving the Pelican in the vault."

"Nuh-no, Master Sergeant. You hah-have our vote."

"Mind you, gentlemen, if this is—in any way—a ruse, I will ensure that the correct people in our command will contact the correct people in your commands so that you will be held responsible under international statutes."

"No worries. Please make your verification of the signatures. I believe that you will fuh-find all is satisfactory."

"Be advised, that if these signatures do not match *exactly*, you will be immediately detained, compliments of the prison system personnel at the Mannheim Detention Facility. Is that clear, sirs?"

"Bluh-Bluh-Bloody clear."

"Then you'll excuse me as I verify these signatures." Master Sergeant Roman moved to a separate computer with a scanner. *Something is not right about these two. Major Michaels-Keyes was here earlier, roaming the halls prior to the Liberian colonel's arrival. Yet now, the Liberian had to call Major Michaels-Keyes when I initially declined his request.* The master sergeant eyed the hotline bat-phone. *If Major Michaels-Keyes was already in the building with a second signature, why didn't he and*

Colonel Worjedee make that correct request first? And how did the Liberian get the major's signature when no one can locate him? I sure would like to know what Colonel Christiansted noticed in her frequent passing through the hallways and hospital this evening. Is she still in the Radiology Department? I'll be glad when she returns … hopefully sooner rather than later. Master Sergeant Roman pressed his lips into a tight line and then turned to face the counter.

"Sir, the scanner confirms the validity of these signatures. If you give me a moment, I will go retrieve the Pelican." Master Sergeant returned quickly and placed the Pelican on a small table inside the counter near the scanner.

"I believe you'll need this." The Liberian colonel held out a key.

"Colonel Worjedee, there's a problem. It appears that your key only fits on the right keyhole. I assume you have another key?" Master Sergeant Roman looked expectantly at the stone-faced colonel.

Major Michaels-Keyes inched closer, chuckling, "I believe you will need this kuh-key as well." He reached his thumb inside his shirt collar. "This key is imprinted with the word *Left*."

Grimly, the master sergeant accepted the other key. "Gentlemen, I will need the combination lock's number sequence as well."

"I'd rather not guh-give that to you, Master Sergeant. Would you juh-juh-just allow me to open it myself?"

"No sir, I would not." Master Sergeant widened his stance and set his jaw. "If you find this unsatisfactory, we'll wait until Major O-stadt can come and open it himself."

"That won't be nuh-necessary." Michaels-Keyes shot a sideways glance to Colonel Worjedee. "The sequence is one, one, zero, nine, and nuh-nuh-nine."

"I confirm: one, one, zero, niner, niner?"

"Correct. Duh-Did I stutter?" Michaels-Keyes winced a grin.

"We have unlocking, sirs." Lifting the Pelican lid and turning it to shield the contents from view, the Master Sergeant drew in a deep breath. "What document do you desire?"

"There should be a brown manila folder with some papers."

"Yes, Colonel, there is." Master Sergeant Roman continued to shield the contents. "How many of these documents will you need copied?"

"There should only be three. Please copy all three."

"I don't understand."

"What is there to understand?" Colonel Worjedee looked at Major Michaels-Keyes and then back to the master sergeant. "Make one copy of three documents. How difficult can that be?"

"Sir, the first and third sheets are essentially blank. Only the middle page has typewritten information." Master Sergeant watched as Colonel Worjedee and Major Michaels-Keyes exchanged animated whispers. After a few moments both faced forward.

"You said, 'essentially blank,' Master Sergeant. Correct?"

"Yes, Colonel."

"How so?"

"The first and third pages have scripted page numbers on the bottom." Master Sergeant observed another brief exchange of coarse whispers followed by the pair facing again frontward.

"We'll only need a copy of the middle document. The others are just pruh-pruh-protective spacers."

"Okay, sir. I confirm. You desire one copy of the middle page. No more. No less."

"Correct." The two officers looked at each other and nodded.

"I must use a classified document copier. This will take a minute." He moved to make the copy, never turning his back to the Pelican. *This feels about as right as eating a gravy sandwich. However, these two have all the access capabilities, the supporting documents, the keys, and the code. They already know the Pelican's contents. Why does it feel amiss? Maybe it's their insistence and impetuousness—the anxious haste.* He approached the counter again. "Sirs, here's one copy of your requested document. I remind you, gentlemen, it needs to be carried in a secure manner." Master Sergeant watched Colonel Worjedee produce a locking cylinder from his briefcase.

"Thank you, Master Sergeant. I trust that you have a good rest of the evening." Colonel Worjedee nodded, and the two officers headed for the door then disappeared into the night.

"Gravy sandwich ... definitely a gravy sandwich," the master sergeant said to himself as he re-secured the Pelican. "I guess I'd better call it in. European Command Headquarters Strategic Operations Center in Stuttgart, coming up." He pictured the familiar face that would answer the bat-phone at the far end. The dialing sound hummed in his ear. *What if this attempt to foster good international relations was a total miscue?* He heard a click.

"EUCOM SOC, Airman Morell speaking."

"Morell, this is Master Sergeant Roman at Heidelberg. I need to first tender a report and then gather more information on no good deed ever going unpunished."

33

Under My Skin

X-ray room number one
Heidelberg Hospital
Germany
Current day

"Nothing? Nothing at all?" Bridgette leaned closer.

"No, ma'am." the MP sergeant leaned backward away from the imposing colonel.

"Nobody, not a single person, has mentioned anything about keys?" Bridgette furrowed her brow.

"No, ma'am." The MP sergeant scanned his clipboard. "What keys are you talking about?"

"It is my understanding that Major Oberstadtmeyer was to pick up keys from the victim, Dewayne Cameron Sweeny."

"What kind of keys, ma'am?"

"I don't know."

"Pharmacy keys were found on Dewayne Cameron Sweeny."

"Were car keys and house keys found on the victim as well?"

"Yes, ma'am."

"Who holds the keys to radiology?"

"I would think the radiology technician on duty and the head radiologist would, ma'am."

"Yes, that's what I'm thinking as well," said Bridgette. "Did you locate the duty technician in radiology?"

"No, ma'am. He's not been located yet."

"Has anyone talked to the head radiologist?"

"You might ask the chief of radiology, Colonel Christiansted," a new voice monotoned. "His name is Bernard Livingstone Tupelo." A doctor looked over the top of his glasses. "Chief of the Radiology Department at your service, Colonel." Tucking a clipboard under his arm, Tupelo held out a pasty, white hand.

"I didn't see you earlier, Dr. Tupelo." Bridgette forced a smile but kept her hands to herself.

"Colonel Christiansted," Dr. Tupelo clasped his unshaken hand, "how may radiology be of service to the European Medical Command's best?" Dr. Tupelo motioned, and the MP sergeant excused himself.

"You might consider helping with the murder investigation."

"Terrible thing to happen. Isn't it, Colonel?"

"Where were you when all this went down?"

"I've been in the radiograph reading room with the hospital commander, Colonel Birdsong, until a few moments ago, ma'am."

"Why would the chief radiologist be reading x-rays when there has been a murder in his department?" Bridgette raised her eyebrows.

"Because they need to be read." The doctor pushed his glasses up the bridge of his nose.

"So, Doctor, who holds the keys to the Radiology Department?"

"Keys?"

"Yes, keys, Doctor, who holds them in your absence?"

"Door keys? Computer keys? Monkeys? Really, Colonel, if you need my help, then you need to be more specific." The doctor picked at something stuck in his teeth and then sucked on his fingertip.

Bridgette felt her face go flush. "Doctor," she barked, "I have data indicating that some undefined keys are part of the crime scene associated with your department. I would greatly appreciate any information you might have on the matter. Are you following me, Major Tupelo?"

"Colonel Christiansted," Dr. Tupelo licked his pale lips while continuing in his toneless voice, "there are no specific keys, locks, combinations, or computer passwords that are specific to this department relative to the normal locks and chains provided by hospital security personnel."

"No monkeys either, Major?" Bridgette thrust up her chin.

"No, Colonel, none of those either." The doctor formulated a grimace that looked like a grotesque attempt at a smile.

"Well, this seems to have been a waste of my time and yours, hasn't it, Doctor?" Bridgette slapped a counter with her hand and turned to leave.

"Maybe not, ma'am." Dr. Tupelo tapped his lip and then pulled out the clipboard from under his arm. For a moment he flipped the clipboard papers, studying them.

Bridgette could barely contain her frustration. She spoke without turning around. "Is there a key that you have in mind?"

"A key person, if you will, Colonel."

"A person with a key?" She faced the major.

"I guess you could say that."

"I did say that. What do you say?"

"Major Preston Michaels was here this evening. Are you aware of that, Colonel?"

"I am. I heard the Military Police brief that to Colonel Birdsong. Is Major Michaels a key person in your department?"

"Not that I am aware. Have you heard that he was?"

"Dr. Tupelo, you are annoyingly answering my questions with other questions. We are getting nowhere fast."

"The interesting thing about NATO Major Preston Michaels is that he appears as a sign-in patient this evening."

"This is not news, Doctor," Bridgette sighed, pressing her index finger and thumb to the base of her eyebrows.

"May I continue, Colonel?"

"By all means and quickly," Bridgette gesticulated with one hand while the other tried to stop her twitching eye muscle.

"Although the major appears on the sign-in register, he did not appear in the computer patient encounters." Dr. Tupelo picked at some dead skin on his neck. "Want to know why?"

"I do indeed, Doctor. Please be advised that this time with you was not intended to be the longest part of my evening."

"Of course not," Dr. Tupelo coughed. "Interestingly, Major Michaels does not appear in any of our computers as Preston Michaels. I thought this odd, so I did a name search by his first name. This kind of search would be difficult with the name John, Harry, or Tom. However, considering the name Preston … only one name came up as a hit."

"I am guessing the name was not Preston Michaels."

"Correct, Colonel Christiansted."

"Is there a name forthcoming anytime this century, Doctor?" Bridgette nearly growled.

"There is." From his clipboard, the doctor plucked a sticky note, holding it so the writing could not be seen.

"May I have it?"

"You may, ma'am."

"Now?"

Dr. Tupelo flared his nostrils. "Preston Michaels is also in the system as Preston Michaels Keyes and Preston Michaels-Keyes, with the last two names hyphenated." He passed Bridgette the note. "I believe you have your *keys* now, Colonel Christiansted."

Bridgette snatched the note and turned it over. "That's genius, Doctor."

"Hardly," the doctor sniffed.

"Thank you, Dr. Tupelo."

"Will that be all, Colonel?"

"For me? I don't think so. But I trust the rest of your evening will be less eventful."

"Thank you, ma'am. Is there anything else the Department of Radiology can provide the colonel?"

"No, I don't think so ... wait." Bridgette flicked rhythmically at the note in her hand. "Actually, yes. What was the nature of Preston Michaels-Keyes's radiograph?"

"A clinical question?" Dr. Tupelo shook his head. "I truly am sorry, ma'am, but I don't believe I can answer that. It would be a violation of patient confidentiality."

"Not at all. Radiology is a crime scene undergoing a probable murder investigation."

"Indeed."

"Wouldn't you say that this warrants an exception to the confidentiality rule?"

"It's really a gray area, ma'am."

"Considering that the head of radiology's career is highly in danger of being the next victim, does an exception now exist?"

"It would, Colonel Christiansted." Dr. Tupelo stepped into a blackened doorway. "Please, this way." Bridgette stood just inside the dark room watching the clipboard-wielding radiologist glide through the darkness like some nocturnal animal predator on a hunt. With amazing agility, Dr. Tupelo slid onto a rolling chair. Then, with careful dodging of assorted tables and floor lamps, he spun his away in front of a rather large radiographic reading machine. Propping the clipboard on a holder, Dr. Tupelo's hands moved quickly, spinning the screen with an eerie screech. Digital radiographs flew from top to bottom and sometimes from side to side. "I'm pulling up the digital data now." Dr. Tupelo's spidery fingers weaved across the keyboard skillfully. "Here we go." Dr. Tupelo locked a digital image into the center of the screen.

"Is that a belly film?" said Bridgette, now completely in the radiology room peering over the shoulder of the radiologist.

"Very good, Colonel," Dr. Tupelo nodded. "I'm surprised a medical service officer would harbor the skill of radiograph reading." He winced a grin. "Do you need an official reading or just the knowledge of the involved body system?"

"Both, please."

"Nonspecific bowel gas pattern," Dr. Tupelo answered in his flat voice as he panned the film. "No acute pathology." The doctor spun his chair. "Apparently, it was just a case of loose bowels. Must be running rampant through the foreign officers. No humor intended."

"None received, Doctor."

"It may interest the colonel that this was the second gastrointestinal case filed today. Anything else, ma'am?"

"Nothing now. Thanks." Bridgette turned, hesitating again. "Actually, can you tell me the patient's name for today's other case of bowel issues?"

"Yes, Colonel Napoleon Moses Worjedee, a Liberian officer. Ring any bells?"

"With a name like that, I would think it to be quite memorable. However, I have no recollection. Could you pull his film up?"

"I can." Dr. Tupelo flew through the files then slowed to a stop. "Yes, same nonspecific gas pattern."

"Why does his film look so different from Michaels-Keyes's?"

"Colonel Worjedee's abdominal parameters are significantly different. Moses Worjedee is a tall, thin, long-waisted fellow. I find that many Liberians have this body habitus."

"If you would, Doctor, please write his name down for me so that I can reference it if need be." She passed him the sticky note and the doctor scrawled the Liberian's name across it.

"Will there be anything else, Colonel?" Dr. Tupelo asked as he pushed his glasses back up on his nose.

"No. Thank you, Doctor." Bridgette watched Dr. Tupelo spin around and within seconds he was flying though films and mumbling into a microphone. She backed away slowly.

Bridgette paused in the brighter light of the hallway near the Patton memorial case and added this note to her pocket alongside the one sent to Major O-stadt. "A Liberian officer?" *That tall thin foreign officer in the atypical uniform pattern. That might have been a Liberian uniform.* She spoke out loud while drawing in her palm. "The Liberian was leaving the hospital going this way," she traced. "He was going toward … my building. My building, where just minutes before a British soldier—with a stutter, if I recall correctly—had just saved me from face-plant. Two foreign officers. Coincidence?" Bridgette tapped her palm. "Maybe yes. Maybe no."

She headed off down the hallway. *G3 should be finished with chow. Let's see what information Master Sergeant has regarding today's visitors during my time out of the office. Hopefully, the missing people have surfaced, been interviewed, and more information has been gained.* Bridgette headed for the north stairwell. *I still need to know what a British and Liberian officer were doing in and around the hospital and the European Medical Command building earlier tonight.* Bridgette crossed the parking lot, heading for her building's main doors.

On second thought, perhaps the biggest question tonight is whether I'm going to make it up those steps without a second shot at a face-plant. Bridgette muttered aloud, "What kind of fool falls *up* a set of stairs?"

34

Pelican Again

G3 Operations Office
European Medical Command
Heidelberg, Germany
Current day

"I hope that something goes right tonight," Bridgette grumbled as she walked up to the G3 Operations counter.

"Good evening, ma'am." Master Sergeant Roman stood and sighed with relief. "I sure am glad you're back."

"Master Sergeant, I need to officially report a soldier's death as well as multiple personnel missing."

Master Sergeant changed his tone to match Bridgette's. "Yes, ma'am. What name are you reporting as deceased?"

"Dewayne Cameron Sweeny."

"DCS?" Master Sergeant's knee buckled, and he threw out a hand to the counter to steady himself.

Taken aback by the reaction, Bridgette leaned slightly over the counter, "Yes, the hospital pharmacist." Her voice softened, "Was he a friend of yours?"

"No, ma'am. Not really." Master Sergeant exhaled loudly, then grimaced. "And the soldiers missing?"

"Major Amos Oberstadtmeyer," said Bridgette as she righted herself in position and tonality. "Also the on-duty radiology technician whose name I still haven't heard."

"Major O-stadt hasn't been found yet? Lord Jesus." The master sergeant rubbed the back of his neck and squeezed his eyes shut.

"I don't think that was the name," Bridgette muttered as she rounded the counter. "Master Sergeant, I need to confirm that the courier case Major O-stadt placed in our vault is still there."

"Yes ma'am. I confirmed that twenty minutes ago."

"Routine check or were you concerned it wasn't there?"

"No, ma'am. I was involved in a personnel action."

Cocking her head, her eyes narrowed. "What kind of personnel action?"

"Transfer of classified information."

"How does that involve Major O-stadt's courier case?"

"The classified document I transferred came from Major O-stadt's Pelican." At the look on her face, the master sergeant dryly swallowed, and immediately turned his boots to the vault room.

Bridgette entered immediately behind him. "Master Sergeant, I know you go by the book, so I'm not going to jump to conclusions and fly off the handle. Let's take this one step at a time. Who requested the contents?"

"I had two requests, ma'am. A Liberian and British officer both presented supporting documents authorizing them to access the contents."

Bridgette clenched the notes in her pocket. "On whose authority?"

"Major O-stadt and Mr. Sweeny both provided authorization via their signatures."

"They gave consent?"

"Yes, ma'am. Here are the documents with their signatures. I validated their signatures using the files and a scanner."

"Let me guess—the validation checked out."

"Yes, ma'am. Greater than ninety-five percent accuracy."

She nodded mutely and passed the documents back. She lifted the case, her thumbs resting on the two locks. "You would have had to have keys to open this. Where did the keys come from?"

"They came from the Liberian and British officer."

Bridgette's jaw clenched. "Did it cross your mind to question why these two international officers would have the keys while the courier was unreachable?"

"Ma'am, I only look to see who has authorized possession of the keys and a valid access document."

"Transfer of keys and signatures can be coerced."

"Of course coercion must be considered. However, it can't be proven at the G3 counter."

"We must remain skeptical."

"Ma'am, I understand what you are saying, however I'd ask you to try not to Monday morning quarterback this issue," Master Sergeant tapped the Pelican. "Skepticism is a very slippery slope when it comes to items in this vault. I could begin being skeptical about a courier that is on his way to Africa yet finds the time to come to Heidelberg to see you. I can even question the selection of Major O-stadt as the best possible choice to be said courier. Is he really the selected courier or did he coerce possession of this Pelican from the originally selected courier? Ma'am, you yourself could have gone into the vault while the G3 and I were at chow. See what I mean?"

"I hear you," Bridgette sighed. "Continue."

"So, in my experience, it comes down to who has the proper documents at the time access is requested."

"So, Master Sergeant, you're telling me that you released the classified documents because access was approved."

"I didn't release anything except access to information." Master Sergeant bit his inner cheek for a moment. "Ma'am, I will tell you that these two international officers already knew what was inside the Pelican. Nevertheless, I only gave them a copy. The originals remain inside."

"Well, that's something at least." She gazed hard at her trusted soldier. "I believe that all access parameters were obtained through coercion by these two international officers."

"You have two counts of a valid argument, ma'am. Major O-stadt is missing and Dewayne Sweeny is dead."

"Sweeny's body was found strapped to a wheelchair. He had been given a solution of penicillin intravenously."

"Penicillin kills, ma'am? I thought—"

"Yes, Master Sergeant, especially in the presence of a severe allergy."

After a long pause Master Sergeant spoke again. "First, the Liberian colonel had Major O-stadt's signature. Then the British officer provided Sweeny's signature as a second verification. If I had known Sweeny was dead, I obviously wouldn't have accepted his signature."

"Sweeny was the one who sent Major O-stadt that note earlier. He signed it too."

"I didn't open the note, ma'am. I just delivered it."

Bridgette rolled her lips inward and then sighed. "But you did try calling Major O-stadt when his signature was presented, correct?"

"Yes, ma'am. Of course I did. Colonel Worjedee said that Major O-stadt told him he was having issues with his phone chip. It seemed a plausible explanation at the time. I know I have phone chip issues when I travel internationally. The Liberian also couldn't tell me where I could reach the major. So, without the major's voice verification, I denied the Liberian access to the Pelican unless he could provide a second signature."

"Have you traveled internationally as a courier?" Bridgette massaged her temples.

"No, ma'am."

"Well then you might want to think about how plausible that phone chip explanation really was."

"Satellite phone?" The master sergeant grimaced.

"I would think so." She twisted her lips and looked down at the case. "There are a lot of moving pieces here and even more unknown variables. Are the originals still here?"

"Yes, ma'am. They are locked inside."

"That's something in our favor. What are the documents?"

"There is one document set between two virtually blank spacer sheets."

"Virtually blank? Was it blank or not? If it had *any* writing on it, then it's not a spacer sheet."

"That bothered me too, ma'am. Even though there were scripted numbers on them, Major Michaels-Keyes called them spacer sheets. He was only interested in the middle document."

"But you didn't release the document to him."

"Correct, ma'am. I did not release the document to him."

"You said that after they left, there was something that troubled you."

"Yes, ma'am. Initially, I was troubled by the fact that they weren't interested in the spacer pages with the numbers scripted. After giving them the requested copy, they left, and I locked up the case. When I returned to the counter, I noticed they had left without these." Master Sergeant Roman held up two keys still on the beaded neck chains. "It's like they didn't care who went in after the originals once they got what they needed."

"That is odd." She took the keys in her palm. "But to our advantage. We can open the case and see if it helps us understand what's going on around here." Bridgette looked down at the case, clenching the keys in her fist. "Wait. No, we can't. We don't know the number sequence combination."

"Well, ma'am, that was another odd thing." The master sergeant shook his head and clicked his tongue. "When I gave Major Michaels-Keyes the choice of telling me the combination or waiting for Major O-stadt, he verbally told me the number sequence."

"Tell me you still remember it!"

"I do, ma'am." He glanced down at the keys and the case. "Are you sure we should be accessing it again?"

"Yes, Master Sergeant, I am certain. One person is dead and others are missing. Let the feathers fall where they may; it's Pelican time."

"Break a leg, ma'am."

35

Of Ravens and Lions

Maternity hospital
Saint-Quentin, Somme River Valley
Vermandois region, France
Current day

"Really? Is that all you see, Annie?" Douglas asked the hypnotized Loni in tandem to the hypnotized Queen Anne of Brittany—who was now calling herself Annie.

"Yes, green, green, and greener," Queen Anne of Brittany squeaked in an excited voice of a six-year-old child. "Here in the Tower of London, the pretty green grass covers all the bailey," she sighed happily.

"It's true, Douglas," Mickey whispered. "Today the bailey is heavily criss-crossed with trimmed walkways and pedestrian crossings leading from one tower to another. What isn't stone gray is overwhelmingly green."

Douglas leaned over and passed the battle book back to Mickey. Mickey propped the phone closer to Loni so Jillian could hear from her location at the Cloisters and resumed taking notes at the small table in the room.

Loni's head turned, following a sound none in the hospital room could hear. A troubled look spread across her delicate features.

"What's happening, Annie?" Douglas squeezed Loni's hand.

"I don't know, Douglas. There are men shouting from the far side of the castle wall. I can't see them, but they are shouting that they have found something."

"Annie, can I get you to go in the direction of the shouts, and tell me what you see?"

Loni shook her head sternly. "Mother said to stay here until she came back, Douglas."

"Where did your mother go?"

"She went to find Isabeau."

"Who is Isabeau?" Douglas looked at Mickey for a clue, but before Mickey could answer Annie did.

187

"She is my little sister." Annie beamed. "She was named after my Grandmother Isabeau of Scotland, the most beautiful daughter of the king. Everyone loves her. Everyone always loves her. The castle children took her to go see the ravens."

"Who all went?"

"Isabeau, Richard, and Bran. I don't know the names of the other children. Sean was another, I think. There were four or five more."

"Only children?"

"No, the raven master was going to show the children the raven babies."

"Any other adults?"

"I don't think so. All the other adults are working at their jobs."

"Where is Edward?"

"He was with Mother and me. But he left with Mother to see what made the men shout." Loni uttered Annie's groan and craned her neck as if trying to see something far off. "Mother told me to plant my feet here. I have done so." Loni furrowed her brow, her eyes tracking something across her field of vision.

"What do you see now?"

"I see the raven master, and he is being held tightly by two of the strong yeomen. They are being very rough with him."

"Is he hurt?"

"Yes, he is hurt. The yeomen are hurting him." Annie's voice went shrill.

"Why are they hurting him?"

"I see Edward now. He is crying. Why is he crying?" Annie whined. "Mother is coming back. She has Isabeau with her. She is pulling my sister by the hand."

"Is Isabeau all right?"

"Yes, she looks fine." Annie sighed with relief and then pursed her lips. "Isabeau is dirty. Beautiful but always dirty. Mother says she is not a very good ermine. Mother says a good ermine is a spotless ermine." Loni primped her hospital gown as if it were a fine frock.

"She's right," Mickey nodded. "I've read that an ermine, by its very nature, would give itself up to its hunters rather than soil its white coat. Given the choice between an escape to ultimate freedom across, say, a muddy stream, or keeping its fur clean, an ermine will choose the latter."

Loni gave a short, sweet nod in agreement. "See, Mickey knows."

Douglas gave a skeptical eye roll and continued his line of questioning. "Annie, have you discovered why Edward is crying?"

Loni tilted her head up and to the right, speaking toward the ceiling tiles to someone beyond their vision. "Mother, why is Edward crying?"

Loni went silent for a few moments while the team in the Vermandois edged closer to the hospital bed waiting to hear what befell the royals at the Tower of London.

"Come, child. Let us go back to our room." Margaret of Foix cinched her scarf. "There is mischief afoot, and there may be more deaths before the day ends."

Annie followed obediently at her mother's heels. "Where is Froggie?"

"Froggie is gone." Margaret's voice broke into sobs. "There is no more Richard of Shrewsbury, child. Froggie is gone, forever."

"Don't cry, Mother." Annie reached for her mother's hand to soothe her. "All will be fine. You'll see."

"I never liked the look of that raven master," her mother hissed. She stopped abruptly and looked down at Annie. "You are not to go to see the ravens anymore. I don't want you near the ravens, even if you are in a group of children. Understand?"

✠ ✠ ✠

Loni nodded in silent compliance toward the ceiling.

"Annie, what is happening?" Douglas whispered, interrupting her silence.

Loni blinked hard and looked straight ahead. "Edward is crying, Douglas. Mother says, she says … " Her voice hitched for a moment. "Froggie is dead—Prince Richard. I hear some people saying the raven master did it. Maybe that's why the yeomen took him." A look of pain crossed Loni's face. "I guess I won't ever see Froggie again."

"Annie, can you go to where the grown-ups are talking? I need you to tell me what they are saying."

Loni bit her lip. "Mother said I couldn't go see the ravens, but she didn't say I couldn't go elsewhere."

"Douglas," Clarisse whispered, "do you think you should be sending that child where her mother has already forbidden her to go?"

"She didn't specifically say not to go to other adults," Douglas whispered.

"Don't worry, Clarisse," Loni paused, looked slyly left and then right, then she whispered, "I'll go now." They watched Loni reach out as if opening a door.

"Don't put that child in danger."

"I won't, Clarisse," Douglas nodded. "I—"

"I can hear the men, Douglas."

"Good, Annie!" Douglas shrugged at Clarisse. "What are they saying?"

"These men are talking to the yeomen."

"What are they saying, Annie?"

"Shhh. I'm listening." Loni closed her eyes, her face full of concentration.

"What happened here?" a gruff voice asked.

The group in the hospital heard the man's voice from 1483 in their own ears as clear as day. A nod of acknowledgment passed between them—this was not the first time they had encountered such a phenomenon.

"It appears that a group of children went over to the raven's nest to see the birds," a second, gravelly voice answered. "Richard of Shrewsbury was among them."

Clarisse swiftly went to the hospital room's door, closed it silently, and returned to Douglas's side. Mickey gripped his pen, preparing to take notes. Douglas kept his eyes trained on Loni.

"Was the raven master with the children?"

"Yes, but I am not sure in what capacity," said the voice, coughing. "Some say he gathered the children there. Others say that he came when he heard shouts from the children."

"I thought he was supposed to be in town today to procure food for the castle."

"Who knows what governs the raven master? He comes and goes as he pleases. He seems to answer to no one except Duke Richard."

"Why is the raven master being detained?"

"The constable has asked the raven master to explain why he is not in town doing his duties. He must also explain why so much mischief occurred to the children whilst he was in a supervisory presence and why he was unable to prevent the outcome of Richard of Shrewsbury."

"Was Richard the only child slain?"

Loni's eyes grew wide with terror; she held her breath.

"No one said the child was slain."

"Well, what happened?"

"As far as we can tell, Richard and a group of children were visiting the ravens and Richard fell—"

"—or was pushed...."

"Yes, he fell or was pushed over the wall. The raven master was there either during or after the fall—"

"—or the push...."

"Either way," the voice said gruffly, "only he can verify what happened. If the children's story corroborates with his, then he will be vindicated. Otherwise, he will have to answer to the charge of murder—first to the constable and ultimately to Duke Richard."

"I have heard it said that Duke Richard could benefit from the death of the two princes."

Loni covered her lips with her hand.

"Indeed, I have heard it too. Are you saying that Duke Richard directed the raven master to kill Richard of Shrewsbury?"

"No, I would never make that accusation," the voice stammered.

"It's a weak accusation at best." The voice loudened, causing Loni to cringe slightly. "It doesn't make sense for him to bring the two princes into a publicly announced location just to have them murdered. Duke Richard has had ample opportunity and a million ways to kill the children before now. If anything, this was an accident."

"Well, it really doesn't matter what any of us believe. The facts are these: Richard of Shrewsbury is now one of three children found dead on these grounds; he died under the protective custody of Duke Richard; he died in the presence of the raven master who has a strange affiliation with Duke Richard. What matters here is what England chooses to believe. This could spell ruin for the reigning credibility of the House of York, especially if this information leaks to the House of Lancaster."

"Annie, who are these speakers?" Douglas whispered.

Loni drew in a gasp and turned her head sharply. "I must go, Douglas. Mother calls. She's noticed I am missing."

"Annie, where is your mother?"

Loni leaned her head as if peeking around a corner. "She is calling from the window to our room. There is someone with her."

"Who is with your mother?"

"I will tell you when I get there."

"Be careful, Annie."

Loni nodded and set her jaw—a determined child on a mission. The sound of rapid footfalls slapping against stone wavered throughout the hospital room. The sound shimmered like light on water.

Douglas observed the faces of Mickey and Clarisse, noting their increasing worry lines and anxious tells. "Don't worry, she'll be okay."

"She'd better be safe, Douglas." Clarisse crossed her arms over her chest and scowled.

"You act like she's your kid."

"Little girls in that environment aren't safe."

"Apparently little boys aren't either, Clarisse."

"Douglas," Loni panted for young Queen Anne of Brittany, "are you there?"

"Yes, Annie," Douglas exhaled. "Take a breath."

"I see Mother, Duke Richard, and Edward's mother—the queen of England." Annie's breathing slowed. "I don't see anyone else."

"What are they saying?"

"I can't hear," Annie whispered. "I'll get closer."

Douglas waited a moment. "Can you hear them yet?"

"Shhh. I'm listening." Loni tilted an ear as if she were pressing it against a door and waved for Douglas to be silent.

The voices started quietly but then grew as if the very speakers themselves were standing in the hospital room in the Vermandois.

✠ ✠ ✠

"I'm sorry, Margaret." Duke Richard folded his hands. "I regret that Richard of Shrewsbury won't marry your daughter Isabeau. However, regarding the Duchy of Brittany and the House of York, at present, this is the least of my concerns."

"Should we continue to pursue the marriage of Edward with Annie?" Margaret gave a sideways glance to the princes' mother, Elizabeth Woodville.

"It's difficult either way, ladies." Duke Richard looked from one mother to the other. "It may be seen by the Lancastrian sympathizers as a premise for war." Duke Richard locked his gaze on his sister-in-law. "Are you willing to risk losing another son, my queen?"

"I need a plan that guarantees the safety of Edward." Tears welled up in her eyes. "He's the only son I have left."

"Do you care if he is the ruler of England?" Duke Richard's non-dominant hand rested on the hilt of his sword.

"I have already suffered so much. First, the loss of a husband." The widowed queen choked her tears back. "Some say it was *not* due to natural causes. Maybe it was. Maybe it wasn't. Now this raven master has seen to it that my younger son has fallen prey to an early death." She gave a deep, shuddering sigh. "The only thing I can think of right now is that I don't want to lose my last son. If you tell me that his life is endangered because he is the heir to the throne, then England needs to have a king's mother with more sons than me."

"My job as the lord protector is to guard the heirs of the royal family. I will continue to do this as long as I draw breath." Duke Richard squared off with Elizabeth Woodville. "Majesty, it has not been determined that any involvement by the raven master is foul play. Nonetheless, I can tell you that there is foul play in the minds of those who would seek the throne. So long as Edward is heir to the throne, he will always be at risk. It is the risk of any ruler and his heirs."

"What are the options?"

"Edward would have to abdicate as king."

"How can a child abdicate a throne to which he has not yet ascended?"

"That could be difficult. Some actions may have to occur prior to his coronation date to prevent his ascension to the throne."

"What kind of actions would prevent his ascension?" The queen arched an eyebrow.

"Four that I can think of."

"Four?"

"Death, disappearance, discrediting, or dishonor."

"Eliminating the first one as a viable option, what if Edward disappears?"

"If Edward should disappear after the death of his brother, it will seem as if he left from fear. All of England would see him as a coward for all time."

"This ties into the last option of dishonor."

"Yes, however," the duke continued, "I cannot see any scenario where Edward would accept dishonor as a plausible option, even if his mother wills it—begging your pardon."

"Agreed. The child is entirely honorable. What of discrediting him?"

"We would have to find a way to make him ineligible for the throne."

"What would this entail, exactly?"

"We would have to question his birthright. We would have to question any legal claims he might have to the throne."

"This sounds the least painful … at least to him," the queen bit her lip.

"It is, but it isn't, my queen. To question his legitimacy as heir to the throne is a most odious process." Duke Richard's lip curled back in disgust. "You would be seen as, forgive me, a tramp and he a bastard. In the end he would be amidst a royal scandal which could leave both him and you destitute, impoverished, and discredited."

"Destitute?" Elizabeth Woodville raised a brow.

"Possibly."

"Impoverished?" She pursed her lips.

"Probably."

"Discredited?" Elizabeth Woodville sighed heavily.

"Absolutely."

"But we could still draw breath."

"Yes," Duke Richard said as he splayed his hands, "it is most likely that you both would."

"He would be alive, yes?"

"Yes, Edward would be alive, but think, Majesty." The duke shrugged. "Is it a life truly worth living?"

"Well, as long as there is life, there is hope."

"What do you wish to do, Majesty?" Duke Richard clasped his hands together.

"Let me talk to Edward first." Elizabeth Woodville placed a hand at her heart. "He has a right to know what is being planned."

"Are you sure you want to involve him in the planning?"

"If you were him, would you want to be considered?"

"I would, Majesty." The duke bowed.

"Then do nothing until I return from conversing with my son." Twitching her skirts, Queen Elizabeth Woodville turned to leave.

"A parting thought, Majesty."

"Speak, my brother-in-law." Elizabeth Woodville turned back, her jaw set.

"What good is to have saved your son's life at the price of losing an entire kingdom?"

Elizabeth Woodville gripped her skirt tightly with one hand; on the other hand she held one finger aloft. "Have you ever been a queen?"

"No, Majesty, that's impossible."

"Have you ever been a widow?" She raised a second finger, her eyes fierce.

"No, Majesty. For the same reason, I have not."

"Have you ever been a mother?" A third finger raised.

"No, Majesty."

"Ask me that question again when you have been," she said, tucking each finger back into a fist one by one as she drove home her argument, "a queen, a widow, and a mother who has lost so much of what is precious in life in the mere blink of an eye." She forced her trembling fist to relax. "My dear duke, for all the joy of being queen, I would happily give it away to keep the life of my husband and my sons."

"I understand."

"Understand this," Elizabeth Woodville said, interlocking her arm with Margaret's, "despite being destitute and impoverished, by keeping my son alive, I would then truly be the richest that there could be."

36

And Den She Went

Maternity hospital
Saint-Quentin, Somme River Valley
Vermandois region, France
Current day

"Annie, where are you now?"

Loni didn't respond immediately. She seemed frozen. Douglas glanced down to see the white tips of his fingers in the hand clenched by Clarisse. Only now did he notice the pain. "Clarisse?" Douglas mouthed, holding his gripped hand up.

"What?" Clarisse mouthed back, then, realizing her vice grip, she released his hand. "*Mauviette*," Clarisse muttered.

"What did you call me?"

"It does not have an exact English translation, Douglas." Clarisse's eyes searched inwardly for a moment. "Wimp."

"Oh, that's classy—"

"Douglas!" Loni whispered for the young Queen Anne of Brittany.

"Annie? I'm here." Throwing a look over his shoulder at Clarisse, Douglas shook out his hand and turned back to Loni. "Where are you, little one?"

"I am walking across the bailey to the Garden Tower. I am supposed to meet the raven master." Annie puffed as if walking quickly.

"What?" Clarisse gasped.

"Where, Annie?" Douglas scowled at Clarisse, putting up a hand to shush her.

"He wrote that he wants to meet in his den."

"His den?"

"Yes, the raven master calls his special room in the Garden Tower the raven's den. I told him some time ago once that I would like to see it. Now he has invited me."

"Why would you go now? You know what has happened—"

194

"He sent a message that he had been released from questioning and that he wanted to meet me right away."

"Annie, I thought your mother said not to—"

"Don't worry, I don't fear the raven master, Douglas," Annie answered with a sing-song voice. "He likes me."

"Annie, the men there at the tower feared that he did something wrong to young Richard. They felt so strongly about it that they sent soldiers to capture him and bring him in for questioning."

"Douglas, anyone who helps the little or the sick, like hurt ravens and baby birds, cannot be bad. I like that about him. Maybe that's why he finds it in his heart to like me?"

Pushing Douglas back, Clarisse lurched forward. "Annie, liking people is one thing. *Trusting* them is another. There are people who can be liked but not trusted with important things."

"Hi, Clarisse." Loni hummed for Annie, looking surreptitiously to her left and right. "Important things like what?"

"Like your life, child."

"Clarisse, you sound like my mother." Loni shooed with her hand.

"I'm sure your mother told you that there are people who seem quite nice on the outside, but then when you see what they are really like on the inside, you find yourself staring at evil. People like that would think nothing of hurting you."

"I think you're wrong about the raven master, Clarisse."

"Annie, please listen to me. Your mother knows this, as do I. Please go back to where it is safe."

"Clarisse, it's safe. I know it is."

"No child, you don't."

"The message said that the raven master wanted to show me something."

"Did he say what it was?"

"No."

"Had he told you earlier, before the accident, about something that he wanted to show you?"

"No, Clarisse."

"Trust me, child, when I tell you this: There can be nothing he has to offer that you need to see." Clarisse leaned in farther and took Loni's hands, imploring, "Please, go back home—now."

"Too late, Clarisse. I'm here."

37

Where Ravens Nest

Maternity hospital
Saint-Quentin, Somme River Valley
Vermandois region, France
Current day

"Annie, no, don't!" Clarisse's hands trembled.

"I am in the raven master's quarters. It's a dark room and very grimy. Only one sputtering candle. It smells too—like old food and...." Loni's focus drifted to something beyond what those in the hospital room could see. She leaned a little to the side and tilted her face.

"What is it?" Clarisse asked.

"I thought I heard shuffling from beyond the partially closed door across the room."

"Who is there with you?" Clarisse released Loni's hands and milked the warmth back into her own.

"No one is here, Clarisse. It is just me. I'm waiting."

"Go back to your mother!"

"I can't."

"Annie, you listen to me right now. You are being an impudent young lady. You get yourself up and leave that room right now. You—" Clarisse cocked her ear closer to Loni's face. "Are you singing, Annie?"

"I am the Duch-ess of Brit-ta-ny. My land sits between dol-men and sea ... "

"Annie. I know you are a duchess. However, you are still a child and as a child—"

"Shhh. He's coming." Loni sat up straight, as did Annie, fronting a regal face.

"Duchess Annie," a deep baritone boomed in the space around Loni. Clarisse clutched her fists to her chest as her face lost color.

"Fly on the wall, Jillian," Mickey muttered near the phone's microphone. "Things are getting dicey."

196

The deep voice continued, "Again, I must say that I am so glad you accepted my invitation. I wasn't sure I would see you. But here you are."

"You sent me a message, Raven Master. You said it was important. You said you needed me. So, here I am."

"You honor me, Duchess, more than you know."

"Well, I am here without permission. I will be in trouble when I get back. But your message said it was life or death."

"It is a matter of life *and* death, Duchess. I need to show you something— something only for your eyes. There is no one in the world that I could show this to except you."

"What is it that I need to see?"

"Come here. It is in my back room."

"Annie, don't go with him!" Clarisse barked.

"Can you not bring it here, into the front room?"

"Come, little Duchess, you don't think I would harm you? Do you?"

Loni lifted her chin. "If I did, I would not be here."

"Now that's the spirit, Duchess." They heard the raven master click his tongue. "So, you will come with me into the back room?"

"You didn't answer my question. Why can't you bring it into the front room?"

"Well … it's too large for one man to carry, Duchess. Certainly, you wouldn't expect an old man to injure himself trying to do a good deed. Duchess, come. Follow me to a place where all your answers can be received."

"Annie," Clarisse whispered through gritted teeth as she gripped down on Douglas's shoulder, "there is mischief afoot. For God's sake, run away."

"Fine, Raven Master." Loni shook an admonishing finger. "But mind yourself." The fear creeping into Loni's eyes threatened her façade of control.

"Always, Duchess."

"You go first, Raven Master."

Little Annie of Brittany stood up from the bench and walked across the short length of the front room. She cocked her head as she peered ahead. A scratching noise echoed from the darkness.

"What's that sound?"

"You'll see soon."

"I can't see." Annie craned around the raven master. He stepped to the side. Through the far doorway, the back room looked even darker and more uninviting than the front room. As she approached the doorway, Annie heard a new sound.

"What's that shuffling noise?" Annie stopped at the doorway. She began to turn around and leave but by now the raven master stood squarely behind her.

"You'll see, Duchess." The raven master placed his large, rough hands on her shoulders.

"Stop! Don't push!" Annie cried as she was forced toward the stifling darkness. "Stop it," she pleaded. "I said stop pushing!" Squeezing her eyes tightly and, drawing in a deep breath, Annie plunged through the doorway.

38

Not Just Another Brick

Maternity hospital
Saint-Quentin, Somme River Valley
Vermandois region, France
Current day

"Annie, tell me where you are right now, young lady!" Clarisse commanded, willing some sense into the young girl so far away in space and time. "Who pushed you? What is the strange sound you hear?"

"This room is the strangest room I have ever seen." Loni's voice seemed to drift and sway.

"Are you in the back room?" Clarisse's breath grew rapid and ragged. "Where are you exactly?" Clarisse noted Douglas's look of concern but ignored it. Her eyes and ears served only the young duchess.

"I thought so," Annie continued in a calm whisper, "but I don't know now."

"Thought what? Don't know what? Annie, are you okay? You don't sound right." Clarisse soulfully pleaded, "Please say you're okay."

"I was afraid of the back room because it was dark." Loni squinted her eyes and peered around the hospital room. "But now...."

"But now what? Did he do something to you? Tell me that you didn't drink anything the raven master gave you."

"No, Clarisse, but I am thirsty."

"Is the raven master there?"

"No. He went behind some kind of wall."

"What? A partition?"

"Clarisse, this room is so strange. It has a wall in the middle of the back of the room." Loni pointed ahead of herself. "It's a long wall, but it's open on each side with archways. It's mostly dark, but—"

"But what?"

"But there are tiny, strong streams of light pouring in from each of the two-door arches."

"Is the raven master behind that wall?"

"Yes. I can hear him shuffling back there."

"What is he doing?"

"I don't know, Clarisse. I can't see behind the wall."

"Of course, child." Clarisse gasped and put her hands on her cheeks in dismay. "I'm sorry. I'm a wreck. I wish I could help you. If only I were there with you too—"

"Can you hear those rustling sounds?" Annie interrupted. "They are the same ones I heard from the front room."

"We do hear them, but only faintly," said Douglas, tugging at the stubbles on his chin, hoping especially now that the unexplained mechanism within the psychic bridge would remain linked and locked so they in Loni's suite could still hear from Annie ears. "Where do the sounds come from, Annie?"

"The come from behind that wall." Loni eased forward, leaning over her gravid belly. "I'm going to take a peek." She reached her hands out in front of her as if groping in the darkness.

"No! Don't! Annie, please," Clarisse bawled. "I am pleading with you. On bended knees, I'm begging you to stop and leave." Clarisse shuddered an inhaled breath. "You don't know the raven master. No one knows the raven master. What has just happened at the bailey wall may have been an accident. I really don't care. Please don't place yourself in danger."

Loni's hands stopped in midair and went to her chest. "My life's in danger?"

"Yes!"

"How?" Fear flitted across Loni's face.

"The raven master could hurt you like he did the other children."

"*My* life is in danger?" Loni repeated.

"He may hurt you in ways you can't imagine, Annie, and if he does your life will never be the same."

Loni's hands dropped to her lap; her face utterly confused. "How do you know he has taken the lives of the other children, Clarisse? The soldiers released him."

"I don't know but—"

"Well then, how do you know he is planning to hurt me?"

"I don't know but—"

"Well then, silence! Please!" Loni covered her ears with her hands. "Clarisse, I have to know what the raven master wants to show me."

"Annie—"

"Quiet, he's here," Annie whispered.

"Go in the other archway, Duchess." The raven master's deep voice emanated from the nooks and crannies of the hospital room in the Vermandois, traveling all the way to Jillian's corner of New York. Douglas, Clarisse, and Mickey steeled themselves again for the sensory onslaught they knew was coming and for the disturbing scene they all expected. The smell of the musty tower crept in tendrils across the room and filled their lungs. The rustling grew louder around them, and it seemed that the hospital lights, succumbing to this powerful surge, dimmed themselves.

Annie blinked hard in the darkness toward the raven master as he motioned from the far left of the room. Annie took a few steps but stopped.

"Can't I go in this side?"

"No, Duchess," said the raven master, backlit into a shifting shape framed by the left arch in the wall. He emphatically pointed toward the right archway. "I need you to go in the far entrance."

"Why?" Annie twisted her hands together anxiously, Clarisse's warnings still echoing in her mind.

"You will understand when you enter on the other side."

Annie spoke with all the courage she could muster. "Are you planning to hurt me?"

"Why would you think such things of me?" soothed the raven master in warm sweet tones that contrasted severely to the burning bright light behind him. His body outline pulsed rhythmically.

"You didn't answer my question."

"Duchess, I need you to go through the far arch." The raven master's tone became cold steel, each word poking her into a forward gait. "It would be best if you walked, not talked."

"Fine, Raven Master. I will do it." A sudden fluttering preceded a screeching sound and Annie jumped reflexively. "What was that, Raven Master?"

"Duchess, tarry a moment longer." The honey voice returned. "I'll tend to it and prepare what you have been brought here to see." The raven master pointed again to the far archway. "Starting now, please count to twenty. Then walk there and come through the far archway."

"Start now?"

"Yes." The raven master disappeared.

"One ... " Annie counted, shuffling past the center of the wall where she saw a pinhole of light squeezing around the edges of a loose brick.

She heard Clarisse's beckoning voice in her mind again. "Annie, it's not too late to leave."

"Three ... four ... "

"There is so much danger that a child faces in this world."

"Seven ... eight ... " Annie wiggled the loose brick with her tiny fingers. Pieces of mortar and grit bounced and slid down the front of her dress on the way to the floor.

"You don't know what he's doing back there."

"Eleven ... twelve ... " The brick ground against its neighbors and slowly began to pivot.

"Annie, why go into unseen danger when whatever he wants to show you can be seen later, with an adult, in greater safety?"

"Nineteen ... twenty." The brick edge rotated out and a bright ray of light streamed in through the aperture. It illuminated swirls of dust in the air. Annie tentatively peered into the hole. Her scream echoed off every wall.

"Annie? Annie! Are you okay?!"

Clarisse's voice, which was yelling in her head, and the face that filled the hole on the other side of the wall caused Annie to throw her arms up over her head and crouch down in terror.

"Duchess Annie," said the raven master's voice from the hole in the wall. "No peeking!" He placed both hands over the gap in the rectangular hole so that only a few rays of light streamed through his fingers. "Slide the brick back and go through the arch at the right side of the room."

"Fine! Some surprises aren't fun," said Annie panting. She rotated the brick and pushed on it as it creaked and moaned back into place. She paused until her rapid breathing eased to shaken inhalations. "In through the far archway or out the front exit?" Annie mumbled softly. "No duchess would hide with God at her side." With her left hand sliding against the wall, Annie turned and proceeded toward the far-right archway.

"Though I walk through the valley of the shadow of death...." Annie walked slowly, feeling each brick pass under her fingers.

"Please, Annie, you don't have to do this," Clarisse's voice pleaded in Annie's mind.

"I shall fear no evil for thou art with me." Annie held her breath and rounded the leading edge of the archway. She was immediately blinded and threw her hands up to block the streaming, brilliant white light. From behind the shield of her arms as her eyes adjusted, she could see a row of windows positioned high in the wall to her right. To her left was the back of the wall with the loose brick. She squinted straight ahead, unable to make out what lay before her. There was something between her and the dark shape of a man.

"Raven Master, is that you? I can't see well." Annie braced her left hand on the wall, squinted her eyes, and groped into the whiteness with her right hand.

"Your eyes just need a few more moments to adjust, Duchess."

Annie turned her head slightly, her eyes still barely open. "I keep hearing that same rustling sound."

"Yes, it's the same."

"It's all around me."

"Yes, relax your hand, Duchess. You will see shortly."

"My eyes hurt." Annie rubbed her eyes with the heels of both hands.

"Apologies, Duchess, it takes different people varying amounts of time for their eyes to adjust." As the girl forced her eyes to open, the raven master nodded and splayed his hands widely. "Duchess Annie, this is my special room."

"I see blurry, Raven Master. Can you see?"

"Yes, of course, Duchess. I guess my eyes are used to the transition as I gave them a little extra time."

"My count of twenty extra time?"

"Yes, Duchess."

"I'm starting to see you." Either the sun outside the windows had gone behind a cloud or Annie's eyes had just finished adjusting. "I see you now, Raven Master." Tentatively Annie surveyed the rest of her surroundings. She felt a slight draft of gently blowing air and wondered if there was another entrance to the tower—or more importantly, another exit. There was a strange smell in the air, one with which she was not familiar.

"What is on the table there between us?"

"You'll see … soon."

Annie took a few steps away from the wall toward the table and its contents, but then immediately retreated. "Those are tools—hooks, probes, sharpened blades!" Annie tore her eyes away from the table's top and looked up into a strange smile. "What are these? Why are you showing them to me?" she whispered.

"Why, these are surgical instruments, Duchess."

"Annie, run now!" Clarisse's voice pleaded. "Please. Run and don't look back!"

Annie, finally heeding the warnings, turned her feet ever so slightly toward the archway through which she had entered. "Why do you have them?"

"That is why I brought you here. I want you to understand firsthand what I do."

"Stop the conversation, Annie. Now!" Clarisse begged, tugging at Annie's subconscious.

"Are you a healer?" Annie asked, buying time as she shifted her weight to the balls of her feet, hoping that her skirt would hide her movements from view.

"No, Duchess. Unfortunately, I have no such training. I only have the skills God has imparted upon me." The raven master pointed to a cross fastened on the wall.

Annie broke eye contact, glancing where he indicated. She saw other things in the room which she had not noticed before. "You are an animal doctor?"

"I am."

"And did you intend to hurt the children?" she narrowed her eyes at the strange man.

"No, Duchess. They hurt themselves. I told the captain of the yeoman that."

Annie relaxed her muscles some but stayed poised on the balls of her feet, prepared to flee. "How did it happen?"

"The children have always been amazed at how I am able to heal the hurt animals here on the castle grounds. They have seen the bandaged squirrel foot, splinted tail, or repaired raven wing. They wanted to know how I did it. So I showed them."

"You brought them here?" Annie's eyes flitted to the far archway and back to the raven master.

"Of course not. I took the children to see the ravens I have helped and to explain how I help them. I would never bring children here."

"I am a child. You brought me here."

"Yes, you are a child. But you are a duchess too. For you, the duchess part outweighs the child part."

"I don't understand." Annie rocked back on her heels, perplexed, her escape plan forgotten.

"The children strayed from my side. Children are naturally playful, mischievous, and unruly."

"I am a child, and I am none of those things. Mother wouldn't allow it."

"Exactly! You are a duchess. That is why I asked you to come here. And, I suspect, that is why you trusted me enough to come." The raven master gave a small smile. "I know that what I must show you will be carefully managed and considered in all that you say and do from now on. Unlike you, the castle children tend to get into places that can lead them to trouble. They find things they ought not find."

Annie let her hand slide off the wall, crossing her arms over her chest. "I see these surgical tools and know that you are an animal healer. But I don't know why it is important for me to be here."

"There is more to see and know, Duchess. I have brought you here to show you this." The raven master moved for the first time since she entered the room. He turned slowly around.

Annie's legs instinctively tensed again. "What are you doing?" Her voice gave a slight waver.

"I'm unlocking a strongbox on this small table behind me."

"I can't see."

"I know."

The raven master finally turned around and walked toward Annie, his right hand clenched in a fist. The duchess pressed herself against the brick wall but stared at him defiantly. He stopped more than an arm's reach away and then slowly extended his arm toward her, knuckles up.

"Look." He nodded at his fist.

"At what? A fist?" Annie stood motionless.

"Go on, Duchess, take it."

"Annie, please don't."

The duchess pushed Clarisse's voice to the side of her mind and searched the raven master's face. She reached out one tiny palm below his clenched fist, keeping the other on the brick wall.

Annie watched the big hand open, depositing something crisp and flaky on her hand. "What is this?"

"Have you never seen it before?" The raven master took a step back toward the wooden table, surveying Annie carefully.

"No, it just looks like dried leaves."

"What about these leaves?" The raven master pointed toward several containers of plants near the windows. The tall plants reached up toward the light.

"Those do look familiar." With her curiosity piqued, she let down her guard. "I cannot see well in this light, Raven Master. Do those plants have yellow flowers with purple veins?"

"Yes."

"And sticky hairs on the leaves?"

"Yes. They are the same as the leaves you hold. And they are responsible for that somewhat unpleasant smell in the air." The raven master twitched his nose and smiled. "Where have you seen this plant?"

"The one I saw belonged to the royal alchemist in Saint-Servan. I asked him why he kept it separate from the other garden plants."

"Did he ever tell you how it was used?"

"He did. He said it was something used to make beer. However, he warned that it must be used very carefully as it can cause death." As she spoke the words, Annie again felt anxiety creeping over her.

"Correct, Duchess. This plant is called henbane. It has been seen to kill the chickens that accidentally feed upon it. It has been used for four centuries in the making of beer." The raven master circled behind the wooden table once more.

Annie stayed rooted to the spot, holding the dried leaves gingerly. "Why would something that causes death be used to make beer?"

"It is all in the skill of the master brewer." He held out his hand to the duchess, beckoning the return of the leaves.

Annie glanced again at the strange metal instruments on the table between them. She took a carefully measured step away from the wall and placed the leaves on the corner of the table then backed away once again. "Why do you have it, Raven Master?"

"I go into town at my leisure. I spend some of that time in the local pubs where I buy beer and ale for the yeomen here. The brewers told me about how henbane was used in Chelsea's Pub to make the best beer in London." He reached across the table and picked up the delicate leaves. "I took some plants to cultivate them. After some study, I learned I could use it to heal hurt animals."

"You grow it here and keep it under lock and key?" Annie inclined her head in the direction of the strongbox.

"Yes, Duchess. It was a hard lesson."

Annie gave him a calculating look. "You killed your children."

"Many think I did." The raven master shook his head. "It was an accident."

"But your children died."

"Yes. The henbane killed them."

"It killed your wife too?"

"She died of the grief."

"Is the henbane the reason for what happened to the children at the wall?"

"Yes and no."

"Did the plant cause what happened to Richard of Shrewsbury?"

"Yes and no."

"Be forthcoming, sir! What happened to the children at the wall?" The duchess stepped forward and put her hands firmly on the table between them.

"Sometimes henbane will grow in the cracks of walls like these." He put his hand upon the rough-hewn stone of the tower. "Often it grows out of reach, but when it can be accessed, I take care to remove it and bring it here. I use it in small amounts to make animals go to sleep so I can reset bones or sew up cuts. I know now that on that terrible day when the children wandered from my side, they found an errant plant that I had missed."

"Did the children eat the henbane?"

"From what I can tell, the three children who died handled the henbane, breaking off the leaves and flowers. Then they touched their faces, near the nose, lips, and mouth. One was Richard."

"Did it kill them?" Annie glanced down at her own hands.

"No, it made them very dizzy and then they fell off the wall." The raven master moistened a cloth at a basin in the room and held it out to Annie across the table. "Here, Duchess, wipe your hands."

Annie accepted the cloth and wiped her hands vigorously, her eyes still on the raven master. "So they fell and died?"

The raven master grimaced. "The two castle children fell first and landed on the sharp rocks on the far side of the bailey wall. Richard fell on top of them, crushing them. After I was released, I was allowed to see the bodies. That's when I saw bits of henbane leaves on their hands ... then I understood what must have happened. I tried to see if I could save them, but I couldn't. If they were dead of just the poison, I might have saved them."

"You have a cure for the poisonous henbane?"

"I have access to frogs."

Annie glanced around but saw no frogs. "How would frogs help?"

"There are many who say that frogs can cure poisoning."

"How would you use the frog?"

"I would take the frog and strangle it over the poisoned bodies of the children. Then I would the tie the dying frog in a bandage for an hour."

"This cures the victim from poisoning?" Annie's eyes were wide with a mixture of wonder and fear.

"Yes, in fact, the children would be safe from poison for a year and a half."

"Really? But you couldn't save the children?"

"Well, there were two problems. One, when I was allowed to see the bodies, I had no frogs with me. Two, when Richard fell on top of the other children they died instantly. There was still hope for Richard—all I needed to do was reverse the poison of the henbane."

"So Richard did not die from the fall?"

"No, Duchess. He just never woke up from the poisoning."

"You could not get a frog?"

"No, Duchess, by the time I was released and discovered the henbane on the children too much time had passed."

The color drained from Annie's face. "So you brought me here to see this plant and tell me of your failure? You could have sent all this in a message!" She slammed the cloth on the table.

"No, Duchess, I didn't bring you here to just see my work area and my plants."

"Well then, why was I brought here? To see a useless frog?" Arms akimbo, Duchess Annie squared off with the man across the table from her.

"Well, yes, in a manner of speaking...."

"I don't understand you, sir! Why am I here?"

"Let me answer that, Mr. Crippen." A voice from behind Annie spoke.

Annie started and turned quickly. "Duke Richard?" The duchess curtsied. "Did the raven master call you too?"

"Hello, Annie."

"How long have you been standing there?"

"A bit."

"Is Mother with you?"

"No, not your mother. Richard's mother."

"The English queen?" Upon seeing the monarch step into the light, Annie again curtsied. "But, if you please, why? Why am I here?"

"We needed to see." Queen Elizabeth Woodville nodded.

"It was an accident, Majesty. The raven master has just explained it. It was the henbane. And although I was fearful at first, I believe he is telling the truth. If you please, let him tell you—"

"We know, Annie," Elizabeth Woodville interrupted. "The loss of a child's life is horrible even if it is an accident."

"Please don't hurt the raven master. He tried to help, honest—"

"Hurt him?" A new voice came from the archway. "Why would we hurt him?" Using his hand to block the light, a boy entered and stood blinking rapidly.

"Froggie!" Annie ran toward Prince Richard and hugged him tightly for a long moment. She kissed his cheeks and stared at him in awe. "You were dead! We all thought…." She hugged him again.

"I know. But I'm not." He smiled and extracted himself from Annie's hug. He embarrassedly rubbed at the places where his face was kissed. "And I guess I can never be called Froggie again."

"Why?" Duchess Annie cocked her head.

"It's true, Annie," another voice chimed in, "a frog kissed by a princess can never be a frog again." Edward entered and kneeled in front of the pair of children.

"I'm not a princess, Edward. I'm a duchess."

"No, Annie, you are my princess."

39

The Haves and the Have-Nots

L'horloge fleurie
Lake Geneva
Geneva, Switzerland

"Meeting that owl woman bothers me on so many levels," Monique Meriwether grumbled as she brushed back her sweeping, gray-streaked blonde bangs. "I truly don't know where to begin." Holding her sunglasses to the light, Monique looked for spots on the lenses.

"Okay, darling." Her husband, Monty, tapped on his watch crystal. "You have been lamenting since we left the Owl Church in Dijon. We came to Geneva to relax and enjoy the beauty of the place, Monique, not lament. However, since you are insistent to perseverate over the Owl, let's just start back at the beginning. Vent from there, then you'll feel better." He leaned back against the grassy hillside and propped up on one elbow, facing his lovely wife.

"Right." Monique tossed her hair and straightened her posture. "First, I don't like the fact that the woman was scrutinizing us outside the church while we were looking at the owl sculpture. That's stalking."

"Maybe. Maybe not." Monty plucked a sprig of grass from the hill.

"Have you changed your definition of environmental awareness, soldier boy?"

"No, Monique. Since we've been sitting on this hillside, I have noticed three helicopters fly over the big Rolex sign on the city skyline." Monty stuck the grass between his teeth. "There have been three ambulances and five police cars pass by the Floral Clock here."

"Come on, Monty, I'm talking about at the Owl Church." Monique leaned over and cleaned her lenses with Monty's shirt tail. "You have always prided yourself in keeping an eye on our surroundings. But at the church, it appears you failed."

"The Owl is a tiny, ambling gypsy woman with a walking stick. How dangerous could she be?"

"I never said outright dangerous. However, the stereotype is that gypsies are a shadowy people."

"So you believe in stereotypes now, do you? Since when?"

Monique rolled her eyes dramatically. "That's not what I meant. Even this non-threatening, strange woman could have been a danger."

"Did you categorize her as a threat when you first saw her?"

"That's exactly my point, Monty. I didn't—but not because I saw her and dismissed it. I never even gave her a second notice."

"Well, honey, if it makes you feel better, I didn't either."

"Actually no, that doesn't make me feel any better at all. It just means that *both* of us have lapsed badly in our environmental awareness. Have we gotten old or just carefree?"

"Yes."

"Yes, what?"

"I'm sorry, Monique. I honestly can't say that I noticed her at all, even as she came in and sat behind us inside the church. I was so involved in the reverent beauty all around me." He rested his hand upon Monique's leg. "The Owl Church does that to me. If that makes me old or complacent, then so be it. I can think of worse places to be negligent in security."

"That's the next thing, Monty. This gypsy woman with a walking stick clacks in on the stone floor of the church completely undetected by us. For God's sake, insects that land on a stone wall create an audible echo. How could it be that neither you nor I were able to hear her?"

"I do have a hearing deficit, Monique." Monty tapped his ear.

"Yes, yes, of course I know that. But still."

He looked down at his illuminating army watch. *How much time do I have left in the hearing world? I really need to tell Monique. Better for her to hear it from me than a doctor.*

"Monty?"

"Yes?"

"Is that your answer?"

"That depends. What was the question?" Monty forced a laugh and focused on her lips as she spoke.

"I asked how bad your hearing was. You never told me after the last exam."

"Do you remember that brass mantel clock over your mother's fireplace?"

"Sure, it was a very precious gift from a dear family friend."

"Well, I don't hear its chime very well—sometimes not at all."

"Sometimes I don't either, Monty."

"Well, there's more."

"More?"

"There's good news and bad news."

"What's the good news, Monty?"

"The doctor says it's discrimination over acuity."

Monique put her hands to her temples and gave an exasperated sigh. "What does that mean?"

"Well, that's the bad news. I don't really know."

"How can you not know?"

"Well, I know that it's harder for me to distinguish words that sound alike."

"So if I ask for seven of something, you could give me eleven?"

"Sure."

"That's not so bad."

"See? The bad news is not so bad." *Well, at least not this part of the bad news. No need to worry her yet I suppose.* He rolled another piece of grass between his fingers until his fingertips were stained green. *It can wait. Let's just keep Lake Geneva calm and unperturbed for now.* Monty's eyes scanned back to the skyline across the lake where the letters *R-O-L-E-X* sat as an advertisement high on the building to his right. The sign graced the building like a crown. He remembered something from his bucket list.

"You know, Monique, a Rolex would make a great Father's Day gift."

"I agree. Rolex makes ladies' watches too, right?"

"Yes, of course." Monty took Monique's hand and gently caressed her wrist. *It looks as dainty as the day I married her.*

"Monty, say yes."

"Ask your question first."

Monique pulled the grass blade from his teeth. "No, Monty, not until you say yes."

"Okay, yes." Monty nodded. "Absolutely yes."

"Would you get me a sleek little Patek Philippe for my special day?" Monique pursed her lips.

"Sure, I said yes. One great Swiss watch is as good as another."

"Monty," she chuckled, slapping his hand playfully, "the last watch to my taste made by Antoni Patek and Antoine Philippe sold for six-and-a-half million dollars."

"What was that?" Monty made a confused face and tapped his ears.

"Not funny, Monty." She tried unsuccessfully to restrain her smile.

"What do you think about his and hers Swiss Army Knives?" Monty chewed on a newfound grass blade. "Their price tags should be something in the Meriwether range."

"Patek Philippe watches don't have price tags." Monique winced and adjusted her sunglasses again.

"Really?"

"Honey, if you have to ask the price," said Monique, "then you probably can't afford it." Monique pouted as Monty chomped harder on his grass stem.

"Monty, did you hear me?"

"What? Yes. No. I don't know."

"Look, let's just get me a new pair of sunglasses." She removed the glasses and tried to rub her eyes without disturbing her makeup. "This pair has had it."

"Hmmm?"

"Monty...."

"I know. I know. I'm deaf in one ear and I can't hear out of the other. However, *your* hearing is like a rabbit."

"Monique the bunny, right?"

"You know, now that I think of it, you *really* have no excuse not to have heard the Owl as she entered the church."

"*Cherie*, hyper-acute hearing is a deficit also." Monique gestured rabbit ears. "Anyway, maybe the Owl was right. Maybe it was by God's hand we were to meet."

"It was bound to happen." Monty inspected the chewed end of his blade. "After all, we all know Elior Yahel and his uncompromising care and concern for the success of our girls."

"Knowing Elior's admiration for our family doesn't automatically mean that we were predestined to meet the Owl."

"I'm just saying that we tend to have common interests and move in similar circles." Monty pulled at grass bits on his tongue. "Maybe it was meant to be. Who knows?"

"Besides God? Apparently, Mickey does." Monique shaded her eyes with her hand.

"That's right, Monique." Monty's eyebrows furrowed. "The Owl made it very clear that she knew Colonel Dr. Michael Philip Peronne and that he was the DCS."

"How would she know that Mickey was the deputy command surgeon unless he told her? Why was it necessary for her to ensure that *we knew* that *she knew*? And further, how would Mickey even know her?"

"I don't know, but I'm glad she did, Monique."

"Fine." Monique reached over and picked at some green tidbits clinging to Monty's lip. "What about the face veil that she wore?"

"Creepy." Monty mimicked a shiver. "Do you think she was hiding something from us?" His teasing tone played up to his wife's dramatic sensibility.

"Even in the darkness of the church, before she quickly covered her face, I could see the shadows of her pronounced features." Monique swirled her hand in front of her face. "I hate to say it, but it's almost as if her face was disfigured like a ... "

" ... bird?"

"Yes, Monty, she was a bird-faced woman."

"That could warrant wearing a veil."

"But still. There are people with facial disfigurements who don't sneak around French churches wearing veils and eavesdropping on conversations."

"Your point?"

"If I had a bird face—thank God I don't—I don't think I would be a social butterfly. I would hole up in a tower so that I never had to face the public."

"Maybe she does."

"Don't be silly, Monty. What kind of person would make their locale of choice a dank, dark tower?"

"Yeah, true enough." Monty threw down his chewed grass blade, hoisted himself up to a seated position, and offered his hand to his wife.

Monique smiled and reached out, then paused. "Wait, Monty. One last Owl thing."

"Sure, if it means I'm in the home stretch of the Owl discussion."

"Why did she give you her walking stick?"

"I don't really know for sure."

"I'm sure it wasn't for the reason she gave."

"As an apology?"

"No, Monty. The last thing she had was any remorse in interacting with us."

"Well, here's a soldier-boy theory for you. Consider this: What if she initially came from Poland to France with the distinct purpose of passing the walking stick to someone? Maybe whoever she wanted to meet was unavailable or unwilling even. Maybe her coming to the Owl Church was her last hope to pass it."

"Are you suggesting that she was there to meet someone else when we appeared on the scene, Monty?"

"Granted, it is a conspiracy theory that begs more questions than it gives answers."

"Honestly, Monty, I think that what we saw is what we saw. The Owl butted into our private conversation with little more than a smattering of obligatory remorse. By all accounts, she was a rude lady and thought she could gift her way out of it."

"Maybe you're right, Monique. But my idea was a lot more interesting." He gave her a boyish smile.

"No second thoughts, then? About overnighting the package to Mickey from Dijon?"

"Maybe at first." Monty pursed his lips. "I have this deep, burning feeling that the Owl wanted to give me her stick—wanted me to personally safeguard it somehow."

"Lord knows I never made enough eye contact with her to feel her intent." Monique closed her eyes and shook her head haughtily.

"I did. But then she also made that cryptic closing commentary."

"Monty, you know, if she wanted her walking stick mailed to Mickey, she could have just done it herself. Couldn't she?"

"Maybe, in a perfect world." Monty plucked a nearby dandelion. "I think her perfect world had passed. I think she was suspicious of everything."

"When friends and confidants cannot be trusted, one may have to turn to the kindness of strangers."

"Something like that, Monique." Monty tapped the old blossom and sent its seeds bobbing along the breeze. "Anyway, I knew that whatever I chose to do with her walking stick was a better option than the ones Szkolna Gora had facing her there at the Owl Church."

"How do you know?"

"Remember the note under the windshield wiper blade of the car when we left the church?"

"You said it was an advertisement."

"I did, didn't I?"

"Yes, Monty, you did." Monique's nostrils flared.

"Suffice it to say that I when I saw what she wrote, I knew mailing was the best option."

"What did the note say?"

"It was a phrase I have heard Mickey say many times."

"That didn't answer my question, Monty."

"No, darling, it didn't. It's better this way."

"Monty, do you think at least we should call Mickey and tell him about this? You know, to expect a suspicious package?"

"No, not yet." Monty stood up and brushed off his pants. "Although intriguing, I don't think we need to trouble Mickey about it. If Mickey has kept our presence in Europe a secret from Loni, then it's probably best not to reach out to Mickey and Loni. Besides, they aren't home right now, and the military post office will hold it."

"What if they don't?"

"Well then, you'll get your wish."

"Which is?" Monique pouted.

"Spending more time with your family in France."

"Monty, what does that mean?"

"I had to put something for the return address."

Monique's eyes flashed dangerously. "Do you mean to tell me that you put my family home in Oger as the return address on that walking stick?"

"Sure, with my name and the Owl's particulars, of course. Better to keep it close, just in case, than have it sent all the way to—"

"Monty! I don't think I want my family mixed up with this Szkolna Gora woman."

"Monique, my love, it will be fine. The military post office will hold the package. There is no danger here except that we are in danger of falling behind in our task." Monty helped his seated wife to a standing position.

"If you say so," she sighed. After stretching their legs along the lakeside, Monty and Monique headed back to their vehicle.

"What's the next stop, Monty? Oh, look!" Monique pointed out the geyser in the middle of the lake as it shot fifty feet into the air.

"After new sunglasses, we'll see."

"Well, show me on the map so *I* can see." Monique spread the map on the passenger door's window. "Point to it. There are so many roads through these mountains, I don't want to lead us astray."

"Right here." Monty prodded the map, then his smile darkened.

"You okay, Monty?"

"Yeah, just a headache."

"Me too. My eyes ache." Monique tossed the sunglasses in the back seat and forced a smile.

Monty folded the map and handed it back to Monique. "You okay with the route toward Annecy?"

"*Mais oui*, we'll see."

40

Bridge Too Far

Pont des Amours
Annecy, France
Current day

"Is this really such a good idea, Monty?" Monique shook her head, peering out over the water. "How can we justify a gift of art to Jillian, of all people? If she can't find what she likes in her art world, she just makes it herself."

"Hey, don't back down now. We've come too far. We both thought this was a good idea in Oger. What changed, my love?" Monty reached up to his wife's chin and turned her gaze toward his face. "I know she loves winged horses and unicorns. Lord knows that she's made them in every imaginable size. However, I know—no, I *believe*—we will find one that has never been seen. Or one that is unique in some way. Just like our Jillian."

"That's going to be difficult, *mon loup*."

"It's for our Jillian Angel. The challenge just makes the gift that much more precious."

"Maybe we should consider commissioning an art piece." Monique rubbed her forehead. "It might be more efficient."

Monty looked over the bridge's railing and into the calm water below. "Did the grande madame ever indicate where in Florence the Oger garden animal statues were sculpted?"

"No, Grande Madame never said. However, I do know a lot of museums there in Florence." Monique tapped her lips. "Also, now that I think of it, Marquis Du Bois once mentioned that he has ties to Florentine artists. Even if they don't have unicorns or a Pegasus on hand, they can certainly lead us to local Tuscan artists. Perhaps one can provide us with a finished or unfinished product."

"I think I would prefer unfinished so that Jillian can choose to finish it in the manner that best suits her."

"*Oui, mon loup*, so long as the marble used is Carrara marble."

"But of course, Carrara." Monty leaned on the railing, attempting Italian swagger. "Everything else is just plain marble."

"Definitely. Our daughter so loves the Carrara marble." Monique chuckled indulgently. "However, Monty," she hid her smile, trying to be serious, "you may well change your mind when it comes time to pay the bill for a sculpture made with the world's finest marble. A sting to the pocketbook, you know."

"Hmmm, just plain marble can be nice too."

"Truly, before we go too far, have you given a serious thought to the cost, Monty?"

"I have … and I haven't. It's going to be like buying your Patek Philippe watch. You go into it knowing it will be expensive. It doesn't matter." Monty rubbed his forehead. "I was more focused on the issues revolving around shipping items of such magnitude."

"Two full-sized marble statues—a unicorn and a winged horse—will be quite heavy, Monty."

"True, then there is the added weight of the packing and crating materials to protect the treasures."

"I think the cost in cash dollars of the sculptures will probably be matched by the shipping costs."

"Well, Monique, we could always ship the Florentine Carrara versions to Loni and save ourselves in overseas shipping."

"That doesn't make sense," Monique snapped. "The idea was to get a gift for Jillian, not Loni." Monique flinched and blocked one side of her face with her hand. "Monty, is someone taking pictures over there?"

"No, not that I can see."

"From the corner of my eye I thought I saw a camera flash from that group of tourists. It hurt my head. It's so strange…."

"What wouldn't be strange is if Jillian decides to keep the two life-sized unicorns she already made."

"She won't, Monty." Monique flinched again but Monty didn't notice. "She said those would go to Loni as her babies' gifts."

"I don't know, Monique." Monty scratched his chin. "Jillian already calls them by name."

"Calling them 'blue-horned unicorn' and 'brown-horned unicorn' isn't calling them by name, Monty. It just describes the color of the horn."

"Fine." Monty put his hands up in surrender. "Then she'll have enough space in her house for the two we buy."

Monique nodded her head gingerly then looked out over the water, blocking its glare with her hand. "Monty?"

"Hmmm?"

"I know that I asked this before, but why blue and brown horns? I don't get it. Do you?"

"Who knows what significance lurks in the mind of our creative maverick of a daughter?"

"You should know." Monique faced him and placed her hands on her hips. "She's more like you than me."

"I'm not sure whether to take that as a compliment or not."

"See? That's exactly what Jillian would say. Jillian is more like you than me." Monique shook her head dolefully. "If I wasn't sure that Loni was our daughter, I would swear Jillian was—like you, Monty—an only child."

"How does my being an only child help me better understand the thoughts of our non-only-child daughter?"

"Good. I'm glad we agree, Monty. I rest my valise."

"I think, my love, that is the wrong kind of *case*."

"I know, it is more humorous that way, no?"

"What was the question, again?"

Monique huffed, "I see your avoidance tactic. But the real question was why blue or brown when it came to Jillian's unicorn horns."

"And the answer is that I know because Jillian and I share similar thinking?"

"Yes. So, Monty, why should a unicorn have either blue or brown horn … in Jillian's mind?"

"I don't know. That is, if she told me, I can't remember. Maybe I have just chosen not to remember."

"Monty, why would *you* choose to have a blue or brown horn on a unicorn?"

"I don't know. Maybe … to symbolize … the distinctive nature of heaven and earth."

"Really, Monty?"

"I confess. It was a stretch." Monty rubbed his temples. "I need a stretch; let's move off this bridge."

"Will a walk help you to remember?"

"Maybe … sure … why not? What do you have in mind?"

Monique gave a small pout of a smile from her days as an actress. "It is said that sometimes you can't see the forest for the trees. I'd like to test that theory."

"How do you propose to do that?"

"I am told that the Gardens of Europe over the far bridge there have the great sequoia and the ginkgo as part of their collection."

"I love those trees." Monty looked toward the other bridge and aligned the trees in a moving bracket formed by his hands.

"I do too. After we resolve the forest-tree mystery, I know a shaded bench on the lake that would be a nice place to sit and look at the reflections of the mountains in the—" Monique reached clumsily for Monty's arm. "Monty…." She steadied herself for a minute and then took a deep breath.

"What? You don't like the trees?" Monty's smile vaporized when he caught sight of her face. "Monique, are you okay?"

"I don't know, Monty." Monique cupped her forehead. "I suddenly felt kind of strange. That flashing…."

"What do you mean strange? Either you are okay, or you are not—which is it?"

"I don't know. It's like I had a huge swig from Grande Madame's eighty-year-old whiskey. Something's not right. I feel … I feel … not right."

"Look, my love, you must be okay. Okay?" Monty gently took Monique's face in his hands. "We can't do a two-person trip to Florence without two people, right? Furthermore, we both cannot be sick at the same time. Who would do the driving?"

"What do you mean?" Monique's eyes struggled to focus.

"Monique, I just need you to be okay. Okay?"

"Well, I need the same from you."

"Monique, you're looking pale and gray. Honey, I'm going to ease you down on the bridge, okay?"

"Hurry, Monty. I think … I'm going … to…."

41

Greek to Me

G3 Operations Office
European Medical Command
Heidelberg, Germany
Current day

"Why call it a Pelican? It's more like a trunk." Bridgette tugged on her neoprene gloves as she placed the three documents in order from left to right. "You said that all they wanted was a facedown copy of the center document?"

"Yes, ma'am." Master Sergeant Roman tapped below the middle document. "I asked and confirmed a second time. That is what Major Michaels-Keyes wanted."

"Did you mention to them that there was writing, albeit small, on all three documents?"

"Yes, ma'am. He said he didn't need the 'spacer pages,' as he called them. He only wanted one side of one page." Master Sergeant watched as Bridgette carefully took each page in turn and held it up to the light.

"Look here. Except for the faded semblance of watermarks, I see nothing more than the handwritten numbers on the page bottoms and the old-style typewriter data on the middle page."

"What's the meaning of this short list?" The master sergeant leaned on the desk over the center page. "And why is it titled 'Asclepius'?"

"I guess the meaning of the list depends on whether it's a prioritized or unprioritized list—that is, for the German who typed it."

"If it's prioritized, ma'am, then a top-to-bottom read doesn't provide much more intel—'*Afrika, Frankreich, Amerika, Italia.*' What would make Africa more a priority over France, America, and Italy?"

"Relative to the title of Asclepius, I don't know." Bridgette pointed at the header on the page. "Here's another head-scratcher. Why is '66:02 (17) 16' the scripted number written on the bottom of this middle page?"

"It doesn't look like any page number I've ever seen, ma'am."

"Hmmm. It looks like a catalog identification number."

"What era is this document, Colonel?"

"This is before electric typewriters—look at the ink. That would mean probably the 1920s."

"Yes, but manual typewriters coexisted with electric typewriters in homes even after electric typewriters appeared in offices."

"That's true, Master Sergeant." Brigette stood up and crossed her arms, leaning against the desk. "In the military, we used manual typewriters through all the conflicts in Vietnam."

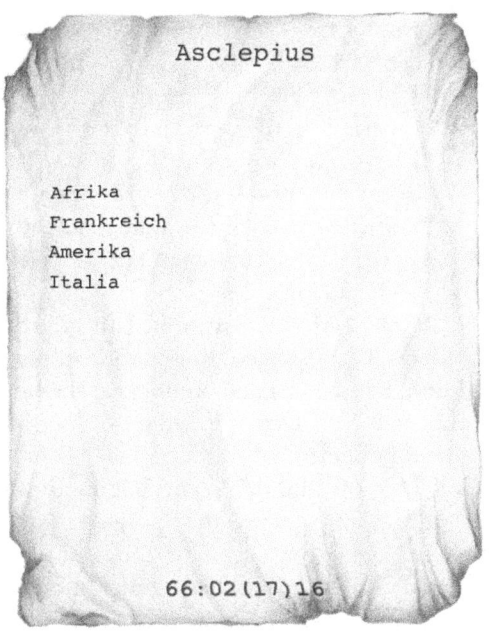

"This is German, though." The master sergeant furrowed his brow. "Are we thinking this is German military?" Master Sergeant stiffened suddenly; his eyes widened. "Ma'am, are you thinking what I'm thinking?"

Bridgette pinched the bridge of her nose and closed her eyes. "I don't know, Master Sergeant, what are you thinking?"

"I wonder if this is one of the documents that Dr. Peronne brought back from the Leaning Tower affair?"

"Back on that are you?" Bridgette gave an indulgent half-smile to the excited master sergeant. "Well, *if* that were true, that would mean this could be a sixty-five-year-old document from an underground bio-medical Nazi laboratory."

"Would this list here be pertinent to that event?"

"I don't know. Those Leaning Tower affair documents revolved around Nazi projects designed to locate a certain population of river people. Also, it involved researching capabilities of achieving immortality through cloning and that sort of thing. I don't see how this list would apply."

"Maybe there are other papers from the lab besides those from Colonel Peronne. I thought there was another American on the ground in Poland at the time."

"Yes, a Lieutenant Colonel Ronald Talbot turned in papers also." Bridgette's eyes moved up and to the left as she tried to recall the details of the aftermath of the Leaning Tower affair. "In fact, Colonel Talbot provided security and chain-of-custody escort until that mission was passed to Mike Winnabe. He confirmed the inventory and ensured its arrival at the Federal Bullion Depository."

"Is Mike Winnabe at Fort Knox now? Maybe he could—"

"No, last I heard Mike was assigned to AFRICOM—somewhere in northern Africa."

"Liberia?" The master sergeant's eyebrows rose.

"Liberia is in the western part of Africa."

"It's still Africa, ma'am. There may be a connection."

"Seems like straws you're grasping for, Master Sergeant."

"Begging the colonel's indulgence, it didn't seem like Major O-stadt and Sweeny were connected, but here we are." He held his hands over the Pelican and the documents.

"Noted, Master Sergeant. I think we should focus on what we have here and now. Clearly, these first and third pages are much more than just spacers. I think that the scripted numbers at the bottom of each of these three pages are connected." Bridgette tapped on the left-hand page. "The number centered on the bottom margin of the first page is 66:02 (17) 08 but on the final page it says '66:02 (17) 06' and that seems out of order to me."

"The left page was the top spacer page, and the right page was the bottom spacer page, right, ma'am? So the only part that changes from page to page is the last part of the numbers, going in order: eight, sixteen, six?"

"Yes, but the significance of this number sequence escapes me. Do these numbers mean anything to you?" Bridgette furrowed her brow.

"No, ma'am. Not a thing. Could there have been other pages in between that were intentionally left out?"

"Possibly." Bridgette tapped below the pages. "Maybe the numbers are grid coordinates or other location identifiers. These names on the center page are countries, written in the German language. The heading is Latin, I'm guessing. But … Africa, France, America, and Italy?"

"There is only so much that these countries share in common, ma'am."

"Yes, but of what interest could this obscure data be to a Liberian and a Brit? What would they need with this data? How would they use it? Most importantly, how *could* they use it against us?"

"It is hard to assess the damage done, ma'am, when we aren't sure what any of this data means … or for that matter, if it is even damaging."

"True, Master Sergeant. We need to study more of the facts as we know them." Bridgette pointed to the whiteboard and pulled off her gloves. "Master Sergeant, write down anything we come up with no matter how disjointed or bizarre."

The whiteboard marker's cap gave a squeak and a pop. The master sergeant poised before the board. "Ready, ma'am."

"These documents are German and of an era that used old-style typewriters. They are of sufficient significance that they were kept under lock and key at Fort Knox." Bridgette massaged her scalp as she rattled off facts and the master sergeant scrawled them on the board in shorthand. "They were released to a courier who was headed to Stuttgart and AFRICOM—wait a minute." Bridgette flexed the fingers of one hand open and closed as she thought. "Who ordered the release of these documents?"

"I don't know, ma'am."

"I don't either, but it would have to be at least a flag officer."

"What need would a general or admiral have for these documents, ma'am?"

"Probably none." Bridgette closed her hand into a fist. "However, the individual needing the information from these documents would need a flag officer's signature."

"There are only a handful of flag officers … but which one and why?"

"This goes back to the significance of the documents, Master Sergeant. One, we find out what this document means. Two, then we can guess who would want or need to have that data. Three, we find the flag officer in that person's chain of command who would garner release of such protected documents under lock and key…." Bridgette sucked a deep breath. "Oh my."

"What do you have, ma'am?" The master sergeant turned from the board to face Bridgette.

"Couriers *never* have both keys. One key is sent to the destination, and the courier is only released when there is confirmation that the first key has arrived."

"This means that either the Liberian or the British officers were previously at the destination point since they had the other key in hand here."

Bridgette scooped up the keys from the desk. "Do you remember which NATO officer had which key?"

"Yes, ma'am." Master Sergeant ran his thumbnail up and down the crest of his nose. "The Liberian had the right key and Major Michaels-Keyes had the left." The master sergeant grimaced. "Why is that important?"

"It's probably me just being a type A personality, but it might have significance later." Bridgette shrugged. "Write it down since we still don't know if the keys were given or taken."

The master sergeant spoke as he wrote, "Only Major O-stadt or the AFRICOM officer at destination could tell us that. How does Sweeny fit into all this?"

"Pull up Sweeny's file, Master Sergeant. Let's see what else is there besides his signature."

The master sergeant capped the marker, dropped into a chair, and pulled himself up to a computer. "Looks like Sweeny had a gambling problem. I see three local-level reprimands involving gambling, betting, and financial mismanagement. Did Colonel Birdsong mention any of this to the Military Police at the crime scene?"

"Negative. What if Major O-stadt was set up on a hit? Would Sweeny set up a hit on a courier carrying protected documents as payoff for a gambling debt?"

"How could he? And if the debt was settled, why is Sweeny dead?"

"True, Master Sergeant. And why would international officers be involved?"

"What if they weren't really international officers, ma'am?"

"Then there would be two dead officers yet to be found." Bridgette shivered. "Let's not go down that road yet." She rubbed her face briskly and shook her head to clear it.

"Okay, ma'am. Besides the verification signatures and that note, how were Major O-stadt and DCS connected?"

"Well, apparently, according to the MP's intel, Sweeny's wife is an old fiancé of Major O-stadt."

"Well, that's a definite connection and possible motive on both sides. I recall Major O-stadt asking me if anything came with the note when I delivered it. What would Sweeny have sent with it?"

"Oh, right." Bridgette took the note from her pocket and passed it to the master sergeant. "Something about keys. Here, tape it to the whiteboard." Bridgette stood and stretched then paced the room. *Maybe I have become more like Lord Doc than I realize,* she thought to herself. She approached the board and read the note again. *Meet @ Hospital Patton's Room. Left Keyes For You.* Bridgette stiffened. "Wait, it doesn't say that Sweeny left Major O-stadt keys." Bridgette pointed. "Maybe it means that he left Major Keyes for Major O-stadt. Was this a lover's triangle? If Major Keyes knew Major O-stadt was traveling to Heidelberg, he might just have been killing two birds with one stone."

"Quite literally, ma'am. But...."

"Now it seems that I'm grasping at straws?"

"Perhaps, ma'am."

"Okay, let's hold on the note and get back to the matter about the Pelican keys. Who is the key holder at destination?"

"Unknown. Whoever it is would be missing their key since both keys are here now, ma'am."

"That means the end point should have, or will be, calling the start point asking where the courier is located so as to abort the mission." The keys spiraled back and forth on the beaded chains as Bridgette dangled them in front of her face. She gasped, "Unless they don't yet realize that the key is missing...."

"Or they are looking around their locale now, thinking the key is just misplaced." Suddenly the master sergeant reached out and stopped the pirouetting keys with one hand. "Wait a minute, ma'am."

"What?" She released the chains.

He flipped each key over in his hand. "If I were going to steal a key, and I'm not saying I ever would or did or—"

"Out with it, Master Sergeant."

"If I was going to steal a key—say a Pelican key—and I didn't want the person to know that I stole the key, I would replace it immediately with a similar key. Ma'am, the end point would never call the start point because the key, in their mind, isn't missing."

"Okay, Master Sergeant," she said as she flipped the keys in his hand, "but these keys have inscriptions."

"Yes, ma'am. But on one side only ... a security feature."

Bridgette's green eyes flashed recognition. "So, if a courier wasn't missing a key, and the key that he has—if it is seen *not* to have an inscription on the one side viewed—"

"—would just be assumed to have the inscription written on the other side."

Bridgette leaned back in her chair and put her hands on her temples. "With no sense of threat, there is no urgency to flip over the key to confirm the presence of an inscription. Oooh, that is so simple but brilliant."

"Indeed, ma'am." He put the keys back on the desk.

"Back to the whiteboard, Master Sergeant." Bridgette cracked her knuckles. "Based on what we know about the Leaning Tower affair, can we assume that these are Hitler-era documents?"

"Back on that, are we?" Master Sergeant gave Bridgette a boyish smile.

She rolled her eyes. "Yes. Just go with it for a moment."

"Yes, ma'am." He cleared his throat. "Based on that assumption, during the era of World War II, all of the countries listed on the middle page there—except America, obviously—were under Hitler's control."

Bridgette nodded. "But how do these countries fit under the heading of Asclepius?"

"I don't know, ma'am. That word's Greek to me." He hit the end of the marker against his open palm while he thought.

Bridgette cradled her head in her hands and muttered, "Asclepius … Asclepius … Asclepius…."

The master sergeant returned to the desk and looked at the middle page's heading again. "Come to think of it. I have seen this word before—though I still don't know what it means."

Bridgette's head snapped up. "Where?"

"When I was stationed at the Medical Research Institute for Chemical Defense, there was a newly arrived doctor there and I was tasked to help set up her office. If I recall correctly, she had a yearbook on her shelf that had that name on it."

"Who would that be?"

"Dr. Suzanne Coletrane."

"See if there's a file on her here."

"No, ma'am. She never served a tour here."

"She was part of the Leaning Tower affair which occurred here in Europe."

"Yes, ma'am. She was brought in as an asset from Maryland to support the mission. We have no file on her here."

"Can you remember where she said she went to medical school?"

"No, ma'am." He uncapped and recapped the marker in his hands repeatedly. "All I remember was that she had a plaque on her wall that read, 'Don't Mess with Texas' and that she was a West Point graduate."

"My husband was a West Point graduate, and since both are colonels, they should be relatively in the same year group. West Pointers tend to know each other."

"Can we call your husband?"

"Can't right now."

"I remember her saying that she was part of the first class of female graduates."

"Well, that puts her at 1980." Bridgette tapped her cheek. "My husband would have been a rising 'cow' that year."

"Excuse me, ma'am?" Master Sergeant stopped clicking the marker cap.

"Juniors at West Point are called 'cows.' She would have graduated two years ahead of him." Bridgette groaned and rubbed her temples. "Another dead end."

"Maybe not, ma'am. We had three research doctors at the ICD. One was Dr. Suzanne Coletrane. Another was Dr. Russell Lange. The last was Dr. Mickey Peronne."

Bridgette snapped her fingers. "Now there's a lead I can follow! Master Sergeant, ring the old man and transfer it to my office."

"It's kind of late to be ringing the boss, ma'am."

"Do it! Bad news never gets better with time."

42

Boss and the Bloody Brief

G3 Operations Office

European Medical Command

Heidelberg, Germany

Current day

"Go with what you feel, Bridgette. I trust the judgment of my chief of staff. Really, I do." Mickey's voice came through Bridgette's desk phone.

"Thanks, Mickey. Appreciate that." Bridgette tapped her pencil on her desktop. "However, I really need your take on this."

"Roger, go ahead. But be quick, okay?"

"In a nutshell, we have a probable murder investigation, a missing courier, and a potential for impropriety involving international officers."

"Sounds like you have your hands full, Bridgette."

"I do, Mickey. But, with Luis and Master Sergeant Roman, I know we can handle this. We have the best G3 Section I've ever worked with."

"Bridgette, I know you didn't call me while I am on emergency leave to tell me you have confidence in our G3 Operations Section."

"How's Loni? Has she gotten any better?"

"I know you too well to know this isn't about Loni. And this call is keeping me from her." His voice softened. "I think this is about Lord Doc."

"No, it isn't really … but, Mickey, he's called in a Broken Arrow. The cancer is overrunning him even as we speak." Bridgette's voice wavered. "I know you probably already know all of this, but … " Her voice trailed off.

"As his physician, I know *most* of this, Bridgette. However, I didn't think this was coming so soon." Mickey coughed and then changed his tone. "Colonel Christiansted, your duty obligations are finished there in Heidelberg."

"Mickey, that's really not what I—"

"Seriously, Bridgette, consider yourself relieved of mission."

225

"But, Mickey, I—"

"Go ahead, Bridgette." Mickey dialed the commander tone down. "It's okay. Turn the reins over to Luis. Your work in Heidelberg is done. *You* need to be with your husband. Have Master Sergeant fax me the emergency leave papers; I'll sign them from here. Being the acting command sergeant major as well as the top sergeant in the G3 Operations shop, he'll have all my contact information at his fingertips."

"Thank you, Mickey. I got it. Before I pop smoke, can I at least close a couple of loops before I turn this over to Luis and Master Sergeant Roman? It's a big mess over here."

"Sure. Make it quick. Both of us need to be taking care of family matters."

"The missing courier is Major Oberstadtmeyer. Major O-stadt might have been set up on a hit. Do you know anything about his mission?"

"I do and, from what I know, what you're telling me is *not good*. Bridgette, he's returning some of the Nazi documents that I transferred to Mike Winnabe when the Leaning Tower affair ended. Since then, both Mike and Russell have been knee-deep in sensitive aspects of historical Nazi research."

"You said 'return.' Are you saying that Mike had the papers initially?"

"Yes. I handed the Nazi papers to Mike. He also got some papers from Chemical Corps Lieutenant Colonel Ron Talbot. All these papers were funneled to Fort Knox for safekeeping."

"So then Major O-stadt was headed to see Mike as the end point and final destination?"

"Right."

"Where's Mike now?"

"That's not easy to answer. He was supposed to be in Morocco by way of western Africa. My information is a few weeks old, but I am guessing Mike is still in Liberia. Hmmm, I want to say Barclayville, but I know other towns were discussed as options."

"How can I find out if he is in Liberia or Morocco?"

"General Bloomfield's staff at the European Command Headquarters in Stuttgart would have that information. The staff elements involved with AFRICOM are the ones who have the mission rose pinned on. I would contact them first. From what I hear, Mike is looking after the medical support for some shepherds and goat herders there. Believe it or not, Moroccan goats live in trees."

"You're kidding, right?"

"Not a bit, Bridgette! They climb right up on the branches," Mickey chuckled.

"I'm not talking about the tree-climbing goats, Mickey," Bridgette snapped. "I'm talking about Mike and his possession of a Pelican safe key. You said to be quick, so stay on point."

"Okay. It's just that you don't hear every day that some goats live in treetops."

"Mickey, *please*," Bridgette groaned. "Clarify this for me. Mike, as the destination point for Major O-stadt, would have one of the two keys to the case, right?"

"Of course. Why?"

"Because I have *both* keys to O-stadt's classified briefcase here now." Bridgette shook her head. "When was the last time you heard from Mike?"

"If you have his key, I guess I need to ask you that question, Bridgette. Unless … " Mickey's voice drifted as the realization set in. "Oh God, I hope Mike's not dead."

"He's not," Bridgette answered confidently. "I just feel it." She listened as Mickey took a deep breath.

"I agree, Bridgette. Even when we were kids, he never died."

"You feel it too, then?"

"Yeah, I do. Only the good die young." Mickey forced a laugh. "Just tell Luis to confirm it, okay?"

"I hope we're right. I'd hate to have to tell Zell…."

"You won't have to. I know Mike."

"Mickey, if Mike is dead, for all intents and purposes, Zell is dead too. I can't lose Prentice, Mike, and my sister all at one time. It's too much. It's too—"

"Focus, Bridgette. Let's worry about what we know and what intelligence we can derive. Did the hit take the courier documents?"

"Yes and no."

"We don't have time for games, Bridgette. Which is it?"

"I wasn't being cavalier. Honestly. The documents are physically here but a copy was made and given out. So yes and no."

"Who received the copied document?"

"An alleged Liberian and an alleged British officer, Mickey."

"You are saying 'alleged' because … ?"

"It is possible that they were imposters. One of them, a Major Preston Michaels-Keyes, reportedly said you would vouch for him."

"Really? Tall, thin guy with a hemangioma on his left eyebrow?"

"I don't know. I didn't see him or his hemangy … whatever."

"You weren't there when the documents were and were not given?"

"No, Mickey. Master Sergeant worked on the issue. I was investigating elsewhere. Bottom line up front: Master Sergeant wouldn't release the documents to the foreign officers. However, since they were friendly allies and they had proper authorization, he made a one-sided copy of one document."

"Ask Master Sergeant about the hemangioma. I'll wait."

"Roger." Bridgette placed her hand over the mouthpiece as she hit the intercom. "He didn't know what a hemangioma was. In fact, Mickey, I am not sure I do either."

"Come on, guys, you are in a medical command."

"Yes, Mickey, but not all of us are physicians."

"Roger." Mickey growled. "It is like a tuft of vein that is curled up under a thin layer of skin."

"Sounds really disgusting. Couldn't he have a thing like that cut off?"

"Not now, Bridgette. Get back to Master Sergeant."

"Sorry. Be right back.

While he waited, Mickey stared out the hospital's hallway window. *I remember it so clearly. The dirty army camouflaged faces of little Mike Winnabe, little Zell Ward, and littlest Bridgette Ward. Little Bridgette always whined because she wanted to play army with her big sister Zell and friends.*

Mickey watched the world outside the hospital. Life continued as normal. Time moved on despite his own personal strife, endlessly unfolding within the hospital room behind him. He sighed and felt the full weight of the adrenaline roller coaster of the last several days.

Thank God for Mike's big sister Kayla, though. She was always the true hero. She'd scoop up the whimpering dejected little Bridgette so that the rest of us could attack a hill or secure a beachhead.

"Mickey?"

"Yeah, go ahead."

"No tuft of veins or anything like that anywhere on his face. In fact, his face was quite nondescript. Except for a very British accent and a noticeable stutter, there was nothing of any distinction he could recall." Bridgette stiffened. "Wait a minute, Mickey, maybe I did see him … earlier tonight on my way out of the building. I ran into—and I mean literally ran into—a man with a British accent who stuttered. It was only a moment in passing and I didn't stop to think … or to ask. Thank God I didn't see a pulsating noodle hanging from his face because that really would have terrified me."

"Stutterer? Did you say 'stutterer'?"

"Yes, why?"

"The Major Michaels-Keyes that I know and that man you encountered aren't the same person."

"How can you be so sure, Mickey?"

"The Preston Michaels-Keyes I know has no stutter, stammer, impediment, or any speech pathology of any kind. In fact, I could probably say he is the most articulate speaker I have ever met."

"Well then, Mickey, I will get with AFRICOM and find out Mike's situation. Luis will get with the MPs and figure out if there are *two* missing international officers. I'm already feeling sorry for your articulately speaking British friend. If the recent holds true to form, then it's likely he's—"

"Bridgette, worry about what we know."

"Roger, Mickey. I will have Master Sergeant fax you my emergency leave form."

"Can you also have him secure fax me a copy of all three documents from the Pelican?"

"Roger, will do. Anything else?"

"No, Bridgette, not unless you have something." Mickey could hear her hesitation through the line. "Out with it, Bridgette."

"It probably isn't important now, but a strange thing did come up. You'll probably ask about it when you receive the facsimile copy of the documents."

"What is it, Bridgette?"

"You served a tour with Army Medical Research, right? With Russell Lange and Suzanne Coletrane?"

"Yes, I served with the Institute of Chemical Defense. Master Sergeant Roman could have confirmed that since he served with us. Let's get to the point. I have a time-sensitive matter here." Mickey glanced back through the hospital doorway of Loni's room. *Douglas is standing and easing back from the bed the way he does when he closes out a hypnosis session. I guess he's close to shutting down for now the psychic bridge between Loni and Queen Anne.*

"*Asclepius* was a word that Master Sergeant saw on a book in Suzanne's office when he served at the institute with you all."

"Okay. I'm not sure I remember that. Asclepius is the Greek god of medicine. You probably know him from his symbol of a snake wrapped around a pole. So?"

"Well, the word *Asclepius* is also on these documents, but it doesn't make any sense in context." She paused and sucked in a breath. "Master Sergeant Roman said he saw a similar word on Suzanne's medical school yearbook. He thought it was the title. He didn't mention anything about a pole-dancing snake though."

"Suzanne graduated from the Medical College of Georgia. Asclepius is one of the gods listed in the original Greek Hippocratic oath that binds all allopathic physicians. It would make sense if the MCG yearbook had his name as part of a title." Mickey's eyes darted up and to the left. "I wonder if Master Sergeant saw the word Aesculapian? It's a variation of the same word with slightly different spelling, but they mean the same thing."

"I don't know. I can ask. Should I also ask him if he recalls a dancing snake and pole?"

"No don't worry about it. Just send me the facsimiles. Cipher it on your end according to protocol. I have deciphering capability at this end. Bridgette, don't tarry. I'm waiting."

"Roger, out."

Mickey punched the buttons on his phone to retrieve the call he put on hold when Bridgette's number flashed on the screen several minutes ago.

"Jillian? You still there?" Mickey moved quietly back to the table in the hospital room.

"Buzz, buzz," Jillian whispered.

"Perfect, little fly. Standby."

Bridgette pushed on the intercom with her pencil's eraser. "Warm up the copier, Master Sergeant. There are some classified copies we need to make and fax to the boss. We've got no time to waste, no money to spend, and he needed these copies yesterday."

43

Up Close and Uncomfortable

G3 Operations Office

European Medical Command

Heidelberg, Germany

Current day

"**D**o you mean catty-corner, ma'am?" With gloved hands, Master Sergeant Roman passed the first of the three documents from the open briefcase to Bridgette who stood by the copier. He held the paper by its opposite corners ensuring safe handling and good copying.

"No. My husband and I spent an entire night discussing this very thing."

"I take it he didn't call it 'catercorner' like you just did, ma'am."

"No again. He called it 'kitty-corner.'"

"I've heard that too. Aren't they all the same thing? Aren't they all talking about the corner opposite from the corner referenced?"

"True enough." Bridgette adjusted her reading glasses. "But only one is correct."

"That would be catercorner. Wouldn't it, ma'am?"

"Correct." Bridgette nodded affirmatively. "One might think this topic might be picked up from higher education, but it wasn't. I learned this from Mickey's father, Franklin, while sitting in their backyard with our neighborhood friends." Bridgette paused with her finger over the copy button. "Let's see, there was Mike Winnabe and his older sister Kayla; my older sister, Zelda Anne; and P. J. Peronne."

"As in pajama?"

"No." She punched the button and the machine whirred. "We called Mickey's little sister P. J. because it was too hard to say Patrice Jewel. On top of that, she would get mad and start crying if you called her by her full name."

"Why so?" The master sergeant chuckled.

"Apparently, Elfie Peronne called all her children by their full names when they were in trouble. Besides that, P. J. couldn't decide which name she hated more, Patrice or Jewel."

"Ma'am, you knew Dr. Peronne when you were both kids?"

"Yes and no. The Peronne family had a fenced-in backyard where we all played until our mothers called us home. Mickey, Mike, and Zell were much the same age, so they played together. P. J. and I were closer in age. We played together and usually not with the older kids." Bridgette sighed. "However, since I had to be everywhere my big sister had to be, I spent a lot of time at the Peronne house." Bridgette passed the first document back to Master Sergeant.

"You see, in Parkersburg, West Virginia, the town has a historic district made up of essentially three streets. Mickey Peronne and his family lived in a beautiful mansion on Ann Street. Mike Winnabe was Mickey's best friend. He and his big sister Kayla lived in a 1917-style block house on Juliana Street. I lived in a Victorian-styled home on Market Street."

"It sounds nice, Colonel."

"It was like growing up in the movie *Gone with the Wind*, except there was no Scarlett O'Hara and Rhett Butler."

"Sounds like a sweet deal for kids growing up, ma'am." Master Sergeant carefully returned the first document to the case. He then handed the second document catercorner to Bridgette. She inspected it carefully.

"I hung out at the Peronne house in the shadow of my big sister until Zell and Mike became boyfriend and girlfriend. After that, they neither wanted—nor needed—little sister Bridgette around anymore. That was one of the rudest awakenings of my early adolescence. I felt like my older sister didn't love me anymore." Bridgette meticulously positioned the second page on the copier.

"I guess since Mike Winnabe's sister was older, she didn't go through that."

"Actually, by this time Mike's sister, Kayla, had disappeared under really bizarre circumstances." She closed the copier's hood and punched the buttons.

"She was never found?" The master sergeant's eyes widened.

"No, she never was. It was awful." Bridgette kept her eyes riveted downward. The light emanating from the copier's hood edge tracked a line across Bridgette's suddenly careworn face. "Mike's dad disappeared soon afterward in the famous bridge collapse. Then Mike's mom went insane and committed suicide. Eleven-year-old Mike changed after that."

"I can imagine."

Bridgette covered her hard sniff with an abrupt opening of the copier's hood. "You know, it's strange, but I almost can't remember Kayla except that she always gave me two lemon drops when I was fussy or miffed. One to 'dry the cry' and the second to 'pin the grin,' as she said." Bridgette passed the original back to the master sergeant. "She had this other playful game for toddlers. It was a teaching tool that made them laugh every time."

"What was that?"

Bridgette leaned against the copier; her eyes went up and to the left. "She would point to places on the face and say, 'Head thinker, eye blinker, nose stopper, soup sipper, chin dropper, gully whopper!' She'd stretch the sound of the last two words and then tickle the kid's chin and neck sending them into a fit of giggling." Bridgette gave a small smile. "It was great."

"It sounds nice."

"I wish I could have gotten to know Kayla more, but I'm guessing Mike feels that way every day of his life."

"I have a similar situation in my youth as well but in reverse." He positioned the second document carefully in the Pelican. "In my case, I can honestly say that my older brother didn't love me anymore. I wish he would have disappeared."

"I'm sure that's not true." Bridgette waved a dismissive hand.

Master Sergeant raised the third and final document out of the case. "I think the clencher was the pitchfork that he threw while trying to impale me against the barn wall. I must admit it was a nice throw; caught mostly clothing."

"Mostly clothing? Ouch!"

"Don't stress yourself, ma'am. I have had worse flesh wounds working here." Master Sergeant gave a wry grin as he handed the last document to Bridgette. "I never kept up with my brother after that. In fact, I can't say that I kept up with any of the folks from my neighborhood. Maybe it was because our family was the only military family in the area." Master Sergeant shrugged.

"We Julia-Ann kids—that's what we called ourselves—had a tight community and maybe that's why we've stayed connected. Or maybe it's fate." Bridgette straightened the last document on the copier's glass. "Later on, Mickey, Mike, and I went into the army—it wasn't the right path for Zell or P. J. And then, what were the chances that we three were assigned overseas positions simultaneously?"

"A hundred percent it seems, ma'am."

"Not the chances, no. But the result, yes." Bridgette nodded as the copier purred. "Get this. Now, my sister Zell—our family seismologist and earthquake expert—has accepted work in France. One could say that almost our entire Parkersburg historic district playgroup has deployed." Bridgette handed the last document back to the master sergeant and scooped up the copies out of the tray.

"Where in France does your sister work, ma'am?" When he didn't receive an answer, the master sergeant looked up from the Pelican. He watched Bridgette scrutinize the first and last copies alternately.

"What did you say?" Bridgette asked without looking up.

"I was asking where your seismologist sister worked, ma'am."

"Ummm," Bridgette pivoted her gaze rapidly between the documents, "in France."

"What's up, ma'am?"

"Master Sergeant, let's recopy these documents with greater contrast."

"Do you see something?" The master sergeant's face lit up.

"There's something familiar … like a faded design … maybe it's nothing at all, but I'm hoping."

"Familiar how, ma'am?"

"I'd rather not say." Bridgette's face blushed. "I'd feel stupid if I was wrong."

44

Faxing the Baton

G3 Operations Office
European Medical Command
Heidelberg, Germany
Current day

"Pole-dancing snake, Master Sergeant. Yes siree Bob, I was right." Bridgette shook her head. "As plain as day."

"Ma'am? Are we still talking about your sister?"

"What?" Bridgette barked a laugh. "No, of course not."

Master Sergeant moved closer for a better look. "What do you see, ma'am?"

"Look carefully at the watermark on page one. Here," she pointed, "after we boosted the contrast. Tell me what you see."

"I don't see a pole-dancing snake." Master Sergeant held the document closer. "Okay, maybe I do. May I see the other document, ma'am?"

"Roger, here." She thrust the high-contrast copies into his hands. "Go fax all these documents to Mickey immediately. I'm going to call him back." Bridgette hurried to her office with a copy of the documents and snatched her phone from its cradle.

"That was quick," said Mickey's voice through the line. "I had just put a call on hold and dialed you. I didn't even hear a ring on your end."

"I was about to call you and there you were, Mickey."

"Great minds think alike."

"Fools seldom differ," said Bridgette, exhaling loudly. "Okay, so Master Sergeant is faxing the documents to you even as we speak. Who will be receiving it at your end?"

"It comes directly into the room here."

"Really? Is that a typical service in French maternity hospitals?"

"What can I say? They love us."

"Really?"

"No. The facsimile in the room is just one less reason for them to have to interact with us non-French speakers." Mickey scoffed. "Okay, Bridgette,

I have page one in hand now. It is numbered 66:02 (17) 08 on the bottom."

"Confirm." Bridgette took off her glasses and tossed them on her desk. "How's the quality of the faxed copy?"

"Quite good. Have you made sense of the number sequence?"

"Nothing meaningful. Master Sergeant says that the number sixty-six reminds him of California—where you get your kicks."

"I am sure that Nazis could care less about a California highway," Mickey grunted. "Did you see the watermark?"

"Yes, Mickey, we made several copies of it here increasing the contrast on the copier. What do you see on your end?"

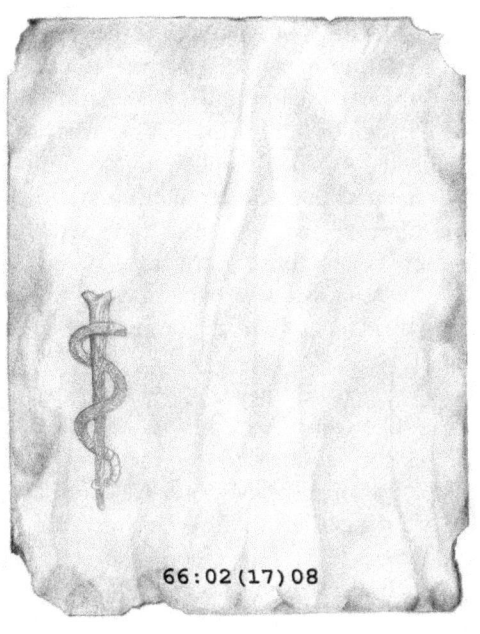

66:02 (17) 08

"I see a pole-dancing snake," Mickey mumbled.

"Sorry, Mickey, I missed that. Have pages two and three arrived yet?"

"Yes."

"Go to page three next. It has the numbers '66:02 (17) 06' on the bottom."

"I'm there."

"Tell me what you see, Mickey."

"Son of a gun. I see another reptilian pole dancer."

"Yes, but...."

"They're not the same snake, Bridgette."

"Exactly." Bridgette pinched the bridge of her nose. "Page one has an unmarked pole that is clearly printed with a single snake."

"Roger. On page three, I see a decorated pole with flowers and vegetation, again with a single snake. Asclepius."

"Why do you suppose different watermarks?"

"Maybe the watermark is the message, Bridgette."

"How so?"

66:02 (17) 06

"The Staff of Asclepius is the true symbol of medicine. It is a single snake on a staff. Purists prefer it to the double snake on the winged staff—the caduceus that we see in the US Army and Navy Medical Corps. The caduceus that we wear on our uniform, Bridgette, is not the real symbol of medicine." Mickey laughed. "When Russell Lange came back from Romania the first time, he commented that the Romanian Army Medical Corps was smarter than we were because at least they had used the Staff of Asclepius as their medical symbol instead of the caduceus."

"C'mon, Mickey, what does all this mean?"

"Bridgette, go to the page numbered 66:02 (17) 16—it's the page with the list."

"Roger. I'm there."

"The word 'Asclepius' is on this page. It's a Greek word. In fact, it is a Greek god's name tied into medicine and medical symbolism."

"Our mistake, Mickey. We said Latin."

"I think the two different staff watermarks and the word Asclepius refer to a power that only the Hebrews possess."

"Hebrews as in Jews?" Bridgette dropped the copies on her desk and tossed her glasses on top of them.

"Roger."

"Well, Mickey, given that parallel, this would now certainly justify the Nazi interest."

"These documents were part of a set of papers that I brought back from the secret bunker in Poland during the Leaning Tower affair, Bridgette. Apparently, this Nazi program searched for more than immortality. They were looking for holy relics."

"Holy relics like the crown of thorns, the blessed nails, the pendant crucifix—things like that?"

"Yes but no. These Nazis would only be interested in relics that are, or could be used as, weapons of power."

"Weapons?"

"Yes, Bridgette, weapons like the Ark of the Covenant or like the Horn of Joshua that brought down the city walls at Jericho. But in this case, it's the Staff of Moses and the Rod of Aaron—so named for its keeper, Moses's brother."

"A staff and rod?" Bridgette mused aloud. "As in 'thy rod and thy staff they comfort me' from the Bible?"

"Yes, that's Psalm twenty-three. We probably have seen and heard about it all our lives. Now it has new meaning."

"That's an understatement. Okay, so the Nazis were looking for this rod and staff. Why, Mickey? They certainly wouldn't be looking for emotional and spiritual comfort. We were talking about weapons. I don't see how these walking sticks could be weapons worth Hitler's time."

"We *are* talking about weapons. Hitler was threatened by the Jews and the power they could potentially wield against him. Inasmuch, he made it his mission in life to exterminate every Jew off the face of the earth."

"Why direct hate against one people?"

"Experts speculate on that every day, Bridgette," said Mickey. "The bottom line is that Hitler personally hated and feared the Jewish people, so he started his genocide there and then it broadened. He knew that Jews are only people who have ever walked in the presence of God. And Moses is one of the few historical figures that conversed with God. The experience transformed him."

"Transformed him?"

"Exactly. After his encounter with God, Moses wore a veil over his face for the rest of his life."

Bridgette gave an exasperated sigh and dropped the phone to her shoulder for a minute. She heard Mickey tapping on the receiver to get her attention and she raised it back to her ear.

"Listen, Bridgette, I'm not going around in circles. The Hebrews are the people who have historically possessed powerful weaponry from God himself. The Ark of the Covenant is deemed formidable all by itself. However, the greatest military weapon of mass destruction ever created were two shepherds' staffs."

"Okay, fine. I yield. I can understand a staff as a weapon of power, Mickey. But why is there a snake in the iconography? And keep it short, Mickey."

"I think that has to do with Egypt, actually." Mickey coughed quietly. "You know—pharaoh denied God's power. So then Moses demonstrated the killing power of the staff by creating snakes. Maybe you don't know though—"

"Mickey … " Bridgette warned.

"Later, Moses also used a staff to cure the snake-bitten in the desert after the Hebrews escaped from Egypt," Mickey rattled off in one breath.

"Okay…" Bridgette stretched the word. "I see the healing power of the staff and snake and why those practicing medicine would choose to use it as their symbol. What about the flowers and stuff on the one watermark?"

"That would be the Rod of Aaron. It was said to have sprouted leaves and vines."

"Which one is the Staff of Asclepius—know what, never mind, it doesn't matter. What I don't understand is how the Nazis knew any of this, or enough of this, to pursue the staff and rod as weapons."

"That answer won't be quick."

"Fire away," Bridgette groaned.

"The second of the sixty-six books that make up the Bible is Exodus. There, Moses leads the Israelites in a battle against the Amalekites."

"Never heard of them."

"Outside of theology, who has?" Mickey laughed. "God told Moses to 'blot out the memory of Amalek from under heaven.'"

"God said that?"

"Through Moses, yes, God said that."

"What did these Amalekites do to tick off the big guy?"

"That's not important right now, Bridgette. The point is that Moses, in Exodus seventeen, sent Joshua to battle. Meanwhile Moses went to an overwatch position with the Staff of Moses and the Rod of Aaron. History has referred to the two combined as the Rods of Power. God promised Moses that if he could hold the Rods of Power above his head, the Israelites would be victorious."

"He got muscle failure, didn't he?"

"Yes, every time his arms dropped the Amalekites began winning."

"I presume help arrived?"

"Yes, Bridgette. Aaron and Hur helped. Each took an arm of the seated Moses and with their help, Moses maintained. Eventually, the Amalekites were soundly defeated and virtually wiped off the face of the earth."

"That's a serious weapon, Mickey."

"The Nazis certainly thought so."

"Are you saying what I think you're saying?"

"Yes, Bridgette, I'm saying once the Nazi searches ended, the Amalekites have been unopposed in their quest for the Rods of Power. They need them for two reasons. First, their existence is assured if they possess the weapon. Second, the Amalekites could then turn the table against the people who tried to exterminate them."

"Those are some serious watermarks."

"I am guessing that this is a priority list for Nazis looking to find the Rods of Power in Africa, France, America, and Italy. It certainly explains the Nazi army's subdivision, *Afrika Korps*, searching for these biblical weapons."

"In light of all this, it seems that perhaps the scripted number sequence at the bottom of the pages could be a biblical reference, correct?"

"I think you've nailed it, Bridgette. The number sixty-six could indeed be a numerical reference to the number of books of the Holy Bible. The two is most likely Exodus, the second book of the Bible."

"Then the number in parenthesis could be chapter seventeen and the trailing eight, sixteen, and six could be the verse numbers. The verses aren't in numerical order on the pages, but … would that general concept be right, Mickey?"

"I am guessing so." Mickey paused. "Bridgette, you told me that the only document that went out was the one with all the country listings. Correct?"

"Roger, the first and last pages were uncopied."

"This center page may or may not be enough for the two foreign officers to go on. However, having all three documents would guarantee full understanding."

"Excellent. Well, that seems to be the only thing in our favor, I guess." Master Sergeant Roman knocked on the doorframe of Brigette's office. "Mickey, stand by for a second."

"Roger."

Bridgette put the receiver against her shoulder as she listened to the master sergeant's report. She sighed deeply and dragged the phone back to her ear. "Master Sergeant just brought in some more news."

"This is bad, isn't it?" Mickey sucked in a deep breath.

"Yeah. Two international officers and a radiology technician were found dead. Their bodies were dumped in hospital laundry bins."

"Let me guess—the international officers were stripped of their Liberian and British uniforms?"

"Affirmative. One body matches up with your description of the real Michaels-Keyes with that bulging thing over the eyebrow. And now I know why both men were in radiology for internal gut issues. Obviously, some kind of poison was used on them."

Mickey groaned. "This isn't looking good, Bridgette."

"Tell me about it."

"Has Major O-stadt been found?"

"Not yet, Mickey. I think it's only a matter of time."

"I worry for Mike Winnabe. He may be a target and not even know it." Mickey groaned. "Bridgette, make the call placing AFRICOM on alert. Have them release Mike to us as essential to a murder investigation. You have enough clout to make that happen."

"I do. Consider it done."

"When Mike is released, send my chopper for him. Have my pilot, Chief Chandra Lamar, take him straight to Brittany to the town of Auray. Have her relay that Mike is to meet me at the *Hôtel de Ville*. Then tell Chief that I will need a pickup here."

Bridgette's face went flat, and she nearly dropped the phone. "You're kidding."

"Why would I kid about this, Bridgette?"

"This is spooky."

"Why spooky?"

"Never mind." Bridgette shook her head and gave a little laugh.

"Bridgette, I've signed your leave form and am sending back right now. You are now on leave."

"Thanks, I appreciate it. Hopefully when I get back from Fort Knox, all will be well with Loni. Tell her I send my love."

"Will do. Say goodbye, Bridgette."

"Goodbye, Mickey. After I make the call to AFRICOM, Luis will have command and control."

"Roger, thanks. Make sure he is commo-linked in with me here."

"He already is. Also, Master Sergeant Roman can fill him in."

"Thanks, Bridgette."

"One last thing, Mickey."

"You are making me tired, Bridgette."

"Taste of your own medicine hard to swallow, Mickey?" Bridgette couldn't resist the friendly jab. "Listen," she continued before he could reply, "when you and Mike get to Auray at the *Hôtel de Ville*—"

"Yes?"

"Remember to order *la bonne reine*. That's 'the good queen' in French."

"What is it?"

"Trust me, Mickey. With it, order a bottle of *Folle Blanche*, served at room temperature. A bottle, Mickey, not a glass. That would be rude."

"Bridgette...."

"Last, be sure to tell Zell that Muffin says, 'Hi.'"

45

The Rest of the Story

Château Royal d'Amboise
Loire Valley, France
1500

"Mademoiselle Louise, have Vaast and I confused you with the story?" Simone asked as Vaast and Strong Charles adjusted a tarp which hung over part of the tapestry.

"Yes, Simone. I don't understand the story I just heard."

"Where did we lose you?"

"I understood all of the first tapestry with the unicorn in the fence and the second tapestry when the hunt begins for the unicorn."

"So is it this third tapestry that is the problem?"

Louise nodded. "Yes, Simone. With it partly covered, I can't see enough to understand the story—"

"Who is this that says Pollixe's tapestry is a problem?" A ruddy cheeked, gnarly handed, robust woman with long, dark braids stood from a bench near the tall windows looking out over the Loire River. She tapped a tapestry brush against her skirt as she approached the group. "Is it you, little lady? You say my tapestry has a problem?" Pollixe raised her eyebrows menacingly.

"This is your tapestry?" Louise asked Pollixe. Louise then looked anxiously between Simone and Vaast. "I thought it was the queen's," she added in a meek voice.

"The child has got you there, Pollixe," chuckled Vaast. "The little missy is unhappy with the tarp that you asked us to put over the tapestry."

"So that tarp bothers you, little lady?"

"I'm Louise." Louise drew herself closer to Simone, unsure of the newcomer.

"I'm Pollixe." The woman dropped her rough pretense and gave a genuine, weathered smile. "I heard you are curious about the story of the tapestries."

"I am, Pollixe, but I can't understand this one because it is halfway covered with the tarp."

"I see what you mean, Louise." Pollixe tapped her skirt again. "That tarp is indeed bothersome."

"Yes, Pollixe, what I see in front of me isn't the same as the story that was told."

"Why do you suppose, Louise?"

"My eyes see peace, quiet, and happiness. The lovely lady sits relaxing on the fainting couch. She has her hand around the unicorn's neck. I think she loves my unicorn. It's the most beautiful tapestry so far."

"Yes?"

"But, in the story I was told, my ears heard words threatening death, danger, and tragedy with the loss of a throne. Why is it that I cannot see in the tapestry the words that the queen spoke? There must be more that is under the hidden half."

"Indeed, there is." Pollixe nodded to Strong Charles, triggering him to reveal the rest of the tapestry. "Now, Louise, without the tarp, what do you see?"

"I see ... " Louise's face contorted. "I see...."

"Go ahead, child."

"Simone, I don't like it." Louise cringed and covered her eyes. "Cover it back up! This is *not* the most beautiful tapestry. It is an awful tapestry. I hate it."

"Wait, now." Simone patted Louise's hand. "It's all right to not like what you see. Perhaps it was wrong to make a judgment before seeing the whole picture, eh?"

"You all tricked me." Louise peeked through her fingers up at the wizened woman chewing on the stump of her pipe. "You showed me only the beautiful part."

"Child, we meant not to beguile you. We wanted that you see the beautiful first before you saw the whole picture." Simone set down her pipe and gently pulled the child's hands down. "Remove your hands. Come on, *pupuce*, settle yourself down." The big hug from Simone helped Louise to ease her cringe. Then, after pressing out creases and fluffing Louise's attire, Simone spoke in a placid tone. "Now, child, tell us what you see."

"I see a horrible dog biting the unicorn. I see a standing woman who is fair and beautiful, but her eyes are evil. She has what Mother calls," Louise raised her eyebrows in imitation of her mother, "'a wayward glance.' That woman is also planning to hurt my blessed unicorn."

Pollixe could not suppress a chuckle at Louise's mimicry. "How do you know she is planning this?"

"Can you not see it? She holds a waving hand as a signal while she looks to the forest behind her where a hunter stands ready to blow a horn to begin the hunt to capture the unicorn."

"How can there be a hunt, child, when the unicorn is already captured by the seated maid?"

"The unicorn is with the two maids because it trusted that they would protect it. The unicorn did not know that the evil maid would signal the hunters to come take it." Louise's fist trembled. "The evil maid is part of a plan which

is bringing harm to my unicorn. She is an evil, evil woman. How could anyone hurt a unicorn? I hate her. I hate her!" The child buried her face in Simone's tunic and sobbed. "I don't want to see this tapestry anymore!"

Simone stood at once and placed the startled child on the seat. "Take it away Strong Charles," the woman waved. "Take it back to the queen ... tell her we said to burn it!"

Louise's shock registered in her eyes as she understood what the weaver was about to do. "Wait, Simone!"

"What?" She held out her arm to stop her son.

"Don't send it back." Louise wiped her tears and sniffed. "Please don't burn it."

The artisan's demeanor softened immediately as she looked down at the young girl. "Ah, child. You see it and understand that it still has value."

"Yes, Simone." The child looked tentatively at the third artisan. "I apologize, Pollixe."

"I understand, little one," said Pollixe, softening her ruddy features into a pout. "Do you think I took pleasure in weaving such a scene? It was hard for me. But it was Queen Anne who asked that this tapestry be made just as it is." Pollixe pointed with her tapestry brush.

"I know, but why hurt my unicorn?"

"You tell us. What is the story here?" Pollixe crouched in front of the seated child. "You know it. You just heard it."

"It's not what it seems, is it?" Louise shifted her position, looking into the face framed by the dangling braids.

"No child, it is exactly what it seems." Pollixe shook her head sadly. "It is horrible, yes. But there is great good in it also. Do you wish me to explain?"

"Please." Louise wiped her nose and scooted over, indicating to Simone that she should sit again. So, being careful not to knock over the nearby goblet on her tool table, Simone settled herself into her spindly-legged chair, with Louise again on her lap.

"Is the little lady ready, Simone?"

"Yes." Simone cuddled Louise firmly. "I think she is."

"Good." Pollixe stood and began recounting the details of the tapestry.

"The seated maid is the young duchess." Pollixe pointed with her brush. "She is holding onto her betrothed, Prince Edward, the Duke of Wales."

"Just as you first appreciated," Simone whispered, "they are blissfully happy. A unicorn in the arms of a beautiful maid will yield its freedom willingly, lovingly."

"Why couldn't the tapestry and the story end there, Simone?"

"It can't, darling. Life doesn't work that way."

"Simone is right, Louise," Vaast nodded as he spoke. "The tapestry is obligated to tell the whole story." He looked at Simone and then Pollixe. "As weavers we must hold to every detail in every story."

"Even if it's not pleasant?"

"Especially so," said Vaast dolefully.

"Is Duchess Anne not happy?"

"No, Louise, the duchess truly is happy. However, she looks beyond her betrothed as she is watching the woman which stands behind the unicorn."

"Who is that woman?"

"You tell us, little lady." Pollixe looked down at Louise expectantly.

"I think she is Edward's mother, right?"

"You are correct, little lady."

"Edward's mother, Elizabeth Woodville, is signaling for the evil of the world to be unleashed upon her son," said Pollixe.

"How could a mother do this to her son?" Louise's eyes welled up and her voice constricted. "Her *only* son."

"Who better to do it?" asked Simone.

"What?" Louise narrowed her eyes at the old woman holding her.

"Remember, God allowed evil to be unleashed on His only son. Why did he do it?"

Louise nodded solemnly. "He did it so that we could return to Him. But what does this have to do with Edward?"

"His mother, the widow queen, had only one remaining son. She released evil on the *name* of her only son so that he would be discredited as king of England."

"He will now have to fight the evil, won't he, Simone?"

"Maybe. Maybe not. Possibly all he must do is run from the ones who hunt him."

"The Lancaster family?"

"No, there are no more Lancasters. However, there are many people still supporting the House of Lancaster, even though it's gone. People like Henry Tudor and his followers."

"How do they know to chase him?"

"Queen Elizabeth Woodville looks to the forest where Duke Richard calls the hunters to chase the fleeing monarch."

"Simone, shouldn't the prince's uncle be helping keep the prince alive? Why would Duke Richard be leading the evil to find Edward?"

"Consider that maybe he is leading them to chase Edward in a direction where Edward *isn't* going. Consider that it is better to lead the hunters down the path where *you want* them to go rather than where *they want* to go."

The child's brow was knit in concentration. "Let me see if I understand."

"Please, child. Go ahead."

"Edward and young Anne's love is shown by the seated maid caressing the neck of the happy unicorn."

"Yes."

"Anne looks to Edward's mother, the queen of England, who is bringing evil to her son—I mean her son's name," she corrected.

"Yes."

"The queen is being *helped* by Duke Richard who is leading the supporters of the House of Lancaster on a chase … away from Edward?"

"Yes, that is the hope."

"Then, why does the evil dog there in the tapestry bite the unicorn until it bleeds?"

"Ah, yes. That is disturbing, isn't it? Let us remember that the price is highborn with many responsibilities and, also, many privileges. Edward suffers the loss of his throne, his home, his family—everything he loves."

"And the pain makes him bleed, Simone."

"Yes, child. The pain cuts deep."

"Yet, he does it anyway."

"He does."

Louise heaved a large sigh for so small a child. "What happens next?"

"The queen tells you in the next tapestry, Louise." Vaast nodded and smiled.

"I am not sure I want to see it." Louise scanned all the artisan's faces.

"What is your judgment now on this tapestry, child?" Pollixe shoved the brush into her pocket and crossed her arms.

Louise paused for a moment and thought, her eyes roving over the tapestry laid out before her. "My eyes have changed. I think they have grown-up."

"I think they have too," said Simone. "I think the queen wants everyone to know the story with all the good and bad that it holds."

"Is there more horror and evil ahead?"

"Yes, honey. I would imagine that there is." Simone joined the other two artisans in a collective nod.

"Why, Simone? How do you all know?"

"Because we have lived longer than you. Like with young Queen Anne and her unicorn, we know that all relationships eventually end in pain."

"Every single one?"

"Yes, darling, every single one."

"How can that be?" Louise's voice edged into sadness and tears threatened to spill from her eyes again.

Simone took the child's face in her hands. "Oh, child. People love each other but few die at the very same moment. So everyone loses the ones that they love at some point in their life."

"Why didn't God make the world a good place?"

Simone gave the child a wry smile and good-natured pinch on the cheek. "Have you ever eaten a nice, sweet cherry?"

Louise sniffed back her tears and rubbed her cheek. "Yes, of course. A sweet cherry is delicious."

"Did you ever eat a sour cherry by accident?"

"Yes." Her nose crinkled.

"By tasting the sour, you can better appreciate the sweet."

"What does that have to do with the world, Simone?"

"The world is a place where both good and evil exist. They battle each other every day. We must experience both to appreciate the good and to decide for ourselves what path to take. The experiences can be hard, scary even. This is why we need a guiding hand. A source to give us strength when we have none. Someone to point us in the direction we need to go when we lose our bearings. One that gives us comfort when we taste the sour cherries in life."

"We need God."

"Yes, child. God the Father, His son Jesus, and the Holy Spirit. And so, in life as in the tapestries, we must have both good and bad parts as well as the one who guides us. Our queen will be the first to tell us that."

"But where is God in the tapestries? I don't see Him."

"Why, in every thread that binds it, just as He is in every part that makes up you and me and all living things. We cannot see God directly except in the beauty of our world and His creations on it."

Louise nodded her understanding. "Gentle artisans, I am ready for the next tapestry."

"Somehow I knew you would be," Simone nodded.

"Strong Charles!" Simone and Louise called together.

Louise smiled at the puffing lad and asked, "Would you please prepare the fourth tapestry?" As Vaast and the young man retreated to the back of the hall to retrieve the tapestry from the travel chest, Louise sighed, "Oh, how I wish the queen was here."

"What makes you think that she isn't?" Queen Anne's voice came from behind them.

46

Roses and Dogs' Pointing Noses

Maternity hospital
Saint-Quentin, Somme River Valley
Vermandois region, France
Current day

"Loni's hands were shaking, Douglas."

"I saw that, Clarisse." Douglas took a calming breath and turned his attention to the flower shop keeper. "So are yours."

Clarisse clenched her quaking hands into fists and moved to cross her arms, but Douglas stopped her in mid-action. He gently held her fists in his hands, his fingers interlaced around them.

He tilted his head toward Loni. "Annie is okay. The worst that could have happened with the raven master didn't happen." Then, looking directly into Clarisse's blue-green eyes, watching them dilate back to normal, he said soothingly, "You are okay too."

"Am I?" She relaxed her shoulders some in response to his tender touch.

"Even if it doesn't feel like it right now, you *are* okay." He looked down at her hands enfolded in his own. "I know a little something about these kinds of things." Clarisse parted her lips to speak but he interrupted her, "However, I would never presume to know what you have been through ... only that we all have our demons to fight and rise above."

Clarisse nodded, watching the tremors in her hands slowly dissipate. "Thank you, Douglas," she finally said. Then she raised her eyes. "But I'm not worried about me."

"I am," he whispered back. Douglas released Clarisse's hands and sat down in front of Loni once more. "Queen Anne, how do you feel?"

"Shhh."

"Uh ... Queen Anne?" Douglas stammered.

248

"Everyone who can hear my voice, quiet, please." Loni clapped her hands loudly twice and all were silent.

"Simone, kindly give me your seat and place that precious, inquisitive child in my lap." Queen Anne sat and then beckoned to her chief lady-in-waiting and keeper of the queen's house, Clare, who stood near the royal entrance door to the queen's right. "Clare, see that these good artisans have what they need to erect another display rack at the other end of the hall. They are to set up the next tapestry there and then roll it to me here when I request it." The queen watched as the group bowed, then moved away from the primary frame situated near her throne. Once the group was at a reasonable distance and engaged in their task, the queen addressed Louise. "Child, do you have imaginary friends?"

"Yes, Majesty," Louise answered nervously, her eyes darting side to side. "Don't all children?"

"I don't know about other children, but I did." Queen Anne stroked the child's hair. "And I still do," said the queen in a whisper. "Right now, I need to talk to mine. Would you mind keeping me company?"

"Not at all, Majesty."

Queen Anne smiled and repositioned the child in her lap. "Hush now." Little Louise gave a nod. The queen spoke.

"Douglas?"

"Yes, Majesty?"

"What were you saying before?"

"I was asking how you are feeling."

"I am happy and sad." Loni pressed her lips together for the queen. "I do remember the day far better now having relived the moments which were once only distant memories."

"Can we now talk about what resulted on that day with the raven master? Is it safe to do so where you now are?"

"Yes, I can. I have managed the situation—for now." Loni cast her eyes about warily. "But this will not be easy in my present time."

"I understand. Can you tell us about what happened regarding that memory you shared with us?"

"I can do so, very easily as I have a visual guide. But can you follow, Douglas?"

"What do you mean, Majesty?"

"Douglas, I am seated here in front of my third tapestry. Today is the day I review the commissioned tapestry series to which Clarisse alluded. They tell the story of Edward and me. My question to you is how are you going to follow along?"

"Majesty, if you give us a moment, I will have that answer as one of us here happens to be in front of the same tapestries as they hang in a museum in America."

"Museum? America?"

"It's across the sea."

"I have heard of this so-called New World across the sea. It is the hidden land of the Templars ... or so the rumors go. The Vikings, Celts, Dutch, English, and French have sailed the seas in one direction while the Portuguese and Spaniards sailed in another. Each met the other in the lands where the Templars have tread. More recently, the Italians Amerigo Vespucci and Christopher Columbus have followed in the wake of the others. This name you use, America, seems to be a derivative of Vespucci's name."

"Those are fine examples of my great countrymen, Majesty." Ottaviano tapped his chest proudly as he approached the queen from where he had been lingering near the royal entrance door to the hall. "Christopher Columbus hails from Genoa and Amerigo Vespucci from Florence." Ottaviano glanced suspiciously at the queen. "Majesty, to whom are you speaking?"

"We're talking to imaginary friends." Little Louise scowled up at the knight then yawned.

"I do not remember beckoning you here to my side, impudent lord knight."

Ottaviano recognized the air of formality upon the young queen's face. "My most sincere apologies, Majesty." Ottaviano bowed low and kept his eyes on the ground as he spoke. "I meant no disrespect. My only thought was to lend humble service to a queen who had," he cleared his throat and then lowered his voice to a whisper, "wandered from Chapelle Saint-Hubert in a trance-like state. Recall, Majesty, I had been asked to wait while my queen prayed. Then, when she left the chapel, I followed Her Majesty on her path here, keeping a watchful eye so that no harm should befall her." He chanced to glance up at the queen who stared back with unsure eyes. "As Your Highness moved in the direction of the great hall and the tapestries, I was loath to deter you on your travel. Believe me, Majesty, I meant no harm nor interruption. Say the word, or lift a finger, and death will follow as atonement for my transgression."

"Do not slay yourself quite yet, my dear Italian." Queen Anne arched an eyebrow. "Though do keep the sword at the ready since, apparently, the day's mysteries have not yet been fully revealed." The queen motioned for Ottaviano to rise. *It seems that today I am to be led about by the spikes of my crown, the voices in my head, and a curious Italian knight.* "Rest assured, Ottaviano, you may yet die or be dismissed due to your impetuousness." The queen shifted the child in her lap, feeling her grow heavy with sleep. "Although, with candor, I have never once heard of a knight who was killed by a sharp word or daggered stare." Queen Anne gave a hint of a smile—a crack in the courtly mask—which was not missed by Ottaviano's perceptive eye. "Mind you though, dear devoted knight, sharpened metal can follow cutting verbiage if the queen wills it so."

"I understand, my liege. I will keep my hand near the sword's hilt to quickly execute the queen's slightest wish, whatever it may be."

"I choose that you join us on the journey of my unicorn tapestries. Please go help the others at the back of the hall to prepare the next tapestry."

"Of course, Majesty, as you wish." Ottaviano bowed and then strolled away, glancing curiously over his shoulder as he retired from the queen's presence.

"Douglas?"

"One moment, Highness." Douglas motioned to Mickey. "The voice from America would like to speak." Douglas rolled his eyes as Mickey nearly dropped the phone in the handoff. Douglas moved the phone closer to Loni so that Queen Anne could hear better.

"Highness?" a voice squawked through the phone in Loni's suite.

"Who is this new voice that addresses Anne, Duchess of Brittany and Queen of all that is France's?" Loni thrust her chin up.

"My name is Jillian Rebecca Meriwether Zimmerman."

"Are you Spanish?"

"No, Majesty. I am American. Why?"

"Only the Spanish have names that take longer to say than any one person has sufficient breath to deliver."

Jillian stifled a laugh, keeping it from echoing off the museum walls. "For simplicity's sake, Majesty, please just call me Jillian."

"Then just call me Anne."

"I don't think I can do that, Majesty." Grunting, Jillian resituated the sleeping octogenarian to better view all the tapestries. "But I'll try." She pulled the charcoal pencil out from behind her ear and repositioned the cardboard coffee sleeve, upon which she had been taking notes, atop her thigh.

"Was that a groan, Jillian?"

"Everything seems a bit of a challenge today, Majesty."

"Are you unwell?"

"No, it's just tough being in a room with no seating." Jillian laughed softly, continuing to mime a discussion with her seatmate. "I imagine windowsills have never been made for sitting comfort."

"I can't say that I know a lot about sitting on a windowsill."

"Worry not about me, Majesty. I'll manage."

"As you like, Jillian. Douglas, may I explain this third tapestry?"

"Please, Majesty, before you start, which is the third?"

"The one with a maiden embracing the unicorn and a woman signaling a hunter."

"Oh," Jillian sighed, "I mean, thank you, Highness. I'm ready now." Jillian stared at the scraps of the deteriorated tapestry and held her breath, pencil hovering in anticipation.

Queen Anne adjusted the sleeping Louise in her lap. "When I saw Froggie alive and standing next to my betrothed, Edward, my young heart filled with joy. I felt at that moment that all was right with the world. However, as adults, we know that moments we love pass all too quickly. It was then that I learned of the plan which would save Edward's life." Queen Anne motioned for a drink from Clare who waited, as always, at a distance to serve her queen.

"What happened next, Majesty?" Douglas blurted.

As Clare approached, Queen Anne whispered, "Patience, Douglas. I am getting to that. Wait a moment." The queen took a drink and returned the goblet to the tray in Clare's hands. With the slightest movement of her hand, the queen commanded Clare to withdraw farther off than usual. "Now let us resume."

"May I take a moment to ask a question from America?"

"Please, Jillian."

"I heard you say the name 'Froggie.' Are you aware that my sister, Loni, who is our, well, our umbilical cord to you, has the nickname Frog Face?"

"None before you has mentioned that."

"It's an odd parallel. I just had to ask." Jillian gave a nervous laugh then cleared her throat. "Please, Majesty, continue with the story."

"As we stood in the raven master's special room, Duke Richard told us the intent of Edward's mother. I remember that I had my arm around Edward's shoulders as if … as if my embrace could ward off all the world's evil."

Jillian tilted her head and squinted at the remnant scraps of the third tapestry in the gallery. "I see that in the third tapestry, Highness," Jillian spoke quietly.

"Yes, Jillian, I asked that it be put there. I asked for much in this tapestry. I asked that my hair be made full and rich, filled with flowers and a crown—"

"But Majesty … Queen Anne … " Jillian interrupted.

"Yes?"

Jillian bit her lip. *How can I tell her that time and neglect has destroyed all evidence of what the third tapestry once held? I can't believe it. The one and only tapestry that captured the child duchess is today only a mere fragment.*

"I'm sorry." Jillian sniffed and then willed herself to switch gears. "Continue, please." She pulled her charcoal pencil across the cardboard coffee sleeve, sketching as the queen spoke to her across the ripples of time and space.

"I asked that my face be bright and full of hope. On my dress, I have an ermine, and a frog worked into the border. In this way, there would certainly be many clues to guide the eyes of the knowledgeable."

"Oh, Majesty." Jillian sighed and sniffled again as she rapidly completed the thumbnail sketch. *Oh why did I leave my blank sketchpads in the car?* she admonished herself.

"Jillian, are you sure you are well?" The queen's voice carried a trace of concern as it came through Jillian's earpiece.

"I'm fine, Majesty, I assure you. Just a bit … um … emotional. Your arm around the neck of the unicorn moves me deeply."

"As it should. Duke Richard told us to keep silent the wishes of the queen and Edward. Also, Richard of Shrewsbury's return from the dead must be kept a lifelong secret. As such, only Edward was to undergo discrediting. And now, finally, after so much time, no harm can come to them as I share this story."

"What was the plan for how to discredit Edward?" Jillian blew her nose and the sleeping man beside her twitched.

"In the raven master's tower, Duke Richard said he would undermine the legitimacy of Edward's birth."

"How so, Majesty?"

"It involved challenging the legitimacy of the marriage between King Edward and Queen Elizabeth Woodville. These actions led to a parliamentary document called Titulus Regius."

"It sounds Latin."

"Yes, sometimes legal statutes were written as such. The duke arranged for evidence to be fabricated to prove that Edward's father had contracted to marry Lady Eleanor Talbot before he married Elizabeth Woodville, thus making his marriage to Elizabeth Woodville invalid. A bishop then verified this evidence, after which the parliamentary decree formally declared that all the children of King Edward IV were illegitimate. Thus, the English crown passed to Duke Richard."

"How humiliating for Edward," Clarisse's voice joined in.

"Yes, but under the circumstances, entirely acceptable, Clarisse. Though since I was a child at the time, I confess it was difficult to accept."

"What happened to Edward, Majesty?" Jillian asked.

"He was made to disappear."

"Where did people think he went?"

"Some thought that he was smuggled out of the country. Others thought that he was murdered in the castle walls. Some believed that his brother, Richard, was murdered as well."

"Didn't people want to see the bodies of the dead princes? To bury or honor them?" Jillian's hand moved across the carboard coffee sleeve as if of its own accord. And Jillian, as an artist, welcomed the familiar pull of the subconscious, allowing it to flow through her as she listened.

"Yes, they would have, Jillian—if they were certain that the princes had died. Remember now, some tongues at the time wagged about seeing Richard fall off the wall, landing dead on the ground. Others contested, saying that he was one of three deathly ill children at the time. Still others said that he was never at the castle at all. Confusion led to great distraction. This played nicely as a smoke screen to allow the princes the time and opportunity to escape."

"I see. But you said some people argued that Prince Richard was still alive. How did Duke Richard stop that?" Swift, minute charcoal lines and dashes added final textures to what Jillian now recognized as a tiny Tower of London thumbnail.

"He put out official word that Prince Richard of Shrewsbury had fallen ill and then disappeared."

"Is this where the bodies of the other two castle children who died of plant poisoning came into play?" Douglas queried.

"Yes, Douglas. Duke Richard buried them under the steps of one of the towers in a shroud of mystery. If discovered, then the confusion would continue. Since the two who died from the henbane-fall accident were boys, there would always be the question of whether the bodies were the princes of the tower who had disappeared. It also lent credit to the subterfuge idea that perhaps, if the bodies were the princes, they were murdered."

"Wait," Jillian interrupted, "wouldn't the people in the castle tell inquisitors that around the same time two castle children died and that these two under the steps could be them instead of the princes?"

"The disappearance of the princes was foremost in the minds of such inquisitors. None cared of the death of castle no-names. Unfortunately, death was, and is, a daily companion during these times. But, as you say, precautions had to be taken to ensure the story. Great care was taken to document a funeral and alternative burial site for the two castle children. Only a few knew for sure that the castle children's funeral and burial was an elaborate ruse—the coffins were empty."

"I'm not sure of the advantage of the stairwell burial."

"There were sure to be searches in every direction. There had to be some accounting for the bodies of the princes once they had disappeared. If the plan to sneak them out of the country succeeded and no one knew they were gone, then there had to be an accounting of the missing bodies."

"I can see there would be many search parties combing the grounds for clues."

"Yes, Jillian, some were from the House of Lancaster. They were looking for any contender to the throne. The House of York had Duke Richard as its new king, but still, some might look to foreign shores for other options. The House of Brittany sent search parties in both places looking for the betrothed of the duchess."

"Yes, Majesty, but how is all of this captured in the tapestry series?" Douglas's voice queried.

"I will do my best to explain." With the sleeping child on her shoulder, the queen looked down the hall, past the four central columns to where the others had completed the frame and hung the fourth tapestry. "Give me a moment," she said, speaking to the voices in her head.

Queen Anne motioned to Clare, and in a moment the tapestry racks were set into motion. A few of the remaining artisans approached the front of the hall and wheeled away the rack near the throne, pushing it past the Loire River windows and back to the traveling trunks. Ottaviano and the other artisans began pushing the rack with the fourth tapestry toward the front of the hall, along the courtyard-side windows, and then into position before the queen.

When all had retreated to the rear of the hall and had begun the work of storing the third tapestry and mounting the fifth, Queen Anne tilted her head as though speaking quietly to the sleeping child in her arms. "I am now in front of the fourth tapestry, Douglas."

"Tell us what to see, Majesty."

"The fourth tapestry portrays the three houses which are being led to search for the absent princes. There is a person in the woods who is motioning to them."

"How are the three houses represented?" Jillian's voice came to Queen Anne.

"The House of York signified by a white rose. The House of Lancaster is signified by a red rose. The House of Brittany will have the symbol of Queen Anne of Brittany."

"A war between those English houses was called a war between the roses," said Clarisse.

"Yes, Clarisse, a war of the roses."

"I see no roses in the tapestries, per se," Jillian added, "but I do see two rose-red hunting dogs, and one white hunting dog. Also, I see two cream-colored dogs and upon their collars they have the symbol of a letter *A* and a numeric three. Maybe? I'm not sure ... they're kinda small."

"I know it's small, Jillian. Sometimes the joy of discovery adds apprecia-tion to the finding." The queen nodded and smiled, swaying slightly as she held little Louise. "This A3 symbol, Jillian, is the symbol for Queen Anne of Brittany."

"Well, honestly, I can understand the A," Douglas interrupted, "but I am having trouble with the numeral three as being part of the symbol for Queen Anne of Brittany."

"I believe the artist among you will be most able to enlighten you, Douglas."

"I will?" Jillian's voice sounded caught off guard. "Um … hang on a minute. Oh, yeah, okay. Yes, absolutely, Majesty. I can explain in terms they understand. I think…. Okay guys, the A3 seen by the person who is left-brain dominant sees only an alphanumeric. You see? Logic first, the obvious first. But a right-brain dominant person who is more abstract and creative will see two symbols. First, of course, the numeral as described, but then as the other hemisphere of the brain kicks in, letter B will appear. The letter doesn't have the vertical backbone, and instead it is sculpted out of the positive and negative space in the design. Brilliant! You all in the Vermandois cannot see it, but there is a quintet of roped A3 symbols in all the tapestries."

"All of them?" Queen Anne questioned.

"Well, no. In one tapestry the roped symbol is missing from the lower-left corner. In another it is missing in the lower-right corner. I am guessing this marks the beginning and the end of the story?"

"You would guess right, Jillian."

"Yes! Score one for the school of artsy tartsy!" Jillian's voice reigned itself in as her jostling of her juxtaposed snoozing companion led to some snorting, shifting, and finally settling. She continued with less animation. "I must admit that, where I am seated, the tapestries are not in the correct order."

"Perhaps one day you will correct the sequence, Jillian."

"Can we please get back to the fourth tapestry and the hunting dogs?" Douglas groused.

"Very well, Douglas. There is one more, and we have already alluded to it. It lies again with the dogs."

"Okay, if it's what we see, it falls to me!" Jillian chuckled. "I see that the two rose-red Lancaster dogs are looking essentially forward. I see that the one white Yorkist dog is looking backward. Last, I see that the two Brittany dogs are divided. One looks forward. One looks back. I see it but don't understand."

"Let me clarify, Jillian." Queen Anne exhaled loudly as she hitched the child up a little higher in her arms and shifted the chain of her crucifix so that it did not press upon the little face. She paused for a moment with the chain of the crucifix in her hand. *I thought I put this in my diary before I prayed in the Chapelle Saint-Hubert … how curious.* The queen lay the chain back on her neck, still and calm, her mind anything but. She continued, "The House of Lancaster is looking to find missing princes in areas forward in time. That is, they feel that the princes have escaped and will eventually be caught in the days to come. The House of York believes that some ill will is responsible for the disappearance. They are looking back in time for evidence to locate the missing princes. These people are combing the castle grounds at the Tower of London."

"What of the House of Brittany? Are they a house divided?"

"Yes and no. The fact is that they are the ones, for the most part, leading the other two houses in both directions to add further confusion to the matter. Having said this, later there was some dispute within the House of Brittany on how the matter of the discredited king should be handled. This leads us to the next tapestry." The queen surveyed the hall behind her and saw that the fifth tapestry was not yet in place on the display rack.

"I'm ready." With a grunt, Jillian nudged her neighbor's head off her shoulder to continue her notes and sketches. Her eyes had been focused on the tapestries while the queen spoke. Now as Jillian looked downward, she noticed more detailed, miniscule sketches on the coffee sleeve. She had unknowingly added a sketch of the A3 in roped knots, and she had done the same with an EZ. She rolled the charcoal pencil from her husband back and forth in her fingers and smiled. It took her a moment to realize she was being spoken to.

"Are you, Jillian?"

"What? I'm sorry Majesty, I was distracted."

"Are you ready, Jillian? How are your ankles?"

"My ankles?" Jillian's eyebrows contracted and she glanced around the room suspiciously.

"Grunting, groaning, needing to sit in a seatless room, and forced to use a sill as a chair?" Queen Anne's voice sighed in Jillian's ear. "I know this all too well. So, I ask again: How are your ankles?"

Comprehension dawned on Jillian she gathered an answer. "They're better now that I have been sitting, Majesty, thank you."

"Have the rings tightened?"

"Oh, Majesty," Jillian laughed, "I stopped wearing my rings weeks ago."

"You are lucky, Jillian. How far are you?"

"Twelve weeks, Majesty. Am I lucky? My swollen joints would claim otherwise." Jillian scrutinized her fingers holding the pencil. "Well, of course, I mean, yes, I am—lucky to be pregnant. It wasn't easy for me."

"It was easy for me to get pregnant, but not easy for my children to withstand this world. I now have only my fifth with me. She has survived her first year. We shall see if she lives longer than my first son; he lived just past three years. My others were not so fortunate as these two."

"I do know that feeling, to some extent, Majesty. Though not as deeply as you." Jillian's voice quavered as she spoke.

The queen filled the silence. "I see we share similar losses, dear Jillian. When I say you are lucky, I mean that you are lucky to have a child with your beloved. I was never so blessed."

"I understand now, Majesty." Jillian swallowed hard, thinking of EZ and how lost she'd feel without him. "Yes, Queen Anne. I *am* very lucky." She blinked the tears from her eyes.

"Indeed. Do not forget it."

"I won't, Majesty."

"I just put my rings on today."

"And your ankles, Majesty?" Jillian seized the moment to change focus and keep herself from dissolving into a puddle.

Jillian heard a sigh in response. "Not as good as I hoped."

"Oh, I'm sorry, Majesty."

"There are things we can control, Jillian … "

" … and things we can't, Majesty."

"Rightly so. So I'll leave that in God's hands."

"You and your daughter will be in my prayers, Highness. Along with all those taken from you too soon."

"You and your precious gift are also in my heart, *petite pupuce*."

47

Queen and the Butterfly

Château Royal d'Amboise

Loire Valley, France

1500

"Why do you shiver so, little one?" Queen Anne smiled down at the stirring child. "Has a cold draft awakened you?"

Louise stretched and yawned. "Hello, Majesty," she said groggily.

"Do you remember any of the story of the fourth tapestry so far, child?" Queen Anne adjusted Louise's hair that had become disheveled as she slept.

"Louise," the child smiled, "my name is Louise. And you're the queen."

"Yes, child, I am."

"I fell asleep staying quiet so you could talk to," Louise dropped her voice so low the queen had to lean in to hear her, "your imaginary friends."

"Yes, Louise, you were most helpful."

"Did they answer you?" As the queen pondered how to reply, Louise peered over the queen's shoulder and down the great hall. "Who is he—the knightly one who interrupted before?"

Little Louise's voice rang clear and bright in the hospital room. Mickey, Douglas, and Clarisse sat on edge awaiting what they would hear and sense from the queen's palace. A cool draft circled around them.

"Fly on the wall, Jillian," Mickey whispered into the speaker on his phone. "We have a new player joining the queen. I leave it to the queen to cue us back into dialogue."

"Of course," Jillian whispered back.

Suddenly, Clarisse jumped up from her seat, motioned that she would be right back, and then left the room abruptly. Douglas tried to protest but was halted by Loni's voice as she spoke to little Louise.

"Who, child?" asked Queen Anne.

259

"The fellow in strange, patterned clothes standing with the artisans."

"Oh, him." Queen Anne nodded. "That knightly fellow is Sir Ottaviano. Quite trustworthy is he. And over there near my entrance door is Clare, the most trusted of my attendants." The queen pinched the child's nose.

"Where are Vaast and Pollixe? Did the knight make them leave?"

"No, child, they left of their own accord. They had preparations to attend to and, it seems, the story of their tapestries has already been told to you."

"I'm happy that you are here, Your Majesty, and I am pleased that Simone is still here too. The weavers all did well telling me the story, but it is *your* story after all." Louise looked over at Ottaviano again. "If you say that knight is trustworthy then I suppose I agree."

"Is that so?" said Queen Anne. "Well, I'm glad to hear it. You see, Ottaviano and I came back just to see you."

"Why me?"

"Why not you? I was watching you earlier. Of all my subjects, you, and only you, showed the greatest enjoyment of my storytelling. So much so that you were willing to scurry up that column there for a better look!" Queen Anne smiled as she straightened Louise's collar. "Tell me what you see and understand about this tapestry here."

"Yes, Majesty." Louise sat up proudly and pointed as she spoke. "I see that the dogs are really people who are looking for our missing princes." Louise rubbed the sleep from her eyes. "But there was a lot more about battles between flowers? And then dead children? And lots of names." She shrugged. "I suppose I don't really see or understand this tapestry."

"Very well." Queen Anne motioned to the knot of artisans standing behind her and to her left, near the trunks at the back of the hall.

"His name is Strong Charles." Louise pointed as the group approached.

"Hello again, Majesty." Simone gave an arthritic curtsey.

"Thank you, Simone, for attending to the tapestries in my absence." Queen Anne nodded. "You too, Strong Charles." The diffident lad blushed at her royal presence while Queen Anne hid her smile. "Simone, my good woman, why have you not gone to tend to your accommodations and prepare for the banquet?"

"Majesty, I had intended to at first, but then I was approached by this curious child. With a little help from some friends, I was talking through the tale of the tapestries. I have lingered since your return to serve you and, should Your Majesty be called away, so that I may take responsibility for little Louise here."

"And a very fine job you have done, in all respects. I especially appreciate you staying to oversee the handling of the tapestries for this private viewing." Queen Anne smiled. "I'd have a hard time of it by myself!" The group chuckled, and Queen Anne continued, "Will you and your trusted few continue to aid us?"

"But of course, Majesty." Simone bowed her head again.

"Thank you." Queen Anne stood Louise up, rose, and took the child's hand. "Right now, Louise, just know that the princes are gone from the tower and there are many people hunting for them everywhere. There is much confusion and mystery, both of which help to protect the princes."

"Where have they gone?"

"Let us see the fifth tapestry to find out." She then addressed the small group. "If you please, my fine artisans, will you exchange the tapestries while this young lady and I take some air?" The group nodded and bowed then began the rotation of the frames. Wooden wheels creaked, ropes slid, and heavy tapestries were brought down and up as Queen Anne and Louise stepped out one of the window doors onto the narrow balcony facing the Loire River.

The wind whipped past them, snapping the flags high on the battlement walls. The river surged far beneath them; the sound of its steady rush of unstoppable emerald water reverberated off the high stone walls. The martins pirouetted in the wind and sang, carefree and wild, over the echoing roar of the water.

Queen Anne drew in a deep breath. "What do you see, Louise?"

Louise's eyes were on her feet. She clutched the monarch's hand tightly, and though her shoulders hunched down in fear, her feet obeyed the queen's lead. "I have never been out here before. Mother says it is too dangerous."

"It is indeed dangerous for a child alone. But with guidance and prudence, sometimes a small danger can bring confidence and courage. Don't you think?"

"I suppose, Your Majesty."

"It is like when you learn to climb a tree. You go a bit at a time—a little higher each time." Queen Anne led them to a small step closer to the railing. "Testing your strength and building your confidence little by little."

"Mother says I shouldn't climb trees—it's not lady-like."

Queen Anne looked down at the flushed face and white knuckles of the trusting little girl. "I was told the same thing. I did it anyway." She took them another tiny step closer to the edge. "But I was sure never to soil my clothes or I'd be in trouble."

Louise squinted up at the queen. "You did?"

"I did! And just look how brave I am now." Queen Anne reached her free hand out into the wide-open air. Tentatively Louise raised her free hand up and out like the queen's, but her eyes squeezed shut and shoulders still hunched.

"Stand tall and you will see farther, Louise," said the queen gently. The girl was frozen with fear, peering from the balcony's railing. "Sweet child, I will not let harm come to you. You have my hand. I will not fail you. Be brave."

Slowly Louise forced her shoulders to drop down. She opened her eyes a little at a time. "Majesty...."

"First, look out to the horizon, far over the land," the queen instructed, "then bring your eyes slowly to where the river begins and as it flows past us, let your eyes do the same. Then look back out to the horizon again." Louise did as she was told, drawing in a deep, shuddering breath. "Good. Now feel the strong stones beneath your feet and the trust in my grip." Louise's eyes were wide open now, her arm raised out in the wind, a smile on her face.

Queen Anne looked back out over the horizon. "Do not fear the winds nor the tides of change. Do not be reckless and do not seek danger for danger's sake but have courage and be strong enough to see what lies before you so that you may navigate it as well as you are able."

"Like the martins?"

"Yes." The queen smiled at the girl. "I ask you again, Louise, what do you see?"

"Everything, Your Majesty."

"Well done. Will you remember what I have told you here amongst the wind and the river?"

"Yes, my queen," Louise beamed.

"Very well, let us see if the artisans are ready for us."

They stepped back into the great hall and sat alone together before the grand fourth tapestry while the artisans continued their work at the other end of the hall.

"Let us begin, Louise. You know my first question."

"Yes, Majesty. What do I see?" Louise scrutinized. "I see the unicorn coming out of water."

"What kind of water? Is it a lake, an ocean, a river?"

"It looks like the streams near my house where I play. You see, I imagine it to be much bigger than it is. I pretend that some people live on one side and different people live on the other. Sometimes, in my games, the people play only on their own sides. At other times, they don't."

"Quite right!" Queen Anne praised. "It is the same with this water here. You see much with those little eyes. Anything else?"

"I see a lot of people on both sides of the water in the tapestry trying to keep the unicorn from climbing out of the water. Why do they want to hurt him?"

"Let me tell you more of the story." Queen Anne looked down as the child leaned back into her arms, the flush of her cheeks dissipating. Queen Anne's voice trailed into a sing-song quality to engage the child and allow her to tell the voices in her head about the tapestry.

"The now discredited Prince Edward of Wales traveled from Portsmouth across the English Channel. Upon landing at Saint-Servan in Brittany, there was a great debacle. Both sides of the channel, both groups of people, found him to be unacceptable as Edward, Prince of Wales. But both sides found him to be acceptable under an assumed name … a new name."

"What was the name?" Louise mused.

"The name was that of his favorite character of Welsh origin. It was a character that his mother told him about in her wonderful bedtime stories."

"I like bedtime stories."

"As do I," said Queen Anne, "and so did Edward. His mother wove fanciful stories that mixed legends of old into new, exciting tales. While I was with Edward and his mother, I heard the stories too and I came to love them as did my betrothed."

"Caradoc." Recalling the stories passed onward from within her lineage of Clares, Clarisse's voice whispered, "Edward became Caradoc."

Douglas jumped from her silent reappearance at his shoulder. She clutched something to her heart—a small square-shaped package wrapped in a brown paper bag.

"Yes, Clarisse." Loni smiled and tilted her head, sorrow in her eyes.

"Is Clarisse the name of another imaginary friend, Majesty?" Louise crinkled her nose.

"Well—"

"So it would seem." Wide-eyed, Ottaviano stood frozen, his gaze fixed on the queen.

"She's your imaginary friend too?" Louise puzzled. "What about Douglas and … Jill? Was that her name?"

Ottaviano watched Queen Anne subtly tap her index finger to her lips. He registered the queen's surprise and her command simultaneously.

"I think so," Ottaviano shrugged slowly.

"Louise, Edward took the name of Caradoc Freichfras, who was a member of Uther Pendragon's legendary English knights. However, when it came time for Uther's son, Arthur, to become king, Caradoc Freichfras joined in the ranks against him."

"That wasn't nice, nor very noble."

"No, Louise, but later he made amends and became one of King Arthur's most trusted knights. There are many adventures that Caradoc Freichfras undergoes—and even more in Queen Elizabeth Woodville's stories—but the most significant is when an evil magician used a snake to bind his arms."

"How did Caradoc get away?"

"The snake was tricked into releasing Caradoc Freichfras with a plan devised by his best friend and his love, Guinier."

"Thank you, Guinier!" Louise clapped.

"It was good, but it was bad too. Because of the lengthy binding, Caradoc Freichfras's arms became shorter." Queen Anne saw the child's brow furrow. "Don't worry, little bird," Queen Anne kissed Louise's forehead, "in the end of that story, all turns out well. Caradoc weds Guinier, and they drink from the sacred horn of marriage."

"Did Edward take that name because of the story?"

"Not entirely. He took that name because of a raven with an injured wing in the tower when he lived there. Even though the wing was fixed by the raven master, that wing was always shorter."

"What happened to Froggie? He secretly crossed the water too. Did his name have to change as well?"

"Yes, Froggie also changed his name. Richard became known as La Piérronne of Brittany, named after a great follower of Jehanne d'Arc. He eventually moved northward to the Vermandois where he built a home in a town on the Somme River."

"Which town was it?" The child cupped the queen's pendant crucifix in her hands, admiring it.

"I believe I can answer that one," Mickey's voice chimed in.

"Yes, Mickey, I believe you can," the queen answered. She nodded to the young knight, watching Ottaviano's face marvel as he listened along with her—the voices in her head clearly broaching his as well.

"It was the town of Péronne, France."

"Was it really, Mickey?" Louise asked.

Queen Anne snapped her gaze to the child. "You heard my imaginary friend Mickey?"

"Yes, Highness." Louise tousled her dress folds. "Not before, but now I do." She looked up at the queen who could not mask her shock and awe. "Was it really called Péronne?"

"Yes, Louise, it really was."

"Is there more of the story in this tapestry, Highness?"

Queen Anne cleared her throat. "Yes. Do you see that almost everyone is involved with the chase in one way or another?"

"What do you mean?"

"Well, child, some are involved in dog handling, others with horn blowing, some jabbing with weapons."

"But you said that *almost* everyone is involved. That means that some are not."

"Two are not," Ottaviano pointed.

"What are those two doing?" Louise bounced her curious gaze between the queen and the knight.

"They are just talking, Louise." Queen Anne smiled and leaned closer as if sharing a secret. "But I wonder, what do you suppose they are saying?"

"I don't know."

"Then let me tell you who they are and what they are saying."

"You know them, Majesty?"

"I do not. But I know what part they play."

"I'm listening."

"Very well. The two men are Lambert Simnel and Perkin Warbeck."

"Are they bad men?" Louise cringed close to the queen's neck, her hand on the crucifix.

"History will decide." Queen Anne stroked Louise's hair consolingly. "They were brought in to add further confusion and to distract the hunters away from the unicorn."

"Why were those two chosen?" Ottaviano twisted his lips.

"That, dear knight, is a very good question. They were chosen because they looked like our escaping princes."

"They look like princes ... but they aren't?"

"Lambert and Perkin are pretenders."

"Isn't that like lying?" Louise tugged at her dress's tight collar.

"Yes, it is. However, the lie they are living was intended to help the princes get away."

"So there can be good lies?"

"That, I can't say, child. The lies that help others are often seen differently than the lies told to help one's own self."

"I don't understand." Louise leaned her head on the queen's chest.

"There are many adults who don't understand either. The important thing is that many plans were put into place to help the princes of the tower escape."

"I can see that in this tapestry."

"Do you see anything else, little one?"

"I do not." Heavy-lidded, Louise yawned and smacked her lips.

"Rest child." The queen patted Louise on the back gently until she felt the girl heavy again with sleep. "Wait a moment my friends." All went silent at the queen's command. She waved Clare over and whispered into her ear. The serving woman left swiftly and returned several minutes later with the queen's book of hours. Once Clare had resumed her post, Queen Anne handed the book and diary to Ottaviano who placed it in his satchel with a solemn bow. "We may resume."

"Highness?" Jillian's voice queried.

"Yes, Jillian," Queen Anne answered, her voice calm so as not to stir Louise. Ottaviano's eyebrows were in danger of disappearing into his hairline, but he kept his mouth clamped shut, concluding that this was the "Jill" the child heard the queen address. He wondered to himself just how many voices there may be.

"I see something else that I don't understand. There are two initials up along the top."

"You are talking about the fancy moniker in the top center, yes, Jillian?"

"I am, Majesty. The *FR* with the knots ... what is that about?" Jillian fished around in her bag for the map and museum information. "My only resource here says it was probably added after the tapestry's completion as a reference to François de La Rochefoucauld? However one says *that* name. But what could that possibly have to do with the princes and the name change to Caradoc?"

"François?" a voice said. "Get outta that garden."

Jillian whipped her head to the side so fast her earpiece became dislodged. The sleeping elderly man beside her pushed up the brim of his hat and peered at her sideways from under its shadow.

"They're throwing shapes at ya."

"Pardon me?" Jillian asked, trying desperately to disentangle the earpiece from her long blonde curls. "What shapes? What garden?"

"Here's the story. *F* is fa Freichfras. Ya follow?" He gave a small jerk of his head in the direction of the tapestry. "*R* there is fa Rhiannon."

Jillian tugged the piece free and gave the old man a wry smile. "Sir, forgive me, but how could you know that? The museum doesn't even know for sure—"

"Museums can't know everythin', ya think?" He gave a gruff harrumph sound. "If they did, they'd be me." Chuckling, he pulled his hat back down over his eyes and was back asleep a moment later.

"Majesty, sorry for that interruption," Jillian whispered as she pressed the earpiece firmly back in.

"It was quite unsettling, Jillian. Are you all right?" Queen Anne's voice asked.

"Yes, I'm fine. My communication piece fell. Anyway, I think I might have the answer to my question. It's the strangest thing...." Jillian cast a wary, interested look at the seemingly placid man beside her.

"If you have the answer to this puzzle, then you will have to break your word as you said previously. You will have to call me by my first name."

"But, Majesty, it doesn't even make any sense to me. What if—"

"Call it another test if you wish. Honor me with your insight, Jillian."

Queen Anne's voice was kind, but Jillian could sense that it was clearly a royal command. Jillian hesitated.

"Take upon yourself the permission previously granted, Jillian."

Jillian gulped. "I will ... Rhiannon?"

"Thank you, Jillian."

"Excuse me. Sorry for breaking up this little party. But I have no idea what you all are talking about," Douglas fumed. "Here in my time, in the Vermandois, we don't have the luxury of seeing what you have at the palace hall and in the American museum. I don't see how we can possibly—"

"Yes, Douglas, we do," Clarisse interrupted, and hastily unwrapped the package she had been clutching in her hand. "I don't know why I didn't think of it sooner. I think I was so worried about little Annie." She thrust the postcards into Douglas's hands and Mickey moved closer to have a good look. "There is one for every tapestry in the series—like the ones framed on my wall."

"From your flower shop?"

"But yes, where else?"

"How do we know the order?"

"The knots tell us the first and last, remember? We know three, four, and five." Clarisse shuffled the cards in Douglas's hands for him. "The queen or Jillian will tell us the rest."

"They're awfully small. How are we supposed to see all the minuscule details?"

"They're *postcards*, Douglas," Clarisse scoffed. "They help the best that they can."

"I see that, but ... really—"

"Douglas," Jillian knifed in from the phone, clearing her throat like a schoolteacher, "don't you have something to say to Queen Anne?"

Douglas swallowed hard and pulled at the collar of his shirt. "Uh...." He looked guiltily at Mickey and Clarisse, each of whom cast a stern glance back. "Yes, I suppose I do." He cleared his throat. "My deepest apology for interrupting, Majesty. I ... I wasn't thinking. I am worried deeply for someone I care about, and I feel helpless. I had no bearings for the situation and the information. I got angry. That is, I momentarily lost my head. It was thoughtless."

"It does seem so, Douglas," said Loni kindly. "I understand to some extent. And as a regal first, I forgive you and return your head to you."

"Douglas," Ottaviano's voice growled. "I do not know you nor from where your voice hails amongst all these others, but you should be glad that we are separated by what I can only assume is time and distance." His voice felt close to Douglas, as though he could feel the knight's breath upon his neck. The unmistakable hissing scrape of a sword being slightly unsheathed grated against the air in the hospital room. "A mercenary for the Duke of Urbino has many ways to *encourage* proper manners."

"Excuse me?" Douglas choked out.

"There is *no* excuse for you, Douglas." Ottaviano's voice rose in pitch. "You offended Her Majesty in my presence. Personally, I do not care for, or accept, your apology to the queen."

"Sir knight ... I uh ... I have openly declared my error," Douglas stammered. "I can do little more than offer my sincere apology." At Mickey's *more* signal, Douglas added lamely, "However, your point is well taken. I am truly very sorry."

"Nevertheless," Ottaviano growled.

"What more can I do than apologize?"

"You tell me." The knight's voice surged around them.

"Okay ... um...."

In his mind, Douglas replayed the conversation that had been occurring before he interrupted, puzzling over this knight's fierce devotion to a queen not of his homeland. Then like cogs in a clock, something clicked together. A smile spread across his face. The others in the room stared at him curiously, but he ignored them.

Douglas began again in his calm, clinical voice. "Consider this, Sir Knight. To show good faith, I will give Queen Anne a gift of knowledge that she would have no other way to gain except by someone who has sight beyond her time and yours. Will that, in some way, move me toward forgiveness?"

"Perhaps. I will hold you to your word, Douglas." They heard the sword return to its sheath.

"The same for me," added Jillian's voice.

"Speak slowly. And weigh your words, strange voice."

Douglas spoke slowly and steadily. "Your Majesty—Queen Anne, Duchess of Brittany, queen of all of France—I offer you a glimpse into the future."

"Tread lightly, Douglas." Mickey gripped Douglas's shoulder and muttered, "Butterfly effect ... butterfly effect."

Douglas nodded his understanding and assured Mickey with a wave of his hand. "It is a gift that honors you even as you hear it, Majesty."

"I am listening, Douglas," Loni tilted her head.

"When the time comes for you to pass from this earthly world, your body will be taken by the people of France to be housed with your royal husband, the king of France."

"I find no comfort in this, Douglas." Loni's voice was flat and her face emotionless.

"Nor do I," Ottaviano's voice added. "Any charlatan can provide that information."

"I understand. May I continue, Majesty?"

"Yes, Douglas, please do."

"According to history, in the preparation of your body, the Carmelite Friars will remove your heart from your chest and take it to Nantes where it will be encased in a gold reliquary—a golden sarcophagus of sorts. Your heart will be first housed in the tomb with your parents, and then later within the Cathédrale Saint-Pierre." Douglas closed his eyes, pulling the image to the forefront of his mind. "On the outside of the reliquary will be etched the following words: 'Into this small vessel of pure gold is resting one of the greatest hearts any woman has ever had in this world. Her name was Queen Anne. She was twice Queen of France and Duchess of the Royal and Sovereign Bretons.'"

"Again, Douglas, I am pleased, but this does not bring me more knowledge than I already can presume."

"Please let me continue, Majesty." Douglas opened his eyes briefly, put his hand on top of Loni's, and closed his eyes again. "What few know is that on the *inside* of the reliquary will be inscribed the following: 'As Rigantona treasures Caradoc, so does the ermine endlessly admire the unicorn, even beyond death.'" Douglas opened his eyes slowly. Mickey and Clarisse stared at him in confusion, their mouths agape.

Mickey leaned close and whispered, "How could you possibly know—"

"Wait! Who is Rigantona? I said Rhiannon." Jillian's voice interrupted through the speakerphone.

Loni sniffed back Queen Anne's tears in the stunned silence of the hospital room.

"Hello? Who is Rigantona?" Jillian asked again.

"Rigantona is the Britannic name that preceded the name Rhiannon," Douglas answered slowly. He offered Mickey a shrugged response to his unfinished question.

"Yes, Jillian, it is so. I did not correct you earlier because, you see ... " Loni sniffed again and sat up tall—despite her pregnant belly—wiping her eyes with one hand. "I am Queen Anne to the French and English. However, to the Celts, Welsh, and Bretons, I am Rhiannon as you said. But to Caradoc Freichfras, I will always be his Rigantona."

"Highness," Douglas closed his eyes and continued, "the etching within the reliquary is a mere hairline within the gold itself. It is hardly discernable until something else is added."

"What would that be?"

"To bring these words to life, Your Majesty—that is, to be able to read them, the writing must be dusted with something fine and dark like—"

"—ashes." Ottaviano's voice rippled around them, completing the statement.

"Yes." Douglas's eyes opened in shock, but he managed to keep his voice placid. "How did you know?"

"I have seen other etchings made legible in such a manner with soot or the like," Ottaviano's voice answered. "It stands to reason also that the ashes used to show the secret inscription should come from the final remains of the beloved Caradoc Freichfras, does it not? He must be cremated so his identity can remain a secret. Thus, the ermine and the unicorn are separated in life, but united in death."

Loni turned her face to someone those in the hospital could not see, her face full of emotion, surging with sorrow-laden hope.

"Yes," Douglas confirmed. He released Loni's hand, leaned back in his chair, and rubbed his chin. *Huh, there is much more to this knight than I expected.*

"Who ensured that this action was carried out?" Queen Anne cleared her trembling voice.

"That I cannot say," Douglas replied. "History says only that it was a deeply devoted bishop."

"Our score is evened, Douglas. I accept your apology to my queen."

"Of the apology I agree. As to the score—I don't think so, Ottaviano." Douglas ran the back of his hand across the stubble on his cheek.

"You don't?" There was a threatening edge to the knight's voice again.

"*I* will be in your debt forever, Ottaviano."

"In my debt?" Ottaviano's voice echoed with confusion. "How so, Douglas?"

"Let us just say that you've taught me something that I have—in all my years and experiences—been lacking: a richer understanding of devoted commitment." *To love brings pain. To lose, disdain. But with rebirth—one's essence regained.*

"Thank you, Douglas," Loni whispered.

"You are welcome, Majesty. I am glad of the chance to assure you of my intent and secure your knight's forgiveness. Is there any more to learn in this tapestry?" Douglas moved the correlating postcard to the front of the stack.

"No. I believe that all that can be gleaned has been gleaned. The story now moves to the sixth tapestry for those who have eyes to see it and heart enough to endure the battle."

48

Flight and Fight

Maternity hospital

Saint-Quentin, Somme River Valley

Vermandois region, France

Current day

"Fight onward, sterling steed. God will honor your bravado."

"Who said that?" Loni asked, turning her head from side to side to locate the source.

"It wasn't me." Jillian's voice carried through the phone and into the hospital room.

"It was me," said Clarisse, lowering the postcard depicting a unicorn mired in a valiant fight for life. "I am sorry, Queen Anne. I saw the battle you spoke of, and my thoughts escaped me." In her hands, Clarisse rotated the postcard of the fighting unicorn sixth tapestry she had taken from Douglas as the slow, steady breath of the child sleeping on Queen Anne's lap in the Amboise Palace flowed around the room like calm waves.

"The sixth tapestry moves me passionately also," said Loni, nodding solemnly with her eyes fixed on a point a short distance in front of her. "Share with me your thoughts, Clarisse. What stirred you so?"

"He is out-weaponed and out-numbered, yet not out-classed. The unicorn fights in all directions knowing that he must hold onto his personal honor. He may have been discredited, but his heart is true. If he wins, he lives to fight another day. If he loses, his soul will be lifted to God."

"Worthy indeed," Ottaviano's voice joined in.

Clarisse traced a finger on the violent scene in her hand. "Was this the intent of the tapestry, Majesty?"

"In part, my dear. My betrothed, Edward, had just crossed the English Channel and arrived in Brittany according to the plan set forth by his mother, Elizabeth Woodville, and his uncle, Duke Richard." Loni sighed. "Upon

271

the disappearance of the princes from the tower, search parties everywhere combed the landscapes, delving into every English nook and cranny for clues. No substantial leads were found." Loni shifted her feet and legs slightly as though she were holding the sleeping little Louise.

"As soon as Prince Edward's feet touched the stones at Saint-Servan, it was known that even the strong Fort d'Alet, the Aleth Fortress, would not be a sufficient defense to keep at bay the hunter's hounds soon to come across the waters."

"Where did Edward decide to go?" Louise's sleepy voice curled around Loni accompanied with the sound of a yawn.

"That's a good question, child. And just in time too. I was afraid you would miss this part of the story." Loni smiled down into her empty arms. "Well, there was only one place strong enough, secure enough, and secluded enough to withstand the war of words which was soon to come. Edward had to go to a place where those who searched wouldn't find and those who hide remain invisible."

"The gulf coast of Morbihan, home of the dolmen," Clarisse whispered. She then closed her eyes and chanted, "Where dreams crash upon the rocks yet ease their way into slumbering heads."

At these words, Loni's face broke into a warm, genuine smile. "Spoken like a true Breton."

"Actually, I'm French Canadian, Highness," Clarisse bowed her head slightly.

"Maybe in where you hang your cloak, you are this … French Canadian … but your artistic heart and fiery soul are undoubtedly Breton."

"Thank you, Highness, I accept that honor willingly." Clarisse's heart swelled in her chest. "Please, Majesty, continue. There is so much we need to hear so that we may better comprehend and our time, as I see it," she glanced at the pronounced fetal kicks thumping within Loni's pregnant belly, "is growing short."

"Of course." Loni nodded, and then she held up a single finger indicating a requested pause. "Are you still with us, Jillian?"

"Yes, Majesty." Jillian's voice issued from the phone nearby.

"Good." Queen Anne cleared her throat.

"Jillian, that was the name," Louise's voice whispered.

"Quite right, child," Loni answered. "In the halls at the Aleth Fortress, among the elder Bretons of Saint-Servan, there were many discussions about the viability of the marriage between myself and the discredited Edward of Wales."

"Oh, they wouldn't separate you, would they, Majesty?" Jillian groaned.

"We both knew that the horn of marriage would only come to us if the Queen of Heaven, Mary the Mother of God, herself deemed it. We waited and listened as the wisest of the land discussed our lives in terms of politics, religion, and practicality."

"How horrible, Majesty."

"Indeed, Jillian. We shuddered at the fact that no one pleaded our case in terms of the affection that began at the bailey wall and grew in the hours and days which followed. During the day we held hands and walked along the walls and turrets. In the evenings we prayed our solitary prayer to the Queen of Heaven to lead the great minds debating our future in the direction of joining our hearts in marriage."

"Ah! I see this in the tapestry, Majesty," Jillian interjected. "The hunter carrying the horn and the scabbard. The scabbard says, 'Ave Regina C.' The other letters can't be seen on it. Apparently, scholars figured that the entire text would be," her voice paused as the crinkling of paper could be heard, "'Ave Regina Caelorum'—Hail, Queen of the Heavens. That fits in with what you are saying. But here's something I don't understand. The dog near the man with the scabbard—it has a collar that reads 'O-F-A-N-C-R-E.' What does that mean?"

"May I, Majesty?"

"Mickey, you have the answer?" Loni's eyebrows rose and a smile played at her lips.

"I have *an* answer, Majesty." Mickey cleared his throat. "May I?"

"Proceed."

"Jillian, there are two historical references that I know. One is the Ancre River which intersects the Somme River to the west of Péronne. Which could be important here because of what we know of the former Richard of Shrewsbury. The other use refers to the writing of a will."

"Your Highness, is it the river or the will?" Jillian queried.

"Both and more."

"How can they be both?"

"Jillian, aren't they one in the same?"

"I don't think so...."

"Isn't a river a living testament to the passage of time? What makes it so much different than a will?"

"Yes, but why the Ancre River?" Mickey frowned as he underlined the name in his notebook.

"Why not the Ancre?"

"Why not the Somme?" Mickey countered.

"Have you been to the Ancre River?"

"I have not," Louise's voice chirped, "but now I hope to someday!"

"You will love it." Loni smiled indulgently at the child only her eyes could see. She then redirected her gaze. "Well, Mickey?"

"Yes, well, Mickey?" Louise giggled.

"I have been nearby."

"Nearby? Hmmm. Well, when you go and return, perhaps then you can tell us why."

"Majesty, you said 'more.'" Jillian's confusion rang clear. "In what way more?"

"The 'more' part is not ready to be discussed. Let us wait for another tapestry to see that fleshed out."

"Why does the unicorn have no ears?" Louise's voice asked with great concern.

"The unicorn has no ears?" Jillian blurted. "How did I never—"

"That is strange! Well noted, child," Ottaviano's voice resounded in the room.

"I agree, Sir Knight. Excellent, my sharp-eyed wonder!" Loni laughed for Queen Anne. "As always, *pupuce*, it is because the queen wished it that way."

"Why, Highness?" Clarisse asked, holding the postcard close to her face.

"It's part of the tapestry's story." Queen Anne raised her voice a notch. "It is an artistic demonstration of something that was said at the meeting held at the fortress. In that meeting, counselors all around Edward were advising him to move in one political direction or another. They used platforms such as 'for the sake of your people' or 'in the best interest of your family.' Finally, Edward had his fill of the opinions brought before him. He climbed up on his chair, stood up on the table, and then shouted at the elders."

"No!" Louise's sharp intake of breath whisked around the hospital room and all the occupants understood her fear and wonder at the audacity of such an action.

"Yes, Louise, he did!" Loni nodded. "I will never forget it. He said, 'I'll understand better when I have no ears to hear such wisdom. At present, I trust only the beating of my heart as it echoes off the dolmen and menhirs. Worry not, I'll know what to do and when to do it, when I know it. Believe me when I tell you, I will arrive at it without ears. Speak what you may. For the wisest counsel, I go among the three thousand that Merlin silenced. I'm taking my betrothed. We'll go to the Gulf of Morbihan.'" Loni's face flushed.

"I am guessing that the reference to Merlin," Douglas spoke, "would be to Merlin the Magician."

"Yes, Douglas. Merlin the Magician had great legacy everywhere among the Welsh, Celts, and Bretons. His home and final burial site is in Brittany."

"Who are the three thousand?" Douglas mused aloud.

"That refers to a great Roman army turned to stone by the magic staff of the great magician. They stand as dolmen in the city of Carnac in the region known as Morbihan."

"Wait, back up. Did you say that the Merlin we know from King Arthur's legend is Breton?"

"Yes, of course, Douglas. Does history not see it that way in the future?"

"Actually, in general, Merlin seems to be more related to the English."

"Interesting. That may partially be my fault. It was I who brought yet another English royalty to an association with the magician."

"How could a child duchess do that?"

"The route to be taken to the dolmen passed through the Forest of Broceliande, the very forest of Merlin. It is also called Paimpont Forest. I have it symbolized in the tapestry."

"Really? I don't see it," Jillian said. "It looks similar to the other forests in the tapestries."

"I think the Jillian voice is right, Majesty," Louise's voice chimed.

"The forest does seem the same." Clarisse held the postcard under a lamplight. "However, Majesty, I do see something in the forest that is quite out of place."

"Yes!" Jillian shouted, then immediately whispered, "Ooops!" Her voice continued muffled as though speaking from behind her hand, "There *is* something amiss. Evil is attempting to harm the unicorn at every angle except for one."

"The male figure in the upper-left quadrant of the tapestry, Jillian?"

"Yes, he is clearly not one of the many evildoers. He is an elderly man with a staff, not a weapon, on a journey through the forest. He carries what looks like a canteen. A woodsman with an axe seems to be pointing the direction for this old man to travel."

"Yes," Queen Anne praised, "you all have it."

"That is Merlin?" asked Louise skeptically. "The great magician?"

"Not exactly, child. I asked that Merlin be symbolized with his staff which is not a weapon, but an instrument of greater power. Just like Aaron and Moses with their rod and staff, Merlin's staff can affect the thinking of kings. And so, our journey overlapped with the life and times of Merlin as we approached the dolmen." Loni moved her hands in the air, drawing two overlapping circles.

"Then Edward did not delay long in Brittany. At Saint-Servan, was it, Majesty?"

"Correct, Douglas, he did not. There was an incident that led to an immediate departure."

"I smell death." Douglas grimaced.

"Yes, in the tapestry there remains one last documentary. Look at the dog speared by the unicorn's horn."

"I don't like that part." Louise's voice registered fear and disgust. "I don't like that the dogs want to hurt the unicorn, but I don't want the dogs to get hurt either."

Queen Anne sighed deeply. "I understand, little one. But such things happen. The night of our departure was a night filled with great wind and the channel surf pounded the walls of the Aleth Fortress. The spray from the impact reached high into the air—as tall as the tallest of the castle turrets. From the darkness stole a Breton hunter whose heart was blackened with malice. He pounced on Edward and Richard with the intent of murder. As he stabbed Richard, Edward stabbed him."

"Was Froggie all right?" Louise squeaked.

"Yes, child. Froggie survived. But Edward willed it then and there that his brother Richard, now La Piérronne, would flee to safety in the north to where the Ancre and the Somme Rivers meet. Richard left immediately. We were all very sad that the moment had come for us to be separated."

"It was time for Edward, as Caradoc Freichfras, to go southward to the Gulf of Morbihan," Clarisse added solemnly. Loni nodded in response.

"Did the brothers ever meet again?"

"Jillian, as queen there are many things I know. However, this I do not." Queen Anne sniffed. "At that time, I knew heading south with Caradoc was the only thing on my mind. It seemed forever before our traveling party arrived at our destination within the shadow of the dolmen."

49

The Richest That There Can Be

Maternity hospital
Saint-Quentin, Somme River Valley
Vermandois region, France
Current day

"I'm here, honey. I'm right here." Mickey swiftly crossed the room in a few strides and knelt, taking his precious Loni's hand in his unbandaged one. "What happened? Is she okay, Douglas?"

"I don't know, one second she was attending to things on her end in 1500—you know, for the seventh tapestry—and then the next second she just started crying inconsolably."

"Did she give any clue as to why?"

"She muttered something about La Piérronne being attacked." Douglas scratched his scalp.

"To Loni I'm not La Piérronne; my dad is. For Queen Anne, Edward's brother, Richard of Shrewsbury, is."

"Fine, okay. But, Mickey, since you came closer, she's calmed down." Douglas pointed at Loni's less frantic breathing. "I can't explain it. She may sense more about your presence than any of us realize." Douglas gave a half-smile and reached out to pat Mickey on the back but then changed his mind and executed an awkward redirect into a stretch.

"I like the notion that I provide comfort to Loni, Douglas ... even if she doesn't know it's me." Mickey bounced his gaze from Loni to Douglas and then back. "Continue doing what you do best. I'll just hold her hand a while."

"Good idea." Douglas pulled a chair closer so Mickey could sit. After a nod from Mickey, Douglas touched Loni's arm and asked, "What do you see now Loni?"

"I see my small hands and another pair of hands holding onto the handrail of a ship."

Everyone in the hospital room shared the same look of confusion and shock. *We're not in 1500 anymore*, Mickey thought. He gave another nod, and Douglas took the reins.

"Where are you going, Annie?" Douglas winced as he added the name, hoping that Loni's consciousness hadn't strayed further than he could follow.

"Someone said Paramé on the north shore of Brittany." Loni's head cocked to the side and her face scrunched. "No, wait. That is where we left from."

Douglas sighed with relief. "Is that all you see?"

"No, I see the lights of numerous campfires to the seaward side of the boat."

From prior studies of the construct known as OFANCRE and its relation to Templar sites in Saint-Malo/Mont-Saint-Michel region, Mickey easily recalled the local geography. He spoke quickly and with quiet confidence to the others in the room. "Those would be the sentry posts of the forward watchmen housed on the two islands of Grand Be and Petit Be. She would see them flickering in the seaward blackness."

"What a lonely job," exhaled Clarisse.

"Maybe, but maybe not." Mickey added, "These night watchmen are nonpareil. They walk to work from shoreside at low tide when the islands are literally connected to the land. Then as the tide rises, both Grand Be and Petit Be become islands. Once at work, these watchmen are locked in place until the sea recedes, and then they walk home."

"Wouldn't that make them feel stranded and all alone even if just for a while?"

"Perhaps," Mickey shrugged, "if they critically needed something or someone from home. I see your point, Clarisse."

"Annie, what do you see on the landward side of the ship?" Douglas redirected.

"I'm on the portside of the ship with Edward and most of the ship's crew. We are watching the glowing windows of the fortress of Aleth. Its stony towers rise high above the crashing shores." Loni's eyes squinted as if peering through thick darkness. "Though it is warm in there," Loni pointed with her chin, "I am glad to be out here. Glad to be on our way at last."

"Even before Romans had arrived," Mickey whispered, "Aleth Fortress guarded the mouth of the Rance River. In those times, Saint-Servan was the host city."

"I meant to ask before when it came up, but I don't remember a Breton city named Saint-Servan," Douglas replied.

"You wouldn't find it as a solitary city on any maps today, per se. Saint-Servan merged together with Paramé to become Saint-Malo, France."

"I love Saint-Malo," said Clarisse, nodding with closed eyes. She recalled the stories handed down from the lineage of Clares about the crashing waters against Saint-Malo's rock walls, spewing higher than the tallest houses.

"I see a tall tower now," Loni interrupted and gestured with her free hand.

"It is unique in shape. It looks like a tower formed by squishing three tall cylinders together."

"It's on the portside?" Mickey queried.

"Yes, it stands lonely on the shoreline."

"That's Tour Solidor. It is where the night watchmen of the islands would be briefed their nightly orders before the tides came in. That was one meeting that never ran late."

"Mickey, once they are clear of Saint-Malo," Douglas drew in his palm, "will the rest of the trip be a boat ride down the river to the dolmen?"

"No, they would only go a short distance by water. Most of the travel to Morbihan would be done by coach."

Douglas nodded. "What do you see now, Annie?"

"It's still dark, but I can smell the dawn. We are docking at Dinan." Loni giggled for Annie, and her eyes cast left and right mischievously.

"Annie … what are you up to?"

Loni's breath puffed for a few moments, and then she put her head down and laughed. "Edward and I ran to the bridge! He's so fast!"

"What can you see from there, Annie?" Mickey asked.

"I see my mother and sister, Edward's mother, and a dozen of the royal party members disembarking from the ship. They are coming toward us, climbing uphill into this town of sleepy people." Loni rubbed her eyes. "The light before the sun is dancing on the water." She sighed happily.

"Why aren't they with the others?" Douglas hissed to Mickey.

"They're kids, Douglas." Clarisse laughed. "They probably disembarked first and then ran up to the bridge because it looked like a fun thing to do."

"Wasn't there just an assassination attempt at the fortress? Now they are rushing off to a strange bridge in a strange town in the dark."

Clarisse rubbed Douglas's back with one hand. "What part of *they're kids* was not clear, Douglas? The things that worry adults often do not linger in the minds of children."

"But," Douglas dropped his voice so only she could hear, "when Annie was in the raven master's tower…."

"I know." Clarisse stopped rubbing his back and stared at her shoes. "As I said, a child's mind does not worry about such things." Douglas reached up and squeezed Clarisse's hand.

"I smell fresh bread baking," Loni sniffed the air, tracking the scent.

"It sounds pleasant, Annie." Clarisse blinked and looked up, grateful for the diversion. "It must be beautiful."

"We're going under a Roman viaduct to get to another part of the town."

"Let us know what you see when you get there, Annie," said Clarisse. She then whispered to Douglas, "If only we could be that young and full of frolic."

"We're at the foot of the city tower, Clarisse," said Annie. "In the morning light I can see there are four horse-drawn coaches parked nearby." Loni's eyes scanned the view before Annie. "Coach doors are being opened." Loni's gaze narrowed; her face pinched in focus.

"What are you looking for, Annie?"

Loni leaned forward, squinting. "Mr. Red Squirrel?" she whispered. Suddenly, Loni's face went slack, and her eyes slid out of focus.

"Red Squirrel!" Annie squealed as she dashed ahead of the group and into the arms of her favorite driver. "I knew it was you the moment I saw that red beard."

"Hello, my future duchess, I am surprised that you see my beard in the dim morning light." With a ruddy hand, Mr. Red Squirrel tipped his hat.

"Dear, dear, dear, Mr. Red Squirrel!" The child duchess gathered her skirts, righting the layers that had gone askew in her run. "I didn't know you were going to be here to meet us. Now our trip will be rich, rich, rich, and the richest that there can be!"

"Where else would your favorite coachman be excepting at the beck and call of his favorite future duchess?"

"Anne," Duchess Margaret of Foix motioned, "come here."

"Yes, Mother?"

"How are you going to be a duchess when you are running up bridges and bowling over coachmen?" Duchess Margaret tapped her daughter's nose and gave a small smile. "I am glad to see you here, Red Squirrel. Is everyone aware of the route as I requested?"

"Yes, m'lady. I have engaged the full tenets of OFANCRE. I have informed every coachman and every assistant so that there will be no mistakes."

"Very well," Margaret nodded. "There is much more that I can't tell you now. I will need your ear alone."

"Yes, m'lady." Red Squirrel nodded and then squatted down to look Annie in the face. "Little duchess." He scratched his beard. "If you will forgive your most devoted servant, Mr. Red Squirrel has to receive the duchess's guidance now." He ended his sentence with a playful frown and a wink.

Annie caught his sleeve as he made to rise. "Can I ride in your coach, Mr. Red Squirrel?" she pleaded.

"That, little duchess, is up to your mother. She determines what serves best for the trip from this point onward." Winking again at Annie, his voice changed to an intentionally loud whisper. "Not to worry, little duchess, I'll put in a good word for you, I will."

50

Of Squires, Squirrels, and Squirms

Château de Dinan
Dinan, France
1483

"With all the lumps and bumps on the road, m'lady, how do you suppose children will stay asleep in the coach?" Mr. Red Squirrel combed his scarred, stubby fingers through his red beard.

"You are not a mother, I take it, my sturdy driver."

"No, Duchess. I am but a humble coach driver."

"Come now, Mr. Red Squirrel, you are much more than that. I can't thank you enough for being here for us."

"Where else should a red squirrel be?"

"Gladly not in a tree," laughed the weary Duchess Margaret. Red Squirrel tipped his hat and climbed up into the driver's bench as the duchess entered the coach and drew the curtains. Pulling away from under the shadow of Dinan's city tower, the four horse-drawn coaches began the trek across the width of the Breton peninsula. Three hours later, they stopped near the edge of a dark forest.

As the carriage slowed to a stop, Red Squirrel heard the latch from the compartment door click. Looking down and over the side of the coach, he spoke in a gruff whisper, "Duchess, please remain inside until I give the word that all is secure."

He heard the door's latch re-engage as his eyes roved over the caravan of carriages and the woods edging one side of the road. Red Squirrel watched each driver as they disembarked and walked in his direction. Once the guard on each coach had shifted into the driver's position and gave the signal, Red Squirrel himself climbed down, and his guard took the reins. The drivers and Red Squirrel huddled together speaking in quick, clipped whispers. After a few moments, Red Squirrel gave final orders, pointed ahead down the road, and then dismissed the drivers. He returned to his own carriage and quietly tapped on the door.

"All clear, Duchess."

The duchess yawned as she slipped out of the coach and closed the door softly behind her. She sheltered her face from the bright daylight.

"How are the children, Duchess?"

"They are fast asleep, Red Squirrel." She blinked to adjust her eyes. "Where are we?"

"We are at Paimpont Forest, m'lady. The town there on the far horizon is Ploërmel."

"Is this a scheduled stop?" The duchess's eyes darted up and down the caravan. "Why have we paused?"

"The horses are lathered. They need a rest, Duchess." Red Squirrel took off his gloves and tossed them to his seat. "The coach drivers need to stop and stretch their legs, and a change of guard is in order. It's been fifty miles since any foot touched the ground. We all must stay alert." Red Squirrel stretched then surveyed the coach through a crack in the curtain. "They look like little angels, sleeping there."

The duchess nodded and smiled. She stepped toward the edge of the road, surveying the other coaches in the party. "How is the English queen in her coach?"

"According to the driver's report, the queen is sound asleep, m'lady. She's holding her little girl in her arms as they rest." Red Squirrel shook his head. "Exhausted as mothers get, they manage to keep their children safe and secure."

The duchess nodded. "Come, let us walk." Margaret took the coachman's steady arm—her courtly shoes were no match for the rutted road. Together they proceeded along the dirt road for some time before she broached the easy silence between them. "Forever and a day, Red Squirrel, I have longed to ask you one single question. Either opportunity or motive were not aligned. However, it seems as if now in the oddest of time and places, I have both the motive and opportunity to do so."

"What would that be, m'lady?"

"Your name. One day, I heard someone mention the name Red Squirrel. I had no idea why it was applied to you. Why is it that you go by this name?" The duchess then lowered her voice and leaned closer. "Can you answer or is it tied in with OFANCRE?"

"Actually, that name was given to me by the little duchess."

"Little Annie?" Duchess Margaret frowned.

"Yes, m'lady." Red Squirrel laughed. "I was telling Annie how I was a squire to the Red Knight. Inasmuch, people referred to me as the Red Squire. The child duchess transposed the words squire and squirrel, and it has stuck with me ever since."

"But you were called Red long before Annie was born, if I recall."

"Indeed, Duchess." Red Squirrel tugged on his beard and twisted his lips to the side. "Some people have called me Red for the redness of my hair or my ruddy complexion. It was only by chance that the knight I served dressed in red. Like it or not, ultimately I became known as the Red Squire." The driver gave a throaty chuckle.

"Correction, my dear coach driver, ultimately you became known as the Red Squirrel." They both laughed. "Your animal name suits you."

"Is the duchess saying I look like a squirrel?" The driver paused and gave a look of pretend shock.

"No, the duchess is saying you bring warmth to any conversation just as a squirrel does when he joins the company at a feast table." The duchess smiled. "A squirrel is always received as a good friend and companion."

"The duchess is much too kind." He continued to lead the duchess along the path, avoiding the large potholes.

"What is your given name, Mr. Red Squirrel?"

"Ah, m'lady. The ruse is over. You have learned that my first name is not 'Red' nor my last name 'Squirrel.'"

"Indeed." She then added in a jokingly commanding tone, "Out with it, man."

"It's … " The driver averted his gaze to the forest's edge. "That is to say…." He raked his top teeth over his bottom lip, causing the bristly red hair of his chin to flare up. "Is the duchess really asking the question?"

"Why do you hesitate?"

"Hesitate?"

"Yes."

"An interesting word choice, Duchess."

"Well, you paused. Why? You have nothing to fear."

"Can we leave it at Red Squirrel, Duchess?"

"I've upset you." The duchess studied the man's face, deciding how far to push. "Red Squirrel, you don't have to tell me if you don't want to." They continued their walk.

"Thank you, I appreciate that," the driver nodded. But a few paces later he paused and took a deep breath. "Duchess, I feel I *must* tell you. I am Alain de Keranrais."

"Is that name supposed to mean something to me?"

"You don't know it, m'lady?"

"No."

Red Squirrel sighed in relief.

"My dear Alain de Keranrais, it is a pleasure to know you by your name. I fear though that I am still compelled to call you Mr. Red Squirrel. That name seems to roll off my tongue just as sweetly."

"The choice is yours, m'lady."

"So it is." The duchess cocked her head and looked over the driver's countenance. "Mr. Red … Alain Squirrel … Squire Red…."

"Mr. Red Squirrel will do, ma'am. You have called me that for years. That will certainly be easier for both of us."

"Agreed. Mr. Red Squirrel it is." The pair resumed their walk. The duchess's eyes were drawn to the edge of the dark forest whose foliage was so dense that any stream of light which managed to battle its way to the ground was met with great vegetative competition. The tree branches seemed to sway though there was hardly any wind. "Mr. Red Squirrel, the forest here reminds me of your earlier comment regarding the bumpiness of the travels and the ability of the children to sleep. Why did this puzzle you so? Even as the trees swing their branches and your coach rocks its passenger in travels, does not your wife bob and sway your children gently in her arms?"

"I have no wife, my duchess."

"Oh, please forgive my presumption. I didn't know you were not married." The duchess's neck flushed.

"No need for apology or embarrassment, m'lady. My life is spent on the road traveling from point to point across Brittany." He waved his broad hand about to include all the landscape before them. "Any wife I might have would easily fall into the arms of another if for no other reason than sheer neglect."

"Red Squirrel," Duchess Margaret's embarrassment crept to her cheeks, "how could I have known you for so many years and not known this fact?"

"We rarely know such things unless we take the time to ask, Duchess." Red Squirrel laughed. "Come now. You're a busy duchess. You handle problems I couldn't dream of solving. The personal life of a ruddy-faced coachman should be the least of your concerns."

"I see your point, but I still think it inexcusable on my part. Well, then, tell me now. Didn't your mother rock you gently when you were small?"

"Duchess, I...."

"Come, Mr. Red Squirrel. Have you no mother as well?" She smiled in her jest, but the smile melted to concern as she looked to the coachman's face.

"I have a mother, my duchess." Mr. Red Squirrel turned crimson. "She was one fine lady, but—"

"Of course you have a mother," the duchess interrupted, hoping to spare her driver any more discomfort. "I am sorry if I made sport at your expense. I meant no harm, my dear Mr. Red Squirrel." She patted his arm consolingly.

"I took no offense, m'lady."

"My point was but a simple one, Mr. Red Squirrel. The supports of a coach are like the arms of a mother—albeit a bit more intense. A sleepy child could appreciate the rocking of a coach much more easily than you and I could as adults. As for me, I am most glad that these blessed children have rested in the arms of your coach. This has been a trying time for them."

"Yes, m'lady. I will do my best to avoid the worst of the potholes and rocks as we continue our journey south toward the dolmen."

"I know that you will." The duchess gave a warm smile. Her eyes were drawn back to the wild woods crouching along the side of the road. "How long will we tarry here in the forest before we go on into town?"

"Not long, m'lady." Red Squirrel read the concern in the face of the duchess. "I know there are many who fear this forest, but I have never in all my life done so."

"The man who hesitates to give his name fears not the enchanted woodlands of Paimpont Forest? The very home of Merlin?" the duchess laughed. "I find that interesting."

"Yes, m'lady." Red Squirrel nodded. "I fear this forest not. As I boy I walked all the hills and woodland of this part of Brittany. Merlin has never frightened me as he might another. I have even been to his tomb which lies not far from this very spot. Maybe at another time I will take you and the children to the tree which wrapped its trunk around Merlin imprisoning him for many a year."

"Hearing this brings gooseflesh to my skin," she shivered. "Yet you seem unmoved, Red Squirrel."

"Yes, m'lady."

"Why so?"

"For God and Saint Hubert are with me." The coachman crossed himself.

"But Mr. Red Squirrel, Saint Hubert is the patron saint of hunters, not coachmen."

"I have not always driven coaches, m'lady." Red Squirrel gave a coy smile before continuing. "As a younger man I spent all my days in this forest. Honestly, m'lady, I feel more at home among the bushes and trees than I ever did behind stone and mortar." Mr. Red Squirrel released the duchess's arm and stooped to pick up a fallen branch. "There is little to fear when sleeping with the forest animals. They have no intent to willfully injure. They harbor no malice."

The duchess stood still, her hands resting on the waistline of her travel dress. "Did you find that you were closer to God in the forest?"

"I confess, m'lady. I was not the Christian I am now when I first visited the woods. That changed on the day I saw the stag of Saint Eustace and Saint Hubert."

"You actually saw the blessed stag with a cross that rested between its antlers?"

"Yes and no, m'lady. What I saw was a stag whose antler branched in such a manner that, when I caught sight of it, I saw the shape of our blessed Lord as he would be standing with his arms extended to his right and left."

"Amazing."

"Fortunately for me, the stag remained still for many minutes and so I had time to carefully study the image in the branches of his horns. Then the stag moved ever so slightly, the branching pattern shifted, and the image was gone."

"So, in a moment of hesitation, what you saw was no more than an unusual branching of deer antlers. Nothing more."

"Yes, m'lady. Though it was not there, I saw the image of our blessed Lord. And I felt His presence in my heart." Red Squirrel walked to the edge of the road; his eyes panned the expanse of the forest. "I didn't ask to see the image. I had no idea the deer was out there. Yet I looked. I saw. And I received great comfort seeing the image of our Lord who was, and wasn't, there. Does it matter if it was a trick of the light and twisted antlers?"

The duchess shrugged. "Perhaps it was an image generated by the spirit of Merlin?"

"Do you really think Merlin generated the vision or the thoughts which followed, m'lady?" He returned to the middle of the road.

"What I think is not important. What do you think?"

"Hmmm. I say no." Red Squirrel scratched his beard. "This was no instance of Merlin's magic." He took a step back and began snapping off the spindly branches from the main portion of the branch he had collected. In a few moments, he had fashioned the branch into a long stick. "Merlin was a man. He could take a branch and make a staff like this." Red Squirrel held the stick out for inspection. "The power in his magic staff conjured images to best further the causes of his people." Red Squirrel drove one end of the stick into the hard-packed dirt of the road and leaned on the stick. "The image I saw with the deer was of a man whose sole purpose on earth was to help us achieve a better life for ourselves while working to gain oneness with Him, the blessed saints, and our heavenly Father."

"Spoken as a true Christian. What makes you believe God and his saints protect Breton people here on the edge of a forest filled with supposed magic and sorcery?"

"The Combat of the Thirty."

"Were you there, Mr. Red Squirrel?"

"I was indeed … but only in spirit. The combat took place many generations ago."

"This, I feel, I must hear. But my shoes are not fit for this promenade." The duchess held out her hand and nodded in the direction of a tree trunk along the side of the road.

"As you wish, Duchess." Red Squirrel removed the stick from the road and assisted the duchess to her seat. "I was named after the Alain who participated in that battle."

"Tell me the tale as you best remember it." The Duchess arranged the pleats of her dress and sat with perfect posture as though sitting in a great hall awaiting the performance of a ballad.

"Is the duchess sure about this?" Red Squirrel pushed his hat back on his head and leaned against the stick again.

"Do we have time?

He cast a glance up and down the road. "Yes, m'lady. The horses need to rest a bit longer."

"Then I'm sure."

"There is good and bad in the tale."

"There always is in every story." The duchess then gave a small laugh. "Just look at mine." She held her arms wide to include the coaches and their precious cargo.

Red Squirrel nodded wisely. "It was the end of March in the year 1350. There was great strife here in Brittany—Breton against Breton on opposite sides. The Bretons in my family were supported by the king of France. We fought against the Bretons supported by the English crown. In this Combat of the Thirty, the entire conflict was to be resolved. A combat of champions as it were. They fought halfway between the two sister castles of Josselin and Ploërmel near this very forest."

"Ploërmel, the town on the far horizon?"

"Yes, m'lady. Josselin is a bit farther on and can't be seen from here."

"Your kinsman, Mr. Red Squirrel, fought with the French."

"Yes, Duchess, our thirty faced their thirty. The men fought with arrows, spears, swords, daggers, and at the very end, with bare hands."

"Fights between knights can be vicious."

"Certainly. Dressed in heavy armor, both sides grew weary and thirsty, having only their own blood to drink. In the end, our champion—a squire, no less—mounted a horse and bested seven of their knights, seizing victory."

"Did your namesake survive the battle?"

"Yes, sadly so." Red Squirrel looked down at the road and scraped at the dirt with the long stick.

"Sadly?"

"Moments ago you asked my given name."

"Yes, you hesitated."

"I am always hesitant to give my real name."

"Why so?"

Mr. Red Squirrel looked up from the gouge he was making in the earth. "Hesitation seems to be in our lineage. On the field of battle, our family squire Alain was already mounted on his fallen knight's horse and poised to take victory. But he hesitated to face seven knights in battle."

"Hesitation in that instance doesn't reflect cowardice, Red Squirrel."

"You are correct—he was no coward." Red Squirrel held the stick out like a sword. "He just took an extra moment to think rather than act, and ... " Red Squirrel snapped the branch over his knee, "in his moment of hesitation, another squire—Guillaume de Montauban—swung himself on a knight's horse, galloped maniacally, and crashed into the seven unmounted knights leaving them in a pile of twisted metal." One at a time, Red Squirrel threw the broken branch pieces into the forest. "It's not what Alain did. It's what he didn't do. Thus, in my life, I think about this every time I come to any crossroad and hesitate."

"What happened after the battle?"

"Alain was captured but released under the respected auspices of chivalry."

"There were many heroes on both sides that day."

"Yes, m'lady. God favored the French Bretons that day. Inasmuch, I give the glory to Him."

"As should we all." The duchess gathered up her dress and stood. "If the horses have had sufficient rest, may we now go into town?" She smiled wearily. "I need personal supplies for myself and the children."

Red Squirrel took the duchess's arm, peered farther down the road for a moment, and then began to lead the way back to her carriage. "We are waiting for the return of a driver sent out to scout the safety of the city."

"Do nearby cities have problems of such a nature that scouts must be dispatched?"

"As you know, Duchess, now is the time just before Lent. It is Shrovetide. As people prepare for the sacred time of penitence and fasting, they often indulge in raucous and—"

"Say no more, Mr. Red Squirrel," Duchess Margaret interrupted, holding up her free hand. "I am quite aware of these festivities. There are times when it is necessary to proceed with caution. This is certainly one."

"Duchess, if the situation dictates, we will dispatch my deputy on another horse for the sole purpose of getting supplies as we bypass the city. Pierre is both resourceful and responsible."

"Pierre? That name sounds familiar. Do I know him?"

"I'm not sure. He is Pierre d'Aubusson from the Limousin region. He is quite trustworthy, as I said. He is of the Knights Hospitaller."

"No, I don't think I know him. However, Red Squirrel, if you trust him, then so must I."

"Thank you, Duchess."

"How much longer do you anticipate the wait, Mr. Red Squirrel?" The duchess paused with her hand on the coach door's handle.

"Not much longer, Duchess. I hear the horse's footfalls now."

"Then now is not the time to hesitate." The duchess smiled.

"And with the tenets of OFANCRE at stake, hesitate we won't."

51

Of Anchors and Offenses

Paimpont Forest

Ploërmel, France

1483

"It's not safe, Duchess." Red Squirrel shook his head as he returned from speaking to the scout.

"There are supplies that I require, Mr. Red Squirrel."

"Sorry, Duchess." Mr. Red Squirrel held the coach door open. "The celebrations in the town seem to have resulted in some unexpected violence." Red Squirrel helped the duchess into the coach.

"What of my supplies? You said you could send a rider to fetch them."

"Sorry, Duchess. It is not safe for any of us. You will have to wait until we arrive in Vannes." Red Squirrel closed and latched the door.

The duchess poked her head out the window. "How far is that?"

"Three hours, m'lady." Red Squirrel signaled the coaches in front and back. "Longer, if we don't get moving."

"Who works for whom, Red Squirrel?" the duchess groused.

"I'm just thinking of everyone's safety." Red Squirrel paused in his climb to the coach seat. "You would expect no less from your head coachman."

The time spent on the edge of the forest at Ploërmel was brief. But even as the coaches passed by the towns along the route, drunken voices and shouts could be heard though it was only midday. Within a few hours, the royal entourage had arrived at the port city of Vannes, the home city of the court of Brittany.

"Annie, wake up darling." The duchess rousted her firstborn. "We're home."

"We're in Vannes, Mother?"

289

"Yes, look. There is the royal residence."

"I love Le Château de l'Hermine."

"Yes, *pupuce*. Everyone does. Now, go in quickly and change out of your traveling clothes. Pick out another set and hurry back."

"We're not staying here?"

"No, Annie." The duchess lifted the child from the coach. "The hunt for the unicorn will certainly come here. We are just stopping briefly, picking up supplies, and heading onward."

"All right, Mother." Annie gathered her skirts and entered the palace.

Annie made her way through the corridors where the polished floors bounced light around the hallways. She looked at the portraits of the many family members who began their lives at the palace. For many of the girls in the paintings, later marriages to distant nobility had carried them to the four corners of Europe. A short time later, Annie returned to the coaches at the driveway, followed by servants carrying her things.

"I thought we were traveling on?" Annie asked her mother.

"You are, *pupuce*."

"Where are the other coaches? Why does only Edward's coach have horses?"

"Annie." The duchess wiped at her tear-stained face. "Please put your things into the carriage. Please dear. Hurry."

Duchess Margaret turned to conference with Queen Elizabeth Woodville and Red Squirrel while Annie climbed into the coach.

"Edward, are you still asleep?" Annie watched as the young prince rolled over in the seat. "There's something strange going on. Don't you want to know?" Edward rubbed his nose and turned his face into the seat. "Listen, Edward, they're talking about the trip ahead." Annie leaned toward the carriage window trying to hear the whispering adults.

"Maybe I should come along." Duchess Margaret shuffled her feet beneath her skirts.

"No, Duchess." Red Squirrel shook his head. "We made this plan at a time when our hearts were not ruling our heads. We need to accept the wisdom of those decisions."

"Yes, but Annie is just a baby."

"She's a little duchess now. She'll be fine." Red Squirrel tugged at his beard and twisted his lips. "Anyway, this is where the trip becomes most perilous."

"You will be extra cautious?" Duchess Margaret's face was drawn with anxiety.

"Yes, m'lady, of course." Red Squirrel pulled his bottom lip into his mouth, bristling his beard as he weighed his next words. "But you know, m'lady, the road has many eyes. Not all of which are friendly."

"It is not the wicked eyes that worry me most. They are easily seen and avoided." She dropped her voice even lower. "It is the few faux friends with blackened hearts that I fear most—those who would sell out our children for any perceived advantage."

"I know the type, m'lady."

"Do you know the safest route to the dolmen?"

"Yes, m'lady. Be assured, our plan is well laid. I have men of honor stationed along the way and they will come to our aid if need be. As you have asked, I shall go to the Dolmen de—"

"Silence! Say not the name here and now. We can't take a chance that someone overhears." The duchess hardened her gaze at the driver. "These men along the way, do they know the end point of this journey?"

"As per the duchess's instructions, I have told none of them the destination. Their loyalty will be tested only in the part of the path for which they have responsibility."

"Do they know the precious cargo that you carry?" The duchess reached out and took Queen Elizabeth Woodville's hand in hers.

"They know only of the child duchess's presence and the execution of the standing plan OFANCRE. They will ensure the child's safety and preserve the lineage of the duchy. They have been told to watch out for those who may try to harm her. Rest assured, m'lady, these men have been trained to execute OFANCRE with maximum efficiency."

"Mr. Red Squirrel, I have great fear...."

"Forgive me, m'lady. You know that OFANCRE has been twice tested before and both times the rusty old anchor dressed as a child was brought to safety to the end point without delay."

"I remember." Duchess Margaret forced a smile, and her tension eased somewhat.

"In both tests, the Bretons along the way were meticulous in their execution of the plan and fervent in their loyalty to the duchy. The Breton heart knows not the difference between practice and reality. They have sworn their loyalties, and the children could not be better positioned except in the hands of God and the saints—which guide us daily in our tasks."

"Enough said, Red Squirrel. My journey ends here along with that of the English queen." Margaret patted the hand of Queen Elizabeth Woodville and released it. "Take the children to the convent, do what must be done, and then continue on to the completion of OFANCRE."

The duchess nodded, and Mr. Red Squirrel bowed low to take his leave.

"I'll take care of the children, m'lady." Red Squirrel began to rise from his bow when he felt a hand stop him.

"Kneel, Red Squirrel." The duchess beckoned, and a sword was brought to her. She raised her voice as she spoke. "Red Squire and Head Royal Coachman Alain de Keranrais, by the power of the Duchess of Brittany, I knight you in the service of your Lord and Lady of Brittany." The duchess tapped the sword on each of his shoulders in turn and then on his head. "I do this in the name of the Father, Son, and Holy Spirit and in the place of his royal servant Frances II, the Duke of Brittany. Rise and perform your tasks as befitting one of your stature and position."

Mr. Red Squirrel began to rise again only to be interrupted.

"Sir Red Squirrel, please remain kneeling." Queen Elizabeth Woodville cleared her throat. "Because, Sir Knight, you carry with you the Prince of Wales, I am compelled by honor to bestow upon you a knighthood in the service of England."

Red Squirrel kept his eyes on the ground, entreating the queen. "Your heart is kind, Majesty, but you must know that I have wielded my sword against your kinsmen and would do so again in the name of Brittany."

"You would do no worse than that which has been done already in the name of the war between the roses."

"Please, Majesty, I must insist. I cannot accept this honor." Red Squirrel looked up. "I fear the time will come when I must raise a weapon against anyone who would harm my homeland of Brittany. Your Majesty must certainly understand my conflict."

"I fully expected that you would be reticent to accept this honor, Red Squirrel. However, since I will not take no for an answer, let me ease your heart's worry. As you stand, Sir Red Squirrel, you rise also as an English knight to Edward of Wales."

Sir Red Squirrel said nothing aloud but arose with his complexion ruddier than ever. *Majesty, what have you done to me? Drat it, Red Squirrel, you are in a fix now. What will you do when you come to the crossroad where English and Breton swords are both raised in battle?*

The group broke apart. Mr. Red Squirrel attended to all the final preparations while the two royal mothers showered their departing children with hugs and kisses. Edward roused long enough to hug his mother tightly and receive her blessing before collapsing back on the coach seat—his body, mind, and spirit drained from the heavy burden of the ordeals faced and those yet to be seen. Annie held on to her mother and sister for a long time, unwilling to release them, and unsure when she'd see them again. After Queen Elizabeth Woodville led Annie's sister a little way off, Annie looked up into her mother's face and saw her own fear reflected back.

"Mother ... " Annie began, but her throat seized and would allow no other sound.

"We must be strong, my darling." The duchess knelt before her child and held Annie's face in her hands, memorizing every soft feature. "Both of us." Margaret moved one hand slightly and with her thumb she traced the sign of the cross on her daughter's forehead.

Annie buried her face in her mother's neck, hot tears racing down her pink cheeks. "I'll try," she choked out.

"As will I," Margaret's voice quavered. She helped her daughter into the carriage and gave Annie's hand a final squeeze through the window. "I love you."

"I love you too, Mother."

From within the coach, a teary-eyed Annie watched as her sister, her mother, and the Queen of England, standing together hand-in-hand, faded from view. Annie sighed as she watched the Cathédrale Saint-Pierre pass along the Rue les Chanoines.

Annie poked her head out of the carriage window and called out, "Can't we stop, Red Squirrel?"

The coachman kept his eyes on the road but tilted his face to call down an answer over the noise of the horses. "Maybe when you come back, little duchess. At that time, you will be able to pay homage to Saint Anne."

"She's the mother of the three Marys and grandmother of Jesus Christ."

"Yes, little duchess, and if Saint Anne were here, she would wave us on by."

"Will he ever wake up?" Annie shot a glance at Edward.

"He's been through a lot, little duchess. Try not to wake him."

"I thought you were a knight now. Knights don't drive coaches."

"This one still has that responsibility, little duchess," Red Squirrel laughed. "Next stop is the Couvent des Trois-Marie." Red Squirrel turned his attention completely to the road.

Annie huffed and withdrew from the window. *I hope the prioress at the Convent of the Three Marys remembers me. Then again, how could she not?* Annie arranged the folds of her dress. "I'm her favorite cousin."

"You're what?"

"Edward? Are you awake?"

"You're whose favorite cousin?"

"Prioress Françoise, wife of Duke Peter II. She was Duchess of Brittany but now she is a blessed personage within the church. She's my favorite of any of the family members on Grandfather Richard's side."

"Who? What?" Edward squinted and rubbed his eyes.

"You're not listening, Edward. My next favorite, after the prioress, is Great-Uncle Arthur Richemont. I never knew Uncle Arthur in person, but through Prioress Françoise's stories—"

"Annie, I'm going back to sleep now." Edward laid back down on the seat.

"Don't worry, I can tell you again once we get to the convent. Or, even better, you'll get to hear it directly from Prioress Françoise."

"Yes, that'll be better ... so much better...."

52

Stag and the Crossroads

Couvent des Trois-Marie
Vannes, France
1483

"It wasn't supposed to be this way, Mr. Red Squirrel," Annie whimpered as she followed Edward.

"There are things we can control and there are things we can't, little duchess." Red Squirrel guided the precious cargo back to the carriage.

"But I was told that Prioress Françoise would be here."

"I was told the same."

"Why isn't she here?"

"The assistant prioress said Françoise made the obligation to be at another place for an undetermined amount of time."

"But didn't she know I was coming to visit her?" Annie stopped and held her ground.

"I'm sure she did, and I'll bet she thought that whenever you arrived, she would be here waiting."

"Why don't we wait?"

"For how long?"

"As long as it takes." She crossed her arms, but her quivering bottom lip belied her show of force.

"Little duchess, I know you don't understand me when I say that we don't have the time, but we don't have the time to wait." Red Squirrel put his hand on her shoulder and steered her to the carriage. "Messages have been sent ahead. People have come from their homes to wait for us."

"I know, but I heard the acting prioress say that the plan wasn't for Edward and me to travel alone."

"She's right and you're right."

"But we're not waiting?"

"No, child. I have heard both your concerns, and I have made my decision." Red Squirrel opened the coach door and placed Annie inside. "We go now."

"You are no longer my favorite coachman." Annie scowled, an angry flush creeping up her little, delicate neck.

"I'm sorry to hear that, Annie."

"Don't you call me Annie!" The duchess buried her face in her hands as the coach door clicked. "Don't ever speak to me again!"

The carriage swayed to the side a little as Red Squirrel heaved himself up to the driver's seat. A moment later the carriage lurched forward, and Annie brought her hands down from her teary face.

"Annie, you were very hard on Mr. Red Squirrel."

"I'm not talking to you either, Edward." Annie shifted resolutely toward the window, her nose up in the air.

"Why? What did I do?"

"Nothing."

"So why am I in trouble?"

"I just told you. *You did nothing.*"

"What was I supposed to do?"

She turned a haughty face to the prince. "He's a knight in *your* service."

"He's a knight in *your* service too, Annie."

"Well," she faltered, "you're older."

"What does that have to do with anything?"

"Well, I don't know." Annie let out an enormous sigh, the bubble of her anger popped by logic. "Anyway, that is not the Mr. Red Squirrel I have known." Annie crossed her forearms. "I don't know this man." Annie twitched the coach curtains open and glared at the landscape. "Didn't you hear what the assistant prioress said, Edward?"

"Actually, I was resting my eyes."

"You should sleep less and listen more. She said that if we went now then the trip to Auray would be much more dangerous."

Edward brushed off the insult. "Annie, the only thing different between now and before is that we don't have Prioress Françoise."

"Exactly." Annie's brow furrowed as she pouted. "She was supposed to be here."

"Look, we have a knighted coachman and his strong assistant. I'm not sure how having an old convent prioress would add to our safety."

"You don't know Prioress Françoise. She was once the Duchess of Brittany. If my duchess mother and your queen mother can't be here, at least the prioress would have some royal power—that's something that neither a knight nor his strong assistant have."

"Two pairs of strong arms come in pretty handy in a fight."

"I don't know how strong the assistant is."

"Isn't he one of your Bretons?"

"I have never seen him before."

Edward leaned over the space between the two seats. "You have never seen the assistant coachman before, and suddenly Mr. Red Squirrel is not acting like himself?"

"Yes, so?"

The color drained from Edward's face. "Annie, this doesn't feel right," his voice quavered.

At the change in his demeanor, Annie's anger deflated and was replaced by genuine concern. "Are we in trouble?"

"I can't say for sure, but I am worried that we might be." Edward was whispering now. "Annie, I'm saying that us *not* waiting for the prioress may have put us in more danger than we already were."

"What kind of danger, Edward?"

"Hush!" he admonished, pointing a finger up toward the driver's seat. "And you just told Mr. Red Squirrel that he was no longer your favorite," Edward muttered.

"Yes, so?"

"We could be in a lot of danger." Edward slid closer to the window on his side of the coach. "Are we going the correct way?" he hissed.

"I don't know." Annie felt panic gripping her throat.

"Does anything look familiar?"

"I saw a stag a moment ago."

"Do you usually see stags this way?"

"I don't know. A stag is a stag unless … unless it's Great-Uncle Arthur Richemont's stag."

Edward turned from the window and shot Annie a look of sheer confusion. "Who is Great-Uncle Arthur Richemont?"

Annie rolled her eyes at him. "I told you earlier. He's my second favorite relative after Prioress Françoise."

"Very well, what about this stag of his?"

"When he was fighting alongside Étienne de Vignolles and the Maid of Lorraine at the Battle of Patay, a stag came out into the field of battle—"

"Are you talking about the stag you saw today?"

"No."

Edward turned back to his window with a huff. "Annie, things aren't right. We might be going the wrong way with two men who could have a plan of their own. Let's try and look to see if anything looks familiar." It seemed that the coach had not gone down the road for more than ten minutes when the horses whinnied to a stop at an extremely large road intersection.

"Edward, I see a stag crossing into the road," Annie whispered.

"Is it your great-uncle?"

"How would I know? I don't know what he looks like."

"You can't recognize your great-uncle?" the prince hissed.

"How could I? I never saw him. I only know him through the stories

Prioress Françoise told me." Tears threatened to spill over her cheeks. "See? That's the reason we need her here. She would know what Great-Uncle Arthur looks like."

"No, no, I see the stag too." Edward pointed. "Wait. I hear voices." Edward leaned tentatively out the coach window. He whispered over his shoulder, "Mr. Red Squirrel is talking to someone out there."

"I see the stag again. It's over here by my window." Annie's voice was barely audible. "He's looking at me." Annie turned to Edward and pulled on his coat. "Psst, look. The stag is over by my window." Edward began to draw his head back into the coach as Annie turned back to her window. Her scream rent the air. Edward smacked his head on the window frame. Annie yelled, "Red Squirrel! What are you doing in my window?"

"Duchess, the journey as you know it ends here, at the crossroads."

"Wh … what do you mean?" Annie shrunk back to the other side of the coach, closer to Edward. Mr. Red Squirrel reached for the coach door. Edward eased himself in front of Annie.

"Sir Red Squirrel, as a knight in my service, I command you *not* to open that door."

"That's not going to happen, little prince." The handle creaked.

"I know not what is in your heart, Sir Red Squirrel," Edward raised his voice, "but no harm by your hand should ever come to Annie."

"What makes you think that it is the duchess I intend to harm?"

"Well, I … " Edward swallowed hard. His bravado faltered. "I guess, if the journey has to end, it really doesn't matter where." Edward moved slowly toward Red Squirrel's side of the coach.

"I never said that the journey ended here, little prince. I said the journey as the duchess knew it ends here."

Annie put her hands on Edward's shoulders, stopping his forward motion. "What does that mean?"

A cloaked and hooded figure spoke from behind Mr. Red Squirrel. "It means that you children are not to be traveling alone anymore." Prioress Françoise stepped forward, pulling back her cloak hood. "That is, darling Annie, if you wish it."

"I wish it! I wish it!" Annie climbed past Edward as the door opened. She leapt into the prioress's arms.

"With your permission, my future duchess, may I ride with you all from here?"

"Yes, please!" Annie beamed as the prioress set her down in the carriage doorway. She pulled the woman into the carriage and sat down beside her. "Françoise, that's Edward."

"Is he well?" The prioress raised an eyebrow at the young prince who collapsed back on the other seat, rubbing his head where he struck it on the window moments before.

"I think he's glad to see you."

"He looks terrified."

"He does indeed," Sir Red Squirrel nodded, standing by the open doorway.

"Perhaps it was the casting of your words, Mr. Red Squirrel, that caused the children anxiety."

"How so, Prioress?" he asked with genuine concern.

"These dears are full of shock and fear in the face of all this uncertainty. Think over your words again, kind driver."

Red Squirrel looked away for a moment, thinking. Then his pallor changed. "Sorry, children. I see it now. I will choose my words more carefully in the future."

"Please do," muttered Edward.

"If you'll excuse me now, Prioress and Your Highnesses, there is coachman's work still needing to be done. There is much more road and night that lay ahead for this knight."

"You do that, Sir Red Squirrel." Prioress Françoise hugged Annie again. "I believe I need to catch up with this little one and learn about that little one." She nodded in the prince's direction.

"Perhaps that part can wait a bit, Prioress." Red Squirrel extended a hand into the carriage. "Young prince, why don't you join us men up in the driver's seat? I think that the ladies will appreciate some personal time."

"I ... uh ... " Edward cast a wary glance at the ruddy coachman.

"Come on, Highness," Red Squirrel beckoned. "I'll show you some tricks with horse teams that few princes ever get to learn."

Edward gave a quick glance to Annie and at her almost imperceptible nod he took the coachman's hand. Red Squirrel shut the coach door and helped Edward scramble up to the driver's seat.

As the coach bounced along, Annie gave a rambling account of her recent adventures. "The bailey was the greenest green I have ever seen." So excited was the young duchess, it seemed that the only thing keeping Annie in her seat was the tight grip she had on the prioress's hand. "You should have seen Edward near the fountain! He told the truth, and the water never rippled." Annie's eyes widened with awe. "Oh, and then the children fell off the tower wall. But then the raven master showed me that Froggie was safe. And then this whole journey began and—"

"Annie?"

"Yes, Françoise?"

"You know that I love you right?"

"Of course, Françoise, I've always known it." Annie sighed contentedly.

"I never had any children but if I did, they would be you."

"And Edward."

"Yes, and Edward, for sure." The prioress smiled. "You two will be married one day."

"Yes, Françoise, I know that he will love me forever."

The prioress stroked Annie's cheek tenderly. "You're so young, but I need to tell you something about love."

"Oh, there's plenty of time for that, Françoise," Annie replied dismissively. "You can tell me when I get older."

"Annie, there was a reason that I wasn't at the convent when you arrived."

"Yes, I know. The assistant prioress said you had to be somewhere else for a while. I was not happy about it." Annie dropped her voice, "I was scared, Françoise."

"I know, and I am sorry. But I'm not well, *cherie*."

"You'll get better."

"Actually, no, I won't." Françoise leaned closer. "The doctors are doing what they can, but I know that I won't be able to spend as much time with you as I want." Annie leaned against the prioress, trying to hide her face. At the sign of distress in the little face, the prioress lightened her tone. "So I need to teach you the secret about love now so that we can ensure that you and Edward stay in love for all your lives."

"There's a secret?" She glanced up.

"It's an easy secret to remember." Françoise kissed Annie's forehead. "In your relationship with Edward—and with each child you have—love God with all your heart, all your soul, and all your mind."

"I do that already with Jesus and the saints."

"I know, child. But sometimes as we get older, we forget this. Especially when we live day in, day out with someone. We sometimes put our love for that person before our love for God."

"Why do I have to love God, Jesus, the Holy Spirit, and the saints more than Edward?"

"I know it is confusing. We must do so because our purpose in this world is to love Him first. Once we do that, the love we have for others grows stronger."

"I don't understand." Annie wrung her hands.

"That's all right, you don't have to understand." The prioress stilled the little anxious hands. "All you have to do is remember it."

Annie wrapped her arms around the prioress. "I want you to be around to always remind me."

"We aren't guaranteed tomorrow, Annie." She squeezed the child lovingly.

"Well, I'm glad I have you today."

"Me too, *cherie*." The prioress spasmed into a coughing fit causing Annie to pull away in both fear and concern.

"Are you all right, Françoise?" Annie held out a handkerchief which the prioress accepted gratefully.

"For now."

"How did you get ill?"

"You remember that I go into the homes of the sick?"

"Yes."

"Well, sometimes I also get the sickness they have. Sometimes I heal and all is well. This time, I won't heal."

"Then you shouldn't have gone to that house. Not if it could hurt you." Annie pressed her lips into a line.

"I love God. All people are His children. As Prioress, I have promised to tend to their bodies, their souls, and their spirits—even if a sickness is strong and even if it means I might become sick myself."

"But ... but now you...." Tears welled again in Annie's eyes.

"Yes, my time here in this world may be shortened, but my time with Him will be longer." Françoise wiped Annie's tears and pulled her into an embrace.

Annie hid her face against the prioress's cloak, trying to blot out the sun and the sounds of the carriage and, most of all, the hopelessness she felt.

"Annie, there is something I want you to do for me."

"What?" Annie spoke from the folds of Françoise's cloak.

"When I die, the Carmelites from the new monastery that I started will take my heart and place it in a special urn."

"Why?" Annie hugged Françoise tighter.

"That's not important. I want you to come visit my heart and tell me about how wonderful your faith has grown. I want you to tell my heart about your love for Edward and about all the children that you two will have."

Annie's head rested against the old woman, listening to her heart's steady rhythmic thrumming. "Why your heart?"

"Because that is the place that I keep you and so it will remember about all the times we have spent together."

"Very well, I will do it," Annie mumbled.

"Promise, Annie?"

"I promise." Annie sniffed and raised her head. "Do you promise to hear me?"

"I promise, Annie."

Annie wiped the tears from her eyes. "We will check that when we get to Morbihan."

Françoise's eyebrows rose. "You know how to check the truth of a promise, Annie?"

Holding up her pointing finger, Annie nodded solemnly. "I learned a lot at the bailey, Françoise."

"Apparently you did, child."

53

Reaping the Grim

G3 Operations Office
European Medical Command
Heidelberg, Germany
Current day

"Colonel Christiansted has popped smoke, sir." Master Sergeant Roman nodded firmly toward the G3. *I hope that she arrives in time to find her husband alive.*

"Let me know when she safely clears the area," said the G3 chief of operations, Luis Toro-Calderon, as he placed a commander's plaque on his desk. "There has been too much violence, and frankly, I don't want her to be on any casualty list."

"Roger, sir."

"Confirm the current body count, Master Sergeant." Luis spread out several files across his desk; his eyes roved over their contents.

"Sir, I have four confirmed dead. First, Dewayne Cameron Sweeny. He was found poisoned."

"Roger." Luis did not look up as he slid a file to the left. "That's one. Next?"

"The real British officer Major Michaels-Keyes and the Liberian officer Colonel Worjedee. They were both garroted and stripped of their uniforms."

"That's two and three." More files queued up in order on the desktop.

"A radiology technician was found with a broken neck."

"That's four." Luis flipped open a file, his pen hovering above a paper. "Do we have a name?"

"No, sir. Dr. Tupelo is sending the name over." Master Sergeant flipped through his notes. "That's the current body count, sir."

Luis closed the file, added it to the line, and opened the last file on his desk. "Add one more, Master Sergeant."

Master Sergeant's eyebrows rose, but he kept his voice steady. "Roger. Who?"

"Major Oberstadtmeyer. He was cut down off the Heidelberg Hospital Operations building spire at sunrise today, Master Sergeant."

Master Sergeant scribbled the information into his notebook then flipped it closed and stowed it in his pocket. "Did Colonel Christiansted know this before she left?"

"No." Luis looked up from the manila folder death row on his desk. "I just received the report from Colonel Birdsong himself."

"I'm assuming foul play."

"No one is assuming suicidal intention at this time."

"Sir, Major Oberstadtmeyer was the assigned courier to these documents we've been dealing with all night. The loss of the Pelican key would be career ending. That could have tipped him over the edge."

"Possibly. But who knows if he lost the key or if it was taken? Either way, it would have been difficult for him to hang himself by the neck from the clock tower weathervane and then gut himself from heart to bladder."

Master Sergeant swallowed hard. "Well then, that makes five murders in one night, sir."

"Roger."

"Are the MPs assuming more than one killer here? Especially because we can confirm that there are two men posing as NATO officers on the caserne."

"No one has said. The one thing all the murders have in common is an association with the classified documents brought here from Fort Knox."

"Sir, why the horrific gutting of Major O-stadt? The last time a body was found splayed with entrails hanging was at the Leaning Tower of Niles in the US, right?"

"Negative." Luis shook his head. "There was an update last night from Poland."

"I saw that it came in, but I got sidetracked. What did it say?"

"Szkolna Gora, a woman known as the Owl, was found dead at a leaning tower in Pyrzyce, Poland. She had been gutted and hung in the same manner as these other two murders."

"And we still don't know who did this?"

"No, but a note was found on her body."

"Did the message claim responsibility?"

"If so, cryptically." Luis pulled a paper from a stack on his desk. "The note read, 'By my hand alone Jerusalem suffers. Rise with the Fallen!' It was written in English."

"Was there any note left on the body of Major O-stadt?"

"As a matter of fact, yes." He flipped open the last file in the line, found a copy of the note, and read aloud. "It said, 'They will come up into your palace and your bedroom and onto your bed, into the houses of your officials and on your people, and into your ovens and kneading troughs. Rise with the Fallen!'"

"I'm not tracking here, sir. Who'll be coming?"

"Or *what*, Master Sergeant. I'm not sure. Intelligence channels have the note now. We'll know shortly." Luis closed the file. "Speaking of Poland, Master Sergeant, I need you to go down and pick up a package at the mailroom. The clerk said the return address bears Polish and American names, Polish and French return addresses, and has French postage. Bottom line, it needs an authorized signature to be released."

Master Sergeant Roman scratched his head. "Sir, I don't know anyone in Poland or France. Why would I be getting a certified package?"

"I didn't say the package was for you, Master Sergeant. The mail clerk says that the package is addressed here to DCS. I am guessing it was meant to go to Dewayne Cameron Sweeny." Luis tapped the first file on the desk. "Anyway, since he is a victim, it's reasonable to investigate to see if this might be connected to his murder."

"DCS, our dead chief pharmacist, received a package from Poland where another victim was hung and gutted? That can't be a coincidence."

"The package isn't from Poland, Master Sergeant. The Polish return address is overwritten with a French return address that differs from the place in France where the package was mailed. That's the detail that piques my interest."

"Are you thinking that the connection might explain why Major O-stadt was killed in the same manner as that Owl woman?"

"I'm really hoping to get a clue." Luis shuffled through the victim's pictures from the files.

"Do you have any idea what's in the package, sir?"

"Negative knowledge, Master Sergeant. That's why you're going to pick it up. Let me know what you find."

"Roger, I'm a dot on the horizon."

"Master Sergeant, be careful." Luis held up Major O-stadt's victim photo. "We should be safe here in our own backyard, but we aren't. Without a murder suspect detained, we can't be sure that the killing has stopped." Luis tapped the edge of the photo on the desktop. "I don't need you to be in the next body count. So go and hurry back. Report what you find immediately. I'll update the hospital commander."

"Roger."

"Master Sergeant, I mean it. Eyes wide open."

"Sir, is there something you aren't telling me?" Master Sergeant reached toward his hip but felt only belt loops.

"I'm doing the same thing." Luis released a nervous laugh.

"What's that, sir?"

"You reached where your weapon should be. Since all this came down, I've been doing it too. But we're not in field operations here. Are we?" Luis glanced toward the arms room. "Like you, I guess I'm wondering if we should be."

"I suppose I'm spooked, sir."

"Ditto." Luis nodded. "Although at the time you didn't know it, I think we can presume that you were face-to-face with two murderers."

"I presume the same, sir."

"Further, Master Sergeant, you were handling the same classified documents which, just by association, seem to be getting people killed. Honestly, in your boots, I'd be rattled."

"Actually, sir, those two made my flesh crawl. I tried never to turn my back to the counter." Master Sergeant's eyes went up and left. "It reminded me of the time you and I were in Guatemala, exchanging hostages. I kept my hand on my handgun grip, and both eyes constantly scanning."

"I remember all too well. Get to the mailroom and get back here ASAP."

As Master Sergeant's footfalls grew faint, Luis pulled a pistol from his desk drawer, jammed in a full magazine clip, and set the weapon within reach.

Master Sergeant quickly exited the building, turned right, and then followed the contour of the street directly to the mailroom. Glancing up at the clock tower, he imagined a body hanging from the spire. *The MPs must be finished with the crime scene. The civilian work crew is cleaning up the roof.* As he kept a brisk pace, he found that his hand kept reaching for his non-existent weapon. To still his hand, he clenched it in white-knuckled fist. *Why was a package with French postage and a Polish name sent to DCS? Was he killed for his signature and this package? The G3 never said the package came from this Owl person killed in Poland, but who else fits the bill?* A loud screeching of tires preceded the feel of a bumper against his leg and the resulting jump of shock registering through his body.

"Head's up, Master Sergeant!" a voice shouted. Master Sergeant waved an apology and forced his body to finish crossing the side street. *I don't need to be in the next body count.*

Master Sergeant doffed his beret as he stepped into the darkened mailroom. *Inattentive … distracted…. Come on, Dogface, you're a senior leader. Why are you violating the basic situational awareness that you teach other soldiers?* The motion-triggered light kicked on. *And then there was light … as well as an open window at the mailroom service desk.* Master Sergeant panned the empty room. *Nothing here to be afraid of, right?*

54

Horseshoes and the Ringer

Château Royal d'Amboise
Loire Valley, France
1500

"Your Majesty, are you well?" Ottaviano touched the queen's shoulder gingerly, his eyes swiftly darting between the child's look of concern and the queen's lack of response. "Majesty?" He snapped his fingers in front of the queen's unfocused eyes. There was no response. "Little one," he said, addressing Louise, "talk to the queen."

The child took the queen's hand and gave it a little squeeze. "My queen, are you all right?"

"Loni, are you with us?" Douglas's calm, hypnosis voice was tinted with concern. Mickey took his wife's hand and held it to his chest. Loni's eyes slowly began tracking something they could not see—it seemed to pull her up from the depths. Then she spoke and they heard everything.

Queen Anne blinked and drew in a deep breath as if startling from a dream. "Oh, my." She glanced at the knight and girl, registering the perplexed look on each face. "I don't know what came over me. I'm sorry. Where were we?"

"The seventh tapestry, my queen." Ottaviano's knitted brow relaxed some, but his gaze remained sharp. "The artisans just brought the display rack up to the front of the hall for us." He added in an undertone, "My queen, are you certain you are well? It appears you had an … episode of sorts." The queen gave the knight a nod of acknowledgment and indicated with her eyes that he should remain nearby.

Louise continued to hold the queen's hand and with the other hand the girl pointed. "This is the seventh, Majesty?" Then Louise covered her eyes.

"I'm sorry Majesty," she whispered, "but I hate this tapestry just like Simone said I would."

"Oh, child." Queen Anne stroked Louise's hair. "I doubt she said that."

"Well, she said I would hate to look upon it." The girl peeked at the scene and then retreated again behind her hand. "I hate looking at it also."

Queen Anne hugged the child. "Maybe it was too much to show you."

"I don't want to look at it anymore, Majesty. Please. It saddens my heart."

"That's all right, dear. You keep your eyes closed and I will tell you about the beauty hidden in this tapestry."

"Beauty, Majesty?" Louise rested her head on the queen's shoulder. Keeping her eyes averted from the tapestry, the child traced a finger down the chain of the queen's necklace to the crucifix and then back up again.

"Listen and judge for yourself."

"I don't like that they killed the unicorn."

"Ah, but have they killed the unicorn, my dear?" the queen asked.

"My version in America certainly looks like the unicorn is killed," Jillian commented with a sniffle.

"Same here, Majesty," Clarisse chimed in.

"You see," Louise whispered, "your imaginary friends agree with me."

Queen Anne panned the hall to be sure of their privacy and then chanced a glance at Ottaviano. He gave a curt nod, and she knew that he too could still hear the voices. "Ears open all." Queen Anne cleared her throat but spoke so that only those nearest her could hear. "Let's start at the upper-left corner. Jillian, tell us what you see."

"Must I, Majesty?" Jillian's voice cracked.

"I'll do it, Majesty," Clarisse interjected. "I believe there is more here than meets the eye." She paused then added, "Well, there has been for all the others, let us hope that the theory stands."

"I hope so," Jillian whispered.

"So be it," Queen Anne replied. "Clarisse, tell me what you see."

"I see hunters. Their swords and spears and hunting dogs biting the body of the unicorn."

"Hunters, you say?"

"Yes, Majesty, hunters. They look like the hunters in the other tapestries. They carry the same weapons."

"Do they? Hunters do not hunt with swords."

"I don't understand, Majesty."

"Clarisse, this is the only tapestry where a sword is unsheathed, and further, it is being wielded against the unicorn."

"May I, Majesty?" Ottaviano queried and with a nod of permission he continued. "Hunters would use quivers and bows for fast prey like this. A sword is used to attack a person, not an animal. Hunters would have treated the unicorn as game—once fallen, they would likely have skinned the unicorn on-site."

"What?!" Louise's eyes grew wide as saucers. "Skin him?!"

"No, no, child. Not our unicorn." The queen soothed Louise and turned her eyes from the tapestry. She gave the knight an admonishing glare, but he only shrugged off the scolding with a playful grin.

"If they are not hunters," Clarisse continued, "then what are these men doing to the unicorn?"

"These men represent the political factions that wish to destroy and defame the Prince of Wales."

"Like the hunting dogs in tapestry four, Majesty?" Jillian asked.

"Precisely. Note that all the men surrounding the unicorn wear red and white—"

"—for the houses of Lancaster and York," Clarisse finished.

"Yes, and Edward has subjugated himself willingly to their attacks on his character and birthright. That is why this is the only place in the tapestries where the unicorn kneels in total submission with all four legs bent to the ground. He does not fight back."

"While he is stabbed in the back," added Ottaviano.

"Indeed," the queen replied.

"What of the blood running into the hunter's horn, Majesty?" Douglas asked.

"An interesting detail, Douglas," the queen answered. "Have you ever witnessed how lies and falsehoods can be spread faster than the truth?"

"All too well, Majesty."

"Ah, I hear in your voice more than you say." The queen nodded. "Here the blood of the unicorn, the essence of his identity, is being drained and trumpeted falsely to any who will listen. At the same time, the deception and mystery surrounding his supposed death or disappearance gathers strength."

Queen Anne lifted Louise off her lap, stood, and then settled the child back on the seat. Without the queen to hide her face against, Louise again clamped her hands over her eyes. Queen Anne stood next to the tapestry and continued. "Now let's go to the lower half. Clarisse, will you tell us what you see?"

"Yes, Highness. I see the delivering of the unicorn on horseback."

"What do you make of the men who accompany the unicorn?"

"They dress and bear arms like all the other men, Majesty."

"And yet they are not quite the same," added Douglas.

Ottaviano moved closer to the tapestry, inspecting the three men delivering the unicorn. "What would you say they are?" he asked both the queen and the voices.

"I would guess that they are travelers?" Clarisse posited. "Maybe they happened upon the slain body of a unicorn? Perhaps, in an act of kindness and respect, they recovered the dead unicorn and delivered it to this fortification?"

"Perhaps," Queen Anne replied. "So you don't see them associated with the vicious act of killing?"

"No, Majesty, I do not. I can't speak for the others here, but that is what I see."

"I know!" Jillian's emphatic interruption startled Louise. Though the child was, by now, used to hearing the queen's imaginary friends, their abrupt and excited manner still sometimes caught her off guard.

"These three men, they have the same demeanor as the men around the fountain in the tapestry with the unicorn dipping his horn in the water. In my thinking, I find them—"

"Wasn't that the second tapestry, Majesty?" Louise excitedly interrupted. "Wasn't it Vaast's tapestry?"

"Yes, dearest. Vaast made the second tapestry for me." The queen smiled. "Hush now, I think Jillian wasn't finished speaking." Queen Anne elevated her tone. "Please, Jillian, continue."

"Yes, Majesty. I was just thinking that the men are calm—reverent even— in their interaction with the unicorn. It's as though, in both Vaast's second tapestry and this seventh one, the people are *protecting*, not *pursuing* the unicorn."

"Quite true." Queen Anne smiled. "I wonder, Jillian, do you see any other similarities between those two tapestries?" The queen moved her hand across the unicorn's mane, stroking it delicately.

"Wait a minute…. Yes, yes, I do!" Jillian whispered. "The two birds. The same two birds are above the unicorn in both tapestries. On the edge of the fountain in the second and in the shrub above the unicorn in the seventh."

"You have an artist's eye, surely, Jillian!" the queen praised. "I know your image is small, Clarisse, but do you see my birds? Always one stands still. In the second tapestry the other bird prepares to leave as we left the bailey. In the seventh, the other bird arrives as we did in Carnac. But always they are together."

"I see them, Majesty!" Clarisse replied. "And they are not in flight. I mean, they are not in the act of fleeing like most of the other birds in the tapestries, which supports the idea that the attack in the left corner is metaphorical, not physical."

"Just like the unicorn's death itself," Jillian added. "I don't see a mask of death on the face of the unicorn."

"My friends," praised the queen, "you are exceeding my expectations. Please look closer and tell me if my story has yielded the fruit for which I have hoped."

"Majesty," Jillian continued, "do I see a hint of a smile on the unicorn? I mean, I never really studied this tapestry very closely because the idea of this part of the story always turned my stomach. But now I think I see it differently. More than that, I *feel* it differently."

"Very good, Jillian."

"I see a sense of relief," Ottaviano offered.

"Also correct, my dear knight."

"I see peace," Douglas added.

"Absolutely true. You have all seen the subtle, secret beauty in the tapestry."

"I didn't!" Louise peeked again through her fingers. "If our friends can see, then I want to see too. Please?" Louise scooted off the chair and approached the tapestry warily, her eyes barely daring to rise. Ottaviano took the girl's shoulders and positioned her directly in front of the face of the unicorn.

"Look, dear." Queen Anne pointed. Louise slowly opened her eyes to a squint. "Don't look at anything except our unicorn here," the queen coaxed. Ottaviano turned his body some to block the top-left corner of the tapestry. Louise opened her eyes a little more and kept them focused on the unicorn. "You see? Our unicorn has transitioned from being an animal chased and hunted into an animal left at rest and final peace." The queen watched Louise's expression slowly melt from one of sorrowful anxiety to that of peaceful acceptance.

"Majesty?" Louise reached out and stroked down the forehead and nose of the unicorn.

"Yes, *pupuce*?"

"Why are there dead flowers by our unicorn's feet? I saw no other dead flowers in the tapestries."

"Such sharp eyes!" Queen Anne patted Louise's rosy cheek.

"Well done," Clarisse added. "Even I did not see that, and I care for plants every day."

"As my little friend has seen, our unicorn has death by his feet. Edward was done running, and who he was, his identity, withers like flowers. But look here, Louise. See the plant near his mouth? What do you notice?"

"That plant is alive with three red flowers or fruits."

"Yes, there is life where the unicorn breathes. He is free to live, but he will be a unicorn no more. This part is not unlike our Lord Jesus Christ, with skulls at the base of his crucifixion cross, who dies as a man to be able to live in a new way."

"Is that why the unicorn wears a crown of vines?" asked Louise.

"Vines?" Douglas asked. "Not a rope like on the hunting dogs?"

"Yeah, you're right Douglas," Jillian chimed in. "They could have used rope; they have it for the dogs." They all heard Jillian's snapping fingers. "I've got it. Remember that these men are protectors, not pursuers. If they use a living vine to secure the unicorn, it could suggest protecting what is secretly alive—not prey, property, or prize."

"I could not have answered better myself," Queen Anne replied.

"Majesty," Clarisse asked, "what of this fortification on the right side where the unicorn has been brought? I thought the next destination for Edward was Carnac?"

"There are many clues designed to give this information away. Let us start with the dog that looks away to the left."

"I thought he was looking away from death," Clarisse answered. "Is there more?"

"Always, Clarisse," the queen laughed. "Let us ask my little investigator." She leaned in toward Louise and whispered, "What is in the dog's gaze?"

Ottaviano guided the girl along the tapestry to the left corner. "I see a squirrel!" Louise squealed loudly.

"Mr. Red Squirrel?" Clarisse blurted, recalling the last words Loni uttered before she had zoned out for a few minutes. Douglas sat with his mouth open and his eyes wide, offering only a shrug to Clarisse while the silent Mickey scrawled notes feverishly into the little notebook balanced on his knee.

"Yes," Loni smiled at them. Then her expression turned puzzled. "How did you know?"

"Well, Majesty, you ... um ... earlier ... " Clarisse floundered.

Douglas found his voice. "Don't worry about it, Majesty. Please continue."

"Very well," Loni shrugged. "Our Breton and English knighted Sir Red Squirrel served as driver and guard for Edward and me as we traveled to Morbihan. I recall it so clearly now, though I cannot explain why." Loni laughed for Queen Anne. "We had just left our mothers at the palace in Vannes and collected Prioress Françoise on the way toward Auray. Let us see where the story takes us, shall we?"

The queen returned to her seat in front of the tapestry, beckoning Louise and Ottaviano. Queen Anne lifted Louise back onto her lap as Ottaviano took up his station near the chair's backrest.

"Ready?" she asked. At nods from Louise and the knight, the queen moistened her lips and pointed to the tapestry. "The trip through Auray went quickly. As night settled in, the coach passed through forest and glen. I was too nervous to sleep, even with Prioress Françoise in the coach. Sir Red Squirrel must have known that a turn was approaching because the coach slowed. In the darkness, on the left side of the road, I spied a man holding a lantern—if I could see the man, I knew Sir Red Squirrel could too." The queen continued the story for all who had ears meant to hear it.

"Who goes there?" a voice hailed.

"A knight in the service of the former and present Duchesses of Brittany and the Queen of England."

"Of Margaret of Foix and Queen Elizabeth Woodville?"

"And Prioress Françoise."

"Françoise d'Amboise?"

"Today, yes."

"And who tomorrow, Sir Knight?"

"Anne of Brittany."

"Of Annie, you say?"

"OFANCRE, says I."

"OFANCRE. Indeed. You may pass."

Queen Anne signaled Clare to bring some water and after Clare retreated, the queen continued. "Sir Red Squirrel completed the challenge and passwords which allowed Edward, Prioress Françoise, and me to cross the hilltop and proceed down to an arrangement of dolmen unique in all of Brittany. There, a host of solemn people welcomed us. And just like the little squirrel in our tapestry," the queen tapped Louise on the nose, "my favorite coachman oversaw the safe delivery of his passengers to a place of peace and seclusion. You see him as a squirrel on the left, looking toward the horse—"

"Which is the only horse in all the tapestries, if I am not mistaken, my queen."

"Quite right, Ottaviano. With Sir Red Squirrel at the reins, horses brought us safely to the dolmen. And there on the right stands Sir Red Squirrel as a man."

"I like Sir Red Squirrel," Louise said. "I like that he secretly saved the unicorn from the bad men."

"As do I, little one," Queen Anne replied.

"Is that why there are squirrels over there?" Louise turned and pointed down the hall. "At the bottom of the ceiling vault near the door?"

"What do you think?" The queen winked at the child who laughed in response.

"There is no doubt," said Ottaviano pointing to the tapestry, "that woman with whom Red Squirrel's arm is linked—she who wears the rosary at her belt and the cross upon her neck—is the prioress you spoke of, Majesty."

"Correct again, Sir Knight." The queen nodded her appreciation of Ottaviano's preceptive nature. *I hope his attention to detail will carry over to the tasks yet to come.*

"Pardon me, Majesty," Clarisse redirected, "you say that the dolmen arrangement you went to was unique in Brittany and that it is represented by the destination of the unicorn. But I'm looking at a small print of the tapestry and mine shows nothing of the sort. I see the unicorn being delivered to a walled European city which is typical in every way."

Queen Anne pursed her lips and tilted her head, her eyes roving over the tapestry before her. "As you look at your version of the seventh tapestry, Clarisse, do you notice that there are a series of arches throughout it as well as a horseshoe shape?"

"Well … um … not exactly," Clarisse replied.

"Highness, Jillian here. My version is a *bit* larger than the card Clarisse has for reference. I can tell you all that I see the city arches quite easily—many of them, in fact—all layered and scaled to create depth and perspective. But it is the horseshoe that has me puzzled. Maybe I'm not close enough?"

"I can't say we see any horseshoes here either," confirmed Douglas, "except the ones on the horse itself, I guess."

"No, no. Listen carefully, all. What you are searching for is not a detail but a vast perspective. Follow the story of the images." Queen Anne pointed as she spoke, and Ottaviano bent close to her shoulder to best follow the line of sight. "It begins high to the left, tracks down to the center, and continues back up to the right."

"Ah, yes, the light." Ottaviano smiled. "It is in the light and dark." The queen returned a smile to the young knight.

"The chiaroscuro," Jillian confirmed, "of course. I see it now."

"Little help, please?" Douglas sighed. "Not all of us are artists."

Jillian came to the rescue. "Douglas, listen. Chiaroscuro is the play of light and dark…its flow. Blur your eyes a little bit. When you follow the path of light and the story, you get…."

"Indeed," Douglas agreed, "the entire scene is a giant horseshoe."

"Excellent. Well said, Jillian. Now, turn the horseshoe upside down and what do you have?" the queen asked.

"An upside-down horseshoe?" Louise replied.

"Yes, child, and an upside-down horseshoe is an arch."

"Why the horseshoes and arches, Majesty?" Jillian asked.

"To symbolize the Dolmen de Mané Kerioned, of course."

Clarisse gasped but Jillian cut across, "You lost me, Highness. I've never been to Brittany."

"Think, Jillian. It will come to you."

"Dolmen de Mané Kerioned, the crown of Carnac," whispered Clarisse.

"Yes, Clarisse," the queen replied, "you have it."

"Has your friend Clarisse traveled our lands, Majesty?" Louise asked.

"I don't know, small one, but she is certainly here now, isn't she?"

"Pardon me, but now it's my turn to ask for a little help. Not all of us live in Europe," Jillian said, only half-joking.

"Jillian," Clarisse answered kindly, "this particular dolmen is not arrayed in rank or file."

"Huh?"

"I think she means the stones aren't in lines or rows," Douglas added.

"Ohhh. So, this crown of Carnac dolmen is arranged in a horseshoe—or rather an arch. Right, Majesty?"

"Now she understands, Majesty," Louise whispered.

"Precisely," the queen smiled. "Yes, my friends, though I have heard of stone structures in other lands which are formed of three stones, none of them are arches that, in their layout, also form an arch. But the Dolmen de Mané Kerioned, with its three dolmen set in three groups, form a secondary arch unique in all of Brittany."

"Majesty," said Jillian, "let me just be sure I understand something. This OFANCRE—from the letters on the dog's collar in the … " she paused, and they heard her count quietly under her breath, "… sixth tapestry *also* stood for the plan to get the children safely to this horseshoe-shaped dolmen? In addition to all the stuff you said before about rivers and wills and all that?"

"Yes and no, Jillian. OFANCRE is much more—"

"More?" Douglas and Jillian spoke simultaneously.

Queen Anne laughed. "I suppose then that the secret has been well kept." She cleared her throat. "To Edward the unicorn, OFANCRE began and ended in Brittany as we have discussed. However, OFANCRE in its fullness was a plan that began much earlier—before either Edward or I was born. Also as previously discussed, it is a word that has multiple meanings."

"Please go on, Majesty."

"Of course, Jillian. The word, and its variations, mean different things in different languages. To the Bretons and Danes, *ancré* is a nautical term meaning 'anchor.' The practice exercises for the safe transport of Edward and myself were conducted with a boat's anchor in the carriage."

Louise giggled, "Carrying an anchor in a carriage. That's silly!"

"It is, isn't it? They even dressed the anchor in clothing!" The queen laughed along with Louise. "But oftentimes something a little silly sticks in our minds and helps us to remember. Right?"

"Right," Louise parroted.

"You may also note," Queen Anne continued, "that the knotted designs with letters resemble an anchor. Perhaps, by now, you have even deduced that the *A3* or *AB* with its—how did you say it, Jillian? Negative … ?"

"Negative space, Majesty."

"Negative space, thank you. Might also be seen as an *AE*."

"A turned-over *E*. Like a puzzle," Louise chirped. "*E* for Edward."

The queen nodded, suddenly solemn. "The *E* is there all along and then," she pointed to the top-right corner of the seventh tapestry, "gone. The *A* goes on alone. Edward was free of political turmoil but my path, my mantle of responsibility, took me back into the heart of it." Louise patted the queen's hand sympathetically. Queen Anne shook her head and drew in a breath, commanding her emotions to their proper places. "So back to translations. In Portuguese *a coragem* means 'guts.' To the Norsemen *reiðr* means 'offense.' And what do all these people have in common that made them come to an accord in making this one single word, OFANCRE, meaningful to all?"

"I have a guess, Majesty," Mickey spoke for the first time in a while, automatically raising his hand for permission to speak and then rolling his eyes at how ludicrous the action was given the circumstances. "Danes and Norsemen were Vikings who were the first to sail to the New World."

"Yes, but there's more," Loni as Queen Anne replied. "Mickey, I wasn't sure if you were still with us, so long have you been silent."

"Just listening and learning, Majesty."

"Spoken like a true scholar." Loni tapped an index finger on her lips as if feigning concentration. "Let us see the breadth of your studies, Mickey. Remember that the Portuguese and the Bretons were also sailors who knew about the Vikings sailing to the New World. What about in the late thirteenth century? A time when all these nations with sailing capabilities shared Christian love and respect—"

"—for persecuted Christian soldier-monks," Mickey finished. Loni nodded in his direction. "I see, Majesty." Mickey whistled as he sat back and looked over his notes. "OFANCRE becomes the unified mission among Christian people of many nations to secretly transport, and hide, something precious—like the relics of the Templars."

"Your studies have served you well, Mickey."

"Majesty, may we then surmise that OFANCRE can be applied to any process or instruction that secretly protects and hides something even if it does not involve the New World—or the Americas, as we know them?"

Mickey's cell phone began beeping. Mickey snatched up the phone from where it had been sitting near Loni so that Queen Anne could hear Jillian. *An incoming call from Heidelberg?* He quickly cancelled it.

"For our purposes, yes, you may, Mickey. The OFANCRE plan, as executed by Sir Red Squirrel, was to carry the unicorn—who had fled in secret from England's Tower of London to the Aleth Fortress—from Dinan to safety among the dolmen of Brittany."

"Majesty, there are many dolmens in Brittany. Why this horseshoe one in particular?" Mickey's phone beeped again. He canceled it.

"Mickey, what's going on?" Jillian hissed.

"It's under control," Mickey muttered into the phone to Jillian.

"Well," Loni began, "the Dolmen de Mané Kerioned—" Loni stopped speaking abruptly when, for the third time, the phone began beeping to indicate an incoming call. "Mickey, what is that noise? It is so strange."

"Highness, I'm sorry. Hold that thought. Excuse me." Mickey stepped out into the hallway. "Jillian, I gotta take that other call."

"What?" Jillian hissed a whisper. "Mickey, if I miss something—"

"I'll spin you up."

"What the—"

"I'll catch you up, okay? Just stay on the line. I must answer this." Mickey didn't wait for Jillian's response before he switched to the incoming call. "Bridgette, I thought you left Heidelberg."

"Sir, this is Luis."

"Luis, three back-to-back calls signal an emergency."

"Roger, sir."

Mickey paced the hallway pressing the phone hard against his ear. "This had better be important," he grumbled. "You interrupted my call with the queen of France."

"Dr. Peronne, there is no queen of France."

"Also, I just cut off Jillian from stateside."

"Sir, are you okay?"

"I am far from *okay*, Luis," Mickey groused. "I take it you are also far from being okay?"

"I can't imagine it getting worse."

"Somehow not being able to imagine *worse* doesn't seem to change the outcome."

55

Sticks and Stones

Maternity hospital
Saint-Quentin, Somme River Valley
Vermandois region, France
Current day

"The Owl is dead." Mickey staggered back into the room, dropped the phone on the table and walked to the window. He leaned his head on the cool glass. "Gutted her like a fish."

Clarisse walked over and placed her hands upon Mickey's shoulders. "I'm sorry, Mickey. No one deserves such a death."

"Five dead in my command." Mickey closed his eyes, unable to bear looking his reflection in the eye.

"There's nothing you could have done about that." Douglas rubbed his chin. "Well, looks like your need-to-know status finally caught up. I told you it would." Mickey shot Douglas a look of confusion which Douglas answered with a nod toward the resting Loni. Mickey surmised Douglas must have put her in stasis when he left the room to take the call.

"That's the intel you couldn't share. That the Owl was—"

"Mickey, it was too late to do anything. And we've been through this. Now you know, okay?" Mickey clenched his teeth in response, but Douglas steamrolled on. "You are *here*. Be *here*. Help *here*. Besides, Bridgette is acting commander, right? Certainly she has things under control."

"Bridgette has just departed on a family emergency. It seems her husband, my former patient, is in a death spiral and possibly already deceased."

"Things are just at a low ebb now, Mickey." Clarisse patted Mickey's back. "I'm sure there are a lot of positive things happening too."

"You're right, Clarisse." Mickey cast his eyes sideways at her. "The asset from Liberia, Mike Winnabe, who happens to be a family friend, is *positively* in an unclear accountability status. Also, the Romanian hospital *positively* lost Russell."

"That's not what I meant." Clarisse turned to Douglas. "Don't just stand there, say something."

Douglas grimaced. "Uh … on the upside, Suzanne is well on her way to finding Russell. That's for certain."

"True, Douglas. And that reduced our team effectiveness here by twenty-five percent," Mickey groaned.

"Yet we three are still here making steady progress." Douglas spread his arms out.

"Are we, Douglas? The last update I had on our progress is that Loni, my pregnant wife, still doesn't know me."

"Mickey, that's not fair," said Clarisse with a firm but calm voice. "This team has worked hard through numerous past personalities to bring Loni closer to herself. Douglas has worked continuously at her bedside. Jillian, her sister, has contributed from America. Russell helped from Romania." She moved into a crouched position to be eye to eye with Mickey. "I think you said even Loni's parents have come to Europe to assist." She smiled warmly at him. "Come now, all hope is not lost."

"Thank you, Clarisse." Mickey gave a sarcastic smile. "I forgot about the Meriwethers! I haven't heard from Monty and Monique since before they left America! God knows something awful has probably happened to them too!"

"Mickey, snap out of it!" Clarisse clapped loudly in front of Mickey's face and then standing, she put her hands on her hips. "I don't know how much evil still hovers on our horizon, but I joined this group because I believed we were making a difference in bringing Loni closer to being Loni."

"Clarisse is right, and you know it, Mickey." Douglas stepped closer. "This is no time for a pity party. Each of us bring a special skill set to this table. Yours is medical, historical, and theological. This is not a time to lose your faith in any of these areas."

Mickey closed his eyes and dropped his head back. "I feel like such a failure, guys. Whereas you all see incremental progress in Loni's psyche, I see only that Loni remains not herself. The endpoint for me is having Loni as I knew her before the terrorist attack hit Péronne. Without that, I'm drowning."

"That's because you are." Clarisse grabbed Mickey's arm and shook it jokingly.

"Thanks, Clarisse," Mickey muttered. "That helps."

"Mickey, sitting in this black cloud of yours, you are *failing* to see the value and contributions we have made. As of now, we've finished off the tapestries with Queen Anne. Douglas thinks we should try to connect again with little Annie to learn more about what happened at the Dolmen de *Mané Kerioned*. We think that's a good plan, but we don't know since we lost our chief historian to a phone call. Can you help us? We need you. Loni needs you. Now."

"The Dolmen de *Mané Kerioned*—the crown of Carnac, right?" Mickey wiped his face with his hand. *Time to compartmentalize again*, Mickey told himself. *Douglas is right. Locus of control. Be here.*

"Right." Clarisse led Mickey to Loni's bedside. "What do you know of the stone structures at Carnac?"

"Well, as Queen Anne said, it is home to over three thousand megalith formations which lie on the north side of the city. Dolmen are shaped like tables, two or more vertical stones supporting a horizontal one. Menhirs are single vertical stones. Many call the megaliths the Carnac Stones, but the truth is that these stones were arrayed in these formations some six thousand years ago, long before Carnac ever existed as a city."

"What is the purpose of the stones?" Douglas asked.

"Same as Stonehenge, I guess. No one really knows with any certainty. Some say they were positioned to represent the constellations in the night sky. Others have speculated that they were seismometers which could relay information on earthquakes. Still others say that they are involved in Druidic memorials to the dead. There are new studies and archeological finds occurring all the time."

"No one likes to hang around places dedicated to the dead." Clarisse shoved her tongue in her cheek. "That is, besides me."

"You tended cemeteries as a florist, Clarisse." Douglas smiled. "Most people don't like cemeteries."

Mickey's eyes brightened. "Exactly, guys. That is what made the place perfect for Annie and Edward. They were sequestered in a place where no one wanted to be and they'd still have, at their beck and call, the prowess of a thousand of stone warriors."

"What exactly are you saying, Mickey?" Douglas picked at his chin stubbles.

"With so many megaliths to choose from, what would be the criteria for the OFANCRE protocol's choice in location—besides the unique horseshoe shape?"

"I don't know how they would choose." Clarisse paced the hospital room. "There are so many funeral stones."

"Yes, exactly! There are three major arrangements." Mickey's eyes went up and to the left. "There is Ménec, Kermario, and Kerlescan. But there are structures farther afield as well."

"Where are you going with this, Mickey?"

"Besides the dolmen and menhirs, there are also tumuli—burial mounds."

"When you say mounds, are we talking small hills?" Douglas asked.

"Sometimes. There are many tumuli that would be considered tall hills—it all depends on the internal structure."

"Are things buried in a tumulus, Mickey?" Clarisse eased over next to Douglas. "And how do the hills stay up?"

"Things have been found within tumuli. And dolmen—the table-shaped stone structures—are sometimes the support inside tumuli."

"Can we assume then that a dolmen visible today is a residual element of a tumulus which once stood there, Mickey?" Clarisse queried.

"Many think so, Clarisse."

"But no one knows for sure?"

"Right, Douglas, no one knows."

"Have human remains been found in these places in Brittany?" Clarisse asked.

"Not that I know, Clarisse. It is claimed that if humans had been buried there, the nature of the soil would have dissolved the bones."

"How many dolmens are there in Carnac, Mickey?" Douglas asked.

"At least ten."

"Of these ten, Mickey, the planners of OFANCRE found the Dolmen de Mané Kerioned the most suitable place to hide a fleeing prince. But why?"

"Don't you see? That's the genius of it," Mickey answered. "Thousands of stones, a large expanse, a place-of-the-dead chill factor, and ten dolmen which at that time might have had suitable, habitable structures built on or around them! It is the ultimate shell game. Even if you knew that the prince was going to the megaliths it would be nearly impossible to find him."

"Very good, Mickey," Loni said for Queen Anne.

"Majesty, we didn't know you were listening," Douglas answered.

Mickey mouthed, *Again?*

Douglas shrugged and mouthed back, *At least it's not Vlad.*

"Mickey, Clarisse, Douglas, and Jillian, to hear you speak of my present as your history is so unusual."

"Oh, crap, I forgot about Jillian!" Mickey slapped his forehead. The momentum of the moment fizzled out. "Just a minute, Majesty." Mickey snatched the phone from the table and fumbled with the buttons until the screen showed a link-up with Jillian. Mickey held the phone to his ear and walked to a corner of the room. "Jillian, are you still there?"

"Yeah, but no thanks to you! What the heck, Mickey?" Jillian hissed.

"I'm sorry, that took longer than I expected. You haven't missed much here. We were—I mean—they were," Mickey tried to disentangle himself from the net of responsibility, "just discussing that there are lots of places in the megaliths to hide and that dolmen sometimes had structures built on or around them."

"Yeah, Mickey, like Douglas and Clarisse came up with that alone," Jillian sniped. "Whatever. Just get me back to Queen Anne, all right?"

"Yeah, let me put you on speaker again." Mickey returned to Loni's bedside to join the conversation already taking place and set the phone nearby.

"Being with you all is like I am again a child," Loni said, "sitting at the table of adults. There I would hear matters discussed that I knew would affect me, yet I had no voice in the process."

"Even I know what that is like," Louise's voice chimed in, "and I am not a duchess."

"Did such discussions continue at the Dolmen de Mané Kerioned? I thought that turmoil had been left behind at the Aleth Fortress," Clarisse asked.

Loni's face grew solemn. "No, we could never truly escape those who planned our futures for us. Our futures were never our own. But at least at the dolmen, we trusted those who made the decisions."

"Can you tell us about it, Highness?" Douglas asked.

"There were many people there when we arrived as you see in the last tapestry. I knew some, but it seemed as if Sir Red Squirrel and the prioress knew them all. I was glad that they were there—as I said, we trusted them implicitly. Even though Edward and I were the subject of the talks, we were expected to only watch and listen, never to question."

"What was discussed?"

"I really can't recall specifics now, Clarisse, especially as I could not participate in the discussions. I remember more how it felt to be there. I have glimpses of memories. Joy and relief—then sadness. I do remember that the faces all looked worried. As the prioress and Sir Red Squirrel spoke, everyone listened carefully. Sometimes the people nodded. Sometimes they smiled. When the talking ended, Annie of Brittany and Edward Prince of Wales were put to rest."

"Wait, what?" Jillian asked.

"Hello, Jillian, I am glad you have been recovered."

"Yes, Majesty, I'm glad to be back too. But," Jillian pressed on, "what do you mean 'put to rest'?"

Loni nodded calmly. "Did you forget, my friends? Annie and Edward became Rhiannon-Rigantona and Caradoc Freichfras. That night we were given our own identities, our own dolmen, and our own new starts on life. Though not the promise of lives together."

"Oh, that's sad. After all that the ermine and the unicorn went through," Louise sniffed hard.

"I can see how living among the dolmen and being together could have been the greatest time in your lives," Ottaviano's voice added.

"Yes, being there among people who loved us and wished well for us was very satisfying. However, it is what we discovered and learned in the base of the dolmen that defined me for the rest of my life."

"Majesty, would you be willing to allow me to—"

"I would like that very much, Douglas," Queen Anne interrupted as Loni's eyes welled with tears.

"I am at your service, Majesty," Douglas replied, understanding the hint.

"Allow me a few moments to prepare myself," Loni answered. "I sense that this is a portion of the journey I must make alone."

"Indeed, Highness. Take your time," Mickey replied. Loni closed her eyes.

"It has been such a joy to share my story with you, Louise," Queen Anne spoke as she took Louise by the hand and walked her over to the aged artisan, Simone, who was directing the storage of the sixth tapestry. "I hope you liked it."

"I did, Majesty. I had no idea that so much could be told in just a few pictures."

Ottaviano followed the ladies at a respectful distance. "For those who have eyes to see it, child," he commented.

"Yes, kind knight," Louise answered. "And your friends, Highness, they were strange, but I liked them too. They were curious just like me."

"Indeed, child. But remember to keep my friends a secret." The queen winked and Louise returned a smiling nod.

"Ah, so the story is done, is it?" Simone spoke while clenching the pipe in her teeth.

"Yes and no, dear artisan," Queen Anne replied. "I must attend to a pressing matter. Would you please guard this little *pupuce* until her mother returns?" The queen tapped Louise's nose tenderly.

"Certainly, Majesty," Simone answered, "we shall wait right here."

"Very well," the queen answered. Louise curtsied to the queen and Simone directed the child to a small table by the fireplace laden with food and drink. The queen turned to face the knight. "Ottaviano, will you accompany me?"

"Always, Majesty," he bowed.

As the queen made her way through the grounds and buildings toward Chapelle Saint-Hubert, Ottaviano walked silently beside her. When they arrived at the chapel doors, the queen paused and addressed the knight. "I do not think that I must remind you of the necessity of silence in all the matters which have transpired amongst these voices." She watched as the knight shook his head. "I cannot explain what has happened nor why. I must believe that whatever this is, it is meant to be. And that it was meant for you and Louise to hear as well."

"Agreed, Highness."

"Good," the queen sighed. "Now, Ottaviano, I must ask a favor."

"You have only to ask, Majesty, and it shall be done."

"Stand guard at the door to the chapel here as you did before. Make sure I am not disturbed. Let no one in—*no one*."

"I understand, Majesty." The knight nodded. He turned his back to the chapel door, leveled his sharp gaze upon his surroundings, and placed a firm hand on the hilt of his sword.

Queen Anne entered the chapel and closed both doors securely behind her. She sat on the middle prayer bench and cleared her mind.

"Douglas?"

"Yes, Majesty, I'm here. Are you ready?" Douglas watched Loni open her eyes, track toward his voice, and nod. A few moments later Loni was Annie.

"Where are you now, Annie?" Douglas asked.

"I see three wooden houses in a clearing in the forest."

"Do you see the dolmen?"

"No," Loni cocked her head, "I don't see any tombs. I am walking toward the houses now."

"Tell me about the houses, Annie."

"They are short."

"What do you mean short?"

"Houses should start at the ground. These look as if part of the house is under the ground. These houses look … short."

"The houses are the dolmen, Douglas," Mickey whispered. "The wooden structures used the stone skeleton as building supports."

"Annie," Douglas touched Loni's arm, "do you know which dolmen is yours?"

"We were told that the dolmen on the left is for the unicorn. The ermine will have the middle one."

"What about the one on the right?"

"It is a place of worship, Douglas. It is much deeper than the other two. It has a long hallway lit up with torch lights. The steps are steep and at the bottom it turns sharply to the left. We are going into it now."

"Let me know when you get inside."

"I will."

The people in the Vermandois waited with bated breath while Loni delved into the secret depths of the dolmen. A few minutes later, Loni spoke again.

"Douglas, I see a giant chamber filled with seated people. The walls are made of large stones. On the stones there is much writing, but in a language that is not French or Breton. I think that the people who made the dolmen put the writing on the walls."

"What are the people in the chamber doing?"

"They are holding a service thanking Jesus for our safe arrival."

"Is someone leading the service?"

"Yes."

"Do you know the person?"

"There is a man and a woman."

"Do you know them?"

"Yes, of course. It is Prioress Françoise and Sir Red Squirrel." Loni's face cracked into a small smile. "He has shaved off his beard … he looks a little funny." Loni then quickly returned her face to solemn piety.

"What are they saying or doing, Annie?"

"They are each holding a large stick, Douglas. When they hold the stick, they speak directly to God."

"What are they saying?"

"Shhh, I am listening."

The smells of torch fire and damp, musty earth filled the hospital room. A murmuring swelled around them before a man's gruff voice entered the air.

"Lord," Red Squirrel prayed, holding a stick above his head, "I speak to you as a man not worthy to be in your presence."

"Equally unworthy, Lord," Prioress Françoise prayed, "I am a woman standing with this man, asking you to grant us a blessing upon the children we have rescued from peril and brought before you."

"The staff I hold is known to you, Lord," Red Squirrel said. "He that first held it was one of the few to ever have heard your voice with his own ear. Your instructions to him were to keep this staff held aloft and victory would be his against the Amalekites."

"Likewise, Lord," the prioress continued in a chant-like voice, "the rod that I hold was made for the brother of that man. To him you taught the Hebrew priestly blessing, the *Birkat Kohanim*."

"Lord," Red Squirrel continued, "make the mission of these two children one that returns your flock into your service."

"In that light," Prioress Françoise finished, "bless and protect them now and for all time."

"Amen." Red Squirrel placed the staff into the corner.

"Amen." The prioress placed the rod next to the staff.

"Amen," answered the gathered people.

After a moment, Annie heard Douglas in her mind again. "Annie, is there more?"

"It doesn't seem so, Douglas," she whispered. Annie was thankful that the sounds of the milling crowd allowed her to answer.

"Can you walk over and look at the staffs? What do you see?"

"They are very tall. One has blue stones and the other has vines and flowers carved all over it."

"Is there a name on either?"

"I don't see a name. I guess the owner is the one who holds the stick at the time. Being connected to God, a blessing would probably come—like it did tonight."

"Out of the mouth of babes," Clarisse's voice whispered.

"We are being called for dinner and bed. It has been a very long day."

"Indeed, Annie. Be sure to say grace before you eat. You children have much for which to be thankful."

"I will, Clarisse. I always say grace and I am always thankful—especially today." Annie held her hand over her mouth and whispered, "I must go, I cannot talk more. They will hear me."

"Though you walk through the valley and the shadow of the dolmen, you should fear no evil, for God is with you, child."

"I know, Clarisse, and also with you."

56

Neither Rain nor Sleet nor Master Sergeant

Unit mailroom
Nachrichten Caserne
Heidelberg, Germany
Current day

I wonder who is sharing the neuron with this guy today? He's killing me. Master Sergeant Roman wiped his face repeatedly, staring at the half door's tarnished *Mail Pick Up* plaque. "You look overwhelmed there, Specialist. Just try keeping your eye on the ball, okay?"

"What was the name you gave me again, Master Sergeant?"

"Roman," he groused. "Master Sergeant Frances Roman. Look," Master Sergeant pointed, "it's right here on my uniform."

"Roger. There is no package here for Master Sergeant Frances Roman."

"I was told by Lieutenant Colonel Luis Toro-Calderon that there was a package being held to my attention at the mailroom, Specialist. Go back into your little hidey-hole there and look again."

"Maybe the lieutenant colonel has already picked it up?"

Master Sergeant drew himself up to his full height. "Why then would he send me to pick up a package if it was already retrieved?"

"I don't know, Master Sergeant," the specialist laughed and pushed his glasses up the sweaty bridge of his nose, "but it happens all the time. Officers task multiple soldiers to pick up mail and packages."

"That's not the way we work at our G3 shop," Master Sergeant growled. "Specialist, I'm not sure if you're being cavalier or if you just have a death wish. Either way, I just need the package."

"I understand, Master Sergeant. I'll look again." The specialist stepped away from the counter and then paused. "However, you do know that I'm

324

going to need Lieutenant Colonel Toro-Calderon's authorization in writing in order to release the package to you ... when I find it."

"Listen well, Specialist. Eyes right here." Master Sergeant pointed his fingers toward his face. "You will not get any further authorization since I am the approving authority in the matter of any soldier *who has died* and cannot pick up their mail."

"The lieutenant colonel is dead?" The specialist's mouth dropped open.

"No, he's not—but that is more than I can say for you if I have to come across this doorway and assist you in finding said package, Private."

"It's Specialist, Master Sergeant."

"Not for long if I don't see a package from France in front of me."

"Did you say France, Master Sergeant?"

"Yes, why?"

"Okay, now that helps," the specialist nodded. "I remember a package with French postage. It had a Polish name."

"You know Polish names?" Master Sergeant cocked an eyebrow.

"Some." The specialist smiled weakly, wiping his sweating palms on his uniform. "Work in a mailroom in Europe long enough and it gets easier to spot the names from other countries."

"Do we get a lot of mail from France or Poland?"

"No, Master Sergeant. We don't get too many of those. That's what makes those packages stick out more."

"Well, if it sticks out, it seems that you would be able to find it quicker, right?"

"Oh, yes, Master Sergeant. Let me think." The mail clerk gave a nervous laugh. "It's not in the mailroom in-box." He pointed in one direction of the backroom.

"Of course it isn't. Why would it be there?" Master Sergeant mocked.

"Because I moved it to the out-box." He pointed in another direction.

"Great!" Master Sergeant rolled his eyes.

"The package that you're looking for was addressed to DCS—Captain Dewayne Cameron Sweeny. It is in the hospital out-box. Can you have Captain Sweeny authorize you to pick it up?"

"Done. He's *dead*." Master Sergeant jabbed the counter with his index finger. "Therefore, as I've said from the beginning: I'm Master Sergeant Roman and I want to pick up the mail being held to my attention. As the G3 Operations sergeant and current acting command sergeant major for my command, may I have the package now?" Master Sergeant barked.

"Absolutely." The specialist swallowed dryly. "It is in the other room. Give me two minutes, Sergeant Major."

"It's Master Sergeant." He tapped his watch. "You have sixty seconds."

"Moving, Master Sergeant." After a brief sprint, the sweaty-faced mailroom specialist returned with a four-foot-long tube. "Here was the glitch, Master Sergeant," he panted, "this label is addressed to 'DCS, European Medical Command.' See?" He pointed. "That's why it was placed into the command out-box for the deputy command surgeon. That is probably the message your lieutenant colonel received. Later, I stumbled upon some mail sent to DCS, but it was addressed to Heidelberg Hospital. So that made me stop and think."

"I doubt that happens often," Master Sergeant muttered.

The specialist nodded, too engrossed in his recounting to be aware of the insult. "Not all mail marked 'DCS' is intended to go to the deputy command surgeon, Colonel Peronne. Some mail, having the same initials, is earmarked for Dewayne Cameron Sweeny." Then the specialist fumbled around with papers on a desk behind the counter. "Also, I have this note.... Ah-ha!" He looked up, waving the paper and beaming. "This note here is from Captain Sweeny saying that he was expecting a package. So naturally, then I moved this DCS package from the G3 box back to the hospital out-box destined for Captain Sweeny."

"Specialist, that note attached there," Master Sergeant pointed, "has *my* name on it."

"Oh, right. I was getting to that." The specialist pushed his glasses up again.

"Specialist, you're making me sad and tired. Just let me have the package already."

"In a second, Master Sergeant. This morning there was *another* note on my desk. It said that Captain Sweeny ... DCS ... had died."

"I told you that as well."

"Yes, Master Sergeant. Anyway, all his mail was relocated to the hold-box. Then I got to figuring that since I was holding mail for a dead soldier, command operations would be coming to pick it up." He smacked himself on the forehead. "So, I moved the package from the hold-box into the command out-box where it should have been all along. How about that!"

"Well, Specialist, in that case, you should have seen it right when I asked for it."

"That's right."

"But you didn't."

"No, Master Sergeant, I didn't." The specialist grinned.

"Am I missing something here?"

"I didn't see it because although it was in the command out-box, it had been placed in a sub-box marked for the deputy command surgeon, Colonel Peronne!"

"Seriously, there are sub-boxes?" Master Sergeant rubbed his eyes.

"Yes, Master Sergeant, lots of them." The specialist gave a serious nod. "In fact, DCS Colonel Peronne's sub-box is filled to the brim with packages and letters. Had you been Colonel Peronne, I would have walked straight over to your command out-box," he pointed toward the mail filing system behind him, "sub-box DCS, and handed you this Polish-named package along with the ton of other mail that is already there!"

"Actually, you are quite lucky."

"Lucky, Master Sergeant?"

"Had I been Colonel Peronne, you yourself would have been stuffed into the out-box marked for immediate court-martial for wasting time with your in-box, out-box, sub-box, re-box foolishness."

"I was just trying to be efficient," the specialist cringed, "and thorough."

"I do realize that, Specialist. And in some galaxy far away, what you did was spot on." Master Sergeant reached over the counter and tugged on the package. "Look. It has been a long night. I'm bone tired and irritated. Just let go of the package and I promise not to rip off your arm and beat you senseless with the wet end."

57

Dears and Roebuck

Maternity hospital
Saint-Quentin, Somme River Valley
Vermandois region, France
Current day

"She's gone, Mother? She's really gone?" said Loni as Annie, wiping the streams pouring from her eyes. "Françoise said she was coming back."

"I'm so sorry, *pupuce*," said Duchess Margaret, as far in the past she held her daughter. "She caught an illness from the people she tended."

"She's been dead for two years. Why did people make false excuses? Why didn't anyone tell me?"

"Well, at first we knew you had to adjust to the life here among the dolmens. Every time we came, you were so happy. We didn't want to spoil that with the sad news of a death which you could not change."

"Yes, but when I asked you if you had seen the prioress, you always said no."

"It wasn't a lie, Annie." Margaret reached out and stroked her daughter's hair. "I hadn't seen her because she had died."

"Fine." Annie leaned away from her consoling mother.

"Annie, at onset, we didn't want to tell you. Then later, so much time had passed that it was embarrassing to admit we kept it from you."

Annie stood abruptly, her cheeks flushing red. "I'm not a child. I'm ten years old."

"I know. I can see you have bloomed into a fine young girl."

Annie paced, the pine needles crackling under her soft leather boots. She spoke without looking at her mother. "How did she die?"

"She passed in her sleep."

"It had been so long." Annie dug the toe of her boot into the dirt. "When she never came back, I wondered if she stopped loving me."

"No! Never! Even now, from heaven she loves you."

"You know, Mother, I should have known it." Annie resumed pacing. "She told me that she was dying." She kicked at a pebble, but it went nowhere, so dense was the carpet of pine needles on the forest floor.

"She did?"

"Yes, in the coach ride from the crossroads. She told me that she wouldn't be around much longer. That was four years ago."

"She became bedridden about a month before she died."

Annie's face fell. "She was so strong," she sighed, "that must have been very hard for her to endure." Annie's pacing slowed and her color returned to normal as the wave of anger ebbed within her. "I am grateful that she was honest with me about her life. I guess, deep inside, I knew she had died. I just didn't want to accept it. Still, Mother, you could have told me."

"What could I have said?"

"Something like, 'Françoise isn't coming back.'"

"That would help?"

"Yes." Annie blew her nose, then stuffed the handkerchief up her sleeve. "You could have told me that she went to God."

"I'll remember." The duchess held her arms open. "Am I forgiven?"

"Yes, Mother." The young duchess fell into her mother's arms and wept until her tears ran dry. Margaret stroked her daughter's hair and held her close.

"You know, your father was afraid you wouldn't forgive us. He asked me to bring you a gift from Tuscany to make you feel better." The duchess lifted her daughter's chin and looked her in the eye. "What do you think it is?"

"I don't know," Annie sniffed.

"Come with me, Annie." Margaret stood and smiled down at her daughter. "A walk will help clear your mind and your teary complexion." Annie felt her own hot cheeks and puffy eyes, then sighed and nodded.

They crossed the old Roman road and walked to a place in the woods where a stable was maintained for the animals of the Dolmen de Mané Kerioned. Along the walk, Annie heard a whispered, garbled voice in her head, and she pulled up short. It sounded like Clarisse.

"Mother, may I have a moment before I see the gift? A moment to compose myself?"

Margaret smiled at her daughter and saw, perhaps for the first time, just how much she had grown up during the last four years amongst the dolmen. "Of course, my ch—my dear," Margaret corrected. "I'll signal you when the gift is ready."

After her mother had disappeared down the path, Annie whispered, "Clarisse? Is that you?"

"Yes. Where are you, Annie?"

"I'm on the path to the animal stables. Mother went ahead to prepare a gift for me. She'll signal when it is ready. I do not have much time to talk."

"Can you see the stables?"

"Yes, I am close. I can see it between the trees ahead."

"Are you expecting an animal as a present? Perhaps a pony?"

"I have a pony and so does Edward."

"Is Edward there with you?"

"No. He isn't." Annie looked down at her boots. "Lately, there have been days that he has been by himself. I think that he needs time to be alone—just to think and talk to God."

"I have days like that myself, child. Did you get the signal yet?"

"No, Clarisse, I haven't—and I'm not a child."

"So, young lady, there's no one there to hint what this present might be. Or if it is safe?"

"We have been safe here for four years, Clarisse. I have nothing to fear."

"Who all is down there, *cherie*?"

"No one. I see no one. Wait. I see someone near the last stall. It is Sir Red Squirrel and Mother is with him." Annie stood on tiptoe, squinting. "They are motioning me to come behind the stables. Clarisse, I guess it's time to see the surprise." Annie wound down the path until she rounded the edge of the stall. "Wow!"

"What do you see?"

"I can't believe it."

"What do you see, Annie?"

"It can't be real." Annie started crying and laughing at the same time.

"What is it, Annie? What is it that you can't believe?" At that moment the crying and laughter abruptly stopped.

"Annie, are you okay?" Clarisse clenched her fists on the back of Douglas's chair. "Annie?"

"Clarisse?" the mature voice of the adult Queen Anne of Brittany came again through Loni.

"Yes, Majesty?"

"I was in a dream." Loni held her hand to her forehead. "I know the dream. It was from my past—a memory made into a dream. I was reliving the blessing at the dolmen with you, and then suddenly found myself at that strange place where fantasy meets reality."

"I know of it," Clarisse answered. "Most people do, though few acknowledge it."

"For you, is it the same place where happiness meets sadness?"

"Sometimes, Majesty."

Douglas leaned forward. "I failed you, my queen."

"Douglas," Loni's face turned toward the sound of his voice, "how did you fail me?"

"I had you in a hypnotic trance and somehow you slipped out of it."

"This has never happened in your experience?" Queen Anne asked through Loni.

"It can happen, but it is rare and usually only in times of great emotion or great fear."

"Yes, that is what I felt, Douglas. I felt great emotion and great fear both at the same time."

"What was happening there?" Jillian's voice was tinny through the phone speaker.

"In the dream of the memory it was my tenth birthday. Mother came to visit me at the dolmen, and she told me that Françoise had died."

"I'm sorry."

"I went with her to the stables to see what present Father had sent me. It came all the way from Tuscany."

"Yes, you had just seen the gift and then we lost little Annie and the hypnosis broke. What was this gift?"

"It was all my joys and all my fears. It was the most dear and horrific gift I could have ever seen with human eyes."

"That sounds contradictory, even for me," Jillian offered.

Mickey, Douglas, and Clarisse exchanged confused glances. "What did you see, Majesty?" Mickey prompted.

"It will take me many minutes to tell you what I saw but, mind you, everything I relate all happened in a span of a few moments."

"Yes, Majesty. What did you see?"

Loni closed her eyes and put her hands at her temples. She pulled in a slow, deep breath. "As I rounded the corner, I saw my dear, precious Edward in a ringed area amongst three animals. He was facing toward me, but his head looked down toward his lap. The three animals were roe deer. Edward wore a white shirt that was opened at the neck. I thought I saw him wearing an animal collar. This confused me. But as I narrowed my eyes, I saw it was a blue scarf with orange and white spots on it." Loni sighed.

Silently, Douglas reached over toward the postcards that Clarisse held fanned in her hand and withdrew the picture of the unicorn in a circular fence. He showed it to Mickey, who peered closely then gave a nod of understanding. Douglas returned the postcard to Clarisse, tapping his finger on the unicorn's collar.

"There was a rope tied to one of the deer—the one on his left, my right." Loni moved her right hand in front of her, reconstructing the moment the same way Queen Anne was in the privacy of her chapel in the year 1500. "I saw the rope as it dangled from the animal's neck and lay across Edward's left shoulder. The brown of the rope lying on the white shirt looked like a snake. Instantly, I feared for Edward until I realized that it was a silly little rope.

"But then I noticed there was blood on the side of Edward's shirt and also on the deer standing to Edward's left." Loni's hand pointed. "This made me silently shriek in fear, my mouth opened but no sound came. Then I realized that what I thought was blood was some flowers or fruit dripping from the branch of the tree above them. I shouldn't have ever worried because an injured animal would not be still as this one was. I was glad my shriek made no sound."

"You saw a total of three deer?"

"Yes. Another lay to Edward's right. It was chewing at the brushy grass in front of it. Fluttering around its nose was a dragonfly. A dragonfly of such size I have never seen. I was again afraid—perhaps it would fly up and spit in Edward's eye? Everyone knows that the spit of a dragonfly will blind a person. I felt fear surge up inside me. But then the dragonfly hummed and flittered away, along with my fears. On the ground jumping away from Edward was a small frog. It made me think of Froggie and then I remembered the night at Saint-Servan when the assassin tried to harm us. My fears rose and then disappeared when the frog jumped away. I seemed to be the only one worrying. The deer to Edward's right was completely at peace; it just quietly chewed and pulled at the grass."

"There was one last deer."

"Yes, the last one was a baby roe. It was probably the baby of the roe buck on Edward's right and the roe doe on his left. It was so small and frail. It curled in Edward's lap and slept comfortably. Edward was looking down at the sleeping fawn. I could only see one of the baby's closed eyes as its head lay in Edward's hand."

"Majesty. This is a beautiful, peaceful scene. I see no substantial horror that could scare a child."

Loni opened her eyes, and though she could not see Douglas, her gaze was harrowing. "I'm not finished yet, Douglas … and I *wasn't* a child at that time."

"Of course, Majesty." Douglas placated, noting the second reference to young adulthood.

"As I said, I walked upon this scene that for me," Loni raised her eyebrows for Queen Anne, "as a young lady, was overwhelming, especially after hearing of Françoise's death. I felt my heart leap with joy and then cringe with fear. As I scanned the scene, the emotions coursing through me made me alternately dizzy and then sharply alert. I felt myself start to fall. I was later told by those who were present that I started to faint." Loni paused for a moment, flattening out her hospital gown as though it were a fine dress.

"I felt my legs go wobbly, but I had the good sense to flex them. The motion caused me to stagger forward and when I did, I stepped on a branch which let loose a sharp cracking sound. Immediately, the whole scene shifted. Edward was no longer looking down at the sleeping fawn. He looked up in terror at me. I didn't know why. All the deer, in unison, snapped their heads toward me. The scene blackened to a tunnel before blotting out completely. I woke up seconds later, looking up at Edward's face framed by tree branches against the blue sky."

"What made you faint?"

"Don't you see?"

"No, Majesty, I'm sorry. It was a peaceful scene with unfounded fears—all of which seemed to disappear until the twig snapped."

"None of you see it?" Loni twisted her hands in her lap.

"Sorry, no, Highness," Clarisse offered.

"Jillian?"

"I wish I could say yes."

Loni's shoulders dropped a little. "When the animals turned and looked directly at me, I saw what my eyes could not believe. It was most wonderous."

"Go on, Highness," Douglas urged.

"Each deer was blessed with a single horn fixed in the center of its head."

"You saw three unicorns?" Jillian gasped.

"No, Jillian, I saw *four* unicorns, and the shock was more that I could bear."

"Edward was the fourth unicorn," Louise's voice tumbled into Chapelle Saint-Hubert and across time to a hospital room. The queen turned to look behind her and saw the child standing timidly with her back pressed against one wooden door of the chapel. "He was sitting inside the circular fence too," Louise continued, "just like in the tapestry."

"How did I not see that?" Jillian's voice muttered.

"Hush, now," the queen whispered to the voices. "Louise, darling, I thought you went back to your mother."

"I did, Majesty. I told her that I wanted to stay with you until the feast. My mother said we needed to ask permission. We went looking for you in the hall and then in the grounds, but we could not find you." Louise frowned. "Then, when I saw the knight outside the chapel, I knew you must be here. While Mother was talking to Ottaviano, I heard your voice through the door. You were laughing and crying. I was worried, so," Louise looked down at her shoes guiltily, "I sneaked in. Then your voice was normal again and I heard *them*." Louise raised her eyes to the chapel ceiling. "I stayed because I wanted to hear more about the unicorns. The real ones, Your Majesty."

The queen smiled indulgently. "You are right, Louise, there is more."

The other chapel door opened a crack. "Little one," Ottaviano's voice whispered, "come out at once, the queen is not to be disturbed."

"All is well, my dear knight." Queen Anne approached the door, and he opened it fully.

Upon seeing the queen, Louise's mother, Lady Anne Pot, dropped to her knees. Her dress dusted the ground where she dropped. "My apologies, Your Majesty! I did not see my child enter. She has disturbed you in prayer. Please have mercy!"

"Your kind daughter heard her queen crying, Lady Montmorency. Being of brave heart, Louise followed her sense of duty and sought to ensure my well-being. Rise, my good lady, there is nothing to forgive." Lady Anne Pot stood, wringing her hands and the queen continued, "As I understand it, Louise seeks permission to attend me until the feast."

"Yes, Your Majesty. If it pleases you."

"Very well. She has proven herself trustworthy, honest, and amiable company. Louise may remain with me awhile longer." The girl beamed up at the queen and bounced on the balls of her feet. Louise's mother bowed, gave a stern look to her daughter that said *You had better behave*, and departed.

Queen Anne turned to Ottaviano; her eyes flashed, her lips a thin, taut line. "A child evaded your guard, Sir Knight. What have you to say for yourself?"

"Majesty, I … " the knight stammered. He swiftly knelt before Queen Anne and cleared his throat. "I knew she had entered the moment she disappeared, Your Majesty. The mother would not stop talking, and I did not wish to appear rude to your subjects. I hoped the child's presence would go unnoticed until I could remove her from the chapel."

"Please, Majesty." Louise stepped between the queen and the knight. She drew herself up as tall as a six-year-old child could and swallowed hard. "It was my fault. I knew better. I should not have entered. Do not punish the knight because I strayed and disobeyed."

Ottaviano looked at the girl in wonder. He raised his eyebrows questioningly at the queen but received no response; she had eyes only for Louise.

"Do you see, my little martin, how one brave action begets another?" Queen Anne's face softened. Both Louise and the knight looked confused. "Had anyone except you, Louise, disturbed me then the situation would be quite different. But do you recall our talk on the balcony, child?" Louise nodded. "You were brave to seek out your queen when you sensed her distress, courageous to sneak past an armed guard to do so, and honorable to take responsibility so that others will not suffer for your choices."

Louise gave a small smile. "Little by little, Your Majesty?"

"Indeed. But remember my warning. Do not take … "

" … unnecessary risks."

The queen nodded and then looked to the knight. "Ottaviano, I believe your words. Rise now and please ask Clare to see that the stables and gardens of the palace are cleared of all servants and attendants. I am sure that the kitchen staff can use all the help available if they are to prepare the banquet in time." Ottaviano nodded and began to turn away, but Queen Anne laid her hand on the knight's arm. "Then you will return here, Sir Knight. You, Louise, and I have a different path." Ottaviano nodded and left. The queen closed the doors of the chapel and then turned her attention to the girl. "Louise, sit here by the door, child. I wish to pray before we take a little walk." Louise smiled demurely in response and obeyed. Queen Anne made her way to the farthest corner in the transept of the tiny chapel and knelt.

"What's—" began Louise.

"Shhh." Queen Anne placed her hands in prayer configuration. She closed her eyes tightly, then opened them slowly.

"Majesty?" Douglas whispered.

The queen glanced back at Louise; the girl seemed not to hear the voices at this distance. "Douglas," Queen Anne muttered under her breath, "I have final things to attend to here. I wish very much for you to hear what I have to say to Ottaviano and Louise, but I must be sure that others will not hear you. I cannot risk that. So please, when I speak again to Louise, listen but be silent. I will address you directly when it is safe for us to converse."

"We understand," Douglas whispered.

"Louise has endured a long trip through seven tapestries—which is more than I can say for my court. For a child, that had to be extremely difficult, yet here she is. Her curiosity and attentiveness deserve a reward. This brave little martin has earned a special place in my heart and that is worthy of recognition."

58

And Dark of Knight

Unit mailroom
Nachrichten Caserne
Heidelberg, Germany
Current day

*O*pening dead people's mail is something I'll never get used to.
After breaking through the seals of the package sent by the names Szkolna Gora and Monty Meriwether, Master Sergeant Roman set down the scissors on the wrapping table in the mailroom.

Opening mail that could potentially belong to the highest-ranking officer in my food chain is also not something I enjoy. It makes me feel criminal. However, these aren't normal times. Five soldiers are dead in the last several hours right here behind the fence where it's supposed to be safe. It's most likely that all of them died because of this tube and that Pelican.

This was packed in Dijon. Master Sergeant pulled out wads of Dijon newspaper from the tube. *And there you are.* He withdrew the contents. *You are not a pole-dancing snake, but most certainly you are one of the Rods of Power that Colonel Christiansted briefed me on before she left.* He turned the Owl's walking stick in his hands, admiring the carved vines and flowers upon it. *When was the last time I held something of such great value?* Master Sergeant nodded. *I remember ... the Institute of Chemical Defense when I was the NCOIC of the Chemical Casualty Care Division. Dr. Peronne, you were there.*

✠ ✠ ✠

"Hey, Roman, come here." Mickey motioned as Francis Roman was passing through the break area where both Suzanne and Russell stood. "There are times when you just know that you are in the presence of greatness. Come. This is one."

"Is this what I think it is, Dr. Peronne?" Roman asked, pulling on the gloves he was given.

"Probably a little more than you expect." Mickey smiled. "In your hand is the last will and testament of John Washington, the grandfather of George Washington."

"He was in the royal lineage of Edward I of England," Russell added, nodding. "The icing on the cake is that probably only a handful of people in history have ever touched this document. Now you, Roman, are one in that vertical history."

✠ ✠ ✠

Vertical history of a lost will and vertical history of a relic that goes back before the origins of Christianity. Why is it here? Why was it sent to DCS—which I know for sure now did not refer to Sweeny? Master Sergeant held the rod in his hands with gentle firmness. *What do I know?*

Well, I know that the culmination of the Leaning Tower affair opened and closed many things. Apparently, this walking stick connects Mickey Peronne and the Owl woman, Szkolna Gora. I suppose that when she felt that danger was closing in, she had to ensure that this walking stick was sent to a safe place. She had to know that even if the DCS was not here, his staff would understand the importance of her gesture if only by her name alone. I need to get this relic to the vault posthaste. Master Sergeant Roman quickly wrapped a few of the stray newspaper pages around the top of the staff and placed the relic back into the tube. *What was that noise?*

He turned to see the legs of the mailroom specialist kick to a standstill. Dropping the body, the imposter in the Liberian uniform approached.

"I need you to pass me the contents of that tube," the Liberian pointed.

"This doesn't belong to you." Master Sergeant Roman eased backward, the tube clenched in his fists. Suddenly, a pair of arms slipped under his armpits and locked behind his neck, pushing his head forward.

"Not so fast guh-governor. We'll be pinching that parcel."

"It's not for you." Master Sergeant grunted as he struggled against the hold. The glint of a blade flashed from the hand of the Liberian and all struggles stopped.

"I believe Haman would quite agree."

59

Upon Death Do You Part

Château Royal d'Amboise grounds
Loire Valley, France
1500

"Why don't you tell me where we are going?" Louise tugged on the queen's dress as the three walked away from the chapel.

"I want you to meet some friends of mine."

"Are they mean or scary?" Louise whispered.

"No, not really. Why?"

"Because you're bringing the knight with us. Is he to guard us?"

"No, I need to talk with him too. Hold his hand and make sure he doesn't wander off." Queen Anne winked at the Louise.

"Can he carry me?" Louise smiled.

"Of course!" With a quick lift, Louise was catapulted up to Ottaviano's shoulder, steadied by one of the knight's hands upon her lower back and the other on her knees.

"This is even better than the view from the pillar in the great hall!" Louise squealed in excitement.

The three continued upon their path toward the main palace. The adults spoke quietly to each other while the child, reveling in the point of view so much taller than her own, pointed out birds and flowers that amused her, paying no attention to the discussion below.

"I can feel her little heart beating against me, Majesty. It is precious."

"As a knight," said Queen Anne, "I take it that this is not something you often encounter."

"It isn't, Majesty."

"Ottaviano, did you know that from time on end, the beating heart symbolizes everything from energy, to life, to love, to unbridled emotion?"

Ottaviano smiled. "You speak of something that is well known to all Latins."

"I see that you understand this as it applies to a physical beating felt here." The queen touched her fingers at her wrist, then paused in her walk and squared off with Ottaviano. "Also, here." Queen Anne pointed her hand upward toward the base of his neck. Along with Louise's, Ottaviano's hand reached up and touched his pulsing neck. Retracting her hand, Queen Anne gathered her skirts and resumed walking. "What I need you to understand now, Ottaviano, is that this energy applies also to a love where the parties are separated and unseen. Nevertheless, the love is forever shared, yet unshared." They passed Église Saint-Florentin and entered the gardens. "I feel love for this child when I am able to touch her, Ottaviano." Queen Anne reached up and touched Louise's leg. "She is not my flesh and blood, but I love her. I see in her what I never had with my other children ... the ones who returned too soon to God the Father."

"I see that, Majesty."

"Even as I take my hand away, my love does not diminish at all," said the queen, smiling. Queen Anne paused in the garden near the rampart wall and gazed out over the Loire River. The water was flecked with the same golden-orange light that stretched across the surrounding fields and splashed over the buildings. Queen Anne sighed contentedly at the scene before her, laying her hand upon her chest. She felt the necklace resting over her beating heart. "Dear knight, what is the greatest gift that can be given?"

"Majesty, would that not depend on the person and what that person has to give?"

"Take me for example. I am queen of France and all that France possesses. I have the richest treasury in the entire world." Queen Anne spread her arms wide. "I am, without question, the richest there can be. What is the greatest gift that I can give?"

"The list is long. I believe, though, that the answer may not be something as simple as it might seem, nor is it found in any treasury."

"A wise answer for a young knight," the queen praised. "The answer is this: the thing that I hold most dearly, yet give freely, is the greatest gift."

"What would this thing be, my queen?"

"The story weaved into the tapestry, the picture that your art master will paint, and my heart—which will be cut from my body when I am gone." Queen Anne turned and led the way to the Porcupine Gate of the outer embattlements.

"Those are several great gifts, Majesty."

"Not really," said the queen smiling sadly. "They're all the same thing." She reached up and patted the girl's leg to get her attention. "We're here, Louise."

"We are?"

"Of course, my lady!" Ottaviano brought the child down to the ground swiftly, causing an outburst of giggling.

"I wanted to share something with you." The queen took Louise's hand and led her through the tower gate and down to a green space hidden from view of the main palace yet still within its outer fortified walls. The three approached the edge of a stable. From around the back of the stable, the unicorn family appeared. "Louise, this is my animal family."

Louise took a sharp breath at the sight. "Oh, my!" the girl whispered.

Queen Anne led the group into the stable and to a rough-hewn bench. "Come, child, sit close next to me. Ottaviano, please stand near." They took their positions and waited patiently. The queen could feel the child's excited energy permeate the air. Finally, the largest of the animals began to approach them. "Louise, this is a roe buck."

"He's big."

"Come, Caradoc," Queen Anne called. The old buck sauntered closer to the bench, followed by a doe and a small fawn. The fawn sidled over next to her mother and neither of these moved another inch. But Caradoc, large as he was, knelt down and submissively placed his head in the queen's lap.

"He likes you, Majesty," Louise breathed.

"Indeed. We are like family, he and I." Queen Anne stroked the buck's head. "Louise, you should know that I first met Caradoc when I was a little older than you are now. At that time, he was part of a family of three and he was the fawn."

"He sat in the lap of the fourth unicorn, right?"

"Yes, child. He was curled up and sleeping in the lap of Edward at the Dolmen de Mané Kerioned."

"He's not a fawn anymore, Majesty." Louise tentatively stroked the deer's head with her tiny hand.

"True, but he is still just as precious to me now as he was then. To the world Caradoc is strange because he is a roe buck with a single horn. However, to me, this is what makes him special and unique from all deer—in fact, it makes him just like the blessed unicorn."

"Is he magic?" Louise looked up at the queen with wide eyes.

"Absolutely, child. He is quite magical. His presence alone is magic." Queen Anne stroked Caradoc's neck. "He appeared to me in a place where roe deer don't normally live. He shouldn't have been there, but like magic, there he was." Queen Anne gently scooted Louise closer. "Whenever I am with him, even for just a blink in time, everything in the present disappears and I am again a child like you. I am back in the forest of Brittany, surrounded by the safety of the dolmen, and with my beloved Edward, knowing that the hunting of the unicorn has ended then, now, and forever."

"This unicorn was the greatest gift ever." Louise lay both her hands tenderly on the buck.

"Although he may not have known it, my father gave me a gift which has made my life eternally happy." Queen Anne wiped her tears. For the first time since Caradoc approached, the queen made eye contact with Ottaviano. "My father gave me something which became a constant reminder of a love that has transcended time. He gave me Caradoc which allowed me to have, to hold, and to cherish the unseen and the forever unshared."

"They are your animal family, Majesty," Louise spoke quietly, "and I love them too."

"Louise, this family of unicorns is the greatest of all my treasures, and I pass their well-being to you."

"Me?" Louise turned her face to the queen. "They're mine to keep?"

Queen Anne put her hand on the child's cheek. "They're yours to care for."

"Oh, Majesty," Louise whispered reverently, "I promise I will take care of these unicorns as long as I live."

"I'll take that promise." The queen tapped Louise's nose. Smiling and wiping her cheeks, the queen continued, "But first, you had better address this with your parents."

At a nod from the queen, Ottaviano helped the child get down from the bench without disturbing Caradoc. "You are now a child in direct service of your queen, Louise. This service is a great responsibility and honor. I need to know that your family gives their consent."

"Great!" Louise grinned and bolted for the path back to the Porcupine Gate but then stopped, turned quickly and curtseyed. "With your permission, Highness, may I be excused?"

"You may indeed." Queen Anne laughed as Louise scampered away with her grand news.

The queen sighed deeply and closed her eyes. She stroked Caradoc, listening to the river pulsing through the land, feeling the roe deer's blood rushing under her hands, and sensing her own life force thrumming within her.

After a few moments, Ottaviano walked over and knelt before her. "Highness, I too am in your service and, by some divine purpose, a witness to the voices you call friends. You have my unyielding devotion. Beyond the art commission, what is it that you would have me do?"

"Since ensuring the health and well-being of these unicorns is now a matter tasked to Louise, I must put a greater responsibility upon you." The queen woke Caradoc from his blissful doze and the buck gently rose then returned to his family.

"Can you see to it that I live forever, sir knight?"

"Pardon?"

"Ottaviano, I will eventually die, and the love I have cultivated through these unicorns will come to an end. Unless, of course, you help me in matters I could trust to no one else."

"I am honored that you wish to place so much trust in me, but why—"

"Are you declining your queen's request even before it has been placed into your ears? What of unyielding devotion?"

"I decline nothing, Majesty. I fear only my own inadequacies in executing your mission."

"But you haven't heard the mission."

"That is true." Ottaviano grimaced.

"You heard my friends. You heard my heart. Will you hear your mission?"

"I will, Majesty."

The queen motioned for the knight to sit beside her. "Then here it is. The day will come when I pass into God's hands. When this occurs, I want you to take these unicorns to Caradoc."

"This is a task far easier than I expected, my queen. Where is Caradoc now?"

"I don't know."

"Is he still alive?"

"I don't know."

"Begging your pardon, my queen, is there anything that you can tell me that would help me complete this quest?"

"When I was with Caradoc in Carnac the world was a daily wonder. We lived in a fantasy and enjoyed life as if there would be no tomorrow. Over time that changed." Queen Anne stared at the roe deer family. "We both knew that one day either Caradoc or I would be required to leave the dolmen for one reason or another."

"What happened?"

"A message came. I was told that I had to immediately leave the Dolmen de Mané Kerioned and that I would not be returning. It was sudden and done without explanation. Caradoc wasn't there at the time and so I never got to say goodbye."

"Why so suddenly? Wait—" Realization spread across the knight's face. "Your father's accident?"

"Yes. What wasn't explained at the time was that my father was dying and that I was immediately to be put in full preparation to receive the official title of Duchess of Brittany as well as all the responsibilities that go with it."

"I'm so sorry, Majesty."

"Indeed, Ottaviano, my heart sank. In a moment I lost my father and Caradoc. I knew that when I became duchess there would be promises of marriage to other rulers in Europe. And I knew that I would once again be at court and unsure of whom to trust." Queen Anne bit her lip. "The only thing I had left to hold onto from that peaceful time was the family of unicorns there at the dolmen."

"You took the unicorns with you from that time onward?"

"Yes, I did. By having them, I still had Father, and I still possessed a tangible portion of the love I shared with Caradoc. The story, as you know, I put into the tapestries."

Ottaviano rubbed his chin in thought. "No one ever indicated the direction that Caradoc took?"

"No. But, I always believed that he went north to where the Ancre and the Somme Rivers meet … or perhaps nearby to the city of Péronne, where his younger brother had gone."

"Is there anyone who can verify this possibility?"

"No. I know that Richard of Shrewsbury became La Piérronne, as I said before. But I don't know what name Edward took. It's possible he kept the

Celtic name, Caradoc Freichfras. Or it might be that he took some name that is revered in the New World."

"Will my path to find Caradoc take me to the New World?" Ottaviano's eyes grew wide.

"I don't know. It might. Who can say?"

Ottaviano pressed his lips together. "I don't know that I can complete this task, my queen. However, I do promise that if I am alive and hear of your passing, I will take the unicorn family and his descendants to Caradoc Freichfras, whoever he has become and wherever he may be."

"I can ask no more of you in this task."

"What if I find that he has passed and cannot care for the unicorns?"

"Well, if that is so and we are both dead, then you must take the deer family back to Tuscany to where Father said he first found the deer." Queen Anne's eyes lingered on the doe near her mother. "In that way, they could potentially be together with any roe deer family that still may reside in the area."

"That is a bit more complex than I had first imagined, Majesty, but I believe I can follow that command. Is that all, Highness?"

"Now, my kind and noble knight, you already know the answer to that."

"Indeed, I do. May I rephrase?" Ottaviano moistened his lips. "What more may I do to serve my queen?"

"I, who will have just departed this world, want you to ensure that my pendant crucifix," Queen Anne stroked the chain at her neck, "which normally marks the pages in my diary and book of hours, is given to my lovely little plum, my daughter Claude."

"What if there are more children at the time of your passing, Highness?"

"It should go to Claude or whichever of my children is eldest at the time."

"Is there a specific time that I should present it?"

"Yes, at a time of sincere acceptance of responsibility. I believe that it should be the day my child is old enough to take marriage vows."

"If he or she do not marry, what shall I do?"

"Then present it at the time when the eldest has given themselves in faith to God. Be cautious." The queen's tone suddenly dour. "Do not present it to my eldest if there are those nearby who are not true or honorable in Christian ways."

Ottaviano gave a firm nod of understanding. "What of the painting to be commissioned and the completed tapestries?"

"The tapestries belong to the people of France. However, the painting of my knight and landscape, when it is finished, should follow the path of the unicorn family as I have previously described."

"If Caradoc and you have both passed, I will take the painting to Tuscany with the herd of roe deer. However, Majesty, I would be loath to leave it there with a shepherd, warden, or groundskeeper. With your permission I will take the painting with me and return it to Master Carpaccio or his pupil understudy. At least they would have an appreciation for the symbolism intended."

"You will do no such thing! Whereas I agree that the painting should not be left where it cannot be preserved, I forbid you to return it to the artist." Queen Anne took a deep breath and softened her tone, placing her hand upon the knight's arm. "Instead, as one who has had a glimpse into my soul, I would ask you to keep it yourself and within your lineage. Can you do this for me?"

"How can I not?"

"Promise me, Ottaviano. I must know that all I have done will not fade with my death."

Ottaviano knelt again at the queen's feet. "I swear it, Majesty." He put his hand to his heart. "But, Majesty, may I be so brazen as to ask why you choose to leave such important matters to me? My intent in coming here to see you was simply to complete a worthy task assigned to my page, yet—"

"Your intent for your journey was one thing, but God's intent for your journey was quite another. We have been connected in a way I cannot explain. You are honorable and true and your way forward from here is clear." Queen Anne locked eyes with Ottaviano. "You know of royal courts and deceit and those who seek to gain power here on earth. You know this all too well. As such, you know that those who can be trusted are as rare as my unicorn family here. I trust in God and His plan. I trust in you. Is that so hard to believe?"

Ottaviano swallowed the rising lump in his throat. "If you believe me to be worthy, Majesty, then I shall strive to be."

"Thank you, Sir Knight." Queen Anne smiled. "I will pray that you learn to see that which I see in you. Now, last of all, my life lies in the pages of my diary within my book of hours." She pointed to his satchel. "I want you to take it so that the instructions you need stay with you always."

"While you prayed, and before your little martin interrupted," Ottaviano gave a small chuckle, "I transcribed all that I needed from your diary, Highness." Ottaviano removed the thick little book from his bag and placed it on Queen Anne's lap. She laid her hands atop the book, nodding. Ottaviano tentatively put his hands over the queen's; with his eyes cast down in genuflection, he added, "With God's help and guidance, I will achieve everything you ask of me. I swear it."

"Now truly, I can ask no more of you except for the honor of your company at the banquet." Queen Anne smiled. "When you rise, rise as a knight in my personal service—rise as a knight in the Order of the Ermine."

With tears in his eyes, the young knight slowly rose. He bowed and kissed Queen Anne's hand. As Ottaviano began walking back to the tower gate to return to the palace, he turned to look back at the stables. The sky was streaked with purple and gold, the last rays of the day making a final stand against the night. He watched as the solitary queen quietly caressed the head of the unicorn who had returned to her, while the remaining two unicorns slowly closed in upon her with loving acceptance.

60

When Hearts Break

Maternity hospital
Saint-Quentin, Somme River Valley
Vermandois region, France
Current day

"Will Ottaviano be able to complete the tasks I have given him, Douglas?" Loni trembled for Queen Anne as she inhaled.

"I don't know, Majesty." Douglas felt a hand touch his shoulder. "You have challenged him greatly."

"He is a proud and competent young knight." Clarisse leaned in. "He has all the talent to succeed."

"True enough, Majesty," Mickey added. "But he has many challenges ahead."

Loni turned toward the sound of Mickey's voice. "Go on, Mickey. I want to know what he faces." Loni's hands continued to stroke the invisible roe deer buck.

"First, Majesty, he serves many masters. This is never an easy task."

"That doesn't sound too difficult yet."

"He must return to Venice with your specifications for the … " he paused to glance at his notes, "Carpaccio painting and then continue to serve the … " he flipped back several pages, "Duke of Urbino in whatever capacity that may be. Plus, he must begin the complicated search for Caradoc—that mission could lead him all over France, Europe, or even to the New World."

Loni bit her lip. "I know his tasks are arduous, but there are few I can trust. Will I live long enough to see the finished painting?"

"I don't know, my queen. History doesn't record such details."

"Would you tell me if it did, Mickey?"

"Yes, Majesty, I believe I would."

"Will Caradoc ever see the tapestries or the painting dedicated to his memory?"

"Again, Highness, I have to say that … "

" … history does not record such trivialities." Loni's eyes welled. "Mickey, these are not trivial matters to me."

"I know, Majesty. I'm sorry. There is nothing I can do."

"Have you, any of you, ever seen my final painting?"

"Majesty," Douglas answered delicately, "we don't know much about the painting you commissioned except what you mentioned to Ottaviano at the stables just now. And, well, in museums all over the world there are probably thousands of paintings of landscapes with knights."

"Oh my gosh, no way!" Jillian's tin voice emanated through the phone beside Loni.

"What is it, Jillian?" Mickey's voice came through the hands-free unit in Jillian's ear.

"Oh. My. Gosh. Guys, I was so focused on the unicorns…." Jillian stuffed both the charcoal pencil and cardboard coffee sleeve covered with sketches and notes pell-mell back into her large bag and dropped it on the ground. "Wait a minute, Majesty." Jillian readjusted the sleeping man on the window ledge with whom she had been pretending to converse for the last several hours. "I think that I might have seen what you are looking for."

"Come on, Jillian," Douglas said. "What are the chances that you saw Queen Anne's painting? Out of all the paintings of knights, in all the museums, in all the world?"

Jillian grimaced as she pushed herself up from the hard ledge. Her body felt stiff, but at least her ankles felt better. She turned her back to the security guard and spoke in the direction of the sleeping man. "I dunno, Douglas," she shot back in a whisper. "What are the chances that you called me about unicorn tapestries while I was standing in the very gallery containing them?" Jillian stretched, adjusted her golden hair to cover her earpiece, and took in one last glance around the gallery.

"Okay, point taken," Douglas answered sheepishly. "It just seems so—"

"After all we have seen and heard, Douglas," Clarisse asked gently, "why do you doubt?"

"Look, I can't explain it, guys. I was supposed to drive to my office; I ended up at The Met Cloisters without knowing how or why. I think, maybe, I saw what Queen Anne is talking about. I just have this hopeful feeling."

"Jillian, darling," said the queen, "I cannot think of any greater hope in my life."

"Bear with me, Majesty, I have a bit to walk." Jillian scooped up her bag from the ground and bolted from the Unicorn Tapestries Room. *Wait! What if the poster on the easel that I saw when I first entered the Cloisters was not it? What if what was, but they took the poster of the boy knight down already? I might be getting everyone's hopes up just to have those hopes trashed.* Anxiously, Jillian passed the guards along the way as her wedged shoes whumped loudly through the galleries. Her heart pumped in time with her quick march, making a whooshing sound in her ears. As she got closer to the bookstore, Jillian felt an old friend nudging her mind. "Um, Queen Anne," she puffed, "what if … "

"What if what, dear Jillian?" came the queen's voice into Jillian's ear.

"Well, what if I was wrong?" Jillian paused midstride, still panting a bit.

"But you *just said*—" Douglas began.

"I know *what I said*," Jillian hissed, "but what if I'm wrong and I mess it all up?" Jillian panted softly. *Like it always seems to happen.*

"Ah, but Jillian," Queen Anne's voice soothed, "what if you are right?"

Jillian took a steadying breath, but her pulse stayed fast from her walk. "Okay, but maybe don't count on this being the correct painting. This may be no more than a wild goose chase, Highness."

"There are wild geese being chased where the painting sits?" Loni whispered.

"Jillian is just using a common phrase, Majesty," Clarisse smiled.

"Clarisse, how will she know if the painter is Carpaccio?" Loni whispered again.

"We will ask, Highness. Giver her time to get there."

Loni nodded and began twisting her hands nervously again. Mickey sat at Loni's side, staring at her writhing hands, clearly wishing to ease her anxiety.

Clarisse took the pause to lean close to Douglas and whisper, "I have a question that has been burning at me for a bit." She then turned and retreated to the room's window.

Douglas turned away from Loni and followed Clarisse. "What is it, Clarisse?" he asked, keeping his voice low.

"You said something before to Ottaviano with regards to being indebted to him."

"Yes, what about it?"

"You said you would be forever in his debt."

"Yes, I believe I will."

"Why?"

Douglas waved off the question and made to return to his chair, but Clarisse caught his arm and pulled him close again.

"Tell me, Douglas."

"Look, I'd really rather not."

"Douglas," Clarisse pressed, "why are you forever indebted to him?" Douglas sighed and his shoulders slumped. "Come now, you can tell me anything," she whispered.

"Okay. Okay. It's because of you."

"Me?"

"Yes, you, Clarisse," Douglas whispered, "and Ottaviano's fierce devotion to Queen Anne."

"So...?" Clarisse's eyebrow arched in confusion.

"Look, he's a knight, sure," Douglas sighed and looked at the ground, "but Queen Anne wasn't even really his queen except by politics and yet, when I was rude to her, he was willing to reach through a time continuum or whatever to fight me and defend her honor. And ... well ... I've never been in a relationship like that. Never felt that kind of support or had someone defend me like that, except for maybe Loni."

"And your angel?"

"Suzanne?" He scoffed. "She should have done that for me, but she never did."

"And ... " Clarisse prompted as she lifted Douglas's face.

"And I ... I never supported her like that either." Douglas winced at his confession, guilt sweeping over his face. Clarisse took his face in her hands until he looked her in the eye. He swallowed hard and his voice cracked as he spoke. "Ottaviano and Queen Anne barely knew each other but she trusted him with so much that was special and sacred to her. I realize that I've never had that—I feel like there is a giant hole sitting in the middle of my body."

"Now that you have learned this lesson, what will you do with this hole in your heart?" She moved her hands to his chest, one on top of the other.

"I want to fill it with that kind of knightly devotion," he whispered, leaning close to her ear, breathing in her fresh, clean floral scent.

"To whom, Douglas?" she brushed her cheek against his.

"Like I said, I owe him because of you."

"I'm here, folks," Jillian gasped. "Sorry, wait a minute." She leaned against a wall and hitched her purse up on her shoulder. "Let me get my breath." She sucked in air and exhaled loudly. "I've got a stitch in my side and my belly is cramping." People passing her in the museum's entryway shot her wary glances before hurrying into the galleries. Jillian ignored them.

"Jillian, please be careful, *pupuce*. I have waited a lifetime. I can wait a few moments longer."

"I'm here, I'm good. Just tired. Okay." Jillian pushed away from the wall and peered around the hall. "Oh, no. The easel is gone. I don't see the poster print!" Jillian's voice quavered. People stared but she didn't care; all that mattered was that print. "Oh my goodness, how can things change so quickly?" Jillian panted. "Why couldn't I have stopped longer on the way in when I first noticed it?" Jillian gasped and whimpered. "Sorry, everyone. I let you all down, just like I knew I would."

"Don't worry, *pupuce*, you did the best that you could." The queen's voice was thick with emotion, and in it, Jillian felt both the monarch's and Loni's disappointment in her.

"Jillian," Clarisse's voice came through the earpiece, "can you talk to someone there? Maybe it was moved or maybe there is another print available? Surely, they have more than one."

"Wait, the bookstore lady is putting up a poster." Jillian bit her lip, waiting for the woman to finish the task.

"A poster?" the queen sniffed. "What is that?"

"Majesty," Mickey answered, "a poster is an image or copy of the painting made from the original."

"This can be done?"

"That and much more," Douglas commented.

"She's done," Jillian interrupted the chatter in her ear. "It's the same one!" She bolted over to the window display and bent over to see it clearly. "I see a young knight standing near a castle by the sea."

"Is the copy signed?"

"I'm looking, Clarisse. Hold on. Bending over makes me nauseous. Let me squat down to get a better look." Jillian squatted in front of the poster. "Nope, I can't see a signature. Wait a minute, there is a lady here. She's walking over to me. Let me see what she says." Jillian looked up and gave a winning smile.

"Ma'am, I'm going to have to ask you to move away from the doorway. The fire marshal has directed that this exit cannot be blocked."

"There's a New Yorker for you," Mickey coughed. "Direct and straight to the point."

"Shut it," Jillian whispered.

"Excuse me, ma'am?"

"What? Oh, I was just saying, it must be hard to *shut it*—the door I mean—with me in the way." As she rose, Jillian surreptitiously pressed her earpiece to put the call on hold while she spoke to the shop attendant.

A few minutes later, after Jillian had moved over near the window but not in the way of the door, she reactivated the call. "Come on, guys," Jillian scolded, "I've got people around me here, jeez."

"What did you discover, Jillian?" Queen Anne's anxious voice asked.

"The lady said that the poster is of a Venetian painting which was completed in the early fifteen hundreds and—"

"Jillian, that must be it!"

"Hang on, Majesty, the original is currently housed in the Thyssen Museum in Madrid, Spain. The title is *Young Knight in a Landscape*."

"Spain?" The queen's tone turned grim. "If this is my painting that would mean it never came to me."

"We don't know," Clarisse added, "and we don't know if this piece is truly the one that Carpaccio made for you."

"We shall know soon enough. Jillian, please," Queen Anne urged, "look for the following details. Are you close enough to this ... poster?"

"Yes, Majesty, go ahead."

"There must be a fantasy version of a waterside landscape and a castle on the coast."

"Yes, there is a seascape that borders the right side. I wonder why it wouldn't be titled *Knight in a Seascape?*"

"I asked Master Carpaccio to express the concept of death over dishonor and it must be obvious, even in your time."

"Obvious?" Jillian's eyes searched the image starting at the top. For the moment she forced her mind to overlook all the obvious-to-an-artist symbolism and hunted instead for what would be obvious to the layman. "Well, there's nothing much more obvious than a sign."

"A sign?"

"Yes, Majesty, two actually. And they are more like parchment scraps."

She bent closer for a minute. "One on a branch on the right says, 'Victor Carpathius' and has the date in Roman letters." A pang shot around her side, and Jillian held her breath for a moment. "Let me see how well I remember my Roman letters … *M* is a thousand … plus *D*…."

"*D* is five hundred," Mickey offered.

"Plus *X* which is ten." Jillian stood up quickly and shouted, "The painting is from 1510!"

"And the name is the Romanized version of the Italian Vittore Carpaccio," Mickey added. "Nice job, Jillian."

Jillian smiled, then winced at the stitch in her side. *Idiot, running in wedges. That's what you get.*

"So, the painting is signed."

"Yes, I was wrong, Majesty." Jillian groaned, "I'm struggling here. Please bear with me."

"What does the other parchment say?"

"Hold on a sec. I'm reading it now." She leaned over again to see the bottom portion of the poster. "It is also in Latin. It says, 'MALO MORI QUAM FOEDARI.'"

"Rather dead than be dishonored," Mickey translated.

"Yes," Queen Anne's voice gave a sigh, "just like my ermines who would rather die at the hands of hunters than be soiled in an escape to freedom. Jillian, this is my painting. You have found it!"

Loni clapped and raised her hands into the air. "God be praised! I lived to see my painting even if only at a distance!"

"Majesty," Jillian's voice came through the phone, "let's be sure. Tell me what else to look for. There is a white ermine, like in the fountain tapestry."

"Yes! There must also be a frog and a large buck." Loni counted on her fingers.

"Richard-Froggie and Edward-Caradoc," Clarisse interjected. Loni nodded smiling through her tears.

"I see both, Majesty."

"Yes!" Loni shouted and clapped again. "This is my painting! It is! There can be no doubt! You all have done it!" Loni swallowed hard, trying to force herself back into appropriate royal behavior but nothing could contain her smile. "The buck, it also symbolizes Saint Hubert."

"Majesty I … " Jillian paused, and they heard her suck in a breath and hold it for a moment before continuing, "I see many, many birds. Like in the tapestries."

"I feel I know your answer, but I must ask it." Loni's hands were clasped over her chest. "A peacock. Is there a peacock? Somehow connected to a squire?"

"It is standing on his head!" Jillian answered.

Loni laughed for Queen Anne, a pure, relieved, joyful laugh.

"The knight is young, handsome, with auburn hair and a strong cleft chin," Jillian added.

"Ottaviano Riario!" Loni gasped. "Jillian, may I ask you one thing more?"

"Go ahead."

"This will be very subtle. It will require your artist's eye. Look at the branching pattern of the buck's antlers. Is there the shape of a heart hidden within?"

"No, Majesty."

"Not even a little?"

"Not in any stretch of the imagination. Sorry, Highness."

"Oh."

"Wait a minute, Majesty. There is a sprouting plant at the knight's left foot."

"Sprouting plant?"

"The plant's multiple leaves are on long-necked stalks but many of the leaves are clearly heart-shaped."

"Oh, how I wish I could be there with you, Jillian."

"Majesty, even though the leaves are in different orientations, I see the presence of a heart within them."

Jillian heard the quiet muffling of a sob. "Majesty?" she whispered. The sounds of crying and consoling came through Jillian's earpiece. "Majesty? I honestly believe this to be your painting and that I was sent here to find it for you."

"Yes, Jillian. I believe it is and that you were," the queen's voice sniffled. "Now the painting belongs to all of you as well. Thank you all."

"You don't sound happy, Highness." Jillian winced again and tried to stretch her core muscles.

"I don't want to be an ingrate … but one question pulls at my heart strings."

"You want to know if Caradoc ever saw the painting," Clarisse's voice whispered. Jillian nodded to herself as she stood in the entryway, wondering the same thing.

"Yes … is that too much for Rigantona to ask? I have all the riches in the world and this answer cannot be bought."

"Highness, we have no way of knowing if Edward ever saw the painting. However," Clarisse continued, "you should take great comfort in knowing that we now have knowledge of a young knight in a landscape which came into existence by the sheer power of a timeless love between a young prince and his beloved ermine … and this knowledge shall not be forgotten."

"Touché, Clarisse, touché. That will have to be enough. Already it is so much more than I could have hope for. Clarisse, Mickey, Douglas, Jillian, and this Loni that connects us, I want you all to know that I love you. Thank you for making me the richest there can be. Jillian, to you I send my most special love and deepest appreciation. The heart you found swells deep within me."

"I know the heart-shaped leaf is allegorical, Majesty, but remember … the artist could have chosen from many types and shapes of plant leaves. I really believe these heart-shaped leaves were intended for greater meaning by the artist."

"Thank you. Thank you all."

"You're most welcome, Majesty," said Jillian, muffling a slight groan of her own. "Hey, Mickey," she clutched her side. "I'll catch up with you later. I need a break."

"Sure thing, Jillian," Mickey answered. "Thanks again for the Cloister's connection."

Clicking off her phone, Jillian stared at the poster and the stalked leaves of the plant. *What if I'm wrong? No. It's a heart—I know it's a heart. If it isn't, I would never tell her. It would shatter her.* A strange sidestepping motion of a couple of tourists caught her eye. Jillian's eyes panned to the floor. *What's that?*

"No ... no ... it can't be," she muttered. On the floor near where she had squatted, right below the poster, was blood. Jillian's eyes followed the red dots on the floor and tracked them back to the source—a tiny stream on the inside of her leg. Her belly cramped again, more severely. She melted to the floor, clutching her bag to her chest. Jillian covered her face with her hands and sobbed silently.

61

Queen's Knight to Queen's Bishop

Château du Clos Lucé
Château Royal d'Amboise grounds
Loire Valley, France
1519

"The mysterious instructions were written but then not taken, Old Father?" Salai leaned forward on the prayer bench, stroking his smooth cheeks as he mused aloud.

"Apparently. Otherwise, they would not remain here in the secret diary pages of the book of hours." The old father tapped the book's cover. "Salai, we need to know the person who was granted the authority to write in the queen's most private book as he may have the answers to many of our questions. We need to know why our departed queen asked for this painting. I also confess that I am curious to know why this crucifix was kept separate of all her jewelry and not managed by the queen's chief chamberlain. But, most importantly, was this painting ever completed?"

"And if it wasn't?"

"Well, then, there may be a new project in our future."

"Would there be a reason to paint it now? After all, the queen is dead. I think it would be quicker and easier to solve the mystery than to create something which may or may not be what the queen wanted."

"True enough, that would be easier." The old father stroked his white beard. "Yet here I am in the departed queen's private chapel," he spread his hands wide, "where she grieved the death of her children, and I paint frescos for her. The paintings honor God, yes, but they are for her." He brought his hands together in prayer and lowered his eyes. "As I work in this place, I often think that I hear her voice, her soft, muttered prayers. Her sorrow and faith have permeated these walls. These benches have been baptized in tears from the secret, hidden ocean of her soul. This place … in this place … she was Anne. Not a queen or a duchess, just Anne, a woman communing with God." The old father opened his eyes and brought his hands down to his lap. "I don't know if the frescos are enough. I feel that she needs more from me. I cannot explain it, Salai. Perhaps someday you will feel as I feel now." The old man cleared his throat. "However, if we do not paint, my dear Salai, where do we plan to begin the unraveling of this mystery?"

"Why not start with me, Master Piero?" Clare spoke from the other side of the openings in the wooden doors.

"Clare, come in. I did not hear you approach. Is there something you need? Has Melzi misbehaved in the kitchen?"

Clare closed the door behind her and moved through the narrow doorway into the chapel. "I sincerely apologize for intruding, Master Piero, and you will be glad to hear that Melzi has been on task. I interrupt because the mystery you seek to solve is one I have been following for many years."

"You know of the queen's dairy and the jewelry tucked within?" Master Piero's eyebrows rose in surprise.

"Yes, Master Piero. It is her tandem book of hours and personal diary. The cross is her bookmarker which she also occasionally wore. She entrusted both to me upon her death. I am the one who wrapped, bound, and placed it in your bed frame."

"I can see the queen placed great trust in you, Clare—you are truly a woman of honor." Clare bowed her head, flushing slightly. "But why would you choose to do this?" He held up the book of hours and its wrappings. "You could have just brought the book to me openly."

"If I came to you directly, would you have taken me seriously? A mere housekeeper? I think not." Master Piero attempted to interrupt but Clare headed him off. "Perhaps now, after all these years you may have, but not at the start. You know that to be true. Those worthy of trust must earn it." She glanced sidelong at Salai. "But I knew if you happened upon the book, Master Piero, then the mystery would burn within you. You would not stop until you had to solved it, or resolved it, yourself."

"Well, I have to admit, the mystery has plagued my mind," he chuckled. "And you are right, I have been ruminating upon how to meet the queen's wishes. However, for all the burning, I have no answers. I have only questions … and now more questions."

"I have many questions also. Some are linked to answers."

"And yet you have not solved this mystery?"

"With your help, Master Piero, I suspect that will all change." Clare told the old father and Salai about Ottaviano and the day that he interrupted the evaluation of the tapestries at the main palace down the hill. She spoke of how she had served the queen throughout the day with great attentiveness, but also at a distance which was irregular. Clare relayed the story weaved into *The Hunt of the Unicorn* tapestries as it was shared with the court over the days that followed Ottaviano's appearance at court. She told the artists of the long-standing love that forever existed between Caradoc and Rigantona even though their paths never crossed again after Anne's father had died. Finally, she explained the queen's lengthy process of choosing artisans to complete the work so dear to her heart and how that method had guided Clare's own actions since the queen's death.

"Once I came to know your character, Master Piero, and I understood your ability to create deep, meaningful art, I knew what must be done. I knew that if my queen's commissioned art had not been completed, then the only artist alive who could fulfill her last wishes would be you."

Master Piero stroked his beard and nodded at the housekeeper. His eyes were rimmed with tears. "Indeed, trust must be earned." When he spoke, his voice was thick with emotion. "I understand, dear Clare. I am flattered by your trust in me." He sniffed hard to draw back the tears. "I take it then that Ottaviano is the knight who wrote in the diary?"

"Yes, Master Piero."

"So, Clare, the painting was never completed?"

"I thought not, Master Piero."

The old man's wrinkled forehead creased deeper. "Thought not?"

"What does that mean?" Salai cut in.

"It means that I now have reason to believe that the painting *was* completed and *has* been delivered to the palace grounds."

"When? Where is it, Clare?"

"Several days ago, Master Piero." Clare bit her bottom lip. "I saw it in Melzi's room, behind his chessboard table."

"The wrapped painting?"

"Yes."

"Clare, how can you be sure of the identity of a painting that your eyes have never seen?"

"The words in the diary have burned the image into my mind these five years. When I unwrapped a corner of the painting and saw the knight, I knew it to be Queen Anne's commissioned piece."

"Now who is a little devil, Clare?" Salai teased, waggling two fingers above his head.

Ignoring Salai, Clare continued, "It was like meeting a person whom you always knew, yet never met."

"Bring it to me, Clare, please," Master Piero requested, then he growled, "and bring Melzi to me as well."

"Master Piero, the painting is there no longer."

"Then where is the painting?" The old man threw his hands up pleadingly.

"For me, that's where this new mystery begins. I have no knowledge of it except that it was here one day and not long afterward it was gone. When I saw that Melzi had it, I thought he was bringing it to you." Clare dried her hands on her apron. "Then I heard that there was a Spaniard in town talking about the purchase of a painting from Melzi. Only too late did I suspect that Melzi's intentions were self-serving. Whatever he did with the painting, only he knows."

"Did you ask him about the painting?"

"I did not, Master Piero. It is not my place as housekeeper to make such inquiries. I was hoping to hear Melzi boasting from his art studio near the kitchen. But he has been silent—which is even more shocking. This is why I have come to you now."

"You did what you thought was best." Master Piero sighed and rubbed his forehead, suddenly seeming haggard in the eyes of those who cared for him. Clare stepped toward the old man and took his hand in hers. He gave her a weak smile and pat her hand kindly. "It seems that once trouble is found, eventually all paths lead to Melzi," he mumbled.

"So it seems, Master Piero. Should I go get Melzi now?" Clare asked.

"Get Melzi?" a voice laughed from the corridor. "There's no need to." The doors flung open. "I have brought him here myself." Bowing, Melzi smiled and entered the chapel. "I came to ask Clare the next kitchen task needing attention, but now I sense that you have need for my attention. How can the humble artist-turned-kitchen-maid, but no less the junior protégé to the master, Melzi be of service to you, dearest of all hearts?"

"Melzi," said Master Piero, the old father, cutting across, "do you know of a painting that was delivered to this house?"

"Yes, Old Father. The messenger that delivered it said it was for the departed queen, may God rest her soul."

"I wonder what made the messenger think to bring it here?" the old father, Master Piero, mused.

"You alluded to it yourself, Old Father," Salai nodded. "Although the queen is departed, her presence still fills these spaces."

"Thank you, Salai. You are right," said the old father. His nostalgic smile withered as he dragged his eyes over Melzi's face. "So what did you do with the painting?"

"I told the messenger, a very handsome bishop from Viterbo, that Queen Anne had passed." Melzi cupped his chin between his thumb and index finger. "He was an odd clergyman. Although he was clergy, he carried a sword. He carried it well. You know what I mean? He carried it with … " Melzi sucked in a breath and posed, "confidence. He looked like a soldier-monk. Maybe he was a Templar." Melzi relaxed his pose, shrugged, and leaned carelessly against the arched wooden doorway. "Then again, Templars have been scarce since the papal purge two hundred years ago. Nevertheless, I didn't ask. Frankly, that would be none of my business. He seemed quite distressed about the queen's death. He said he was now in search of someone named—"

"Caradoc," The old father growled. He released Clare's hand and clenched the prayer book.

"Yes." Melzi snapped his fingers and smiled at the old father. "Caradoc. The bishop said that he had business at the dolmen but that he would soon return."

"And did he return?"

"Yes, Old Father, he did a few days later."

"What happened then?"

"He said he had to journey to Nantes and then to the Vermandois. He asked me if I would hold the painting for him until he returned. I said I would."

"Did you?"

"Yes, I did, Old Father."

"Then bring me the painting. I want to see it."

"I can't, Old Father. I don't have it anymore." Melzi gave a roguish smile.

"What mischief have you done, Melzi?" The old man slammed his fist into the wooden pew. "Has some Spaniard purchased the painting at a price set by you?"

"Mischief? You cut me to the quick, Old Father." Melzi grimaced melodramatically. "Melzi, your beloved junior protégé an incorrigible rascal? Is that truly what you think of me?"

"I know you, Melzi," Salai hissed as he stood up. "You have broken your word with the bishop and, in turn, marred the memory of a queen."

"You know this, Salai? How could you know this? Is it because that is what *you* would have done in my stead?"

"I would do no such thing. I resent the implication." In one step Salai moved swiftly into the other part of the double doorway, and with his hands on the central support frame he leaned menacingly toward Melzi. "You scoundrel, how dare you—"

"Salai, your name fits you well," Melzi snarled. "You may have the old father fooled, but I know that you are still the living devil."

"Cease, both of you! Stop it now!" The old father pointed to one, then the other, then back to the first. The old father paused, clutched his chest, and took a few deep breaths. "My apologies to both of you. I have tried to raise you two apprentices to be honest and noble. If either of you have failed, then I, as your mentor and sole benefactor, am to blame." Old Father turned his face away from the youths and toward the altar.

"You have not failed with me, Old Father." Salai tapped his chest and leaned back on his side of the doorframe.

"Nor with me," Melzi echoed.

"Melzi." The old father sighed and looked back to the young men. "I ask you directly: Where is the painting now?"

"I gave it back to the soldier … knight … bishop when he returned from Nantes and the Vermandois. He said that he had to take it to the new owner."

"Very well. I ask you now: What did you sell the Spaniard?"

Melzi's smug look returned. "An old painting of mine—*Flora.*"

"The partial nude I painted with you?"

"Yes."

"Is this the truth?"

"As God looks down upon me, Old Father, I swear it."

"When did you give the painting back to the bishop, Melzi?"

"Not more than a couple of days ago."

"Ottaviano is in the area, now?" Clare drew in a quick breath.

"Yes, Ottaviano, that is his name." Melzi picked at his cuticles. "He called himself, His Reverence Ottaviano Riario, Bishop of Viterbo."

"Melzi, did he say when he learned about Queen Anne's death?" Clare moved closer.

"No, Clare, he didn't. He also didn't say when the painting was finished. I think this was the source of his distress."

"In what way?"

"I sensed that he had the finished painting before the queen died but did not bring it back timely. Thus, when he heard that Queen Anne had died, he knew that he had failed to bring the commissioned painting to her."

"Did Ottaviano say why he came at this time?"

"No, Clare. He just said that he knew he had to leave his bishopric in Lazio within the Papal States. He said he was an ermine and that he had work to do in Queen Anne's service. He said that he would be in Amboise a week longer to gather provisions to go to the south."

"He is here right now? Where is he staying?" Clare pulled on Melzi's sleeve.

Melzi leaned back and spoke quickly as Clare bore down on him. "I don't know. Bishop Ottaviano said that once he had enough provisions, he would be taking the queen's special herd of roe deer with him. He also said that he needed to meet with you, Clare. Something about a bookmark?"

Salai laughed at Melzi's discomfort. "Is there anything more in this mystery to be solved, Old Father?" Salai asked. Clare released Melzi's sleeve, and he scampered away back toward the kitchen.

"I think all will finally be known after the meeting with Clare and the bishop." The old father, Master Piero, smiled and chuckled with relief.

Clare approached the old father and sat beside him. "Master Piero, I want so very much to introduce you to Ottaviano. I am convinced that the stories he can tell you will bond you two immediately."

"I believe you to be the wisest among all housekeepers, Clare." Master Piero patted Clare's rough hands. "And one of the most honorable women I have had the pleasure of knowing in my lifetime."

"I am a housekeeper by choice. I am wise only by chance. I am honored by those who place their faith in me. God has chosen wisdom to be my talent. If I have served you and Him equally well, then I rejoice."

"I can't speak for God," Master Piero pointed his index finger up to the bright blue ceiling of the chapel strewn with golden stars, "but for my part, I say that you have. For His part, however, I will ask Him when I see Him." He squeezed Clare's hand as sorrow crept into the corners of his eyes. "And, Clare, I fear that time is rapidly approaching."

"You have been saying that for years, Master Piero." She squeezed his hand back.

"Then my prayer would be that I remain the old father for many years yet to come."

"Lord, please hear that prayer." Clare smiled.

62

Clos Calls

Château du Clos Lucé
Château Royal d'Amboise grounds
Loire Valley, France
1519

Balancing the kitchen basket on her shoulder, Clare fumbled at the door's lock and lost her grip on the keys which then tumbled to the ground.

Isn't anything going to go right today? Clare stomped her foot and looked up in frustration. The carved dove at the door's apex looked down at her, holding its ribboned message out to her as if it were an offering: *Dieu Avant Tout.* She wiped the tears from her reddened eyes with the back of one hand. "Yes, God above all," she whispered to herself. Then, scanning the ground for the keys, she saw a dirty little child perched on the stone outcropping under the window to her right.

"Who might you be?" Clare sniffed, drawing back her tears. The cherub's face was streaked with grime and sweat but she smiled as she held the keys up toward Clare. "Not talking today, child?" The little girl tapped her gathered fingers to her lips. "I'm guessing you're hungry, little green eyes." Clare sniffed again and set the basket at her feet. "I'll make a deal with you. You give me the keys and then you get to choose any one thing from the basket." The child beamed and pointed to the large bread loaf protruding from under the basket cover. "You have chosen wisely, little one," said Clare grinning as, if in a prisoner swap, she handed the loaf of baked bread with one hand and tentatively received the keys in the other. "It looks like we both benefited from that exchange, no?" Clare blew her nose with a handkerchief as she watched the child scamper off through the gate to the main road.

Just as the child turned out of sight, the thunder of approaching hooves clattering on the road came to a halt within the courtyard. Clare securely locked the door as a rider dismounted and strode up to the entrance of

358

Clos Lucé. Wiping her face clean with the handkerchief, she turned to face the traveler.

"Even though there is a lot of road dirt on you, I believe I know that strong chin and the kind face to which it is attached," she said to the traveler. His face had lost its youthful blush over the past nineteen years, but his eyes burned with the same intensity as Clare remembered. "Good morning, Your Grace." Clare gave a curtsy and held it as the knight approached.

"God's blessing, dear housekeeper."

"Sir Ottaviano, Your Grace, I am so happy to see you." Clare rose and gave a small smile.

"You don't look happy, Clare. Why do you cry?"

"It's not a good day. I stepped on the cat. I burned myself while cleaning the hearth. I dropped the keys...."

"It's not any of that, Clare. What really troubles you?"

"My heart is broken." Clare clutched the apron at her chest and sobbed. "I have lost one dear to my heart."

"Come now." Ottaviano hugged the housekeeper until she quieted. With his ring and pinky fingers curled, Bishop Ottaviano motioned the sign of the cross toward the closed door. "Easy, my child. Have faith." He led Clare over to the small set of semicircular stone steps outside the queen's oratory. He sat beside Clare in the cool shadow of the holy place and held her hand. "Our Lord will guide you through your sorrow."

"Thank you, Your Grace," Clare sniffled. "I do know this, but in the iron grip of sadness it can be hard to remember." Clare cleared her throat, but a tremor remained in her voice while she spoke. "I am told that you asked to see me, Your Grace. I just missed seeing you on your previous visits. How long before you will be pope?"

"Clare, I will not achieve that personal goal. Giovanni di Lorenzo of the house of de' Medici holds that position with the Duke of Urbino at his side. As for me, you can see God has had other plans. I am the Bishop of Viterbo. I provide for His Holiness during his summer recess from the Vatican."

"I see, Your Grace." Clare bowed her head slightly. "I am sorry that you have come too late to see Queen Anne of Brittany. I was with her until the end." She wiped her eyes with the back of her hand.

"Was it the birthing of her last child that caused her death? Did she never heal fully?"

"No, Your Grace. But it was a difficult birth and, sadly, the baby boy did not survive to see this world." Clare sniffed hard. "In the last year of her life Queen Anne suffered greatly. Doctors said it was her kidneys. It has been a dark time for me, these last several years, Ottaviano." Clare was silent for a moment and then added, "And yet, Queen Anne's linage continues since her daughter Claude is now queen."

"This I have learned, and I am sorry for your many losses. I come now for Queen Anne's precious roe deer family, the one that the child was given the mission to protect. I imagine that Louise is no longer little."

"No indeed. She has blossomed into a beautiful young lady."

"Well, this beautiful young lady must now relinquish her charge over the herd to me."

"Oh, she won't do that," Clare chuckled.

Ottaviano was taken aback. "She must. Queen Anne willed it."

"Where that herd goes, so will she. She doesn't understand the depth of your mission regarding the moving of the herd, but she understands her oath to her queen just as you do."

"You, Clare, are the one person left in this world who knows the reason this must now be so. Such is the trust the queen had in you."

"And in you, Sir Knight. If the herd must be moved it can only mean that Caradoc is dead."

The bishop nodded solemnly. "Yes, Clare. I found the ashes that remained of him inside the Dolmen de Mané Kerioned. I took some of the ashes and gave them to his brother in Péronne. The rest I have brought with me to take to Nantes and the Carmelites. If my sources are correct, I believe Queen Anne's heart now rests there. You remember what needs to be done, don't you?"

"Yes, I remember well. I am glad you are the one to be doing it. Do you have the commissioned painting from Master Carpaccio?"

"Yes, I will take it and the roe deer herd with me. Thus, I will fulfill the promises that I made to Her Majesty, Queen Anne."

"With that herd goes my eldest daughter, Clarisse, as well. She has joined Louise in caring for the herd. Please, Bishop, take care of my babies." She squeezed his hands in entreaty.

"Young ladies are always seen as babies in the maternal eye, eh?"

"Most certainly so," Clare nodded and released the bishop's hands. "Will you take with you the queen's diary and her pendant bookmarker, Your Grace?" Clare produced the small, hefty book from an inner pocket behind her apron.

Ottaviano shook his head. "Taking the queen's personal diary and book of hours was never agreed to by me, Clare. All those years ago I transcribed everything I ever needed. Perhaps it should be passed to the queen's daughters—Princess Rene or Princess Claude?"

Clare smiled. *Even though he knows Claude is queen, he still sees her as the little princess he remembered.* "You are right. I will hold it in prayer for further guidance. What of the bookmarker?"

"I will take that from you now as I am obliged to take it to the eldest of her living children."

Clare carefully removed the pendant crucifix from the diary and passed it to the bishop. As he secured the necklace in a pouch at his waist, Clare brought her basket closer, retrieved something, and held it out to the bishop. "Here, take this as well."

"I've never seen this. What is it?"

"The old master called them paper cutters." Clare slipped her thumb and fingers through the wooden loops. "He used them to remove the rough edges of canvases. I thought maybe in your work you might find use for it?"

The bishop took the strange contraption. "It cuts like two knife blades coming together," Ottaviano scrutinized. "Are you sure you don't need it? It could cut yarn very easily."

"Worry not, the old master made many."

"Thank you, Clare." He rose and stowed the paper cutters in his saddle bag then returned. "After my duties to the deceased queen are complete, I will give the bookmarker to Princess Claude."

"That would be Queen Claude, Your Grace."

The bishop smiled at his mistake and nodded. "Quite right, as always, Clare." He offered his arm and together walked a short way across the courtyard, out of earshot and away from the loaded wagons near the entrance. Ottaviano turned to his right and peered across the gardens toward the main palace down the hill near the water. Chapelle Saint-Hubert was just visible between the trees, its antler-pronged spire reaching up as if in supplication to the heavens. "Well, it looks as if Her Majesty's mal-shaped little plum now owns all of France and what France controls."

"Come now, Bishop. The curvatures in Queen Claude's back have failed to limit her, just as Queen Anne's short-leg problem failed to slow her successes, may God rest her soul." Clare crossed herself. She then glanced around cautiously and dropped her voice to a mere whisper. "Queen Claude's lady-in-waiting is Mary Boleyn. Be wary of her. I would not leave the pendant book-mark with her, nor give it to the queen in Mary's presence."

"So, Mary is not to be trusted. I understand, thank you, Clare."

"It grieves me to see Queen Claude so dutiful to our king when he betrays her so. Under the queen's nose, Mary Boleyn shares her feminine favors with the king. That Mary has no respect for herself or the pregnant queen she claims to serve." Clare scuffed her shoes on the gravel. "Our queen deserves better."

"Unfortunately, such seems the way between kings and queens the world over." The bishop patted Clare's arm consolingly while in his head he whispered a silent prayer. He then brightened into a smile and guided them back toward the main building. "By the looks of your basket there, it seems as though I caught you amidst your errands, my dear Clare."

"Actually no, Your Grace, I am closing the house. The old father, Master Piero, died last night. I am sure the king is distraught because he so loved the old man."

"This man Piero is the source of your grief?"

"Yes, Your Grace. He was beloved by all who knew him."

"Would this Piero be the king's engineer?" Ottaviano's face tightened.

"Yes, he was the king's chief architect and chief engineer. His skill brought many French victories in the battlefield."

"Yes, I know him and the battles that were swayed to victory by his hand."

"Ah then, you love him too."

"Sorry, Clare, but I do *not* love this man." Ottaviano's voice ratcheted in intensity as he continued. "It was his engineering skill that brought defeat to our Urbino armies at the hands of the French. It was by his hand that I was not able to return to dear Queen Anne while she still drew breath and complete the task that she had bestowed upon me. It was he—a man that shares the same Italian blood as me—who wreaked havoc and death upon his fellow countrymen. No, Clare, I do not love him." At the look on Clare's face, he paused and regained his composure. "I can respect him for his skill. I can grieve that you have had a loss. But I cannot love such a traitor to my country."

"Please, Your Grace, do not say such things. You do not understand this man. He does not start wars nor promote them. He never turned his mind or heart against his fellow Italians. He was a man of better mettle than that."

"He held the title of chief engineer of war for the French king."

"Yes, he was a chief advisor in engineering. What he provided was to give the edge of victory in war. He did not give war—we do that ourselves. If he had designed for Italy, you would call him a hero and patriot. Since he gave his loyalty to the French, you call Master Piero a traitor. I think this is not just, Your Grace."

"Not just?"

"Your presence here is proof of that."

The bishop's forehead wrinkled. "What does my presence here have to do with Master Piero?"

"You are here because of a promise you made to Queen Anne—a *French* queen. You placed your skills and talents in her service because of the richness of your Italian heart. She saw such qualities in you and trusted you, above all her own countrymen and court, even beyond the span of her life. What makes you so different than your countryman and my good-hearted Master Piero?"

"I am different in that I do not wage war against my countrymen under the flag of France," Ottaviano grimaced.

"If Queen Anne had asked you to do so, would you have done it?"

"She would not have done so." Ottaviano turned away slightly.

"True, Your Grace. But *if* she had," Clare laid her hand upon the bishop's arm, "would you have raised your weapon against a fellow countryman in the name of Queen Anne's honor?"

The bishop pressed his lips together in a firm line. He then sighed and looked at Clare. "Yes, I would have done so, even at the expense of my very life."

"Such is your honor and integrity, Bishop. And so too is it for my master, Piero. His promise to King Francis I was strengthened by his Italian heart as was yours to Queen Anne."

A small smile twitched at the corner of the bishop's mouth. "You have bested me with great apologetic skill, Clare. How is it that you do so?"

"It is not I that subdued a bishop-knight. It is I who understands that loyalty is not a quality that one produces like the light of a candle. Loyalty is a presence of mind and depth of heart that is the very wick of the candle. Loyalty burns deep and guides the hand of a bishop-knight of Italy who will see to it that promises are kept to a French queen, even though no one watches."

"God is always watching."

"Yes, *Dieu avant tout*. Your Grace, you are a man of loyalty and honor. As such, God watches you intently."

"Indeed, Clare." He paused and then added reverently, "I will pray for the soul of your Master Piero."

Clare nodded her thanks, closed her eyes, and added, "God, please hear that prayer."

"I will pray for your Master Piero because he served with the depth of passion imparted to him by his Latin blood."

"God, please hear that prayer."

"Clare, I will also pray for your soul and fiercely loyal heart."

"God, please hear that prayer."

"Clare, I will even pray for that little street urchin who stole your bread."

Clare's eyes came open at the accusation. "It wasn't theft, Your Grace. She gave and received in kind. God, hear that prayer for the poor and forsaken above all others."

Ottaviano nodded and as he crossed himself, so too did Clare. "Will you be all right, Clare? What will happen to you now? Who will take charge of the Château du Clos Lucé?"

"Queen Claude has not said. She knows that now because Master Piero has passed, I will leave the court and palace. Without him, I have no need to stay. Further, they have nothing to keep me here. As for Master Piero's effects, Melzi is the principal heir and executor of the will. He has given away all of Master Piero's paintings, tools, books, and notes as the will dictated. Salai and Battista each received half of Master Piero's vineyard. Maturina received a black, finely stitched, fur-lined cloak."

"What did your master leave you?"

"Besides the memory of a deep friendship?" Clare sniffed. "He returned to me the queen's book and the pendant." Clare patted the interior pocket of her dress. "You see, Your Grace, I did not know if the commissioned piece had been completed in Italy and, thus, after careful deliberation I entrusted the diary to Master Piero as an alternate artist. Now I hold the book and you hold the pendant. Each of us has our tasks set before us and may God guide—"

"Ah! There is my mysterious Templar!" From around the corner of the residence, Salai and Melzi approached, arms laden with the final contents of the house. "Working with you, sir, has caused me great grief and disfavor."

"Give it a rest, Melzi!" Salai said as he rolled his eyes and proceeded to Clare's cart near the courtyard entrance to deliver the items in his arms.

"For my part," the bishop replied, "I am sorry for what grief befell you due to our encounters, Monsieur Melzi. As for being a Templar, how did you know?"

"I assumed, Your Grace." Melzi reshuffled the items in his arms to free a hand with which he pointed to the bishop. "You carry yourself as such."

"How do you know how a Templar carries himself?"

"Another assumption." Melzi gave a roguish grin. "Perhaps in the benevolence of your soul."

"It's not always good to makes such assumptions, Melzi," the bishop warned.

"No harm done, Your Grace. The situation and my assumptions only served to prove to one and all that I had changed my mischievous ways. Master Piero must have seen me to be a changed man as, upon his death, he trusted me with the dispensation of all that was precious to him in life."

"As I have been recently reminded, no greater trust can be given, Monsieur Melzi." Ottaviano looked at Clare and smiled.

"Yes, Melzi has been reminding us of it all day," Salai grumbled as he rejoined the group.

Unfazed, Melzi continued, "I understand the contracted painting *Young Knight in a Landscape* is now with its rightful owner, Bishop?"

"No, Monsieur Melzi, it is not. I will take it with me back south to the Papal States along with the small herd of roe deer."

"I see." Melzi gave a wry smile then held up a small, dingy portrait in front of the bishop. "Will you take this painting along with you as a symbol of my gratitude for the part you played in my life, Your Grace? It was one of Master Piero's favorites. It pains me so very deeply to part with it. However, as I understand your role in all matters, none would be greater suited to receive the blessing of this masterpiece."

"I am sorry. I must decline. I have no room for anything more except provisions for myself and the livestock that will accompany me. I earnestly thank you, though."

"Well, Salai, then I guess the painting belongs to you." Melzi shoved the painting toward the other apprentice.

"I have said no to you before and I say no to you again, Melzi." Salai pushed the painting back. "That which I have already, coupled with the time spent with Master Piero, is enough for me. The painting is yours."

Melzi twisted his lips in irritation, then pasted on a grin as he moved toward Clare. "Clare, there are so many times that you have done such wonderful things for me. I never found the words to thank you—until right now. I believe you to be the best person to possess this heartfelt gift."

"Thank you. I thought you would never ask, Monsieur Melzi. The answer is the same no that you heard numerous times before. You have left this portrait behind in the house twice. Once hidden behind the bed and once behind the garden stand. Lucky for me I have ensured that it has always found its way back to you." Clare poked Melzi in the chest to which he playfully mocked great injury.

"And so you have, dear Clare, and so you have. Well then, there is no more than for me to bid everyone a safe and happy journey." With those words spoken, Melzi turned with a flourish and walked to his wagon. He passed Clare's cart and teasingly pinched the cheek of young Camilla who stood near it. He then glanced around the cart and courtyard. "Where is Little Clarisse?"

"She is with her father," Clare answered. "I could not have her at my apron strings today."

"Of course," Melzi replied. "Well, do tell her adieu for me." Melzi gave a deep, exaggerated bow which made Camilla giggle. Then, using the cart and his free hand, he vaulted himself up to his wagon's seat and got situated for a long ride southward.

Salai stooped to kiss Clare on both cheeks. "Goodbye, Clare. Farewell." He then turned to the bishop. "I am glad to have met you, and I am sorry you had to meet Melzi." Salai shook the holy man's hand, shouldered his pack firmly, and strode away.

"Unfortunately, I need to make a trail as well, Clare. God bless you." Ottaviano kissed Clare's hand and bowed. He mounted his mud-splattered steed and waved a final time before he passed through the gate and turned onto the main road.

"Goodbye, Ottaviano!" Clare called as she waved. *I know your mission continues from here. The roe deer unicorn family and their caretakers must be prepared to travel. This will take time yet. Perhaps we shall see each other again.* Clare glanced over at the basket near the steps and let her eyes rove over the residence. *Except for Melzi, straggling as always, it looks like only Camilla is here with me to say a final farewell to Clos Lucé.*

Clare gathered the basket and walked to her pushcart near the outer wall where her daughter stood patiently waiting. When Clare lifted the tarp to stow away the last of the things to be delivered to the Amboise Palace, she cringed.

"Melzi! Curse you! This painting is yours!" She struggled to dislodge it from the items in the cart.

"Clare, my former housekeeper, why say no when it is so easy to just say yes? You are a loving soul, and the painting belongs to you. After all, since you have retired, you have an abundance of time to consider why Master Piero found the least bit of interest in that sad little oil painting." He made a clicking noise and his horse began to pull.

"Melzi, don't you dare drive off," Clare threatened, shaking one hand at him while the other pulled at the canvas. "You come back and take this painting. If Master Piero loved it so much, he would have taken it with him in death." Clare groaned and then begged, "Please, Melzi! Camilla and I have enough to push in the cart. I have no use for a portrait in my house."

"Nor does the artist par excellence the world will come to know as Monsieur Francesco Melzi!" he shouted to the empty courtyard as if it were full of cheering spectators. "Camilla, will you please tell your mother to listen to reason. I, Melzi, trained by Master Piero himself, have already posed for Salai's version of that painting. It should have been a striking nude, but Master Piero wouldn't listen. Why would I want to keep his dark, dreary portrait when Salai's version featuring Melzi is so much better?" He pulled on the reins before entering the road and called back over his shoulder, "In fact, when the world can have the beautiful *Monna Vanna*, why would they ever care to see this pitiful, sad *Mona Lisa*?"

63

Arrivals and Departures

Maternity hospital
Saint-Quentin, Somme River Valley
Vermandois region, France
Current day

"Queen Anne? Queen Anne?" Douglas's hailing quickly morphed into pleas. "Your Majesty, please … speak to me. Folks, I'm not getting any response across the psychic bridge!" Douglas stood aghast; his eyes widened with terror. "What in hell's kitchen is happening, people!?"

"It looks like Loni's monitor feeds are changing!" Shoving his phone into his vest pocket, Mickey cut all communication with Jillian and ran over to the monitor to check the output strip that was being spit out. Loni herself began groaning with each wave of birthing contractions. "I don't think these are Braxton-Hicks contractions!"

"Neither do they!" Douglas sprung out of the way as the French maternity staff swarmed in. The doctors and nurses positioned themselves in their respective roles, jostling Mickey and Douglas roughly and pushing them to the edge of the room.

Mickey shook Douglas's shoulders, "I thought you said that Loni shouldn't begin the birthing process until she psychologically regained herself."

"I … I…."

"Mickey!" Loni's eyes were wide open and searching. "Where are you? Mickey? I want my husband!"

"Loni!" Mickey began shoving his way toward the head of the bed.

"Mickey, I need you." Loni clawed in the air. "Where are you?"

"I'm here, darling."

"I don't see you, Mickey. Stand where I can see you. Come here. Give me your hand."

"Almost there," he said, clawing a path from the outer fringes of the room. Mickey plowed against the tide of maternity staff until he arrived.

"Mickey." Loni grabbed Mickey's hand and pulled him close to her. "I have been living my life in a dream … all these faces flashed … a bearded king." She paused and drew in a shaky breath. "It was a long … winding dream…." Loni's voice dropped off as another contraction swept over her.

"Yes, I know! Oh my God, I can't believe you are finally back!"

"Back?" Loni groaned.

"From the dream—you kinda talked your way through most of it. We all have been following you through it." He held her hand tightly as it shook uncontrollably during the contraction.

"We? We who?" Loni panted in the brief respite.

"We—Douglas, Suzanne, and Clarisse."

"There is so much I want to tell you, Mickey, but I can't."

"Don't worry, now isn't the time. There'll be time later. We will talk later. Right now, just breathe, keep breathing. Don't push until they tell you."

"Okay, okay." Loni nodded, her eyes only on Mickey's face. "How will I know when to push? I don't speak French."

"Good point." Mickey looked up and found that Douglas had migrated to Clarisse at the side of the room. "Douglas!" Mickey yelled over the mess of French being spoken around them. "Send Clarisse here next to me!" Then he looked back to Loni. "She is the only one here who is French and can speak English." Another contraction stole Loni's focus.

"I am *not* French," Clarisse grunted as she shoved through the crowd. "I am French Canadian. Why is that such a hard concept—"

"Fine, you are French Canadian." Mickey swallowed hard as the fingers of his good hand, interlaced with Loni's, were vice-gripped by his wife. "My error, Clarisse. I'm sorry. Can you please be the liaison between this staff and Loni? Please."

"Yes, of course." Clarisse finally reached Mickey's side. She straightened her hair wrap, an abbreviated bonnet, which had been knocked askew. "Why would you think—"

"Clarisse!" Mickey groaned.

"I'm right here." Clarisse looked over at Douglas and rolled her eyes. "I thought *she* was the one having the babies." With her eyes, Clarisse drew Douglas's gaze to the hands of the soon-to-be parents. Douglas looked pale but nodded as he bit his nails.

"By the way, Mickey," Loni grunted and huffed in the break. "Who is Clarisse—a specialist?"

"Clarisse Saint Vincent." Mickey pointed with his bandaged hand. "She's housekeeping."

"Housekeeping is delivering my babies?" Loni's red face scrunched up.

"No, she's a florist too." Mickey gave a big cheesy smile, but his wife only groaned and dropped her head back into the pillow.

"Mickey, we have to talk," said Loni, speaking through clenched teeth. "We *really* have to have a talk."

"Yes, honey, I know, but later. Just breathe now. Relax your jaw. You must breathe, and push when Clarisse says to."

"Okay, okay," Loni panted. "Is Douglas here? I gotta talk to him." Loni cast her eyes around to find him but couldn't due to the bustling staff. "DIA business ... why wasn't he at Péronne? He was supposed to ... we were supposed to...." Her body began to shudder uncontrollably.

"Loni." Mickey urged. "It's mommy time. Focus."

"The babies," she winced, "they know it's time to leave me."

"Breathe, honey, keep breathing."

"I am. I am. I'm so ... so ready. Tell the housekeeper florist lady, I'm ready." She moaned as her body shook harder. She squeezed her eyes shut. "I need something. It hurts," she choked out.

"They know ... I know." Mickey soothed her and tried not to look at their interlocked, bloodlessly white knuckles.

"Mickey!" The veins in Loni's neck bulged and her eyes shot open. "You're ... a ... doctor! Give me ... something ... for pain!"

"I'm not your doctor." Mickey clenched his jaw. "I wish I could, but I can't."

"Mickey ... tell them ... get the babies ... out now!"

"They know. You can do this, Loni, I know you can."

"Clarisse, drop your mop and flowers!" Loni screamed. "Here they come!"

THE END

Sneak peek of the next book in the series:

Mercenary of God (Novel 5 of 12)

1

The Croak Room

US Army Hospital Morgue

Heidelberg, Germany

Current day

"**Y**ou didn't deserve this, Master Sergeant." Pressing his knuckles into the metal autopsy table, Lieutenant Colonel Luis Toro-Calderon looked into the dead eyes of his operations sergeant, Francis Roman. "When I catch the slime that did this to you, their mothers—if they had any—will wail." Luis looked at his reflection in the glass partition. *Don't try to wriggle free of it. It was you that placed him in harm's way.*

"The cause of death appears to be a rapid deoxygenation." The pathologist spoke without inflection, her eyes sharp as a scalpel, her voice just as cold.

"He lost the ability to breathe?" Luis grunted. *We huffed and puffed through Central American rain forests, breathing just fine. How many times can warriors face death before this tragic eventuality?*

"Yes sir. He quickly lost oxygen to his cells—he asphyxiated. He had an obstructed airway."

"Obstructed airway?" *So many times, either I saved him or he saved me. We always came through relatively unscathed ... till now.* "I've never known Master Sergeant to have any breathing problems."

"I concur with that, sir. I didn't see any residual effects of a chronic long-term lung condition." The doctor held the clipboard with her report close to her chest, locked behind crossed arms.

"So, you're telling me all of the sudden his airway just shut off?"

"Yes, sir. It appears that the airway collapsed."

"Collapsed? Why would a healthy airway collapse suddenly?"

"The medical evidence supports the theory that the airway collapsed secondary to direct cervical trauma. Which was likely—"

"What are you saying, Doc? Someone crushed his neck?"

"As I was about to say before, sir, the medical evidence indicates that Master Sergeant's neck was forcefully snapped and thus the airway collapsed."

"All right, now I want to know how that happened."

"It's hard to say." The doctor shrugged and the papers on her clipboard crinkled. "It could have been done manually, bluntly, or by the hanging."

"Hanging? What hanging? I heard nothing about Master Sergeant being hanged."

"Yes, sir. It appears so. I cannot say definitively if the hanging itself was the source of the airway obstruction," she pointed with her pen to the markings around the corpse's neck, "or if he was killed and then hung. And then there's the matter of the other—"

"At least it was in the mailroom and not a tower or a clock spire," Luis muttered.

"What was that, sir?"

"Nothing." Luis dragged his cold hands across his face. "Look, I've just lost the number one master sergeant in the entire command, there's a heap of bodies from the last forty-eight hours, and you are parrying words with me. Walk it out for me, will you? Tell me everything you know—now," he growled.

The pathologist averted her eyes to her clipboard and flipped through a couple pages of notes. "Fractured cervical spine, collapsed trachea ...."

"Now, Doctor!" Luis's voice echoed loudly off the walls of the morgue.

"Sir, I know this is your friend." The pathologist pushed her thick, smudged spectacles up beyond the reddened imprints on the bridge of her nose. "But, I am trying to do a thorough post-mortem here and answers don't come just because we yell for them." Clearing her throat, she proceeded. "Master Sergeant was found hanging by his neck from the rafters in the mailroom. His body was suspended by the neck using thin packing cord. Amongst the many unanswered questions here, I keep circling back to one in particular: why was the mailroom clerk killed too, but not in the same way?"

Luis's dark eyebrows became a solid line. He spoke through clenched teeth, "So, there are *two* dead bodies. When were you going to tell me about that?"

"Sir, you didn't ask."

He slammed his fist against the autopsy table causing the instruments to bounce and flash in the fluorescent light like lethal metallic fish. "Doctor, I take it you don't have much of a life here in the morgue and you probably don't see many living people due to the nature of your profession. Maybe outside of this metal death-box you call an office you don't interact much with the walking and breathing either." Luis walked around the table, easing nose-to-nose with the pathologist. His breath fogged her glasses. "I really don't know, and I really don't care. I *do* know this. Unless you want to join your clients here, you'd better start briefing me with the facts that I need to know."

"Sir," the pathologist gave the slightest of nods. She licked her dry lips and sidestepped towards the table. She pulled back the sheet to the master sergeant's hips.

"Damn it, another one," Luis closed his eyes and sighed.

"Another one, sir? How did you know—"

"Just lay the facts on me, Doc. Please."

"The facts as I understand them are this: Master Sergeant was approached from behind and his neck was broken either by compression or by a blunt object of significant weight. My gut tells me that his neck was locked and snapped by a pair of strong arms, but I haven't had the chance to examine him thoroughly enough to prove that."

"How was this different from the mailroom clerk?"

"I have only had a cursory glance at the clerk's body so I can't answer that."

"But I thought you said they weren't killed the same—"

"One body at a time, sir. May I continue?"

"Go on."

"Looking at the abrasions there, I am guessing that Master Sergeant's dead body was hoisted up by his neck using the redundantly twined postal cord mentioned in the police report. The photos of the scene show the body suspended from the rafters."

"The photos showed something else too, didn't they, Doc?" Luis's eyes tracked down the slice in the master sergeant's body.

She nodded, pointing again with her pen towards the pale, stiff corpse. "That cut you see there was done to him in the mailroom. After his neck was broken and he was hanged, the contents of his belly were ripped out of him."

"How do you know he was eviscerated after he was killed?"

"The blood on the floor was minimal compared to the amount that would have been there had he still been alive."

"That's what I feared." Luis turned away from the table, his eyes scanning the morgue. "How many bodies do you have here now, Doc?"

"Only three. Why?"

"Since last night, seven people were killed here on the caserne. Did you see any of them?"

"I processed one of the two in the cooler. My intent was to finish evaluating and processing this body here next, then do the same for the clerk's body. Since our morgue only holds four bodies that means that four corpses were shipped out to Landstuhl Hospital this morning at the zero six hundred hours pick up. The particulars of those bodies would have been handled by my colleague on duty last night."

"Were you briefed as to the circumstances of their deaths?"

"No, sir. We never got to do a verbal report or handoff. The moment we sat down to officially pass the baton, two more bodies—"

"Yeah, fine. Where are the medical files or records regarding the bodies that were processed last night? Did you read them?"

"I saw that reports had been written on those four bodies, but I didn't get to read them yet. I have only evaluated one of the two bodies currently in the cooler," she checked her notes, "a Major Amos Oberstadtmeyer. Then, there's Mater Sergeant on the table here now. As for the clerk in the cooler, even from a cursory glance, I can tell you he wasn't murdered in the same way as these other two." The pathologist paused for a moment, scrutinizing Luis's drawn features. "Since you seem familiar with the similarities in the first two bodies I have here, it appears that you have more insights about this situation than I do, sir."

"As the acting commander of the European Medical Command, I guess that is a fair assessment." Luis looked down again at the autopsy table and tapped his fingers methodically on the cold metal.

"What, sir?"

"Was there a note on Master Sergeant's body?"

Like a curious pigeon, the pathologist cocked her head before answering. "Oddly enough, yes, there was."

"Did the note contain a message that talked something about rising and falling?"

"Roger, sir. It did. It said, *'Rise with the Fallen.'* How did you know?"

"May I see the folders for the bodies that you have in your possession?"

"Certainly, sir." The pathologist went over to an unkempt desk and sorted through several folders lying in a document tray. After a few moments of searching, she returned with a folder labeled *Oberstadtmeyer, Amos US Army Major.* She handed the folder to Luis. "Sir, this folder also has a copy of the military police report."

"I know. That's fine for now. I just need to know the specific wording of the sign on his neck." Louis flipped through several pages, "Soldier found dead ... hung from the clock tower ... Hospital Operations Building ... abdomen eviscerated ... sign hung around the neck ... here it is. *'They will come up into your palace ... into the houses of your officials and on your people, and into your ... kneading troughs. Rise with the Fallen!'* There you have it."

"Sir, this is horrible, just horrible. Seven deaths and two eviscerations in the last twenty-four hours—"

"I know. What kind of raging animal ..."

"Sir," the pathologist blurted, "there's one more thing I think you ought to see. I don't know what to think about it. It's ... strange."

"Strange? Coming from someone in your profession, *strange* makes me nervous. Are you sure I need to know this?"

"Yes sir, you have a need to know. It's about Master Sergeant there. However, I am not sure that you are going to understand."

"Why, Doctor?"

"Because I think it defies explanation." The pathologist walked over to a rolling metal table and brought back a large, capped gallon jar in one arm and a stainless steel pan under the other.

"Before I started working on him, my eye caught movement in his neck."

"Don't dead bodies twitch from time to time?"

"Not as much as they do in the movies," the pathologist scoffed and rolled her eyes.

"What did you discover, Doc?"

"I found these in the oral and aboral cavities."

"Oral meaning mouth and aboral meaning …."

"Yes sir, aboral means the rectum and anus." The pathologist opened the jar and poured out the contents into the steel pan.

"Jesus Christ, son of Mary," said Luis, grimacing while turning away. His eyes watered as he fought through the gagging. "That smells putrid." He shoved the back of his hand against his flaring nostrils.

"Yes, sir." The pathologist remained unmoved. "That is a voluminous amount of blood and rancid human waste."

"What about that?" Luis pointed with one hand while the other clamped over his mouth and nose. "Are those what I think they are?"

"Hard to believe, isn't it, sir?" Using the alligator forceps, the pathologist fished out one of the larger objects from the pan and held it up for inspection.

Luis turned and gagged.

"Sir? Are you okay?" The pathologist adjusted her glasses.

"I'm fine." He attempted to speak but gagged again.

"Sir, I think that—"

"Oh, for God's sake," Luis interrupted, "cover that up. Will you?" Wiping his eyes with the back of his hand, Luis shook his head and rolled his lips inward into a severe grimace as he swallowed the bile rising in his throat. "Make it official, Doc. For the record, what was in Master Sergeant's throat and bowels?"

"Sir, meet *Hyla heinzsteinitzi*."

"In English, Doc, not Latin."

"Jerusalem tree frogs, sir. They're dead and dying Jerusalem tree frogs."

About the Author

B. Albertill is the author of the twelve-book historical fiction series, Lost Books of Benjamin (LBoB). Albertill is a retired US Army physician-scientist, educationalist, science researcher, theologian, historian without portfolio, and a modern-day Templar. Having served in the military from Viet Nam era (1973) to his last posting in Afghanistan (2014) before retiring in 2015, he has trained/worked in clinical, research, and operational military medicine, the field of chemical warfare, and the history of military medicine. His writing is underpinned by a worldview defined by this professional education, military training, Christian faith, and resulting personal experiences.

Albertill writes historical fiction supported by years of travels and residence throughout Europe and the Mediterranean countries in Northern Africa and the near east. As LBoB novel protagonists Mickey Peronne, Suzanne Coletrane, Russell Lange, and the numerous historical characters move throughout these regions, Albertill literarily walks shoulder-to-shoulder with them. The gift given to the reader is the robust flavor of credible historical fiction from novels penned by one who has firsthand appreciated the numerous historical settings.

The Lost Books of Benjamin

3 Benjamin 4:1-63

The Richest That There Can Be

Novel 4 of 12 in the 3rd Book of Benjamin

B. Albertill

Publisher: SDP Publishing

Also available in ebook format

 SDP Publishing

www.SDPPublishing.com

Contact us at: info@SDPPublishing.com

www.ingramcontent.com/pod-product-compliance
Lightning Source LLC
Chambersburg PA
CBHW051635050726
47502CB00011B/407